UNDISCLOSED
Submission

CARLY MARIE

CONTENTS

Prologue	1
Chapter One	9
Chapter Two	21
Chapter Three	31
Chapter Four	41
Chapter Five	53
Chapter Six	65
Chapter Seven	79
Chapter Eight	93
Chapter Nine	105
Chapter Ten	117
Chapter Eleven	131
Chapter Twelve	143
Chapter Thirteen	157
Chapter Fourteen	169
Chapter Fifteen	179
Chapter Sixteen	189
Chapter Seventeen	197
Chapter Eighteen	207
Chapter Nineteen	221
Chapter Twenty	233
Chapter Twenty-One	247
Chapter Twenty-Two	259
Chapter Twenty-Three	273
Chapter Twenty-Four	283
Chapter Twenty-Five	295
Chapter Twenty-Six	309
Chapter Twenty-Seven	319
Chapter Twenty-Eight	331
Chapter Twenty-Nine	343
Chapter Thirty	355
Chapter Thirty-One	367

Chapter Thirty-Two	379
Chapter Thirty-Three	389
Note From Carly	401
About the Author	403

Editing Services: Jennifer Smith

Cover By: Quinn Ward

Copyright © 2021 by Carly Marie

All rights reserved.

This book or any portion thereof may not be reproduced or used in any manner whatsoever without the express written permission of the author except for the use of brief quotations in a book review.

This is a work of fiction. Names, characters, businesses, places, events, locales, and incidents are either the products of the author's imagination or used in a fictitious manner. Any resemblance to actual persons, living or dead, or actual events is purely coincidental.

PROLOGUE

MERRICK

Mid-December

"Hey, old man." Dean's eyes sparkled with amusement as he took a seat across from me at Brodrick's, an old burger joint a little south of Nashville that just happened to be one of our favorite meeting spots for a meal and a beer. There would be no meal or beer today. The restaurant was closed, the lights off, the normally busy kitchen quiet. We were alone.

To Dean, the decade I had on his thirty-five years probably did make me an old man. "Don't call me that." I ran my fingers through my silver hair as I surveyed the dining room.

Over the last two decades, I'd seen countless restaurants around the world and had lost track of the cities, states, and countries I'd visited. I'd built my career in the bar and restaurant industry. My experience as a flair bartender in some of the busiest nightclubs and most elite competitions through my younger years had paved the way for my success as a highly sought after restaurant consultant. When it came to bars, pubs, restaurants, or dives, there was very little that would surprise me. I'd seen it all. I'd saved it all. I'd been in places in far worse shape than Brodrick's. I'd pulled small failing bars and restaurants in huge bustling cities back from the brink. My team and I had rehabbed, rebuilt, and rebranded countless holes-in-the-wall.

Looking around the outdated restaurant, it was hard to believe that those days were behind me. I was now looking at my future, embarking on what could be the craziest thing I'd done since I hitchhiked from my childhood home in Missouri to New York City as an eighteen-year-old kid fresh from high school graduation. Back then, I'd been fearless—and maybe a little stupid—with no plans beyond finding a job and popping my gay cherry.

Twenty-seven years might as well have been a lifetime. Missouri felt like it was a million miles away, not a day's car trip. There were twenty-seven years of lessons, heartache, and heartbreak separating me and the impulsive high school graduate. After two successful careers and a nomadic lifestyle, I was getting ready to embark on what might be my retirement.

Here.

In Franklin, Tennessee.

For the better part of two decades, I'd found myself coming back here. My college career brought me here the first time, and then my tight-knit group of friends kept me coming back. At some point in my travels, this was the place I'd come to think of as home. And this was the place where I was ready to settle down.

That eighteen-year-old kid seemed so far removed from the man I'd become that I didn't know if we had ever been the same person. But looking around this restaurant, this place that I'd come back to over and over again, I felt a spark of the adventurous kid I'd once been. Maybe settling in Middle Tennessee hadn't been where I'd seen myself landing when I jumped into that first pickup truck that had taken me from my childhood home in Watson to the Missouri-Iowa line, but this was where I was.

Dean scrubbed at his well-trimmed beard, the noise bringing me out of my thoughts. "You're serious about this?"

I lifted a shoulder, portraying a casualness I didn't feel on the inside. "How do the numbers look?"

My friend smirked at me, rolling the sleeves of his white dress shirt up enough that the bottom half of the sleeve tattoo on his left arm was visible. The vibrant ink still surprised me.

Part of me would always remember Dean as the young guy who'd helped me pass a business course as I finished up my degree. At the time he hadn't been old enough to go to the bars, barely old enough to drive. The genius had started college at sixteen and by the time I'd met him eighteen months later, was already well on his way to finishing up his undergrad degree.

He'd been tutoring a group of guys when I realized I'd never pass the course without help. The professor had given me the name of a tutor, and I'd joined the group that night. Once I got over the shock that a guy who wasn't yet eighteen was leading the group, we all became fast friends, so close that even my nomadic lifestyle after graduation couldn't drive a wedge in our friendship. The farther I went from Tennessee, the more often I was pulled back, until finally I couldn't keep leaving.

The frequent travel meant I hadn't seen Dean grow up like the others had. It led to me sometimes finding myself surprised that the lanky teenager had grown up to be an attractive man. If I was being honest, Dean was sexy as hell, and his intelligence only made him hotter.

Dean could have been a brilliant scientist, engineer, or doctor, but his love had always been numbers. He could have made an amazing mathematics professor, but no amount of begging from the faculty had been able to convince him to trade his love of accounting for academics. He'd started an accounting business before he'd started college, had taken over my accounts within a month of our meeting, and all these years later was still in charge of both my bank accounts and stock portfolios.

His accounting skills were ultimately what had led me to be able to comfortably step back from the business I'd literally started from nothing and had built into a successful consultancy. In a roundabout sort of way, the man grinning at me from across the table was why I'd found myself setting down roots here in Middle Tennessee.

A folder I hadn't seen him holding was placed on the table between us. Gesturing vaguely around us, he transformed from my friend to my accountant. "You know as well as I do that there's enough money in the accounts. If I move a little around in your portfolios, you could probably do the renovations here without getting a loan. We can bring Travis's company in. You know damn well he and Ben would be all over rehabbing this place."

Dean stopped for a light chuckle. "So long as you don't plan on running Steve out of business."

Travis was one of the guys in our circle. Another small businessman, he owned a construction company that specialized in home construction and remodeling. Ben was his young but incredibly driven associate. And Steve? Well, that was Travis's dad, who also happened to be the owner of Steve's Tavern, a bar down the road that had become the unofficial gay bar south of Nashville. There was no way in hell I was going to compete with Steve, and Dean knew that as well as I did.

"If the numbers make sense, I'm down for talking with them. I have to make sure I'm not going all in on a money pit."

Dean closed his eyes, a sign that he was considering his words carefully, and the hair on the back of my neck stood on end. "That's a complicated answer, Mer. First off, this place, as is, *is* a money pit. But three years ago? When it was being taken care of? This place was a moneymaker." He flipped a page over so that I could see the graphics that spanned two pages. "About eighteen months ago, sales began to decline."

I nodded. He wasn't telling me anything I didn't know already. I cut him off before he could get onto a tangent. "The *real* old man just can't keep it up anymore. He's been giving the staff a hard time about making any changes at all."

Dean leaned back in his chair, lacing his fingers behind his head and sighing. "Rod's aging. He really should have sold this place about ten years ago."

The statement made me laugh. Rod wasn't just aging—he was a dinosaur. A stubborn old goat who thought that Brodrick's was fine just the way it was. It had taken his manager reaching out to me three times before I even thought about coming to help this place. It was the reason I was sitting here instead of in another little bar, in another little town. "Let's be honest. Rod's an ass. And ten years ago is being generous." I pointed to the table and chairs we were sitting in. "This place hasn't been touched since the late eighties. It was in style when you were born."

Dean blew out a breath as he abruptly sat forward and placed his hands flat on the table. "Alright, fine. I'll cut to the chase. This place is a hot fucking mess right now, but you've told me that the staff is amazing, talented, and willing to put in the work to change. You know as well as I do that that's two-thirds the battle in this business. If the staff isn't willing to change, you're sunk before you start."

I hummed, liking the frankness Dean was now delivering. Everything he'd said was true and the sooner we cut to the chase, the sooner I could decide if this was what I wanted. My gut was saying yes. This place, this staff, was worth every risk. When I'd ignored the third email from Brodrick's manager, she'd shown up to Steve's with the cook, bar manager, and hostess. It hadn't been worth asking how they knew where to find me. Franklin might have been a suburb of Nashville, but we'd been going there long enough that any local knew where to find us on Thursday nights. The passion the staff had shown that night had swayed me into considering it.

Rod had been another challenge. At first, I'd thought about taking Brodrick's on as a client, but when I'd finally thrown the numbers down on the table, the black, white, and very red reality of things changed. The first number was the cost of a new kitchen to replace the sorely outdated space, the second was the price to update the dining area, and the third was the yearly figures that he was bringing in. The discrepancy was startling to the old man. Two days later, he'd called with an ultimatum of sorts.

All or nothing.

Either I bought the place and did it all, or nothing was happening.

And that was how Dean and I had come to be sitting at Brodrick's at nine in the morning in the middle of December. And that was how I found myself nodding my head as we talked about the numbers I'd seen before. Dean was nothing if not prepared, and I appreciated his insight into everything from my finances to the projected costs.

"The real question in my mind is if you're all in. Mer, this isn't a take-the-job-then-leave-it-six-weeks-later thing. This isn't a rehab-and-move thing. This is a commitment. A commitment to stay in one place. A commitment to Tennessee. A commitment to this staff and the area. You do this and you, a self-proclaimed commitment-phobe, will be committing to all of it."

I'd been running from commitment for as long as I could remember. That was why the consultancy had been so good for me; I'd found something I was good at, but I'd never had to commit to any one place, one restaurant, one bar, or one staff. The only thing I'd committed myself to since I was eighteen had been Tom, and I knew how that had ended.

That was why the words coming from my mouth were as shocking to me as they were to Dean. "Yeah, I know. I know, but this feels right. I think I need this." What I needed was a reason to stop running. What I needed was to find my footing. What I needed at the moment was stability and consistency. Like Dean had helpfully pointed out earlier, I was getting old. My body no longer liked the random beds, the odd hours, and the uncertainty of the next place I'd land. Committing to a restaurant wasn't the same as committing to a man.

I could do this.

Dean pursed his lips, studying me for a moment before slowly nodding his head. "Then I think you've already got your answer." He closed the file, hesitated a moment, then looked at me with a giant smile on his face.

"Welcome home, Merrick."

CHAPTER ONE

DEAN

Two Months Later

A pounding at my front door pulled me from the spreadsheet I'd been poring over. It was early on a Sunday morning, and no one sensible would be up at this hour, so I ignored it. After three knocks, it was clear that the person on the other side wasn't going away, so I reluctantly dropped the blanket wrapped around my shoulders and placed my laptop onto the coffee table.

My back pinched as I stood. The constant, dull ache was an ever-present reminder of who I no longer was. A daily reminder of how much worse it could have been and how lucky I was to be able to walk to the door while I stretched my back and silently cursed the sore muscles.

Still annoyed and stiff, I flung the door open without looking at who was there. "I'm not—" My mouth clamped shut when I noticed I'd come face-to-face with Merrick, his silver hair tamed to a perfect just-rolled-out-of-bed coif that likely took him twenty minutes to get just so.

Since Christmas, he'd been a permanent staple in our lives. After having one foot out the door since he'd graduated from Tennessee State, having Merrick around constantly had been a shock to the system. Well, maybe a shock to my system more than the other guys. Our little five-man study group from college had grown to over ten, picking up friends and boyfriends along the way, to the point that Merrick and I were the only two single guys left.

I had a feeling that *single* seemed to be the qualification Merrick had deemed important when he'd attached himself to me before the clock struck twelve on New Year's. He'd been showing up at my house so frequently, I'd actually given him the code to the garage door. He was always good about knocking and waiting for me to answer, but after he'd been left waiting in his car for nearly a half hour one evening, I'd given him the code.

He had his phone to his ear, having an animated conversation with an unknown person yet grinning at me. "Give us twenty." Cocking his head to the side, studying me closely, he amended his statement. "Make that thirty. Dean's still in his pajamas." He pulled the phone from his ear, pressed a button, then shoved it into his pocket at the same time he held a coffee cup out to me. "Some bean for the bean."

"What?" I took the coffee with my left hand, quickly running my right hand around the shirt hem to make sure it was pulled down. I missed the days of walking around without a shirt on, proud of my muscular chest and stomach, not self-conscious of the unsightly scars that marked the lower half of my back.

He watched with a furrowed brow as I tugged on my shirt hem. Whatever he was wondering about stayed in his head as he lifted his eyes to meet mine. His smirk made me worried about what was going to come out of his mouth next. "Cute shirt." His hand gestured to the oversized shirt I'd slept in the night before.

I looked down at the T-shirt with a huge coffee bean wearing sunglasses, and the words *Cool Bean* scrawled across the front. Flipping him off, I stepped back and allowed him to enter the house. "Fuck you."

He shrugged casually. "I mean, I wouldn't normally say no, but sleeping with friends is a bad idea."

The cup of coffee he'd handed me was not big enough for this conversation. "Wha… You know what, I'm not going to go there. Why are you here?"

"We're meeting at Canyon's for brunch. Everyone's going. Haven't you checked your phone?"

My blank stare said enough, and Merrick's expression turned knowing. "You got lost in work again." It wasn't a question, so I thankfully didn't have to deny it. Merrick knew I liked numbers, knew I didn't often take days off, and knew I often forgot the world around me when I got into my work.

"Drink your coffee, Bean. I'll brew you more while you get yourself ready. Knowing you, you haven't had anything to eat or drink all morning." He shooed me out of the living room. "Go. And put on something nicer than sweats and a baggy shirt."

Arguing with Merrick was pointless. If our friends were all going to Canyon and Larson's house, they would expect me there. No amount of stalling or arguing would get me out of it, only delay the inevitable. Instead of fighting, I sighed dramatically and headed to the steps. "Yes, Dad."

Merrick's laugh followed him through my living room and into the kitchen. "I'm pretty sure you're supposed to respect your elders."

And I was pretty sure I'd had this exact conversation with my mom when I was about fifteen. Something told me I'd lost that argument as well. Probably because I hadn't discovered coffee until college, and my uncaffeinated brain functioned no better in the mornings at fifteen than it did at thirty-five.

It didn't take me long in the shower, and I wasn't particular about my hair or clothing. Drinking coffee in the shower might not have been the best idea I'd ever had, but at least I was feeling more alive as I walked down the steps twenty minutes later. Jeans that fit me well and a snug screen-print shirt passed for the nicer look Merrick had demanded. The baggy flannel button-up over it made me feel more comfortable.

Merrick didn't look as pleased as I had been about my outfit. "I know you have shirts that fit you somewhere. Ones that don't have ridiculous graphics and sayings on them and aren't too big."

I grabbed a pair of Chucks from the organizer by the

door and slid my feet into them. "I'm a millennial. I'll leave the grandpa attire to you Gen-Xers."

He growled, but I still got the promised coffee as we headed out the door to his sparkling white Range Rover. My snipe about his age had gotten him to lay off my clothes—win one for me for the day. Of course, I wasn't sure how much of a win it really was as we were heading to spend time with our friends. I scolded myself for being such an asshole, that was usually Merrick's job anyway, but the more of them that had coupled up, the harder it had become for me to spend time with them.

Confidence was something I'd had in spades in my teens and twenties. I'd learned the skill early. Starting high school at twelve forced me to find it. Entering college before I'd gotten my driver's license had been a shock to the system once again. *Fake it 'til ya make it* had become my mantra. Within a few years, I'd made it. In the process, I'd found a group of guys who hadn't batted an eye at my age.

At first, they'd been too grateful for my knowledge of the material to care about my age. The longer we'd met up, the more they'd begun to open up. As soon as one came out as gay, they had all been open about their sexuality, often laughing and talking about a club they'd been to, a hookup they'd had, or a boyfriend they were seeing. It hadn't taken me long to come out to them.

From that moment on, we'd become more than classmates. They'd taken me under their collective wings, by my side through every turn life had taken me. We were closer than friends, through thick and thin, ups and downs, and as we'd slowly discovered we were all kinky—some of us more than others.

Well, everyone but Merrick. Aside from being a control freak, he was about as vanilla as they came.

In the sixteen years that I'd known him, he'd never been in a relationship. He talked about hookups, said he didn't do relationships, and had just thrown out that he didn't mix friends and sex, but that was the extent of it. At least he'd never minded that he'd ended up with a bunch of friends who shared various alternative lifestyles with each other as naturally as most people talked about the weather. Daddy, little, pup, lace, Dom, sub, none of it bothered him, but he had never expressed an interest in any of it, or anything else.

Being surrounded by a group of men who were confident in themselves and their interests had helped me discover early on that I liked pleasing my partner and taking care of them. By the time I'd hit twenty-five, I'd discovered Daddy Doms. While I wasn't the most traditional Daddy, and I sometimes found it hard to set firm limits and boundaries, nothing made me happier than the moment I'd see my partner light up because of something I'd done for them.

Over seven years after my last relationship had ended, the memory of pleasing my lover in that way still made my cock swell, but I no longer had a pull toward domination. I wasn't sure I had a pull to anything kinky anymore. Sometimes, the lack of desire to find anyone made hanging out with my friends difficult. They'd found happiness in various nontraditional relationships, and I'd found—

"You okay?" Merrick's concern surprised me, but when I blinked to find that we were already in Canyon and Larson's driveway, I could understand his worry.

"Yeah, sorry, just lost in thoughts." In case I hadn't been convincing, I tried for something that sounded believable. "Thinking about the file I was working on this morning." That would be something plausible. Plausible and easier than admitting to Merrick that I'd felt out of balance for a long time, and the happier my friends got, the more I was struggling to find my footing and place among them.

He studied me for an uncomfortably long time. "You know, you can talk to one of us if something's wrong. You haven't been yourself lately. You aren't as loud and opinionated as you used to be." Giving a casual shrug, he tried to downplay his intent. "What I'm trying to say is we haven't been scared away yet. There's nothing you can say or do that will scare us away." He pointed toward the house with a grin on his face. "Case and point."

Larson had only recently admitted that he was a little. It had been a surprise, even knowing others in our ever-growing group were littles. It was obvious that Larson was still a bit uncomfortable, but he was trying hard to be more open with us. "Thanks, Merrick. I appreciate it."

He pursed his lips, like he wanted to say more, but sighed and changed the subject. "Let's get going. I'm kind of surprised we're the first ones here."

Canyon was standing next to his boyfriend when we arrived at the door, looking as imposing as ever in a black Henley and dark wash jeans. The warm smile that graced his face softened his features and made him look no more intimidating than the puppy tumbling around his feet. Of course, I was pretty sure their new dog was going to turn into a horse before long. He'd doubled in size since they got him four months earlier, and he had already been an impressive size then.

I'd been standing there when Larson had met the dog, and remembered laughing all the way home that he'd called him *little*. There had been nothing about him that was little even back then, but I guessed when he was used to Marley, Merrick's full-grown mastiff, the puppy would have been small.

Larson wandered off toward the kitchen as Marley pushed his way past Canyon's legs to greet us. He sniffed at Merrick, growled once, then turned to me and sat down to be petted. I stuck my tongue out at Merrick, enjoying the opportunity to tease him. "He likes me better."

Canyon rolled his eyes. "He's one persnickety dog. I wish I could figure out why he likes some people and is so damned impassive toward others." Directing us to the hall Larson had disappeared down, he shook his head. "No offense, but he was hoping you two were either Aiden or Caleb. He wants to show them the new mushroom houses my mom sent."

Merrick and Canyon had formed an immediate friendship when Larson introduced Canyon to us. The two were close in age and had a lot in common, so it wasn't surprising. Merrick reached out and slapped Canyon's wide shoulder as we entered the house. "I know how much you love those."

Their shared laughter told me I'd missed something

funny between them. When Canyon stopped laughing, he shook his head fondly as he glanced to where Larson had sat down in front of what appeared to be a village made of fabric mushrooms. "And I know how much Larson loves them."

Looking closer, every piece of the village, from the little mushroom homes to the tiny mushroom-shaped people and animals, was impressively detailed. A bucket of cars had been dumped over on the edge of the rug, a few of them placed within the village.

Cross-legged on the floor, wearing a pair of striped pajamas with a ratty blanket beside him and a sippy cup on its side a few feet away, Larson no longer looked like the giant lumberjack I'd known for so long. He looked younger, happier maybe. Even Larson's giant puppy, Lennon, toppling a few of the mushrooms hadn't dimmed his smile.

We followed Canyon automatically, and Merrick ruffled Larson's hair lightly and gave him a big smile before sitting down on the couch. "Hey, Lars."

Larson looked up and smiled at him. "Hi." His cheeks turned a bit pink when he saw me, but he offered a little wave, then turned back to his toys.

Merrick jabbed a finger into my side and shot me a look I didn't understand until he gave a pointed gesture toward the couch beside him. I sat quickly and forced myself to look away from Larson. This was the first time I'd seen him as anything other than a towering man with huge muscles and an uncanny ability to blush at nearly everything. This was the first time I'd seen Larson for who he was, and he looked... Well, he looked relaxed.

"Coffee?" Canyon had made his way to the coffee maker while I'd been watching Larson.

A voice from the floor in front of me spoke before Merrick or I could open our mouths. "Yes, please."

"Not a chance, little bit. You've got juice in your cup, and I'm pretty sure Trav mentioned something about bringing chocolate milk."

Larson shrugged and turned his attention back to his village. No matter how hard I tried, I couldn't take my eyes off Larson, and I couldn't help but be surprised at how quickly he'd forgotten all about Merrick and me.

He'd always been quiet with a stiff posture. The man playing with the toys in front of me was nothing like that. He wasn't the first little I'd spent time with—hell, I'd dated a little. I knew better than to assume a personality based on one headspace, but Larson relaxed and making noise as he played was so different from the man he was at dinner, I was struggling to believe what my eyes were seeing.

Okay, calling Evan a little was probably a stretch. He had liked the roleplay. He swore he liked rules in and out of a scene, but the truth had been Evan was awful with rules. His submission was sexy in a scene, but outside of the bedroom he was a handful who pushed my buttons. Hindsight was clear; it was for the best that our relationship fell apart before the car wreck.

"Dean?"

Hearing my name had me turning around to see Canyon holding a mug and the coffee pot up. Before I could accept, Merrick spoke. "He's had two coffees since I got to his house and judging by the sound of his stomach on the way here, he should probably eat something before he has more coffee."

I stuck my middle finger up at Merrick but couldn't argue with him. "Food first is probably a wise idea."

Canyon brought a mug to Merrick and sank down on a small couch that began to rock slightly. He fell into easy conversation with Merrick as I got lost in my head once again.

There had been a time that sitting in Canyon's position would have been ideal. A boy happily playing with his toys in front of me as I chatted with another Dom or a friend would have been a dream come true.

So why didn't it feel right anymore?

Larson must have felt me staring at him because he turned around and gave me a soft smile that I tried to return. He picked up a car and began to hold it out as the front doorbell rang. Dogs barked, Canyon stood, and Merrick laughed as Lennon barreled toward the front door to greet whoever was on the other side. Within seconds, voices filled the entryway and my thoughts were lost to a chaos too hard to ignore.

No sooner had everyone gotten into the house than I was sucked into a conversation with Trent about his raise at work. The man could do almost anything he set his mind to, but numbers were a foreign concept to him. After the first checking account nightmare I'd had to decipher for him, I'd taken over paying his bills.

We'd teased him relentlessly, but he'd taken the ribbing

with grace and still paid me fifty bucks a month. I'd given up telling him that he didn't have to pay me to do something that took me twenty minutes every two weeks, and instead put the money into his investments.

With Marley curled up on one side of me, Trent on the other, and conversations everywhere, it was hard to pay more than a passing glance toward the men playing on the floor in front of me. Even Logan was more pup than human, alternating between begging someone to throw a ball, asking for belly rubs, and occasionally jumping into a conversation one of us was having.

Pandemonium. It was the only way to describe it. Then again, we'd gone from a group of young gay college guys to a group of slightly older single gay men to mostly partnered middle-ish-aged men. We weren't as young and crazy as we once were, but our group had grown considerably as well. A quiet gathering wouldn't be in the cards for a number of decades.

CHAPTER TWO

MERRICK

An hour and twenty minutes after arriving, I stood in Canyon's huge kitchen and watched the scene around me. Brunch had just ended, and all I could do was wonder how Logan had ended up with syrup in his hair. It had to have been when he and Aiden were trying to see how high they could stack the building block waffles Canyon had served up.

At least the syrup removal hadn't been my issue to deal with. Trent was bouncing back and forth between his boyfriends, trying to get them both clean enough that they didn't leave sticky goo all over the house.

"Pup, stop squirming." Trent had uttered some variation of that phrase at least five times in the last two minutes.

As soon as he focused on Logan, Aiden would reach for another waffle and the process would start all over again. "Baby boy, fork! Your fingers are not a utensil."

Larson had found the entire interaction hysterical as he held his own sticky fingers out for Canyon to clean off. It wasn't a surprise that Larson had been cleaned up and sent off with a new cup filled with the earlier-promised chocolate milk before Trent had been able to get his men cleaned up.

Better him than me.

Domestic bliss was me and my cat, Mooch. This circus was enough to give me hives. Trent, Aiden, and Logan's house had to be insane. Scratch that, their house *was* insane. Trent had been friends with us since college, and Logan had joined the group after getting out of the Marines. It was hard to believe the sheriff and his deputy were able to cause so much mischief and not end up in jail themselves.

They'd shared a house for years before they finally admitted they were madly in love. Of course, that realization—or maybe admission was a better description—had only come after they'd found Aiden, the little who needed a Daddy and a puppy as much as the pup and Daddy needed him. Unsurprisingly, the chaos had only increased now that there were three of them together. A hyperactive pup, a curious little, and a Daddy who could be as stern as he was ornery was a recipe for excitement.

Again, better him than me.

I glanced over to find Dean laughing at something Travis was saying to him. Travis had wiped his boyfriend's face and hands with a damp cloth and sent him back to the toy area nearly ten minutes earlier. Caleb was a lot quieter than the rest of us, even when he was little, if this morning was any indication.

The chaos around the kitchen hadn't been enough to

fully distract me from Dean. He'd been off all morning and I'd been more than a little concerned about him by the time we'd arrived. There had been a few minutes of awkwardness when we'd first sat down, but after that he'd been mostly the Dean I'd always known. It hadn't stopped me from trying to figure out what was going on in his head.

"Penny for your thoughts?" Canyon sidled up beside me, his eyes tracking toward where I was watching Dean.

"Nothing important. I'd been worried about Dean for a bit, but he seems better after he ate something."

Canyon hummed. He was the newest guy in our group, so I didn't expect him to have much insight into Dean's mood and it didn't surprise me when he changed the subject. "How's the restaurant going?"

This was a much easier subject to discuss than my worries about Dean, and I jumped on the change in topic. Canyon had been a CEO of a major company before he'd stepped down and moved back home the previous summer. He understood all aspects of business and the frustrations that came with owning one. "Actually, I can't complain too much. It took way too long to get Rod to sign the papers, which pushed everything back. We're really just getting started. At least the staff has been understanding. The kitchen manager is super excited to get his hands dirty. He's done with that small kitchen."

Canyon had seen the kitchen. He knew the shoebox the poor guy had been working in for the last three years, and it was a miracle he'd stayed on as long as he had.

All of our group had been involved in helping me

purchase the bar, from estimates, valuations, and temporary jobs for Brodrick's staff members. There were no secrets between us, and everyone was curious as to how the project was going. I'd be answering questions like this all day.

We were a family, a very gay family where some lines got blurred from time to time. Friends falling in love with one another, oversharing kinks and personal lives, and texts that blew up our phones at all hours of the day and night. And I'd be lost without them.

I walked toward the coffee pot to refill my cup and noticed that Dean hadn't used his coffee cup after breakfast. "Hey, Bean, want a cup of coffee now?"

Dean gave me an unamused eye roll but finished with a nod. "Yeah. I'll take one now, *old man*."

Getting under Dean's skin had become a new hobby of mine, and with the new nickname, it had become even easier. After working in the service industry since I was eighteen, there was nothing the man could say that I hadn't heard before. Hell, after my first job in New York, there was little *anyone* could say that would surprise me. Nothing could desensitize a man like working in a gay club in New York City in the mid-nineties. Even the genius I was pouring a coffee for had no idea what it had been like to grow up during the HIV epidemic and work in a gay bar at the tail end of it. The things I heard in Tennessee now were mild compared to what I'd heard in New York then.

Dean had barely been out of diapers when I'd watched my first of many friends die of AIDS.

I wasn't being fair to Dean—he was a little older than

that but not by much. He definitely hadn't lived through the epidemic like I had. He'd come out when HIV was no longer a death sentence.

I shook the thoughts from my head, finished pouring the coffee, splashed some cream in it, and handed it over to Dean with a dramatic bow. "Your bean, Mr. Bean."

"Fuck you." Dean was smiling as he took the coffee from my hand. "Thank you, *Dad*."

I rolled my eyes, kicking myself for being cocky enough a moment before to think that he couldn't say something that got under my skin. As it turned out, there *was*. By the gleam in his eyes, he knew it too.

Three littles rushed past us on their way to get into something else, leaving Logan to chase after them on all fours. At some point he'd gotten kneepads, which helped his speed, but Lennon weaving through his arms and running in circles around him was hampering his progress. The only thing that surprised me was the fact that Dexter wasn't chasing after them. He'd found his husband's lap and was curled up with him as they chatted with Trent.

"You'd think Trent and James would get tired of one another. They work together and now spend their free time hanging out together too."

Dean scoffed around the rim of the coffee mug. "Seriously? Have you ever met these guys?" He gestured around the spacious house. "I'm more than a little convinced that they are in some weirdly platonic poly relationship. I wouldn't be surprised if they all bought a house together one day."

While I couldn't argue, I found myself happy that they'd

all found a way to be themselves. "Point taken. Are you the next to find Mr. Right?"

An unexpectedly dour look crossed Dean's face. "Nope." He popped the *p*, then tugged at the back of his shirt. The subconscious movement had been repeated so frequently over the years, the backs of his T-shirts were all longer than the fronts.

"For a long time, I honestly thought you'd be the first one of us to settle down. Even so much younger, you were always the most settled."

At least Dean laughed. "With this motley crew, that wouldn't be hard. But Evan and I were never perfect. Far from it. Maybe…" His sentence trailed off and when he spoke again, he'd changed directions. "I'm not the same person I was in my twenties."

I wanted to tell him that none of us were, but I knew he didn't mean just his age had changed. It would have been impossible to forget the car accident that he'd been in. We almost lost him that night. Once he'd finally recovered enough that he'd let us see him, we hadn't wanted to pry. Then by the time he'd started coming out with us again, everyone was so thankful to have him around that no one pushed into what had happened to him during those long months of recovery. The accident had changed him. Some of his spark and a lot of his confidence had been left in the crumpled wreckage of his car.

Seven years earlier, we'd played the stereotypical man card a little too well. Years later, none of us felt right pushing for answers. Maybe if we'd been better friends, we'd have been able to help Dean back then. If the accident had happened today, I knew Caleb, Logan, Aiden, and Dexter would have had him opening up in no time, but aside from Logan, none of them knew the way Dean had once been. The outgoing guy who stole the attention of a room and exuded a palpable sex appeal was altogether different than the man standing in front of me that morning.

He opened his mouth to say something else, but a loud smack cut his words off. We both looked over to where a handprint was already blooming on Dexter's thigh.

A faint pink had crept up Dexter's neck, but nowhere near enough to indicate he was actually embarrassed by the way his husband had popped his thigh right below the hem of the almost indecent satin shorts he was wearing. They were so skimpy I wasn't sure how his dick was covered. Then again, by the way Trent's eyes were focused intently on James's face, there was more than a chance it wasn't. And as Dexter wiggled more, I had to assume there was a very noticeable erection between his legs.

Dean smirked behind his coffee mug. "See what I mean? Dexter's about to come from a swat to his thigh, while Trent and James talk like there's nothing out of the ordinary. Weird, platonic polygamy."

All I could do was shake my head and laugh.

Dean turned back to me, somehow ignoring the show in front of us. "I made some trades for you last week based on a feeling I had. It's already paid off nicely. I've been keeping my eye on them, but I think there's a few more days, a week if you're lucky, before I need to sell them again. They stand to be quite profitable."

"Thanks. You know, this entire thing wouldn't have been possible without you." My understanding of the stock market wasn't much more than a basic understanding of the numbers that scrolled across the bottom of the TV screen when I had CNN on. Dean's knack for all things numbers had given him an uncanny ability to understand the stock market. The few hundred dollars he'd bummed off of each of us in college had taken some roller coaster rides along the way, but we all had a nice retirement or rainy day savings.

A commotion in the other room drew our attention for a second, but when we didn't see anything, Dean turned back to me. "For a man who just bought a business in need of massive renovations, you've hardly stepped foot in the place in weeks."

I poked his side with my elbow. "Do you forget that Rod dragged his feet in getting the papers signed? I had to get his kids involved before the man finally signed." *Stubborn old goat.* "It pushed everything back. Trav had us worked in last month, but by the time I officially had keys, it was too late for him to start. We're at the mercy of Trav's team, and when they can fit us in. Thankfully, Trav was able to get everyone at the restaurant a temp spot in his company while we're closed. It's taken a lot of stress off me."

"Good plan. Hate to admit it, but you're a good man, Mer. Aside from bugging the hell out of me three nights a week, what are you doing to keep busy until then?"

Laughter bubbled up from beside us. Canyon had stepped over without our knowledge and had heard at least some of the conversation. "Well, after Trent called and begged me to get the man out of his office, Lars and I put him to work filming and editing for social media."

It was the least I could do. I was the one that had pushed the record button for Larson's very first YouTube video. Besides, I couldn't stand being idle. So when Larson had quit his job as a firefighter to take up woodworking full time, I'd helped Canyon convince him to start posting on social media. Now it was just assumed that I'd edit the videos, but I liked the work and planned to keep doing it.

Dean looked to Canyon, batting his eyes like Aiden did when he wanted something from his Daddy. "Promise me you'll never send him to me for work."

There was no way Dean would let anyone near his spreadsheets. Even as a guy who liked numbers and organization, I thought his job as a forensic accountant was a tedious, exhausting job that required attention to detail that I couldn't comprehend. The challenge had never bothered Dean. He loved it and was damn good at his job. He'd gotten cases from all over the country and had testified in court a number of times. The man was a number whiz, but he was also friendly and sociable.

I made a cross over my heart with my finger. "I will never mess with your precious spreadsheets. The one time you tried to explain to me how it was that you figured out the way that guy embezzled money from his wife's inheritance, I got lost on step one."

Dean beamed with unmistakable pride at my words. "That's why I get paid good money to do what I do."

Canyon scratched at his bald head. "So what you're

saying is that you would be able to commit the perfect financial crime."

"Oh, yes." He rubbed his hands together and cackled like a greedy miser.

Laughter spilled into the room as the group came charging back in, that time with Marley in the mix. Dean and I went our separate ways. He was more relaxed than he had been, but he wasn't happy. Something about the look on his face—his eyes in particular—ate at me. Dean wasn't telling us something, but *what* was the real question.

CHAPTER THREE

DEAN

How could grown men have the energy that Larson, Logan, Aiden, and Caleb all had? They'd played hard all afternoon—inside, outside, with the dogs, with toys, and with video games. I was exhausted from watching them. But as the afternoon turned into evening and pizza was ordered, I could tell the activity was catching up with all of them.

When Logan yawned and stretched, I heard Trent sigh. "Maybe you'll actually sleep tonight, huh?" He placed a gentle kiss on Logan's temple.

Logan gave him a grin, his blue eyes flickering with anything but innocence. "Well, I know Aiden will. You might need to wear me out a little more."

Trent rolled his eyes. "Behave, pup."

"Never!" Logan swiped a bottle of water from the fridge and nearly danced back to where the others were cleaning up the disaster they'd made throughout the day.

For a few minutes, I got caught up in watching them.

All of them were relaxed and smiling, laughing about things that had happened during their day. As Aiden collapsed a tower of LEGO bricks into a bin, I wondered when the last time was I'd built with blocks or played with a toy. I hadn't been a typical kid by any stretch. I'd already finished *The Chronicles of Narnia* when I'd started kindergarten. By first grade, I was doing fifth grade math.

My mom had done her best to give me a normal childhood, but I hadn't been interested in what the other kids were playing with. There were many more interesting things to do and learn. Why would I want to build with LEGO when I could be rewiring the RC car I'd gotten for my birthday?

Natural curiosity had kept me excited for learning, but that meant the elementary school had run out of curriculum for me by the end of fourth grade. The next two years had been spent driving the middle school math and science teachers insane with questions that were well above their ability to answer. The eighth grade history teacher had kicked me out of his class halfway through the civil rights unit after I'd corrected him numerous times.

The rest of the year had been spent completing the course with the guidance counselor, who gave up on the planned work three weeks in, gave me the final test, and told me to figure out something history related to study on my own. The next ten weeks had been spent poring over college texts about World War II.

High school hadn't been much better, but I'd finally found a footing in college. By then, I understood social expectations better and was able to test out of the required classes that I wasn't interested in. Being able to focus on my areas of interest had gone a long way in easing some of my awkwardness. The last bits had slowly diminished when Merrick, Travis, Trent, and Larson had folded me into their group.

These guys, as unique as we all were, were my family, and I never got tired of watching everyone interact. Trent split his time effortlessly between Aiden's and Logan's needs, a smile on his face every time he interacted with one of them. A lesson I'd learned early on was that a Dom had to be in the right headspace to care for a submissive. I hadn't been in the right headspace for years. Pain and self-consciousness played a part in it, but beyond that, there was something wholly unappealing about caring for someone else right now.

Trent's voice pulled me from my musings again. Logan had effortlessly joined the conversation he was having with James and Canyon about five minutes earlier. "Take a juice back to Aiden and actually help them clean up this time."

Logan gave a deep sigh as he approached where I was standing near the stack of juice boxes on the counter. "Yes, Daddy." An exaggerated eye roll accompanied his blatantly sarcastic response.

"Stop calling me that!" Quieter but still audible, Trent could be heard grumbling to James. "You'd think it would get old."

Logan's blue eyes sparkled as he swiped a juice box off the pile and turned to me, whispering conspiratorially. "After all these years, you'd think he'd figure out that it will never get boring to tease him. Hey, Larson got his game system set up in the other room. Want to play Mario Kart? I think they're about to fall asleep."

His question sparked something inside me. How long had it been since I'd played a video game with anyone? I could lose hours of my night playing first person shooters with faceless strangers, but I couldn't remember the last time I'd sat down and played any game with a friend.

A smile tugged at my lips and I found myself opening my mouth to agree when Travis stepped up beside us. "Hey, Dean. You have a second?"

Logan gave another roll of his eyes, that time directed at Travis, and mouthed *Later*. The little furl of excitement I'd felt a moment before left with Logan as he hurried off to go bug the three on the carpet.

My smile was forced as I turned to Travis. "Hey. What's up?"

His bright eyes always pulled me in and his voice soothed me in a way few things did. I found myself relaxing despite my annoyance only seconds earlier. I even managed a genuine smile when he turned a concerned look my way. He was a natural Daddy, a caretaker to everyone, not just Caleb. "You doing alright? You keep rubbing your back."

I felt a flush creep up my neck. "Yeah. I think I spent too much time on the couch last night and this morning."

Travis gave me a teasing grin. "Too many video games last night?"

"If only. Got wrapped up in work." It was easier than telling him that my back always hurt. The physical therapist I'd seen throughout my recovery had pushed me to see a massage therapist, insisting that frequent massages would help keep the damaged muscles and tendons loose. But that meant questions about why half my back was scarred and telling someone that the scars were painful.

What was the point in paying for a massage if they couldn't press hard enough to loosen the muscle?

"Wait until you're my age and you end up waking up with a crick in your back and you're hobbling around for an entire day for no apparent reason."

I laughed because it was expected of me, but I'd known what that felt like since the feeling in my back and legs had returned a few days after the accident. My thoughts turned melancholic and my eyes drifted to where Logan had sunk back onto the floor, sitting with his legs outstretched as he watched them cleaning up.

"Enjoying watching them play?"

"Yeah. They're having fun."

His hum was understanding, but I didn't look over at him. "I enjoy watching them play. Hell, Logan has a blast too. Half the time I think he does it because he likes to drive them nuts, half the time is because I think he just likes to stop thinking for a bit. Talking with Trent, James, you, or me, he has to be on."

My head tilted as I watched Logan. "I never thought of it that way. You're right, though. As a pup, he's a lot freer. Is it possible that he's calmer as a pup than a human?"

The question made Travis laugh. "You've never seen him at the club on a mosh night. That is something else."

And something I could do without seeing. That level of energy, excitement, and noise had always been too intense for me and a headache started to bloom at the thought.

I knew the club he was referring to. It felt like the entire group had a membership to Nashville's BDSM club, DASH. Back before the accident, I'd also been a member. It was where I'd met Evan, and where I'd had my first real experience with D/s relationships. I hadn't been back since the accident. My membership had expired during my recovery, and I'd never renewed it.

Travis was one of the few people who knew I'd once been a member. He also knew I no longer was. I'd told him years back that I was no longer in the lifestyle. We hadn't spoken much about it since, so the words that came next left me speechless. "There's a littles night coming up in a few weeks. Could I convince you to come with us?"

The four on the rug were forgotten as I whipped my head toward Travis so fast my neck popped. Despite my mouth opening a few times, no sounds came out. When my brain and voice began to work together again, they were half-functional at best. "What? Why?"

Travis gave me a shrug that approximated casual, but I knew him well enough to know that he'd had a reason to ask. "Actually, there's a guy I think you'd like to meet. He's a little who's looking for a Daddy."

I should have known. Despite my best attempts, my answering laugh sounded fake. "Can't let me stay blissfully single now that you're happily engaged?"

Travis leveled me with a stare that saw too much. "Dean, it's been over seven years since you and Evan broke up. I know you said he wasn't the right guy for you. I didn't push when you told me that you weren't in the lifestyle anymore, but it isn't something that just goes away. This guy isn't a brat like your ex was. He's mature, he's polite, and he's got a good head on his shoulders. He went to dinner with us before the last event and told us he's a music teacher and is just figuring out his little side. He's sweet and happy and loves to snuggle. He's made friends with the guys, so you know he's a good egg."

My eyes went back to the four across the room. Aiden had crawled between Logan's legs, Larson on one side, Caleb on the other, and Logan was reading a book to them. Stuffed animals and blankets were still scattered around, but the toys had been cleaned up, and they were oblivious to anything but the story.

My brain was just working out that I wanted to be with them more than where I currently was when Travis poked me in the ribs. I wasn't going to deny that my look might have looked like longing, but I also knew that it wasn't for the reasons he suspected.

"See. That. It's time to get back in the saddle again. It's part of you."

Oh no. It most certainly wasn't time to get back in the saddle again. Definitely not after the thought I'd just had. I wasn't touching that one. Not with Travis. Not with anyone. "Trav, I've already told you. I'm not looking for a boy. Hell, I'm not looking for a relationship. I'm good being single."

"Think about it, Dean."

Knowing that he wouldn't let it go until I at least agreed

to think about it, I nodded my head. "Yeah, sure, I'll think about it."

I sagged against the counter as he left, my mind already far from the conversation with Travis. Scanning the room, my eyes fell on Merrick's. He was watching me closely, a furrow of concern across his forehead. My forced smile clearly didn't convince him because he excused himself from the conversation he was in the middle of to come stand next to me.

Our arms touching, Merrick leaned into me and spoke quietly. "What's wrong, Bean?"

His concern was touching, but not in the way I'd expected. He didn't sound like a friend who was asking because it was expected of him but like he actually cared. The look he was giving me reminded me of how Trent often looked at Logan, and my stomach flipped.

I liked that look. I liked someone looking at me that way. Hell, I liked *Merrick* looking at me that way.

He'd always been off-limits. He was a friend and was clear that he wasn't looking for more. That had never stopped the low-key crush I'd had on him since he'd shown up in my study group. A sexy older guy, world-traveled and exciting. Charismatic and charming in ways I had never been able to be. I was the boy next door; he was the wild child who chased his dreams.

His travels had made it easier to ignore the crush. I'd gotten so good at ignoring it that I'd totally forgotten about it until that moment. The moment his silver-gray eyes looked at me, imploring me to open up and tell him what was wrong. Even if I'd wanted to spill everything, there was no way I was going to tell him the thoughts going on in my head at that moment.

"Just getting tired and thinking about work."

My inconvenient crush wasn't ebbing as he wrapped his arm around my shoulders and squeezed gently. "Come on. I'll get you home. Let me make some excuses for us."

CHAPTER FOUR

MERRICK

I wiped sweat from my forehead with a bandana. Why was I sweating so much in March? Then I looked at my surroundings and remembered why. As of 7:00 a.m., the renovations were officially underway. Travis's team had made short work of the gut job, and I was now looking at stud walls, a few piles of debris, and a blueprint tacked to the area that used to be the back of the bar.

"Whoa." Dean's voice pulled me from my thoughts, and I looked over to see him standing in the front entrance, eyes wide with surprise.

Sweat dripped into my eyes and stung, causing me to pinch them shut and curse under my breath before I could finally greet him. He'd been distant since that day at Canyon's place. The two of us were still spending time together, but despite his easy laughs, his eyes had dulled.

Maybe it was the relentless pain he seemed to be dealing with. While I hadn't come out and asked him directly, he had a tendency to rub his lower back and glutes frequently. I'd caught more than a few winces of pain at quick or sudden movements. But he'd been doing that before his brown eyes had become sad.

There were a lot of layers to him that I hadn't been able to figure out. He had closed-off down to an art. I knew because I did too. My biggest problem at the moment was that I couldn't stop thinking about Dean. More than anything, I wanted to see his eyes sparkle again, but I hadn't found a way to make it happen.

He'd obviously just come from work, his gray slacks hugging his lightly muscled legs and his blue dress shirt still tucked in. He'd lost his sports coat and had rolled the sleeves of his shirt up to his elbows, leaving his tattoos exposed. If there was a rhyme or reason to the design, I hadn't figured it out yet. The lines looked like they'd been placed randomly around his forearm, broader in some places, narrower in others. Despite the haphazard design, they were still striking and gorgeous.

I'd caught myself following the random lines and patterns on numerous occasions. My mind had gone as far as to wonder how far up his arm they went. The day I had caught myself obsessing over how sexy they were and wanting to trace each line just to watch him squirm, I'd forced myself to stop thinking about them. With the tattoos on full display, the inappropriate thoughts were coming back at an alarming rate.

"Bean!" My voice cracked. All I could do was hope he thought it was from surprise and that he had no idea it was because my dick had suddenly swelled and was trapped at an uncomfortable angle. I cleared my throat and tried again. "Wasn't expecting you to show up."

Exhaustion clouded his eyes and he stifled a yawn as I took him in. "Did you really think I wasn't going to stop by and see the progress? The group chat has been going insane today with pictures. I just had to see it with my own two eyes." When he didn't add *Dad*, I knew he was exhausted.

The group chat? Why hadn't my phone notified me? I patted my pockets to find them empty. "Be right back." I hurried to my SUV, hoping like hell that I hadn't lost the phone during the demo process. I'd never find it in the dumpsters, and I was pretty sure a few had already been hauled away. My phone was sitting in the cup holder, the lock screen alerting me to over two hundred missed texts. Well, that explained why everyone had shown up at some point that day when I hadn't told anyone about it.

I waved my phone in the air as I reentered the building. "Do you all do anything but text? How do I have over two hundred missed texts in barely eight hours?"

Dean's laugh lit up his face in a way I hadn't seen in a long time. When a dimple appeared in his cheek, he looked younger. "I had to put my phone on silent by lunchtime because I wasn't getting anything done."

"I could believe it. Did you get enough work done, though?"

The question sounded a lot like something Canyon would ask Larson. Larson liked Canyon's hovering, but something told me Dean wouldn't like mine. To my surprise, he only lifted a shoulder. There was a chance we'd been spending too much time together because I immediately knew what that look meant. Wiping my hands on a rag, I shook my head before he could say anything. "You are not going to spend another night hunched over your computer."

His cheeks heated at my calling him out. "I like my work. Besides, it's not like I've got anything else to do."

"Well, now you do. Follow me to my place so I can shower, then we're going to get dinner."

The snarl he went for would have been more impressive had he not yawned. There was no mistaking the exhaustion in his eyes, and I knew he wasn't in any condition to go out. "Change of plans, let's go to your place. If you don't mind me using your shower, I've got spare clothes in my car. You look like you could use a cold beer, some takeout, and an early bed. Nowhere in there is work included. If that means I have to tuck your ass into bed and wait for you to fall asleep before I head home, I will."

Dean's brown eyes flashed darker and he ducked his head as a slight blush stained his cheeks. His reaction was sweet and to confuse matters more, my cock gave a warning twitch to remind me that it was already unhappy in the current position. Whatever caused his reaction, or my dick's, wasn't important. What was important was that Dean got a night to relax. If it took me sitting on his damned laptop, I would.

"So, can I shower at your place?"

He glanced up at me, the blush still on his face, and managed a small nod. "Yeah, um, that's fine."

"Want anything in particular for dinner? I'll order on the way."

The question made his eyes brighten and he looked up at me with a smile on his face. "Pizza?"

I had a flashback to college nights spent sitting on a couch, eating pizza and drinking beer. At least Dean's house was nicer than the college apartments had been and his furniture wasn't a biohazard. "Pizza's great. I'll follow you. What do you want?"

He gave me a hopeful look, and even before the request was out, I knew I'd be ordering whatever he asked. "Ham and pineapple, please."

Despite his smile when I nodded my agreement, Dean yawned three times between then and the time we climbed into our vehicles. If he had lived any farther away, I'd have insisted on driving him. Instead, I followed him out of the parking lot while telling my car to call the nearest pizza place to Dean's address, keeping a close eye on his car. If he so much as swerved, I'd hit the horn and make him get into my car.

One order of a ham and pineapple pizza and a sausage, onion, and green pepper pizza was placed before we made it halfway to his house. I'd added two six-packs of beer as an afterthought, given them my credit card number and Dean's address, and clicked off in time to see the turn to Dean's complex coming up.

A few turns later, Dean had parked in his garage and I was parked behind him in his driveway, and we headed inside without saying a word. He hung his backpack, which I knew contained his cherished laptop, on a hook by the door, then gestured down the hallway. "You know where the shower is."

I'd already been heading there, but at the steps, I gave him a little push. "Go get changed. I'm going to shower. And I'm not going to come out to find you on your laptop."

I was halfway to the hall bathroom when I heard it. "Yes, Dad. Ugh, you're so strict."

Yup, the word still got to me, but that time it hadn't annoyed me like it had in the past. I didn't care what he called me, just as long as he relaxed that night. "I mean it, Bean. No work."

Dean huffed but didn't say anything else, so I shut the door and showered quickly. To my surprise, Dean appeared more awake when I stepped out of the bathroom. I knew I felt and smelled a hell of a lot better, but Dean was the one who looked like a new person. In a pair of mesh shorts and an oversized T-shirt, he looked like he could be going to bed, but he was stretched out with his long legs against the coffee table. The blanket that normally graced the back of the couch was draped across his lower legs. A game controller was in his hands, a headset over his ears, and he was chatting with an unknown someone as things exploded on the TV.

He was so lost in whatever game he was playing, he didn't notice me as I headed through the house and into the kitchen to see what he had in the fridge. Hopefully he had beer, because I'd drunk my weight in water that day and was tired of it. I didn't find beer, but I did find two ginger beers that would have to suffice until the pizza arrived.

Dean didn't acknowledge my presence as I placed one of the bottles in front of him, then settled into the chair beside the couch to watch him play. His eyebrows had turned downward and little lines creased his forehead as the game continued. It didn't look as relaxing as the racing game I'd been watching Larson play the night before with Logan and Aiden. It definitely wasn't as cute as the one with little animals and villages that Caleb and Aiden played all the time. This was gruesome and violent, and Dean's fingers were mashing at buttons and joysticks in a complicated pattern while he verbally sparred with other players.

Nothing to date had drawn such a sharp contrast to our age difference. Whatever he was playing looked nothing like the 8-bit cartoon video games I'd grown up with. I was willing to bet there wasn't a game cartridge that had to be blown into before it would work. This thing looked more like a high-budget action flick than a video game.

The doorbell brought relief from Dean's constant dialogue and the sounds coming from the TV. I was feeling much older than forty-five as I rubbed my temples on my way to the door. Behind me, I could hear Dean saying goodbye before the living room fell silent. I signed the credit card slip, grabbed the dinner, and turned to see that Dean had headed to the kitchen for plates and napkins.

"Level with me, Bean. Do you work as much as you claim, or do you play that?" I was at a loss for a description. *Hideous, annoying noise* would make me sound like I was old enough to be his dad but calling it a video game felt far too generous.

Dean pushed a drawer shut with his hip, and I caught

his face twitch in unmistakable pain. Ignoring whatever he'd felt, he shook his head. "I work a lot, but I also like not thinking sometimes."

The statement hadn't answered my question. If anything, it was evasive. I was pretty sure Logan had said nearly the same thing when someone had asked why he liked puppy play. There was no time to unpack the statement. Dean had already moved toward the living room with the plates and napkins. "Come on. I'm starving."

I grabbed two glasses from the cupboard and headed back to find Dean already seated on the couch. He'd pulled the blanket over his lap again and had both pizza boxes open on the coffee table. "I love this place. Good choice."

Focused on the pizzas in front of him, Dean couldn't see my smirk. "Glad you approve." If it hadn't been for the name of the place printed on the boxes, I wouldn't have had a clue where I'd ordered from.

"My favorite pizza from my favorite place. Damn, Mer. If I didn't know better, I'd think you're trying to find a way to ask me out." He grinned over at me.

My laugh was harsh as I shook my head. "God, no. No boyfriends. Been there, done that, have the scars to prove it." Even as I said the words, something was shifting inside me. Until that moment, I hadn't considered trying to impress Dean, definitely not to date him, but what if—

The thought didn't have time to fully materialize before Dean spoke. "No interest here either. Trav is trying to play matchmaker with me right now, so watch yourself. You'll end up being next."

That sobered me quickly, pushing the errant thought away.

We sat in silence as we ate, my mind trying to dance toward a place I didn't want to go.

I didn't know if I'd made a noise or a face, but something clued Dean in on my thoughts. "What happened?"

"Hmm?" Dean was focused intently on me, studying me in a way that made me feel seen.

The tilted head and raised eyebrow told me he wasn't going to let me off the hook. "I've known you since I was eighteen and you've never had more than a casual hookup. What happened? Who broke your heart and turned you into Elsa?"

"Did you really just compare me to a cartoon princess?"

Dean didn't stop staring at me. "Would you have rather I called you the Abominable Snowman? If memory serves, he had a toothache, not a frozen heart."

Ouch. "Just not my thing."

"Bullshit."

Tom had done a number on me, and now Dean was on the scent and I needed to get him off it. "Same old shit, different guy. You know how it goes—young gay Midwestern boy meets flashy New York bartender. Boy falls in love, bartender cheats. Love isn't like the movies. Besides, I'm pretty sure Elsa ran a kingdom on her own. She didn't need a prince or a king."

Despite my attempt at flippancy, Dean's eyes had turned soft. The understanding and sadness I saw there made the admission worse.

"Damn, Mer. I'm so sorry. I've never been cheated on,

so I can't imagine what that felt like, but I'm sorry it happened to you." He gave me a smile that matched the look in his eyes, sweet and kind. "First broken heart is hard, but to have it end that way really sucks. Evan and I just grew apart." He shook his head. "Hell, maybe Trav is right. Maybe I just need to listen to him."

His statement confused me, but I was ready to latch on to any excuse to change the subject. "Who is he trying to hook you up with?"

Dean groaned, grabbed another slice of pizza, and flopped back onto the couch. "A boy at DASH."

I knew what DASH was, and I knew what he meant by a boy. But why did Travis want Dean to meet one? "Why does Travis think you'd want to meet this guy?"

The large bite of pizza in his mouth couldn't hide Dean's grin. When he swallowed, he began to chuckle. "The boy needs a Daddy."

As a true Midwestern boy at heart, I knew staring was impolite. I also knew openly gawking at someone was rude, but I was doing both at the moment. Dean's words made no sense to me. Did that mean Travis thought Dean was a Daddy? It was almost laughable. He was so… *not* one. At least not from my experience. "I'm sorry, I'm being rude. I just, I can't imagine you with a boy…"

Dean lifted his eyebrows, nearly daring me to finish the thought. I shut my mouth and Dean grinned. "Yeah, I know. I can't see myself with a boy now either. Before the accident, I'd probably have been all over it, but a lot has changed for me. I haven't found myself in a position where I feel right being a Dom. Hell, I don't think I'm in the right place to date. Physical scars aside, I haven't felt comfortable trying to date since the accident. I wouldn't be a good boyfriend, much less a Daddy who needs to be able to please his sub."

I wasn't going to push about the accident. I was also going to ignore the sudden ache in my chest at Dean admitting that he'd been a Daddy. I didn't have a submissive bone in my body, and if that was what Dean wanted, we would never work.

My logical brain kicked into gear again. There would never be a Dean and me, no matter what my cock thought at the moment. We were friends, and I wasn't going to date anyone, much less a friend.

Desperate to get the idea out of my mind, I asked the only question I could think to ask. "Do you *want* to be in a relationship?"

He tossed the crust of his pizza into the box and reached for another slice. As he sat back, he pulled the fuzzy blanket up a bit higher, his free hand working idly at the fabric. "That's a hard question to answer. I think I would like it, yeah. I always enjoyed having a partner to share things with. Finding that space where I feel like I could be there on an emotional level isn't in the cards, though. I would be a shit boyfriend. And then Travis threw me for a loop and decided it's time for me to find a boy."

He took a bite of his pizza, effectively stopping the conversation on his end, but my mind was now in overdrive. I was a problem solver. I also had too much time on my hands. Sure, Brodrick's had just been taken down to the studs, but aside from overseeing the budget—which Dean was keeping a closer eye on than I was—and being around to answer logistical restaurant questions, I didn't have much to do. Helping Dean find his groove and the ability to date again felt like just the thing I needed. Besides, if he found a boyfriend, I could stop having irrational thoughts about us.

"Well, we're just going to have to find your Zen. Whatever that might end up being."

Dean paused with his beer halfway to his mouth. "I'm going to regret telling you that."

No, he wouldn't. And I wouldn't regret helping. The sooner he found a boyfriend, the sooner I could forget about being interested in him.

CHAPTER FIVE

DEAN

Dexter: What "sips" should we bring?

Logan: Please tell me it's something stronger than wine.

Trent: I cannot believe we're actually doing this. Seriously, Mer, don't you have something better to do with your time? It's like we're old women!

Dexter: What are we painting? Is there a dress code?

Trent: Canyon, you have a rule that dicks need to be covered, right? Asking for a friend.

Aiden: You take all the fun out of things.

Trent: Baby boy, you're not going to go to Canyon's and Larson's house with your dick hanging out. If you're not careful, it's going to be caged inside a thick diaper.

Dexter: And Caleb says I overshare...

Aiden: I never said I wanted to have my dick hanging out... but I mean, free show?

Canyon: Leave me out of this. My boy's dick has been tucked safely inside his training pants for the evening.

James: *Dexter, clothes are required! Travis, make sure he is dressed and COVERED.*

Travis: *Don't get me involved in that one! Besides, Dexter's with Cal right now... you know at their work. Just like I'm at my work, trying to get stuff done so I can meet you nut cases in a few hours.*

Me: *It's three in the afternoon! This thing doesn't start until seven. I'm certain this is an argument best had after work.*

Merrick: *Rainbow tree. Clothes required. We have far too few boundaries as is. I don't need to see anyone's dick tonight.*

I turned my phone to silent, stuffed it in a drawer, and promptly turned my attention back to my laptop. Easier said than done when my friends had been openly discussing what was being worn—or not—under pants. I shook my head, trying to shake the images from my mind.

At some point, I managed to forget about my phone and the crazy texts because an alarm ringing drew my attention. Except my phone was on silent and I hadn't set an alarm. I looked up, surprised to see Merrick standing in my doorway smirking at me. Not for the first time in recent weeks, I was struck by how handsome he was as he leaned against my doorframe with his arms and ankles crossed.

"I knew you'd get lost in work."

Cocky and infuriating but handsome nonetheless.

"What time is it?"

The corner of his mouth twitched. "Late enough that you should be out of here. Come on, Bean. You don't want to show up to paint in that." He gestured at my nice pants and dress shirt.

I pushed my glasses up my nose so he could better see my glower. At a certain point, it wasn't worth arguing over the nickname, but that didn't mean I had to accept it without a little poking. "What time is it, Dad?"

"Four thirty. Now come on."

With my glasses in place, I knew he'd be able to easily see my eye roll. "My workday ends at five."

"You work for yourself. You only have an office because you get distracted at home."

I looked around my office in the co-op space. His words were only partially true. I liked the co-op space because I liked the noise of people around me, but I also got more work done when I was dressed in business clothes. At home, it felt wrong to walk around in dress clothes. In the co-op space, people came to work in everything from pajamas to suits and ties. I fit right in.

"I like getting out of the house some. But I still work nine-to-five."

"You're also dragging your feet. I have a restaurant that is in three million pieces, a crew trying to put it back together, and I'm here instead of there. Take it from *Dad,* you need to focus more on your life and less on your work. The next ten years are going to go by with startling speed. You don't want to spend the next decade pushing people away, only to find that you're lonely."

Unable to unpack his statement, I decided to do the easiest thing and pack up for the day. With my laptop powered down, I slipped it into my bag. "Okay. You've made your point."

"Good." His pleased smile had already sent a swirl of

pleasure down my spine, but the praise made the feeling continue into my groin.

After a quick stop at my place to change and leave my car, we were pulling into Canyon and Larson's driveway just after five thirty. To Merrick's dismay, Marley met us at the door. Whatever he felt about Merrick, Marley had taken a particular interest in him. Merrick swore Marley wanted to eat him as a snack; I thought he just wanted to be friends.

Regardless of Marley's motives, Merrick was unappreciative of the dog jumping up to rest his huge paws on his shoulders as we entered the house.

Canyon was right behind Marley, trying to save Merrick from the bucket of slobber. "Marley, down!"

He'd uttered some variation of those words numerous times by the time I made it through the door. As I passed the group, I shook my head. "Marley, sit."

Marley stepped back immediately, sitting on a whimper and allowing Merrick to finally pass.

"I'm just going to reiterate. You're a pain in my ass, Marley. Why do you sit for Dean and Larson but won't for me?" Canyon shook his head all the way to the kitchen. "Larson's just starting to set the food out. We bought half of the grocery store today."

Canyon hadn't been exaggerating. Containers of food were scattered across the marble. "Leave anything at the store?"

Larson shook his head. "I told him we were buying too much."

"I've seen the way you boys eat. Let me get the others—

they're on the patio. Logan just texted that they're a few minutes out."

Merrick squeezed my shoulder. "Will you help Larson while I step outside with Canyon for a second?"

My head bobbed an automatic agreement. When he gave me a wide smile, the same tingle of pleasure shot down my spine. "Thanks, Bean. I'll be right back."

I could feel my face heat as he left and I was certain Larson was going to mention it. He was staring at me like I'd become interesting over the last few seconds. I prepared for the question that never came. In true Larson style, he observed what happened, didn't push for an answer, and changed the subject to something safer. "I'm predicting an interesting night. Dex is already two drinks in."

Larson laughed as I rolled my eyes. We worked in silence for a few minutes, but I found that the harder I tried focusing on the task before me, the more my attention drifted toward the play space Larson had beside the kitchen. It wasn't hard to picture Larson, Caleb, Aiden, and Logan playing there. They'd been loud and goofy, but I'd found myself laughing more that day than I'd laughed in months, and most of the laughter had been a result of their antics.

I'd been moving on autopilot, lost in my thoughts, when Trent's booming voice echoed through the foyer. "Seriously? A rainbow tree?"

Merrick had just walked back inside and threw his hands in the air. "What's so bad about a rainbow tree?"

Fighting a losing battle against a smile, I found myself

chuckling as I spoke. "I mean, there's nothing wrong with it. It's just, um, very cliché for a group of gay men."

Logan bounded into the kitchen, Marley trotting happily behind him. If a dog could smile, Marley was smiling. "It's such a middle-aged thing to do."

Merrick rolled his eyes. "We *are* middle-aged, asshole."

"Hey! Speak for yourself! Not all of us are old farts. There's a number of us still in our twenties. *Thank you very much!*"

Dexter's exclamation caused James to sigh. "Thanks, Mer. Get the menace all riled up."

Logan and I dissolved into laughter as we grabbed paper plates for ourselves and began piling them with sandwiches, salads, and cookies while the rest of the guys argued. "They'll be at this the rest of the night at this rate. Come on, let's go eat."

I followed Logan, Marley, and Lennon out to the sunroom where we settled into some of the comfortable couches to eat our dinner. Marley somehow fit himself between Logan and me on the couch, his head resting on Logan's lap as he blinked up at him for food. Logan fed him a bite of turkey off his sub, then turned to me. "Remind me again how we all got roped into this Boozy Brushing thing?"

I didn't think the original name of the event was Boozy Brushing, but judging by the amount of liquor I'd seen in the kitchen, Logan's description was better than the Sip 'n Paint Merrick had scheduled. "Mer's decided I need to find a way to relax. I think it's a ploy to get me back in the dating scene so that everyone stays off his back."

Logan shook his head. "He's an intelligent man. I'm seriously stumped about why he thinks focusing on your love life will keep Dex and Trav from trying to pair him up with some—Hey! That's mine!"

Marley had taken Logan's distraction as an opportunity to eat his sub in one huge bite. I found myself laughing so hard I struggled to breathe as I moved my plate away from the dogs. "Correction, that *was* yours. It's now Marley's."

Logan climbed off the couch, heading back into the kitchen. "Canyon! Your dog ate my dinner!"

This was going to be an interesting night. "Down!" I pointed to the floor when Marley's eyes turned toward my plate. He huffed but got off the couch, then slunk away to go torment someone else.

At least with Marley gone, Lennon simply lay at my feet while I ate and listened to the others chastise Marley for trying to eat their dinner.

By the time the event was ready to start, I was pretty sure everyone had managed to get food. Marley had eaten more than all of us, but he appeared content as he slept at Larson's feet.

We'd been placed in a semicircle, and I'd ended up with Logan on one side of me and Dexter on the other. The instructor had her back to us as she explained how to get started. Admittedly, the finished painting she'd brought with her was beautiful, but I highly doubted that many of us would be able to replicate it. There were six trees, each a different color of the rainbow, and a body of water at the bottom that reflected the leaves.

I couldn't think of a single place in any of our homes

that the paintings would fit. And what were Trent, Aiden, and Logan going to do with three of the same painting? I was supposed to focus on the painting, not everyone else. Something about the rhythmic movement was supposed to be soothing. It would have been easier to find relaxation if Logan and Aiden weren't giggling beside me or if Dexter hadn't been humming as he painted.

The six tree trunks on my canvas looked nothing like the instructor's. They were lopsided and unevenly spaced, but they were there and I could at least start on the leaves. My tongue poked out from between my lips as I coated the next brush in red paint. Before I could make contact with the canvas, the laughter beside me drew my attention. A glance over showed Logan's red tree was in the shape of a dick. He was going to great lengths to combine the whites and pink tones to make it look more like the tree we were supposed to be creating, but there was no mistaking the dick shape.

I leaned over so that only Logan could hear as I whispered into his ear. "Size whore?"

He barked. It couldn't even be considered a laugh. It was a bark of surprise that sounded a lot more like the sounds he'd made while running around the house when he'd been Curious. "Aren't we all?"

Aiden leaned forward. "I'd take it!"

Logan reached over and patted his arm. "We know. You take it every time your Daddy offers."

Aiden's cheeks flushed as red as the tree Logan was painting, yet he managed to grin and nod.

I stuck my fingers in my ears. "Lalalalalala."

When I was done, I had the attention of most of the group. Focusing back on my canvas, I tried to ignore their confused looks. This was not going as planned and wasn't going to get back on track at any point once Logan lifted an eyebrow in my direction, a challenge clear in his blue eyes. "Think you can do better?"

"Challenge accepted."

Over the course of the next hour, six distinctly dick-shaped trees appeared on both of our canvases. We'd drawn the attention of Aiden and Dexter, who continued to find reasons to walk by our canvases and critique each different tree.

The poor instructor didn't know what to make of us, actively avoiding our section of the patio after the first time she'd walked by.

As Aiden and Dexter examined my blue dick-tree, Trent cleared his throat. "Pup, do I need to separate you and Dean?"

Logan's eyes went wide, but he shook his head. "No, Daddy."

Trent groaned, Aiden snickered, and Logan grinned at me. "It's so easy to get under his skin."

I found myself smiling, leaning toward Logan and Aiden to whisper conspiratorially. "I call Merrick Dad because I know it drives him nuts."

Logan's head bobbed up and down. "Oh, yes. It's so fun to poke at Trent."

Out of the corner of my eye, I could see Merrick standing next to Canyon, slowly shaking his head. The odds were it was at us, but I didn't care. This was fun. Not the painting, because it was horribly boring, but creating dicks on sticks with Logan had been more fun than I'd expected to have the entire night.

Then I glanced over at Aiden's painting and found myself laughing harder than I was at the paintings Logan and I were doing. He'd painted the trees exactly like they were supposed to be, but the falling leaves were different shapes depending on the tree. Little puppy heads were falling from one tree, dicks from another, pacifiers from a third.

"Trent has his hands full with you two."

Aiden beamed over at me. "He loves us!"

Trent finally put his brush down and walked over to where we were standing. When he took a look at our paintings, his palm hit his forehead. "Can you all not behave yourselves for an hour?"

Logan's lower lip stuck out in a pout. "But we didn't *need* three of the same paintings!"

"We painted the trees. Personally, I think we made gorgeous dickiduous forests."

No sooner had the words left my mouth than the instructor gave up all pretense of ignoring us and burst out laughing. Merrick left his painting and walked over to us. The sigh he gave was unmistakable frustration. "Really?"

I lifted a shoulder. "I know you were trying, but this definitely isn't my thing."

"I don't know that I'd go that far. You obviously have creativity and I'm pretty sure it takes skill to create six unique dick trees."

"It's a dickiduous forest. Get it right." I turned my attention back to the trees, placing the final falling leaves beneath the purple tree. If my falling leaves happened to be more white than rainbow colored and just so happened to look a lot like splatters of cum hitting the ground, well, that was just pure coincidence.

We'd either traumatized the instructor or given her the best painting class of her life. Trees that looked like dicks, a not-middle-aged man in a satin camisole—I had no idea when Dexter lost the T-shirt he'd been wearing at the start—and a guy who barked and answered to Pup. Yup, we needed to come with a warning label.

We also needed to agree to never host a painting night again. No amount of alcohol could make up for this torture. And seriously… "What are we supposed to do with these things?"

Everyone laughed at the question. Looking around at the paintings that were now lined up against the rock surround of the patio, I could honestly say that Larson was the only one of us with a lick of artistic ability. The rest of ours looked like toddlers had made them—then again, in many cases, the artists might not have been in an adult mindset in the first place. This had been a doomed activity from its inception.

CHAPTER SIX

MERRICK

I rubbed at my temples, frustrated at the scene in front of me. Brodrick's was a disaster. Three weeks into renovations and nothing was going according to plan. The flooring was held up in shipment, the drywall was only half-complete, and the kitchen appliances that I'd ordered had come in all the wrong sizes. After double-checking that the order had been correct, I'd taken a little too much pleasure in venting at the shipment coordinator at the supply store.

Now that I'd hung up, I felt bad for unloading on the poor guy, who hadn't been the one to load the wrong things on the truck. He'd just been the unfortunate soul who had ended up taking my wrath when the straw broke the camel's back that afternoon. At least the bar had gone in the day before, giving me a place to hoist myself onto to stew in my annoyance.

The place was silent save for the cooling system

running. With everyone long gone, I had nothing but time to think about the disaster in front of me. This wasn't my first reno rodeo; I knew shit like this happened. It just sucked that I had things personally at stake with this project. It brought a new level of stress to the entire thing.

I was still sitting on the bar top, lost in thought, when the unmistakable click of dress shoes on a hardwood floor drew my attention to the door. In the doorway, suit coat draped over his arm and dress shirt halfway unbuttoned, Dean stood looking around the empty space. "Rough day?"

Too deflated to respond, I nodded.

His footsteps sounded again, this time coming to a halt directly behind me. Before I could turn around, he leaned his arm on the bar top and angled his body so he could look at me. "Don't tell me, let me guess. Renovations going poorly?"

He was way too smug about the state of Brodrick's. I elbowed him a little harder than playfully. "Seriously?"

His eyes sparkled and a grin spread across his face. "It'll get better. But you've worked your ass off this week. Besides, it's Friday night. There's nothing you can do now. Go home, get a shower, feed Mooch, and come over. I know what will cheer you up."

"Mooch is never going to forgive me for spending so much time away from the apartment." The cat had become spoiled with me at home so much the last few months and had been snubbing me since I'd started working again.

A can of wet cat food appeared in front of my face. "A peace offering to Mooch."

The unfinished restaurant was forgotten as I turned to face my friend. "What the hell? How do you know what I feed him?"

Dean's smile was as endearing as it was infuriating. "Because you talk about that cat like he's a person and spoil him rotten."

"He showed up and wouldn't leave."

"Because you treat him better than you treat most people."

I glowered at Dean but it didn't do much good. He just shook his head and pushed the can of cat food into my hand. "My house. One hour." He narrowed his eyes at me. "Actually, make that ninety minutes. I think you're going to need that extra time in the shower."

"You're a pain in my ass."

He nearly danced out the door, calling behind him as he turned the corner. "You only wish!"

With a grunt, I slid off the counter and set to work locking up for the night. The cloud of dust that puffed up from me as I gave myself a quick brush off before climbing into my SUV told me I probably did need the extra time in the shower. If this renovation didn't get better soon, I was going to need to seriously consider buying a work truck. The interior of my Range Rover was going to need to be detailed if this continued.

Ninety minutes later, I was knocking on Dean's door. My arms and legs were sore and my mood hadn't improved much, but at least I was showered, Mooch was fed, and Dean had assured me he'd have dinner for us. My hand had barely returned to my side when Dean flung the door open, his big eyes and smile drawing my attention away from the baggy hoodie and sweatpants he was wearing.

No matter how happy he looked, my nose and stomach honed in on the smell coming from Dean's living room. The greasy pizza and popcorn smelled heavenly. When I leaned around him, I'd expected to see beers on the coffee table, not bottles of soda and... was that apple juice? And Christ, how much junk food could fit on that table?

My eyebrows crept up my forehead, but Dean's smile never wavered. "Come on. Dinner's ready." I wasn't sure I'd ever seen the man so happy. "Time to forget about stress the best way possible!"

"By putting myself in a food coma?" I hadn't eaten like this since I was in college, hell, maybe high school. When I'd gone to college, I'd already owned a business that kept me traveling. I hadn't settled in Tennessee until I'd been about eighteen months from graduation and couldn't do those last few semesters online. I'd been far from a traditional college student.

"Junk food and a good movie. It's the cure for all stress."

We settled next to each other on the sofa. Dean was cross-legged and his knee poked into my thigh. We were closer than was strictly friendly but were both within arm's reach of the food and beverages. As the large flat-screen across the room turned on to display the words *Mr. & Mrs. Smith*, I stifled a groan.

I remembered seeing trailers for the release, but it hadn't been appealing enough for me to actually consider taking time to watch it in the theaters. I'd forgotten about it by the time it was released on video. "Bean, what constitutes a good movie to you?"

Dean already had a piece of pizza in his hand and a bottle of sugary soda resting between his legs. The piece of pizza paused halfway to his mouth and he looked over at me like I was insane. "Anything with a sexy male lead, some action or comedy. In this case, both." He pushed the pizza in his mouth and chewed, effectively telling me to shut up and watch.

This was going to be a long night, and nowhere near as relaxing as having a beer, maybe a good steak, and watching something that was actually interesting. I'd been meaning to watch the latest Ryan Reynolds movie. That sexy salt-and-pepper stubble he'd been sporting the last few years was calling to me, yet I was stuck watching a movie at least fifteen years old while eating pizza and drinking soda sweet enough to give me diabetes.

At least the pizza was good.

Twenty minutes in, Dean's laughter became contagious. The longer we watched, the more tension left his shoulders. By the halfway mark, his happiness had seeped into me and I found myself laughing harder than I should have at the scenes, enjoying myself nearly as much as Dean.

Except the movie still wasn't that good. Actually, it was pretty awful, but I discovered that I liked hearing Dean laugh and liked seeing him smile. Those things alone made the movie better.

The sex scenes were about the only redeeming factor of the entire movie. Not that they were particularly erotic, but there were some sexy muscles on display and the way he took charge of the moment did it for me. Wild, passionate sex with someone I could take control of pushed all my buttons. Brad Pitt's ass in a pair of white briefs didn't hurt either.

I'd gotten so drawn in by that ass and those abs that I hadn't noticed Dean was every bit as hard as I was until he grunted slightly. The noise drew my attention to his lap and the situation in his pants that was impossible to hide.

My underwear and jeans hid the outline of my erection quite a bit better than his worn sweatpants and obvious lack of underwear. I forgot all about the naked body on screen as I felt my lips turn upward. "I'm not gonna say anything if you need to go take care of that."

Dean's head whipped over to me, his eyes wide with shock. Heat crept up my neck and I tried to give a casual shrug, mortified at the words that had come out of my mouth. I attempted to laugh the moment off. "You're a decade younger than I am and you're watching a hot guy walk around in only underwear. I'd be more surprised if you weren't horny by now."

I watched as Dean's brown eyes dropped to my crotch and a smirk slowly formed on his lips. "It doesn't appear as though age has anything to do with it, Dad."

I growled low and watched in shock as Dean's dick twitched in his pants. That was interesting. Forcing my eyes to meet his, I found there was a faint blush on his cheeks. "Like you said, hot man walking around in his underwear." He waggled his eyebrows at me. "And you can obviously appreciate the view as much as I can."

Of course a hot man and some rough sex was going to turn me on. But if there was ever a surefire mood killer, it would have been my friends knowing. Not that I'd had an erection called out by one of the guys in the past—hopefully, none of them had noticed the few times I'd sprung an inconvenient erection. I knew I didn't go out of my way to look at their crotches—but I'd have thought it would have made my erection flag, not grow.

So why was my erection showing no signs of standing down? If anything, I'd gotten harder since Dean called attention to it. If this continued, I'd be the one heading to the bathroom to take care of something.

One more moan on screen and a quick glance up to see firm abs and big muscles on full display, and Dean let out a groan that rivaled the one on screen. "Dammit. This is not going down now. This is all your fault."

My mouth fell open. "What? How is it my fault?" This seemed like some convoluted logic, and I wasn't going to try to follow it.

Dean palmed his dick, his eyes rolling back at the contact. If the movie hadn't been enough, the show he was giving me was now making my jeans uncomfortable. Somehow he forced words out, though I could hear the blatant arousal in his voice. "You just had to talk about the view and bring attention to my boner."

My laughter was so sudden, I forgot about the throbbing in my jeans for a moment. "Boner? How old are we now? Fifteen? Sixteen?"

"Shut up. You brought attention to my erection, then yours. Now I'm hard as a rock and I need release."

That made two of us.

How awkward would it be for me to tug one out in Dean's bathroom? I must be insane to be considering the idea. Shaking my head to rid myself of the ridiculous idea, I made the mistake of looking back at Dean. He wasn't exactly stroking himself, but his hand was on the bulge in his sweats and his cheeks were flushed with arousal.

This was wrong on so many levels, yet my hand still made its way to the front of my jeans in an attempt to relieve the mounting pressure. I must have made a sound because Dean's head rolled to the side and he looked at me beneath hooded eyes. "At least it's not just me."

"Not just you. I was sitting here wondering how many lines we'd cross if I went to your bathroom to jerk off."

His shrug was lazy. "Fewer than the idea I'd had."

My eyes shot open. How many more lines could we possibly cross than if I jerked off in his bathroom while he knew about it? I shouldn't say anything, but all the blood had left my brain in favor of my dick, and my mouth opened on its own accord. "And what idea was that?"

"Mutual handjobs."

He'd said the words casually, like it was no big deal. If it weren't a big deal, my body wouldn't have short-circuited at the mention of it. My brain said *Hell no*, my dick said *Hell yes*, and my mouth stubbornly said nothing helpful. "Seriously?"

He stroked again and my hand followed his movement along my own dick. "It's not unheard of. I used to do it with some friends when I was a teenager."

The hair on the back of my neck rose as I thought of

Dean jerking off with a friend. I hoped like hell he'd been legal by that point or it had been with someone his own age, because I hated the thought of a sixteen-year-old Dean being used by some asshole college senior.

Irrational anger? Yes. Valid concern? Absolutely.

The thought had every chance of killing my erection, but the little gasp Dean let out beside me as he cupped his balls made me forget all about the unwarranted emotion.

"I don't think I've ever jerked it with a casual friend or been jerked off by a casual friend."

The statement got Dean's full attention. His half-closed eyes popped fully open and he gasped in surprise, not arousal. "Seriously? You've never had a mutual handjob, just for release? And you're forty-five?"

"Alright, Bean. Don't rub it in."

"I'd rather just rub it off." He winked at me but quickly sobered. "We should totally do it. You need that experience at least once."

I'd been wrong. There were definitely more lines we could cross. So why wasn't I turning the idea down immediately? I should have been saying no. I should have been taking my hand off my dick. I most certainly shouldn't have been feeling my head nod in agreement.

There was only one thing holding me back. Well, there was one thing I'd voice. The thought that I didn't know if I could keep my brain in the friend zone if I touched his dick was going to stay right where it was. "Nothing changes between us. No awkwardness later, no ghosting the other." I had a feeling that was going to be easier said than done.

His look told me I'd just said something stupid. "Absolutely none. That's not how a mutual handjob works. No feelings, no awkwardness, just two friends helping the other out. Another hand on your dick just feels better."

I couldn't argue the last point. "I can't believe I'm agreeing to this, but you drive a hard bargain."

Dean grinned like he'd just won the lottery. "Mmm. Get that dick out, Mer. I can see how hard it is from here. It can't be comfortable trapped in those jeans."

It definitely hadn't been, but that didn't make it any less awkward to be fumbling with my button in front of one of my closest friends. As though he could sense my discomfort, Dean untied the drawstring on his sweats and pulled them down below his balls.

The cut head of his dick was a perfect mushroom shape, though at the moment it was red and swollen. While his cock wasn't the longest or thickest I'd seen, it was proportionate to his body and had a slight curve to the left. His hairless balls were what really drew my attention. I had no idea if he'd noticed my eyes stray to his balls or not, but he reached down and cupped them, rolling them slightly in his palm and moaning at the sensation.

I'd forgotten what I was supposed to be doing. "Need help getting your pants off?"

"Shut up. This is all new to me." Once my fingers finally got the button of my jeans to pop open, my underwear did little to contain my dick. It pushed out from my body, working the zipper down as it stretched.

"Damn, that's quite an impressive dick you have."

I rolled my eyes. "Do not make me regret this."

He mimed buttoning his lips, but the silence only lasted

until I adjusted enough that I could pull my jeans and underwear down to my thighs. With my dick fully exposed, Dean licked his lips. "Whoa, you've got a gorgeous dick."

If nothing else, he would be good for my ego. While I didn't think it was particularly impressive, Dean clearly disagreed. He was cataloging every inch of it with his eyes, and his hand had already left his dick and was closing the distance to mine.

He made contact with me before I could move my hand to his erection. His fingers encircled the base of my cock, fingertips barely touching. I hissed, my eyes falling closed as he made the first pass up my length.

When his thumb ran over my slit, gathering the precum that had already beaded there, I remembered that I was supposed to be returning the favor and reached out to Dean. My fingers easily met around the base of his cock. While he wasn't thick, he was long and the vein that ran along the underside was pronounced and—if his gasp could be believed—sensitive.

"Fuck, yes."

I had no idea who'd spoken the words, but if it hadn't been me, I totally agreed with Dean. His hand began to work my dick, exploring what made me gasp or moan. I'd been doing the same to him and was pleased to find how responsive he was. His entire body had come alive as I stroked him.

Dean's hand on my dick had me producing enough precum to ease the friction of his hand, yet he was producing even more precum than I was.

My hand was coated in his slick, sliding effortlessly up and down his dick. Occasionally, I'd let my hand dip low enough to fondle his sack, roll his balls, or run a finger over his taint. Those were the moments Dean was the most responsive. His hand would tighten on my cock, his movements would speed up, and his breathing would turn ragged. I paced myself, learning his reactions and how close I could bring him to the edge.

"Jesus. Fuck. Shit. Mer, your hand is magic. More. Shit."

I'd reduced the well-spoken genius to a begging mess with just my hand. I knew then I'd made a mistake. Dean was intoxicating and one handjob on the couch wouldn't be enough to get him out of my system. That realization should have made me stop, but my hand tightened on his cock and I pumped him in time with his strokes on me, knowing it would pull him over.

"That's it, Dean. I know you want to come. You're so hard."

The only sound he made that time was a whimper, though when I cracked my eyes open, his head was bobbing up and down.

"You're so close." I was too, but I was stubborn enough to not come until he did. I was a control freak, and I didn't care what I had to do—Dean would find release before I found my own.

Dean found his voice, though he could only make single-word sentences. "Yes. Close. Please."

Jesus, if the man didn't come soon, I didn't know if I'd last, determined or not. The plea from his mouth was nearly enough to send me over the edge. I jerked him hard and fast, feeling his cock swell in my grip, then slid my hand down his length and cupped his balls harder than I'd normally grab my own.

That did it.

Dean let out a loud gasp as the first spurt of cum shot from his dick. He barely had a chance to lift his shirt out of the way before he was painting his chest and abs. "Fuck. Yes. Merrick. Goddammit."

Through it all, he pumped my cock with his hand, working me for all he had. I pushed my own shirt up, knowing that my release was imminent, though I hadn't expected it to come with two whispered words from the man beside me. "Please come."

His cock was still pulsing in my hand when my dick began to shoot cum onto my stomach. Through a grunt of pleasure, I could hear Dean's sated whisper. "Oh, damn, that's hot."

His words made me smile. The regret I was certain to have later wasn't anywhere to be found as my orgasm faded. Something exploded on the screen, but it sounded far away and I absently wondered how much of the movie we'd missed. Not that I cared.

This had been much better than a movie.

Then Dean's breathing evened out and I knew he was falling asleep. It took effort to push myself up from the couch, and it took longer than it should have to find washcloths in the bathroom. I cleaned myself up, pulled my pants back into place, and took a fresh cloth to the living room to clean the man sleeping on the couch.

He barely moved as I wiped him down, but when I took

my seat after tossing the cloth into the hamper, he curled up next to me. The blanket that had been on his lap earlier was now wrapped around his body, the edge tucked under his chin, as he dozed against my side for the rest of the movie.

CHAPTER SEVEN

DEAN

I didn't remember falling asleep but when I woke up, the living room was only lit by a lamp on the end table. The TV was off, and my pillow was moving. I was trying to figure out what had happened and what time it was when my pillow hummed. Then I remembered Merrick and the handjobs.

I waited for regret to wash over me, but it wasn't there. The only thing I felt was, surprisingly, peace. Less surprisingly, exhaustion was weighing heavily on me.

With no feelings of embarrassment or discomfort, I finally opened my mouth, hoping my words would cut any awkwardness Merrick might be feeling. "Damn, I came my brains out." I pushed myself up off Merrick, who happened to be a very comfortable pillow. "Sorry about falling asleep on you." Literally.

He gave a warm chuckle that didn't hint at any feelings of regret either. "You crashed hard—you must have needed the sleep. Gave me plenty of time to catch up on some emails and the news." He waggled his phone back and forth. "Gotta love technology."

I rubbed my eyes with the blanket in my hand. "What time is it?"

"Late." He glanced back at his phone. "A little after midnight. I really should get home, but I didn't want to leave without your knowing."

"Midnight?" How the hell could that be? We'd just been eating dinner at like… seven thirty or eight. "Seriously?"

He shrugged. "Twelve fifteen, actually."

"Dammit. I slept straight through my game!"

Merrick's scrunched forehead said more than any words could. I found myself waving my hand around the room. "I play a game with a group of guys every Friday at eleven. I'd honestly figured you'd be long gone by then. And you know, I wouldn't be dead to the world."

"Sorry you missed your game night."

I shook my head as I fought a yawn. "Not your fault. I clearly needed to sleep. I do feel bad that I kept you here so long."

He shrugged as he fought a yawn too. "Not like I had anywhere else to be. Though I really should be getting home."

"Oh, yeah. Right." I stood up, feeling an inexplicable loss.

He stood and stretched his back, grumbling about old bones not working like they should. I stood as well, unwilling to let on how much my back ached at the moment. I didn't need to hear another person tell me I was too young to hurt this damn bad. Instead, I plastered on a smile and pulled the blanket around my shoulders as we made our way to the door.

He turned to face me before he got to the porch steps. "Have a good night, Dean. And make sure to go to bed. Don't get on that game."

Given that I was stifling another yawn, I wasn't planning on doing anything but heading to bed. I saluted with one hand. "Bed. Got it."

He gave me a pleased smile that made my stomach flip-flop. I was getting ready to close the door when he called over his shoulder. "See you tomorrow."

I must have been tired because I had no idea what he was talking about. "Tomorrow?"

"Yoga."

I wasn't tired enough to not groan at the statement. *Goat Yoga*. Merrick had been spending too much time with Canyon and Larson. As soon as Larson mentioned that Canyon's mom had started goat yoga classes—yoga while goats roam around and can climb on the participants—Merrick had decided it was worth a try. I thought the goats were cute, but in her front yard or their normal field, I suspected it would involve a lot of poop. The odds were, one or both of us would get pooped on before the night's end.

Merrick had been undeterred by my hesitations and had decided it was the perfect thing to help me relax. I still hadn't figured out how goats climbing on me could be relaxing, but we were going to find out.

"Right. With the goats."

Merrick was already halfway down the walkway.

"Don't sound so excited, Bean. You might burst something."

"You know, I'd laugh but my aunt actually burst a blood vessel in her eye doing yoga."

He stopped, turned to face me, and blinked twice. "You know what? It's late. I'm not going to ask."

Truth was sometimes stranger than fiction, and when it came to my mom and my aunt, the saying had never been truer. He was better off not asking. It was already past midnight, neither of us wanted to be up another twenty minutes while I told the story, and I would never be able to do it justice the way my mom and my aunt could.

As Merrick's headlights turned on, I finally closed the door and headed up the steps to fall asleep.

* * *

I TUGGED at the T-shirt I'd put on. We were going to be doing yoga, which required bending and stretching, and the last thing I wanted was to have to answer questions about the ugly scars on my back when it was over.

I tugged again, questioning if it would stay down. This was the fourth shirt of the afternoon and I was reaching for the fifth when the doorbell rang. "Fuck." I'd run out of time.

A quick glance in the mirror told me I was overthinking everything. My shirt was at least two sizes bigger than I should have been wearing, and there was nothing else I could possibly put on that would be longer. On my way out of the room, I noticed the blanket and grabbed it to take back to the living room.

The bell rang again. "Coming!"

I bounded down the steps, opened the door, and turned to take the blanket back where it belonged. Faster than the blink of an eye, my shirt got hooked on the knob of the door, stopping my forward momentum and pulling me backward suddenly. I didn't have a chance to get my feet under me before the door flung back, smacked the back of my thighs, and pushed me forward. The pain of the doorknob making contact with the top of my thigh was enough to make me forget about trying to stay upright.

My yelp wasn't so much of surprise but of pain, and I fell forward, landing hard on my hands and knees. The blanket I'd been holding landed in front of me, protecting my head from the same carpet burns I could already feel on my palms and my knees.

"Jesus!" Merrick's voice came from right beside my head. He was already crouched down and checking me over. "Are you okay?"

Tears had welled up in my eyes from the pain of the door hitting the sensitive scarring on my upper thigh. "Fuck." The moan was pitiful, but I couldn't be bothered to care. I was in enough pain that I didn't think about the air rushing over my back where my shirt should have been.

"Dean?" Merrick sounded more worried than the rug burn on my hands and knees warranted. I looked up to see his eyes glued to my back, wide with a sudden understanding. "It makes so much sense now."

It took a few beats for my brain to process what I was

seeing, hearing, and feeling, and then reality crashed into me. The hem of my shirt was halfway up my back. That breeze I was feeling was because the door was still open and air was blowing against my skin. Squeezing my eyes shut, I dropped my head against the floor and began counting backward from ten.

Seven years. Seven years I'd kept the disfigured skin from everyone.

"Dean?" Merrick shuffled around, but I didn't look up. Then a hand came to rest between my shoulder blades. "Why haven't you ever told us?"

He'd nearly whispered the words, hurt and shock clear in his tone. I shook my head, not wanting to deal with any of this.

When I didn't answer, he sighed. "Are you hurt?"

The slight abrasions on my knees and palms weren't anything to write home about, so I shook my head once more.

"Can you get up?"

Could and *want* were two very different things. I absolutely *could* get up, but that would mean facing Merrick and questions I'd avoided for years. After a few long seconds, I nodded my head and pushed myself upright, the baggy shirt falling down my back and covering the pale, mangled skin.

Merrick was sitting on the floor, watching me closely as I adjusted. He didn't miss my wince as my ass cheek came to rest on the floor. There was sure to be a bruise from the doorknob.

"Let's get you to the couch. It's going to feel a hell of a

lot better than the carpet." He stood slowly and reached a hand out to help me off the ground.

"I can do it myself!" He didn't deserve the snarl I'd let out, but I hated to be seen as weak or incapable, and at the moment I was having flashbacks to months of physical therapy so intense I'd cry through the exercises. That first month after the accident when the skin was so raw and painful that the therapist had needed to teach my mom how to lift me and help me stand, a feeling of pure helplessness had been my constant companion.

At the moment, I was feeling helpless and touchy, and Merrick had the misfortune to be the target of my anger.

He held his hands up in surrender. "Yeah. I know you can. But below this cocky, city-slicker entrepreneur exterior is a country boy interior. My ma would come smack me if I didn't offer a hand up to anyone who just took a fall like that."

Somewhere in the recesses of my brain, I knew Merrick was giving me something he didn't give many people. He didn't talk about home, didn't talk about his family much. It was as if the Merrick we knew hadn't existed before we met him.

The problem was I simply didn't care at the moment. I'd all but shut down, and no amount of kindness on his part was going to help that. "Seven fucking years." I shook my head at myself as I stood up, rubbing at my thigh as I did.

Merrick only hummed in response, not pushing me for answers but invading my personal space to take my elbow and guide me toward the couch. He settled me where I'd sat the night before—a memory of what we'd done in this exact spot not twenty-four hours before invading my morose thoughts—and disappeared into my kitchen.

Seconds later, he returned with one of the bottled apple juices I kept in the fridge and an ice pack. Merrick placed the items on the coffee table then headed back toward the front door. I watched as he bent to grab the blanket that I'd left on the ground. I'd forgotten all about it for a few minutes, but once he had it in his hand, I couldn't deny that I wanted it wrapped around me.

My mom had bought it for me shortly after I'd come home from the hospital, before I was in any condition to traverse the steps on a regular basis, and it had kept me warm through many nights sleeping on the couch or recliner. At present, it was big enough to wrap around and provide an extra layer of protection between my scars and the world.

Merrick handed the blanket to me, then the ice pack, and finally twisted the top off the juice before handing that to me too. Wrapped in the blanket with the ice on my sore hip, I was feeling a little better.

At least I was until Merrick took a seat on the coffee table across from me. He didn't say a word, just watched as I relaxed, then checked my knees. They stung, so I knew they were abraded, but I didn't think they were in bad shape. Given that Merrick didn't do anything, I guessed they were okay.

I'd drunk half the juice before the silence got to me. "I'm fine."

Merrick's lips pressed into a thin line and he nodded

slowly. "I'm sure you are. The fall itself wasn't bad—your knees are a bit red. Your hip is probably going to hurt for a few days. Though you're used to aches and pains." The words weren't sarcastic, more a statement of fact, but they helped settle some of the unease inside my stomach.

My mouth betrayed my brain as I nodded my head. "Pain is normal."

What I hadn't expected to see was sadness in Merrick's pale eyes. "I've suspected as much for a while now. Why didn't you say something?"

I shrugged as I capped the bottle. "I don't want pity."

Merrick's eyes closed, disappointment clear in the movement. "We've known you since you were eighteen. Do you really think any of us would have treated you differently?"

I didn't have an answer to his question, but my gut said no. When I didn't say anything, he continued slowly. "When Jenny called us that night, we'd already known you were in a wreck. Trent had been on duty; the call had come through dispatch. I was in DC for work. I'd gotten a call from Trav telling me that he didn't care if I was on Mars, I needed to get my ass home. By the time your mom called me, I was halfway through Virginia."

His words surprised me. I had been in so much pain at the time, all I remembered was telling my mom that I didn't want to see anyone. Between the burns, the broken bones, and the relentless pain, I hadn't been a nice person.

"I was coming home from a concert. A drunk driver came into my lane. All I know is what I've been told. I don't remember anything about that night. A witness says I made an evasive maneuver at the last second. The doctor told me later that it was probably what saved my life. Except I'd been knocked out cold. So when the other car caught fire, I was trapped inside."

Merrick was still sitting across from me, but I was so lost in my own thoughts that I wasn't seeing him, just snippets of stories I'd been told about the night and pieces of memories I had from waking up in the ambulance.

"The fire spread, caught my seat on fire. That witness had called 911. The dispatcher told him to stay in his car and wait for help, but he threw his phone down, climbed into my car, and ended up pulling me out through the passenger's side before the whole damn thing went up."

A tear ran down my cheek. "I don't remember it. I have his name from the police report, he came to see me a few times while I was recovering, but I was barely functioning at that point. The burns"—I ran my right hand up my left arm, over the tattoos that hid the disfigured skin—"were extensive. Second- and third-degree burns over my arm, thighs, and back. Did you know that burn scars hurt?"

Merrick shook his head, still not saying anything.

"They do. The scar tissue is thick, and in places that move a lot—like the legs—it hurts more. There's some muscle damage as well. The doctors did the best they could. I somehow managed to escape needing skin grafts, but it's still ugly. For weeks, all I remember is pain. Blisters, medications, itching, pain. And then they made me start to move. I thought I knew pain lying in bed. That pain was nothing compared to walking, sitting, and moving."

"You wouldn't let us see you."

Merrick's words held hurt and all these years later, I felt guilty. "I knew you guys kept asking about me. My mom kept telling me that you all wanted to see me." I scoffed, a bitter, sad sound that came from years of holding the memories in. "I don't have a clue why you all didn't just forget about me."

His lip twitched in a smile as sad as I felt. "We knew you were in a bad place. Jenny and your aunt kept us in the loop. We tried to see you. She said you'd been burned, but none of us had any idea." When words failed, he gestured at me.

"That it was this bad." I shook my head at myself. "I was in a bad place. Emotionally, physically. More days than I care to admit, I wished I'd died in that damn wreck. It would have been a hell of a lot easier than living through what I did to recover."

Merrick winced but didn't interrupt my thoughts.

"I didn't want you all to know. I didn't want to see the sad looks. I didn't want to be looked at as broken, just be seen as normal. To this day, even when I hurt like hell, when I meet up with you all, you still see me as normal. You don't ask how I'm feeling. You don't ask if I've gone to get that massage I was supposed to schedule six years ago. You don't ask if I've used the creams, seen the therapist, spoken to the doctor."

A small laugh bubbled out of him. "Jenny has her hands full with you."

I smiled. A genuine smile. "That she does." My mom was an amazing woman who had worked her fingers to the bone to provide for us. She hadn't planned on having a kid at fifteen, but she'd done her best. My grandparents and aunt had helped out a lot, but I hadn't been an easy kid to raise. It wouldn't have mattered if she had been fifteen, twenty-five, or thirty-five, I would have been a lot to handle.

Merrick was quiet for a long time. "Why don't you do what you're supposed to?"

My chin dipped to my chest. "Because then I have to answer questions. The muscles are tight, they ache all the time, but I'm used to it by now. And why am I going to pay for a massage when they can't really dig into my back and fix anything?"

"I know your mom's told you this, but you're not broken. You're a little beat-up, but you're far from broken. And even if you were, I hope you know that none of us would think less of you."

I scoffed. "Yeah, but you'd treat me differently. Everyone does. You should see how my grandma fawns over me still."

Merrick had the nerve to snort-laugh. He laughed so hard, his cheeks turned red and he had to take a few deep breaths to compose himself. "Oh, you are the light of that woman's life. She's fawned over you as long as I've known you. Nothing's changed in the last seven years, if you believe that or not."

He bit his lip and studied me closely. "I'm a little frustrated right now. Not going to lie. I'm annoyed at all of us for different reasons. I guess I'm more disappointed that we gave you the impression that we'd treat you differently. A little sad that you've suffered in silence for years. And a lot pissed that you've hidden that body under shirts four sizes too big all this time."

The seriousness of the moment broke and I found myself smiling again. "Two sizes, thank you very much." I tugged at the shirt. "And it's comfortable."

Merrick shook his head. "It's also ripped. So you better go change it."

"Seriously?"

He nodded solemnly. "Yup, halfway up your back. You still up for going tonight? If you're not, we can cancel."

I thought about the question for a few minutes. I had never been looking forward to goat yoga, but I needed to get out of the house and away from the memories. Maybe I could find a goat to cuddle while Merrick did the stretchy, touch your toes, turn into a pretzel stuff. "Yeah. I am."

"Is your ass going to be too sore?"

I waggled my eyebrows. "Only if you plan on something more exciting than yoga."

"Get your mind out of the gutter and go change. I'll put the ice pack back in the freezer. Oh, we need to swing by Trent's place. Canyon's there and he asked me to take something to his mom."

CHAPTER EIGHT

DEAN

I never knew what to expect when arriving at Trent, Logan, and Aiden's house. That night, the front door was open and voices were spilling out from the screen door. It sounded like a lot more people than the three cars in the driveway warranted. Heck, James and Dexter were babysitting their niece and nephew, so the entire group wasn't even here.

The noise appeared to be mostly emanating from the living room couch where Aiden, Logan, Larson, and Caleb were sandwiched side by side despite the large couch. All four had a game controller in hand while they yelled, laughed, and called each other names as their characters raced around a track on the screen.

There were three juice boxes and a thermos with a straw poking out of the lid sitting on the coffee table as they played the game. It was the same game Logan had asked if I wanted to play at Canyon and Larson's, and I found myself wondering how awkward it would be for me to join them.

I was watching the game as we made our way toward the open patio door where their boyfriends were sitting. I'd just watched a car cross the finish line when Logan let out a woot and his hands—controller included—shot up and whacked my shoulder.

"Oops! Sorry." Logan turned, his bright blue eyes shining a more vibrant shade than normal. "Oh! Dean! Want to join?"

"Uh?" Technically we were supposed to be going to yoga, but Merrick still needed to grab something from Canyon. I looked over at Merrick, silently questioning what to do.

He raised a shoulder. "You missed your game date last night, might as well get it in now. We've got time before we have to leave. We might just need to go through a drive-through instead of a sit-down place."

Logan's brows pulled together, slowly looking between us before speaking. "Trent's grilling back there. Canyon and Trav seem to think an entire football team is eating here with the amount of food they brought over. There's more than enough for you two."

Aiden elbowed Logan's side, grinning playfully. "They brought all that food over because *you* eat enough for an entire football team."

Logan patted his firm stomach. "It takes a lot to keep my body looking like this."

They were nuts, but I was already smiling. I knew we had to go to the yoga class, but I needed some more space from the events back at my house. Losing myself in the game the guys were playing was a lot more appealing than going out to sit with the others, wondering if and when Merrick would bring up my back. I glanced at Merrick. "You sure you don't mind?"

He gave me a warm smile and pushed me gently toward the couch. "Go. I'll figure out dinner."

Merrick was already moving toward the back door, so I took a seat a comfortable distance from Logan, who was looking at me with all sorts of questions in his eyes. "What?"

Logan's blue eyes narrowed on me, but he turned to the others. "I'm going to sit this round out." Then he waited for them to reconfigure the game and start playing before he turned back to me and nearly hissed. "*What?* You're going to ask me *what?* I should be asking you that!"

"What the hell are you talking about?"

Now he was looking at me like I was an idiot. "Seriously? You two have been spending a ton of time together lately. That exchange sounded a lot like you were going on a date with him!"

My eyes widened so far they began to dry out and I had to blink a few times. "What? No!" Then I laughed. "God, no. We're definitely not dating." I flopped backward and closed my eyes. Not that I would have turned him down if he'd asked, but I wasn't going to let myself go there.

Logan wiggled closer to me, to the point that when I cracked an eye open, he was nearly nose to nose with me. "You're not going to leave me alone, are you?"

He batted his eyes, then placed his chin on my shoulder. "Not a chance. So, what's going on?"

"Honestly, he's just trying to get me to relax… still." That was the shortened version, but I wanted to forget about what was going on, not think more about why Merrick and I had been spending so much time together.

Logan finally pushed back on a sigh. "You're no fun. I was hoping the story would have changed by now."

On the TV, Larson's character crossed the finish line first. Caleb and Aiden were close behind in second and fourth place. Caleb leaned over Aiden to speak to Logan as a bronze trophy appeared on the screen. "Joining?"

Logan shook his head. "Nope. Dean is, though."

Two minutes later, a new round had started and I was chasing the cartoon characters around the track. It had been years since I'd played this game and I was finding myself off the track almost as frequently as on it. It didn't matter that I wasn't any good at the game or that I came in tenth the first two races; it was fun.

Logan had wiggled back toward Aiden and had taken on the role of the announcer. There was a chance he was taking too much pleasure in my failings, but we were all laughing. By the end of the cup races when I handed my controller to Logan, I'd forgotten all about Merrick, the bruise on my thigh, and the yoga class we were supposed to be leaving for.

By the third race, laughter, barbs, and watching the cartoon characters race around the screen were all I could think about. In the back of my head, my brain was telling me this was what I'd needed all along, but all I was focused on was the fun we were having.

When a plate with a burger, grilled veggies, and a baked potato appeared over my shoulder, I jumped in surprise. My shoulder nearly hit Logan's jaw, for the first time drawing attention to how close we were on the couch. I wasn't sure when I'd scooted over toward the others, but now we were all in a line that took up barely half of the couch.

"Sorry to scare you." Merrick was still holding my plate, all signs of the stress he'd been carrying as we left my house gone. The smile on his lips and sparkle in his eyes told me he was relaxed, and I felt happiness bloom inside me.

There was no time to think about why it made me feel that way. Dinner was ready. I placed the controller on the coffee table and made to stand up to head to the deck to eat, but Trent was walking up behind Merrick with two plates in his hands. "Don't get up. You look comfortable, and we're bringing their dinners here anyway." He set a plate piled high with food in front of Logan and a less full plate in front of Aiden.

"You sure?"

Travis's laugh was unmistakable as he brought food over for Larson and Caleb. "Are you kidding? If he's going to let Aiden eat in here, you're fine."

Trent's eyes widened before he disappeared for a moment, returning with an old towel that he placed on Aiden's lap and a large bib that he wrapped around his neck. "Try not to wear everything on your plate."

Logan nearly fell over laughing, but Aiden just grinned up at his boyfriend. "It's finger food! It's supposed to be messy."

I looked at Aiden's plate, surprised to see it was different than the plates Logan and I had. His paper plate had a burger, pasta salad, and chips like our plates did. But where Logan and I had a pile of grilled veggies, Aiden's had raw broccoli and ranch dressing to dip it into. The paper plates were all heavy duty, with the same divided sections on them, but Logan's and mine had everything piled together. Had it not been for the divided sections, the oil from the veggies would have been all over my burger. At least Merrick had thought about that. But on Aiden's plate, everything had been separated nicely with nothing touching at all.

Trent sighed, but the smile he gave Aiden made something in my chest hurt. There was so much love in his eyes that I knew, while he might complain about the mess, Trent wouldn't change anything about it.

Canyon's voice interrupted my thoughts. "What do you boys want to drink?"

Aiden and Larson immediately asked for apple juice and Caleb asked for milk. Logan's mouth was too full to respond, so Canyon turned his attention to me. "Beer, wine, water, apple juice, orange juice, white milk, chocolate?"

"Chocolate milk?" I couldn't remember the last time I'd had a chocolate milk and it sounded perfect at the moment.

Canyon nodded. "I know I saw some chocolate syrup in the fridge somewhere. Give me a minute."

I didn't want to inconvenience anyone. "If it's a problem, I'll just have a beer."

Logan finally swallowed. "Oh! The syrup's in the door. Can I have one too, please?"

Trent groaned. "You, pup, do not need that much sugar."

Logan pouted. "But Dean gets one! I won't go crazy."

I watched as Trent deflated some. "Fine. One. But you better behave."

Logan nodded, then leaned toward me to whisper in my ear. "Don't let me go crazy tonight. He'll fuck Aiden and not me."

My eyes watered when the bite I'd taken went down suddenly. Logan noticed my distress and patted my back a few times until I was breathing normally again. "Jesus, Logan. I'd like to live to see thirty-six. Listen closely—if I'm going to die by meat, I'd much rather it be of the sausage variety."

The room erupted in laughter and from the corner of my eye, I caught Merrick's beer shooting from his nose.

Maybe I'd said that too loudly.

Trent raised his bottle of beer. "Hear, hear. The man speaks the truth! And seriously, Logan, behave yourself."

Before Logan could respond, Canyon appeared with two plastic tumblers of chocolate milk. We both thanked him and turned our attention to our dinners.

Merrick, Trent, Travis, and Canyon headed back to the patio and conversation on the couch turned to our games.

Travis came in as we were finishing dinner. Without a word, he came over with a wet cloth and wiped Caleb's mouth. One glance at Aiden and he shook his head. "Go wash up in the bathroom. I think your Daddy is going to need to give you a bath tonight, though."

Aiden sighed like he was being inconvenienced but got off the couch and headed down the hall. Travis gathered plates and cups from everyone who was done, wiping a few faces and even handing me a washcloth to clean off my beard. I would have been more embarrassed had I not been deep in conversation about the next game to play.

"Oh! That one!" Larson pointed to another Mario game that didn't hold much interest to me, though Caleb and Aiden quickly agreed.

Logan rolled his eyes as he changed the cartridge. "You all play that. We're going to play something else." He turned around to reach into the cabinet below where the TV was hung on the wall. When he returned to the couch, he was holding two different Switch controllers. "How's Minecraft sound? I've been building a world and wouldn't mind some help."

I was too caught up on the number of gaming systems they had to respond with words and just held my hand out for the controller Logan offered me. He settled himself next to me, once again pressed to my side. Throughout dinner, we'd spread out to eat, but that changed quickly once we started playing games again. Logan and I ended up huddled together on the opposite end of the couch, away from the other three.

As we booted up the game, words finally came back to me. "Enough game systems?"

He only laughed. "There are three of us. Trent likes to play Tetris and puzzle games, and we can't always agree on what to play. This saves fights."

It made sense, and at the moment it was handy to have all the game systems. Yoga was forgotten as we built the world and talked about nothing more serious than the creeper in the cave system we were in.

I had no idea how much time had passed when Aiden's voice pulled me from the game. "I'm out of juice."

"I want more milk and I think we were promised dessert." Caleb made to stand, but I was already getting up.

Larson's head bobbed up and down. "We made cookies earlier today. But that definitely requires milk."

Logan's eyes brightened at the mention of cookies.

Once up, I stretched my back and looked at the guys on the couch. "I'll go."

Aiden sent me a bright smile. "You're the best!"

I made it to the kitchen with a smile on my face. It had been a long time since I'd made someone happy just by offering to get cookies and milk. This was what I missed about being with someone: the warm feelings I got when I pleased them. Even setting boundaries and rules wasn't difficult when I knew I was giving my partner something they wanted and needed. My feet stopped moving as I played the thought over again in my head.

I couldn't remember the last time I'd felt like a Daddy. The truth was I hadn't enjoyed it much when I'd been with

Evan. I'd liked making him happy, but being in charge hadn't been all that fun. What did that mean?

As I was thinking, I'd still been focused on the task I'd set out to do. My eyes landed on the large container of cookies on the counter, and my thoughts faded away as dessert took their place. I went to grab a few plates before my hand paused.

Was it okay to give them cookies and milk without their Daddies' permission? And how many cookies could they have? Trent wasn't Logan's Daddy, so he could have cookies and milk if he wanted, but I'd noticed that Logan often listened to Trent's opinions on food and drinks with sugar, and Trent had been clear about Logan not having too much sugar. I didn't want to overstep, but I'd promised them dessert.

After a few seconds of hesitation, I headed to the patio where the others were seated around a gas fire pit as they chatted, each with a beer in their hand. I heard snippets of conversation and picked up on Canyon telling Merrick about plans he and Larson had for the weekend. It was a stark contrast to the conversations taking place in the living room. The conversations in the living room were a lot more entertaining than work, plans, and the shit that we dealt with all day, every day.

I cleared my throat and found myself uncomfortable as they all turned to face me. "Um, there's rumblings about milk and cookies in there. I didn't know how much they could have." Was that a blush I felt creeping up my cheeks?

Trent stood and clapped me on the shoulder. "Thanks.

Should have known they wouldn't forget about them for long."

Everyone else stood and followed him into the house. Merrick headed in last, placing a hand between my shoulders and leaning in to speak quietly in my ear. "How's your back and leg?"

My initial reaction was to get irritated but I reminded myself that he had been worried about me. "A little sore, but I'll be fine."

He nodded once and moved us toward the house. "Go on back to your game. You and Logan were quite engrossed last time I came in."

"You sure?" I glanced back at the living room, then out the back door, noticing the sun had set. "Shit. We were supposed to be at yoga!"

The corner of his lip turned up in a smile. "You were going to hate it, and I can't imagine it would be comfortable after that fall. Besides, you look a hell of a lot more relaxed right now than you did when we got here."

"I mean, I was kind of looking forward to snuggling the goats."

His laughter was warm. "You weren't going to do yoga at all, were you?"

I shook my head. "I'd planned on finding a spot in the back and cuddling goats."

He rolled his eyes and pushed at my back again. "Go. I'll bring you cookies."

"Thanks." I made sure to shoot him a smile before I went back to Logan.

While I was gone, he'd gotten a blanket from somewhere, and he tossed it over me as I sat down. When I let out an *oomph* at the surprising weight, Logan gave me a smile. "It's weighted. It helps me sit still and sleep at night. But it's also great for cool evenings like tonight. And your legs had goosebumps when you got up."

"Thanks." It was a sweet gesture, and after snuggling together on the couch for most of the evening, it didn't feel strange to share a blanket with him. Our focus returned to the game until milk and cookies were delivered to us.

CHAPTER NINE

MERRICK

We sat on the patio for hours, talking and laughing as the others sat inside playing video games. Dean had told me he liked to play them, but I hadn't expected him to get as lost in them as he had. I wasn't sure any of them had moved for more than the bathroom in nearly five hours. Well, the bathroom or the one time Dean had come out asking about dessert.

The temperature had dropped noticeably, and with it the gas fire pit was no longer enough to keep us warm. Canyon stood and stretched. "I should probably get Larson home anyway."

Travis groaned. "It's late. I can't believe Cal is still awake. He's usually dozing off by now, especially when Dexter isn't around."

"He's got Logan to keep him entertained tonight. Then again, I haven't heard from my guys either. Shit, what did they get into?"

I opened my mouth to make a quip about them all

having their hands full with their men, but the words died in my throat as we stepped into the house to find the five men asleep on the couch. Larson had Caleb curled into his side, and Aiden was stretched out with his head on Caleb's lap and his legs across Logan's and Dean's. Logan and Dean were curled under a big blanket, Logan's head resting on Dean's shoulder and Dean's head atop Logan's. On the blanket was a book that looked to be a bedtime story.

Trent's head was tilted to the side as he studied the couch. "Well, that's unexpected. It's only half past ten. I can't believe Logan's asleep."

"I almost feel bad waking Dean up." But I also knew that his back wasn't going to appreciate sleeping upright on a couch. If it hadn't been for that, I'd almost be willing to let him sleep there for the night.

Trent sighed. "I really hope Logan goes back to sleep after this. He never falls asleep this early."

Travis glanced around the living room and kitchen. "We'll help you clean up some before we wake them up. At least you'll have a clean house and can just usher your guys upstairs."

Trent readily accepted the help. For nearly twenty minutes, we worked in silence to clean up as much as we could without waking the men on the couch. By the time we deemed the house clean enough, we hadn't woken any of the men up, nor had they moved. I headed over to where Dean was sleeping and gently removed the book from beneath his hand, then placed my hand on his shoulder. "Hey, Bean."

A sleepy eye cracked open for a moment, then closed again.

"Bean, come on, wake up. I need to get you home."

"Umph."

That hadn't been an answer, and by the way he curled tighter into Logan, I didn't think I was doing a very good job convincing him to get up. "Bean, it's late and you're going to hurt in the morning."

"Stop calling me that, Dad." Even though they were still closed, I saw him roll his eyes. At least while they were closed, he couldn't see my smile.

"Fine, if you get up now, I won't call you Bean again."

His eyes opened, but he was suspicious. "That's too easy."

"I won't call you Bean until we leave at least."

"You just said it again."

I didn't bother hiding my smirk. "And you haven't gotten up, have you?"

He grumbled at me and Logan let out a growl that sounded a lot more like his pup side than his human one.

Dean yawned. "But I'm comfy."

Realizing I wasn't making forward progress, I took matters into my own hands and pulled the blanket down. Dean's grumbled protests were forgotten when my eyes fell on the plush bear between him and Logan, each of them with a hand on it.

Trent's voice pulled my attention away from Dean's hand gripped in the fur. He was smiling as he rubbed Logan's head softly. "Pup, where on earth did you get your bear from?"

Aiden spoke through a yawn. "I got it for him from his bin."

Trent was still smiling when he turned to me. "It's one of Curious's toys. Aiden got it for him a few months ago. I think it's just because Aiden likes cuddling with it and Logan likes trying to pull it from him when they're playing."

Dean finally stretched, but I caught his nearly imperceptible wince as he did so. "Ugh, you two aren't going to shut up, are you? Fine. I'll get up."

I looked over toward Trent and rolled my eyes. He chuckled at my reaction. "Have fun getting grumpy pants home."

"Note to self, Dean does not like being woken up."

Dean humphed but was finally making his way toward the door. "You got me up. Now you have to take me home." He yawned and I suspected he'd be asleep again before I pulled out of the driveway.

To my surprise, by the time we made it to my SUV, Dean wasn't as tired as he'd been a moment before. "Sorry I made us miss yoga. I know you wanted to go."

I buckled my seatbelt and turned the car on before I responded. "No need to apologize. Truthfully, I was only going because I know yoga helps a lot of people relax. Hell, I'm allergic to grass."

Dean let out a snort of surprised laughter. "Yet you were going to get all up close and personal in a field of it? A field of grass and goats?"

"I took an allergy pill earlier today."

"You're such a dork." I couldn't see him, but I could hear

the smile in his voice. "Thank you for trying to help. I do appreciate it, but I think tonight was exactly what I'd needed."

"I'm glad you feel better." I meant the words. Dean had been so stressed when we left his house, I hadn't thought yoga would do any good for him anyway. It probably shouldn't have surprised me that he'd fallen asleep on the couch, especially with Logan curled close to him.

Dean's second wind left as he drifted back to sleep against the window, and I let him sleep until we were parked in his driveway. "Hey, Dean." I'd teased him enough earlier in the night. Not using the silly nickname I'd taken a liking to felt like I was extending an olive branch.

His eyes opened slowly and he looked around, for a moment appearing confused by where he was. Then he sighed and sank back into his seat. "Oh, sorry, I must have fallen asleep again."

"Yeah, you did. Come on, let me get you inside."

"You don't have to do that. I'm fully capable of heading inside on my own."

I stared at him for a moment and he finally relented, shaking his head as he unbuckled. "Fine. Come on in. I can see you're not going to be satisfied until you know I'm heading upstairs. I swear I'm not going to sign into my game tonight. I've played more video games tonight than I have in years."

"Thank you for humoring me."

His eye roll would have been more effective if he weren't yawning as he reached for his keys. With his door open, we walked inside. He didn't make a move to shut the door, so I did it for him, flicking the lock into place. "Go brush your teeth."

"You know I only call you Dad to get under your skin. You're taking it a bit literally at the moment."

That time, I rolled my eyes. "Brush your teeth. I'm going to check the doors and turn off the lights." I also had another plan; hopefully, he was tired enough he wouldn't fight me.

He shook his head, muttering about me being a pain in the ass as he went up the steps. I did as I said I would, leaving only the light above the kitchen sink on. I'd need to be able to see when I finally left. I'd just come out of the downstairs bathroom with the bottle of body oil I'd seen in the cabinet the night before when I heard Dean grumbling from the upstairs hall as he made his way toward the steps.

"What are you doing?"

He jumped in surprise and grabbed onto the handrail. "Jesus. I thought you were gone."

"I was coming up to make sure you were actually going to bed. What's up?"

"Forgot my blanket."

I blinked at his words. "Your blanket?"

Dean nodded. "I left it on the couch."

The only blanket I had seen that evening was the one he'd been holding when he fell. It stayed on the back of the couch when Dean wasn't wrapped up in it. But his matter-of-fact words had a piece I hadn't known was missing falling into place. I felt myself smile as I thought of Dean holding it under his chin the night before, and the way he'd wrapped himself in it after he'd fallen that evening. "I'll get it."

He thanked me through a yawn and turned to go back to his bedroom as I headed for the living room. It wasn't hard to find the blanket. Now that I knew it was special, I could see a few frayed corners and could feel that it wasn't as soft as it looked at first glance.

At the top of the steps, Dean's bedroom door was open, and I turned as I began to speak. "Found Blankie."

He was already in bed, the blankets pulled up to his chest. I couldn't remember the last time I'd seen a man sleep in anything more than a pair of underwear, sometimes pajama pants if he was around friends, but Dean was wearing an oversized T-shirt.

He blushed lightly. "It's not my blankie. It's just my favorite blanket."

His words said one thing; his relieved smile said something else entirely. I didn't press the issue as I walked over and handed him the blanket. Dean took it without hesitation and wrapped it around his shoulders, then wiggled down farther into the bed.

As I watched him, his face pinched in discomfort and I remembered my original plan. It was probably stupid for me to be even considering what I was doing, yet I hated knowing Dean was in constant pain.

"Roll onto your stomach."

Dean jolted, his eyes flying open, and stared at me. "What?"

"Roll over. I want to try something."

"Mer…" He trailed off as I stared back at him.

"Please? I promise, nothing below the waist." If I told him my plan, I knew he'd say no, so all I could do was hope he'd trust me.

"I don't know if that makes me more or less suspicious."

Since he was rolling over, I took that to mean less. With that opening, I sat beside him and began to gently pull the blankets back, exposing his body from the swell of his ass up. He was wearing athletic shorts that covered from his waist to his knees, including the bruise I knew he was sporting on his thigh.

I poured some oil into the palm of my hand, then rubbed my hands together to warm them up.

"Tell me if I hurt you."

"Wh-what are you doing?" Fear was palpable in Dean's voice as I slowly moved my hands under the baggy material of his shirt.

"Just trying something. I did some reading this evening. You said you don't get massages because you don't want to talk about your back, and the scars are painful. You don't have to explain them to me. I know about them. And you're not paying me, so you don't have to worry about not getting the full benefit of a deep tissue massage. Just tell me if I hurt you."

Dean's muscles were tense as my hands ran across his lower back, feeling the uneven skin for the first time. He didn't speak, didn't move, but didn't tell me to stop either. Moving slowly, I began to work my way up his back until I felt unmarred skin beneath my hands. I repeated the process again, that time going down his back until I reached the waistband of his shorts. I moved slower than I thought possible, giving Dean every opportunity to stop me, but by the fourth time up his back, I heard him let out a breath.

A few minutes later, his back slick with oil, my hands moved a little faster and with a little more pressure, and Dean let out a tiny moan. "That feels nice."

He couldn't see my smile, but it was wide as I worked. With each passing minute, my confidence grew. Before long, I was pushing harder into tense muscles. I wasn't digging by any stretch of the imagination, but I was rubbing the knots with my thumbs with increasingly direct pressure.

Each time my thumbs found another knot, Dean would let out a grunt. If I accidentally applied too much pressure or moved to a place too sore to be touched, his sharp inhale would tell me to back off. After fifteen minutes, my hands were getting tired, but Dean's back had relaxed. His occasional hums of happiness kept me working.

I continued to work his muscles for another fifteen minutes until I worried that I'd need a hand massage of my own before I could drive home. Just before I couldn't go on any longer, Dean let out a long sigh and rolled to face me. "Thank you. That felt amazing."

My hands fell to my lap. The oil had been mostly absorbed by his back, so I wasn't worried about oil stains. "I'm glad."

He blinked slowly, exhaustion clear in his eyes. "I actually feel better. Really. Thank you." His eyes closed, and I thought he'd drifted off to sleep. I pulled the blankets up around him and made to stand when he spoke again. "Thank you for not making a big deal out of it."

My chest ached at his words. "It's skin and muscle. We all have it, Dean. Yours might look and feel a little different, but that doesn't mean you should be in pain." I thought about stopping there but pushed on. "I'll rub your back any time."

A smile twitched on his lips. "Better watch out what you promise." He yawned again.

I knew what I'd promised, and I'd meant it. "Hold me to it. Now, get some sleep. I need to go home and check on Mooch, but we'll talk later."

Dean nodded. "Tell Mooch I said sorry for keeping you out so late."

I resisted the urge to reach down and brush the few stray hairs from his forehead. "Will do. Night, Dean."

"Night, Mer."

I made my way out of the house, turning the kitchen light off as I left through the garage. The entire way home, I replayed the events of the evening. The way Dean had trusted me had made my heart pound in ways it hadn't in over two decades. His happy laughter as he'd played video games, his sleepy eyes and yawns over the last ninety minutes, each one had made me smile. I wondered what else I could do to see him smile like that.

"You're helping him get his dating feet under him, Merrick. Stop trying to get your dick involved." It was easier to tell myself that it was my dick that liked the evening more than my heart. If I said it enough, maybe I'd believe it.

I was still trying to convince myself that it was only my dick that had enjoyed the night when I arrived home. Mooch jumped from the arm of the couch, gave a loud mewl of annoyance, then turned and walked away. His dinner had only gone so far in winning him over and by the looks of it, that time had passed about two hours earlier. I gave him some more food, refreshed his water, and headed to my room, leaving the door open so Mooch could come in when he finally decided he'd given me the cold shoulder long enough.

For being a former stray, he'd certainly come to love apartment living. A warm bed, a body to curl up next to, and a pillow to steal whenever he wanted. He'd mooched more than food off me over the last few months, my heart high on the list—not that I'd admit that to anyone.

Climbing into bed, I rolled my eyes at the cat. He'd forgiven me already and had stolen my pillow while I'd been brushing my teeth. "Mooch, move over."

He cracked one eye open, then shut it again, leaving me to climb in on the other side of the bed and fall asleep while thinking about Dean and hoping his back felt better in the morning.

CHAPTER TEN

MERRICK

Monday brought a return to work at Brodrick's, this time with the right parts and pieces where they should be and the wrong kitchen pieces returned to where they had come from. By Tuesday I was stuck, though. I was going to have to wait three more days for the last of the kitchen equipment to arrive, but at least we weren't working around the wrong stuff until then.

Without being able to finish the rest of the job, I was able to lock up for the day just before five, head to the house for a quick shower, feed Mooch, and leave for Larson's woodshop. Twenty minutes after arriving, I was kicking myself for not stopping to grab dinner as I listened to the two debate about what Larson would make for this week's YouTube video. Larson wanted to finish the project from the week before, a gorgeous trinket box made from scraps of various previous projects. Canyon was eager to start on the dog bowl stands.

I suspected his eagerness was because the two horses they called dogs were eating him out of house and home and their bowls were the size of small wading pools. They took up a lot of floor space, and for how big the two dogs were, they looked uncomfortable as they bent down to eat and drink.

Trying to forget about my stomach, I let my mind wander. The topic of choice was, once again, Dean. He hadn't been far from my thoughts since I'd started trying to help him relax. Since tucking him in, my brain had decided that Dean was always the right topic to land on. Except finding ways to help him relax had taken a very different turn the last couple days. His cute blushes and sweet *thank you's* had made me want to figure out just how far down the blushes went and how sweet he really was. I'd totally given up on listening to the voice in my head telling me that he was off-limits.

Canyon turned to me like I could settle the dispute. "What do you think?"

"Think about what?"

Larson laughed. "Told you he wasn't paying attention. He checked out fifteen minutes ago."

In response, I pointed to the camera. "You two have me here to catch the magic of creation, not guide the creation. When you started debating, I tuned you out. Are you two still debating between the feeder things and the box?"

They nodded, looking to me for guidance. I needed to give the question serious thought, so I shelved the Dean topic and focused on Larson's work. "How long will the stands take? People really liked the box thing Larson made last week, but it would be nice to put some storage under the feed troughs you call bowls."

Canyon looked over at his boyfriend. "Oh, I like that idea. Can you make storage under them?"

Larson scrunched his face in thought. "Probably. It would be a bit more complicated. Give me a few to sketch it out." He grabbed a pencil and piece of paper and got to work.

We both knew Larson would lose himself in the sketch until it was done, so Canyon came to sit on the stool next to where I'd placed myself when I'd come in. "You heading to the movies with us Thursday night?"

I lifted a shoulder. "Not really sure, honestly. Maybe? What is it again?"

Canyon pulled out his phone, but Larson answered first. "The new Marvel movie."

"Probably not, then. I never got into superhero movies. I actually haven't seen a single one. It would probably be a bad idea to start with the newest."

"I hadn't seen one until Larson made me watch them. Now I'm caught up to speed. Besides, it's going to focus on Iron Man, and he cracks me up."

I was already confused. I knew who Iron Man was but didn't know why he would be amusing. Larson never looked up, but he'd obviously been listening to us. "You just think he's funny because he's a total middle."

I looked toward Canyon for an explanation, but he looked just as confused as I did. When it was clear Larson wasn't going to elaborate, Canyon cleared his throat. "Little bit, what are you talking about?"

Larson put the pencil down and slowly looked up at us. For a beat, he studied Canyon as though he didn't know if the question had been serious. When he saw we were both lost, he shook his head slowly. "You really don't see it, do you?"

Canyon shook his head.

Larson sighed and adjusted himself so he was standing at his full height. "Tony Stark is a total middle. He's a rich dude with expensive toys, who would rather be playing than dealing with real world shit. Tony doesn't need Pepper to be his... secretary. He needs Pepper to be his Mommy. That man *needs* someone to take care of him."

I swore I'd been part of this conversation from the beginning, but it still wasn't making sense. Maybe I didn't understand the movie, or maybe I didn't understand what the hell a middle was. "Because Iron Man is Tony Stark and Tony Stark is a middle?"

Larson nodded. "Exactly. That's what I said."

I was still confused, and Canyon looked equally so as he pinched the bridge of his nose. "Okay, I'm just going to admit it now. I know what a little is, but what's a middle?"

We were going to be there for a while. I knew the conversation wasn't going to be quick when Larson walked around the workbench and propped his ass against the top, settling in for however long the conversation would take. He might have been Canyon's boy and submissive to the core, but at the moment he looked every bit a frustrated

Daddy who had to repeat himself. I'd seen the look on Trent's and Travis's faces enough to recognize it.

"Little." He pointed to himself. "My regression age is young. Maybe two to three. I like having Daddy. I like the freedom to play, I like the snuggles, I like the routines. It makes me feel cared for when my food gets cut up and Daddy chooses my clothes. Sometimes I might feel more like a curious four- or five-year-old and need a little more freedom, but I still need Daddy nearby. That's usually when Caleb, Aiden, or Logan are around."

I was hanging on Larson's every word, while Canyon was nodding his head. "Ah, that makes so much more sense! I've always noticed that you're a lot more mischievous when they're around."

Larson grinned at his Daddy and nodded. "Exactly. But Tony doesn't give off little vibes. I don't ever see him wanting a bottle or pacifier. He's a lot more like a teenager. He wants to play with expensive toys. Give him a video game to hack into or something that moves to distract him, and he'd be in heaven. Give him something he doesn't enjoy and he gets all pouty. That's why he has Pepper. She's basically his Mommy."

That didn't sound different than many adults I knew.

My thought must have come out because Larson shook his head. "Yes and no. A lot of *adults* relax by losing themselves in video games or RC cars, whatever. *Middles* still need the structure of a D/s relationship. Just like I thrive on knowing what's expected and having Daddy here to help me make decisions, or sometimes make decisions for me, a middle is the same but maybe with not as much hovering."

He paused and thought. "Think of it kind of like Trent with Logan."

"Logan's a middle?" The words were out before I could stop them.

Larson shrugged. "I don't know, definitely not in the traditional sense of middle. Logan's not submissive—we all know that. But Trent still looks after him. Reminds him to not eat all the cookies. Tells him to go to bed. Tells him to stop playing video games. Reminds him to not be too pushy when we're little around him. Those are things that a lot of middles need. They need structure, stability, clear expectations without their Daddy hovering. And sometimes, just like Curious will curl up with Aiden or Trent for snuggles, they need to be able to show their vulnerable side. At their core, they're usually an adolescent at heart. They want independence, but they still need their Mommy or Daddy to catch them when they fall."

Something was beginning to tickle my brain. I didn't understand it yet, but it was coming into focus. The more Larson described middles, the less I was seeing Iron Man or Logan and the more I was seeing a certain brown-haired, brown-eyed man I'd been spending a lot of time with.

He lost himself in video games, pouted when I told him to do things—like going to bed or getting ready to go places. But when he didn't have to think, didn't have the responsibilities of real life weighing him down, only the games to play with his friends, he'd lit up. He'd had fun. He'd been happier than I'd seen him since the accident… possibly longer than that.

Larson wasn't just describing the movie character; he was describing Dean.

I shook my head, trying to make sense of it all. "So what you're telling us is that Dean's a middle?"

Larson paused and cocked his head to the side. "We weren't talking about Dean, but I mean, they are similar in that they are both incredibly smart and like to tinker with things. And yeah, Dean's stubborn and maybe a little bossy. And, come to think of it, yeah… he had a lot of fun that night. I mean, I could see it, I guess."

Now that I saw it, I couldn't ignore it. "You said that middles need structure but independence. Dean is like that."

Larson didn't look convinced as he turned over my words. "That's a leap. Dean's always struck me as strong-willed…" He fell silent, his eyes focusing somewhere on the wall behind me.

Canyon narrowed his eyes in thought. "Does strong-willed mean Dom, though?"

Larson opened his mouth to speak, but when nothing came out, he shut it.

My brain raced to put parts of the previous weeks together. I began talking my thoughts out. "I saw it that day we all came over here for brunch. He'd wanted to play. He was trying to figure out how to join you all. I remember looking over and seeing him watching you guys a number of times. At first, I thought it was just because you all were loud and distracting. But looking back, that wasn't it."

That look I'd mistaken as distraction had been longing.

Larson nodded slowly. "You know? Now that you say it, I've picked up on the same thing in the past. I almost offered him one of my cars that morning, then the doorbell rang and things got crazy, and I kind of forgot."

"He likes structure." I was speaking as much to myself as I was to Larson and Canyon.

Canyon looked between us again. "But that doesn't make him a middle. Doms like structure… I can say that from experience."

Larson bit his lip in thought. "You are both making valid points."

I didn't have an explanation either, but my gut was telling me that Dean was a middle. And what did that mean for me? Was I supposed to help him find a Daddy now? Hell, I knew less about that than I did helping him find a little. Rubbing the heels of my hands against my eyes, I let out a groan. "I'm so confused. How you described that movie guy—"

"Tony Stark."

"Yeah, him. How you described him, it fits Dean so well."

We all fell silent for a few minutes, so lost in thought that Larson forgot about his sketch.

Canyon broke the silence. "Okay, you two make good points, but Dean says he's a Dom. Can you be a Dom *and* a middle?"

Larson looked toward Canyon and nodded slowly.

"Sure. There are little/Dom switches, just like there are Dom/sub switches. But Merrick might be onto something. Think about that paint thing. He and Logan were feeding off each other all night. It was effortless for him. Those were not the actions of a Daddy Dom. You two kept trying to follow the instructions, hell, so were James and Travis, but what about Caleb, Dexter, and Aiden?"

I blinked a few times. "Caleb was behaving himself. Dexter and Aiden were making weird things, though."

Larson shook his head, a wide smile forming on his face. "Caleb made one tree with rainbow leaves, and he used his fingers to make the leaves. It looks really cool but definitely not what the instructor said to do."

I didn't remember that, and from the look on Canyon's face, neither did he.

Blowing out a breath, I tried to come to a different conclusion. Maybe I was seeing something that wasn't there. "Okay, but could it just be that he's comfortable around everyone? He was the youngest in the group until Travis started to date Caleb. And on Saturday, he was in pain. He'd fallen before we left his house. I'm certain he had a bruise on his thigh by the time we got here. It could just be that the couch was a hell of a lot more comfortable than the patio chairs."

Larson shook his head. "A bruise wouldn't stop him. That man knows pain."

The abrupt change in topic threw me for a loop and I couldn't hide my surprise. "You know that?"

Larson nodded, though his focus was far from the room

we were in. "He has to be. Injuries like that don't just go away."

"You're talking about the wreck, right?" When Larson nodded in confirmation, I was left with even more questions. "He recently told me about it, and yeah, he is in pain."

When Larson spoke next, I could tell the memory was painful to dredge up. "The wreck took place in our jurisdiction. At first, I didn't know it was Dean—the call just said vehicle fire. We pulled up and his car was engulfed in flames. Immediately, I knew there was no getting anyone out. Then the wind blew and I saw a glimpse of the plate number. Dean had that NMBRMAN plate. It was the only thing still recognizable on the entire car. I was in the middle of losing my dinner on the side of the road when a commotion in the field caught my eye."

Larson stopped to scrub a hand down his face. "The caller had pulled him out. He was in bad shape. EMTs were working on him; vitals were all over the board. They had the paddles out three times, so sure he was going to code. When they went to move him, I saw the burns, mid-back to mid-thighs. His left arm was blistered. It was horrific."

Canyon's mouth had fallen open at the story. Even knowing what had happened and knowing Dean was safely at his house, my palms had gone damp and my stomach lurched. I'd seen the scars. I'd felt them with my hands. But that was the moment I fully understood how close we were to losing him that night. "You knew all this time?"

Larson nodded slowly. "I'd been shaken up enough that I wasn't up for talking at the time. When Jenny told us that

Dean didn't want to see anyone, I assumed he also didn't want anyone to know how bad things were."

Canyon got up to stand next to Larson and wrapped an arm around his shoulder. There weren't words for what Larson had witnessed that night. I was still struggling to imagine the pain Dean had gone through after having seen the scars seven years after the accident. Holding onto that memory for just as long couldn't have been easy.

Larson shrugged and forced a smile. "He's different now. Like, he's the same Dean, but you must have noticed, Merrick. He's not as… something."

I understood what he meant. "The spark is gone. He's Dean, but like Dean version two point oh."

"Exactly."

Canyon kissed Larson's temple. From the gentle touch, I knew we wouldn't be filming that night. When we finished our conversation, Canyon was going to be taking his boy upstairs to help him decompress. That didn't mean he was ready to do so just yet, because he was still as confused as I was about the entire situation. "Why would he go from a Daddy to a boy?"

Larson's answering shrug left me with more questions. "I can't answer that one."

Finally admitting I was also at a loss, I shook my head. "I don't have an answer either, but you're right. He's different. At the same time, if my gut is right, I need to stop helping him find a boy and help him find a Daddy." I scrubbed my hands over my face. Why did I feel so tired all of a sudden? "Well, shit. How do I do that?"

Larson blinked at me for a few seconds before shaking

his head. "Well, if you're serious about helping him, you'd be trying to find a way to get him to understand that side of himself."

Canyon sighed. "Larson, you have the kinkiest family in a hundred-mile radius of here, and you both know him a lot better than I do, but this is almost hard to believe."

It was… but it wasn't. Dean might roll his eyes and huff, but he didn't fight me when I put my foot down about things. Hell, he hadn't told me to shove it when I'd told him to leave work or not to play video games. I was bossy and used to getting my way, but Dean was an adult who could tell me no if he wanted to. Except he hadn't. He'd agreed.

I was seeing Saturday night in a very different light, from the way he'd looked to me when Logan had invited him to play video games to the way he'd asked for dessert. He'd been looking for guidance and one of us had given it to him without thought each time. I couldn't forget how he'd fallen asleep on the couch sharing Curious's teddy bear, or the way he'd gone looking for his blanket when he'd thought I'd left already.

Larson had made me see something that had been right in front of my face, but I had no idea what to do with the information now that I had it. How did I help a thirty-five-year-old see that he needed structure, cuddles, and rules? Another even more insane thought planted itself in my brain. If Dean wasn't a Dom, would we have a chance?

The thought hadn't left by the time I pulled out of the driveway over an hour later. In that time, we'd decided we didn't have answers to anything, and at the end of the day, Dean's kinks were his own. Larson had given me some ideas to help Dean figure himself out, I'd been told they were there if either of us needed them, and we'd changed the subject. Despite the subject change, the hope that maybe we could make something work was still there.

Turning my brights on, I remembered the biggest stumbling block to my plan. If Dean was a boy, that meant he needed a Daddy. And I wasn't a Daddy.

CHAPTER ELEVEN

DEAN

Wasn't the flu something you got in the winter? Until the day before, I was convinced that was the case.

That was before I'd woken up achy and sore on Wednesday morning. I tried to work from home but by lunchtime had admitted I wasn't getting anything done. After a short email letting my client know I was sick, I shut my laptop, pulled my blanket over my head, and fell asleep.

Things hadn't improved by the next morning, dashing all hopes that it was a twenty-four-hour thing. I was now at thirty and counting and still feeling like death. I'd slept most of the day, at least when my fever wasn't doing crazy things and either causing me to shiver or sweat.

I didn't know if it was better or worse that I fully understood why I was going from freezing to burning every few hours. Sometimes, knowledge wasn't power. The science of understanding body temperature regulation was not going to help me fight off the flu.

My phone going insane on the coffee table wasn't helping me sleep. Though it did remind me that it was supposed to be a group dinner tonight and I needed to let them know I wasn't going to be at Steve's. Thankfully, the meds I'd taken an hour before had kicked in enough that I was starting to feel human again. At least I would sound somewhat functional when I sent the text. There was no need to worry them needlessly.

I scrolled far enough back that I felt like I was up to date with the conversation then sent a text of my own.

Me: *Don't wait for me tonight. Won't be there.*

It shouldn't have surprised me that Merrick was the first to respond.

Merrick: *Everything okay?*

Me: *Flu. I've spent the last thirty-something hours sleeping, or in some sort of fever cycle. I'm starting to feel a little more human, so hopefully it's passing. But I'm not going to be there tonight.*

James: *That sucks. Feel better.*

Larson: *Need anything? Daddy and I are at the store.*

I smiled. We jokingly complained about our lack of boundaries at times, but someone was always there when we were in need.

Me: *Mom is bringing soup over in a bit. And knowing her she'll probably have an entire car filled with groceries.*

Logan: *If you're up for it, we can play Minecraft! I'll send you an invite to the world we were working on last weekend. I'm off today and tomorrow.*

I yawned and rubbed my eyes.

Me: *Thanks. Maybe tomorrow? I'm pretty wiped out right now. Going to pass out again.*

Logan: *Just say the word!*

With another yawn, I turned off my phone and pulled the blanket over my shoulders. I was out in a matter of seconds and slept until I heard my mom and aunt bickering in my kitchen.

Sitting up was difficult, but I had to admit that I was feeling better. I pulled the blanket more tightly around my shoulders and shuffled from the living room into the kitchen. My mom was bent over, putting food in the fridge while my aunt had her head in my cabinet, looking for who knew what.

"Can I help you find something, Aunt Monica?"

She yelped and jumped back. "What are you doing up? You were sound asleep five minutes ago!"

Laughing hurt, but I couldn't help it. "Well, if you were trying not to wake me up, maybe you two shouldn't have been banging around in here like a steel drum band."

Mom stood up and smiled at me. "Sorry, baby. We were trying to be quiet. But Monica couldn't leave until your dishes were put away."

I glanced at the dishwasher to see that it was open. So she wasn't looking for something, she was putting something away. "Do I have any plates left? The way you're clanking around, I wouldn't be surprised if you'd broken them all by now."

Mom snorted as my aunt threw her hands in the air. "This is what I get for trying to help!"

Mom gave me a long once-over, taking in everything

from my disheveled hair to my rumpled pajama pants. "How are you feeling?"

I lifted a shoulder. "Better than I was a few hours ago. Still feel like a train hit me."

Aunt Monica pressed her hand to my forehead and hummed to herself. "There's a nasty bug going around. It's been leveling people for about thirty-six to forty-eight hours. You should be on the tail end of it by now." She worked as an office manager for a doctor's office, so she was always in the know when it came to illnesses.

"Well, I've passed the thirty-six-hour mark already. I guess I'm going for the longer version." I sniffed the air. "What did you bring? It smells amazing."

Mom patted my cheek gently as she bustled past me to the cupboard for a bowl. "Chicken noodle soup. Gramma made it when she heard you were sick. She sends her love but didn't want to come over."

"No wonder it smells so good." I laughed again when my mom narrowed her eyes at me.

"Dean Anderson Nicoles! Are you insulting my cooking?"

I shook my head, but my grin was unable to be contained. "I would do no such thing!"

"If you didn't look like you were ready to keel over, I'd smack you right about now." She was smiling the entire time she threatened me, so I knew she wasn't serious. Besides, it wasn't a secret that my mom wasn't a great cook. She could make a killer chocolate cake, dessert breads, and a cherry pie that was to die for, but main dishes had never been a strong suit for her.

"Seriously, thank you. And don't let Gramma or Pap here. I don't want either of them to get this."

Mom reached into the dishwasher and grabbed one of the remaining bowls, filled it with soup, and slid it across the island to me. "I'd give you a hug, but you look like shit and I spent enough time sick thanks to you when you were little. I've done my time."

"Thanks, Mom. I'm feelin' the love today." This was the way we were. We joked with one another more like friends than mother and son. It was likely because we were so close in age.

By the time we'd gotten our own place, I was already ten and basically a tiny adult. We had talked about current events, problems at work, problems at school. I'd never connected with the kids at school. The ones my age weren't interested in the things I was, and the kids interested in the same stuff I was wanted nothing to do with a guy so much younger.

She blew me a kiss. "I'm just telling you like it is. You need to get better in case Prince Charming walks in that door tonight. You don't want to scare him off looking like that. You know, maybe you should shower?"

I groaned again. "Mom!"

She put the leftover soup in the fridge and turned to smile at me. "I know, I know. You aren't looking for a boyfriend. I've heard you a million times already. But you never know if that perfect man is just going to appear out of nowhere and sweep you off your feet."

At that moment, the garage door went up and I furrowed my brow. Not fifteen seconds later, it started to shut and the kitchen door opened. Merrick's silver head of hair appeared a moment later.

If my smile turned a little brighter at seeing him in my kitchen, it was just because he was saving me from my mom. It had nothing to do with the fact that the sight of him had begun to make my heart race in ways it never had before.

Mom's grin got huge. "See? He might have just walked right in here! Hurry, you have time to shower. I'll cover for you." She made a shooing motion with her hands, pretending that Merrick couldn't see me.

My head hit the counter and I groaned. Mom hadn't been wrong; I looked like shit. Not only was I unshowered, I was also only half-dressed after I'd left my shirt in the living room the last time I'd started sweating.

It didn't help that Mom had had a crush on Merrick from the moment she'd laid eyes on him. There had been many times over the years that I'd been thankful my mom had promised to never date one of my friends. It had been one of the most awkward, uncomfortable conversations I'd ever had with her. However, we were so close in age that it had been necessary.

Promise aside, Merrick was gay, which meant that Mom had decided that if she couldn't date him, I should. While she'd never tried to set us up, she still joked that he was going to be the man that swept me off my feet one day. It hadn't mattered how many times I'd told her he wasn't the relationship type, that I didn't want a relationship, or that we weren't compatible, my mom held firm on her claim.

Sickness was not enough for Jenny Nicoles to lay off the charm.

Merrick looked between us. "Oops, sorry. There wasn't a car in the driveway. I didn't know anyone was here."

I looked up in time to see my mom grab my aunt's hand. "We parked on the street. And it's perfect timing because Mon just got a text from her work and we were on our way out. Glad he's got friends like you all that keep an eye on him."

To add insult to injury, Mom patted Merrick's cheek, giving him a sweet smile.

Aunt Monica's mouth opened in protest. It was the end of the day and we all knew there hadn't been a text, but my mom was pulling her out the door Merrick had just entered.

The door shut behind them before the garage door even began to open. I shook my head. "That woman is a menace."

Merrick was still looking at the door my mom and aunt had just gone through. "She's awesome. But she didn't have to run out through the garage."

"She always uses the garage, but she probably could have used to hit the button for the garage before shutting the door." I yawned and felt a chill run down my spine. "Ugh, not again."

"What's up, Bean?"

"Chills. Again. I thought I was over this fever. Wait, what are you doing here? Shouldn't you be at dinner?"

Merrick ignored my questions in exchange for grabbing my bowl from the counter. "Did you want more?"

All I managed was a weak shake of my head. Another chill ran down my spine, making me pull the blanket tighter over my shoulders. When the chill passed, I had a few seconds of reprieve to ask the question again. "Shouldn't you be somewhere else?"

I didn't know what time it was, but Brodrick's was being completely renovated, and Merrick had been spending absurd hours there. If he wasn't at Brodrick's, then it must be time to go to dinner.

"I backed out. Told the guys I was going to come check on you instead."

I glowered at him but the stare was broken when my teeth chattered. "I'm not a child. I'm fully capable of taking care of myself."

Despite the eye roll he gave me, his smile was more amused than annoyed. "I know you are. But sometimes it's nice to not have to."

Any argument I might have made died in my throat. Not having to take care of myself sounded nice for a change. Reflexively, I adjusted my blanket around my shoulders and slid off the chair. "I'm going to go to the living room."

The couch sounded heavenly at the moment. Merrick wasn't fazed by my abrupt exit, continuing to clean my bowl and tidy the little bit in the kitchen that my aunt had left untouched. There wasn't much there to begin with since I normally kept a pretty clean kitchen. The last few days had been an exception, but I also hadn't been doing much more than drinking and picking at a few bites here or there.

In the living room, I tugged on the hoodie I'd pulled off earlier before I collapsed onto the couch with the remote and my blanket. My head hit my pillow just as the TV clicked on to the channel I'd been watching earlier. Cartoons weren't normally my thing, but the antics of *Dexter's Laboratory* were exactly what I'd needed to forget about feeling like shit.

Before today, it had been years since I'd watched the show, but I'd spotted it while scrolling through the channels. Growing up, many afternoons had been spent with the cartoon on in the background while I did homework or tinkered with something I probably shouldn't have.

A memory of trying to figure out how to make my mom's hair dryer run hotter came to mind. I'd been about thirteen and had needed a heat gun for some shrink tubing. We didn't have one and Mom's hair dryer wasn't powerful enough. With the show as background noise, I'd successfully tweaked the dryer to the point that it worked for the shrink tubing… but it had also melted the plastic casing of the hair dryer. Not being old enough to go buy her a new one, I'd had to explain to her what I'd done when she got home.

A few days later, I had a dedicated heat gun and her new hair dryer got locked in the cabinet. I'd never told her that the lock could be picked with two paper clips because then I wouldn't have had access to it when I'd needed the lower-powered dryer for drying nail polish and paint.

Dexter had been background noise for many an adventure in my youth, but as I watched the cartoon, laughing occasionally, I struggled to remember if I'd ever sat down and just watched it before that day.

With every shiver, I curled into a tighter ball, until I was barely taking up two of the three squares. My eyes felt heavy before the credits rolled on the first episode, and I was just giving into sleep when the couch dipped above my pillows. My eyes fluttered open for a moment to see Merrick getting comfortable.

"You don't have to stay." It was nice to know someone was here—hell, the clanking in the kitchen had been comforting compared to the usual silence—but I also didn't want him to feel obligated to stay. I was an adult and had been living alone since I was eighteen.

I fought to keep my eyes open, but they drifted shut again. Merrick's hum was comforting, as were his quiet words. "I know I don't have to. But I can't think of a place I'd rather be right now."

My lips twitched into a smile, then I felt Merrick move. "I almost forgot something." A bag rustled and he placed something soft and lightweight against my chest.

Despite my exhaustion, I wanted to know what was resting against me. My eyes opened again, that time to find fuzzy light brown fur. I untangled my hand from my blanket cocoon and reached for the object. Without my glasses, I had to pull it back slightly to get a better look. The fur was softer than anything I could remember holding before. When my eyes focused, its big floppy ears made me smile. The inside of its ears was equally soft but white instead of tan, and its eyes, nose, and smiling mouth had been created from thread.

I couldn't explain why it made me as happy as it did, but I couldn't deny the emotion. Looking up at Merrick, tired and still confused as to why he'd given me the rabbit, I opened my mouth without thinking my words through. "You got me a babbit?"

It was Merrick's quirked eyebrow that told me I'd said something he hadn't been expecting. When I replayed the question in my head, I felt my cheeks heat with something different than a fever. One of the only words I'd ever mispronounced as a child had been *rabbit*. I'd gotten bunny and rabbit mixed up and ended up saying babbit until I was nearly eight.

Once I'd figured out they were rabbits, my mom had begun calling all rabbits runny babbits, and the name had stuck. The two of us still called all rabbits babbits, but when I was with someone else, my brain automatically switched it to the right word. Sick, tired, and confused, my brain hadn't made the switch.

As it turned out, I wasn't sick enough to not be embarrassed by my slip.

CHAPTER TWELVE

MERRICK

Dean had been pale since I'd walked into the house, but now his cheeks were rapidly turning an unnatural shade of red. The cutesy name had been so unexpected, it had taken my brain a few seconds to process what he'd asked. He'd already turned red before I'd come up with an answer.

"I mean, rabbit. My mom and I, we—"

I cut him off with a finger to his lips. They were hot to the touch, confirming his fever was still present. Looking at the man lying on the couch beside me, insisting he didn't need me to stay despite feeling like crap, then stumbling over a single word, had my chest tightening. If calling the toy Babbit had embarrassed him, he wasn't ready to know I'd bought it for him earlier in the week before he was sick.

His illness happened to be a good cover for the purchase. "Well, you're sick. Babbit looked like it was a good size to cuddle."

Dean groaned and dropped the rabbit on his face. "Great. Bean's Babbit. I'm never living this down."

At least with his eyes covered, Dean couldn't see my smile. I'd called him Bean so often, it was almost as second nature as calling him Dean, to the point that all the guys knew I called him that. And Babbit was an adorable name for his bunny, no matter the reason he'd said it in the first place. One day I hoped to get the story but for now I just wanted him to get some sleep.

Lifting the bunny's soft ear, I rubbed it along his chin. "You and Babbit really do need sleep."

His groan was no less embarrassed, and he didn't move the toy from his face as he spoke. "I'm going to sleep. When I wake up, you're going to be gone and we're going to pretend this entire conversation never happened."

I didn't miss that he hadn't included Babbit in the things leaving, but even if he had, neither of us were going anywhere. Not until his fever broke, at the least.

Being sick was miserable. Being sick and alone was possibly the only thing worse. I knew that from personal experience. Mooch had clean litter, dry food, a generous portion of his favorite canned food, and plenty of water to last at least twenty-four hours. If Dean wasn't feeling better by then, Canyon had a key to my place and could go check on the cat.

With an overnight bag already at the base of the steps, there was no getting rid of me.

Glancing down, I found Dean sleeping. At some point while I'd been lost in thought, he'd pulled Babbit from his face and it was now tucked firmly in his arms and resting under his chin.

All the reading I'd done the last few days—and it had been a lot—had made me more convinced Dean was a middle. The way he was holding the blanket and stuffed animal only cemented the feeling.

The night before had been spent at Canyon and Larson's house, peppering them with countless questions about littles and middles. Three hours of questioning later, my brain had been swimming with information, but I'd left with a better understanding of the differences.

There were things that overlapped, and others that weren't very clear. Canyon and Larson had continually repeated that there wasn't a right or wrong way to be a Daddy or a boy, and that nothing was ever concrete. The only thing I knew for sure, regardless of age, was that boys liked rules and structure. Judging by the information I'd found on my own, they also needed security.

Dean deserved someone to give him that security. I wasn't known for providing anything more than a warm body to men. I was an overbearing asshole who ran guys off after a few nights. My track record was not a ringing endorsement for my personality. I'd spent more time with Dean since January than I could ever remember spending with another man—Tom included.

Knowing all that I did about Dean and myself, I still wanted to be the person Dean needed. Whether he knew or accepted that he was a middle was still up for debate, but the more time I spent with Dean, the more certain I was that there would never be anything that could get him in the headspace to be a Daddy.

With his pillow pushed against my thigh, a blanket wrapped tightly around his shoulders, and Babbit clutched in his arms, I could easily see Dean curled up with a Daddy of his own. He shivered in his sleep and I reached for the blanket that had been dropped on the floor at some point.

I placed it over him and watched as he nearly burrowed under it. Then he wiggled closer to my leg, his cheek coming to rest on my thigh as he mumbled an almost incoherent "Thank you."

When he finally settled down again, I reached for the remote, switched the channel, and propped my feet up on the coffee table.

Twenty minutes later, I didn't have a clue what was on the TV. My hand was gently stroking Dean's head, and I was contemplating a text to Travis to ask him when I should worry about the heat radiating off Dean's head. He needed a Daddy, someone who knew the answers to the things I didn't. He needed someone who knew how to help him relax and let him simply exist.

I didn't know what he needed or how to help him. I didn't even know how to help his fever.

I ran my hand over his head again. He let out a little huff as he readjusted himself further onto my lap. By the time he'd relaxed once more, he'd ended up with his head and shoulders over both of my legs.

When a growl sounded, it took me a few seconds of looking around to figure out the sound had come from me. I'd been thinking about what Dean's ideal Daddy would be like and had gotten frustrated at a hypothetical man that I couldn't even picture.

Try as I might, the TV didn't hold my interest. I finally gave up and texted Travis.

Me: *At what point should you worry about a fever?*

The response came quickly and I relaxed knowing that he'd have an answer.

Travis: *Three days, or not controlled by a fever reducer. Dean still fevered?*

Me: *Yeah. He was looking okay when I got here, but he got fevered shortly thereafter. He's been out for about an hour, and the man is like a furnace.*

Travis: *When was the last time he had anything for it? How high is the fever?*

Me: *I don't know, and I don't know. I didn't ask.*

Travis: *Find the thermometer and have him take his temp.*

I looked down at Dean, still draped across my lap and sleeping soundly, his arm still gripped around the plush toy.

Me: *That would require waking him up. I feel bad doing that.*

Travis: *Mer, just dig through the medicine cabinet. You're both gay men. Shy of a dungeon in his medicine cabinet, there's not much that could surprise you.*

It was hard not to laugh. Worrying about what I'd find in a medicine cabinet had not been top on my priority list. My biggest concern was disturbing the man on my lap. Though now that he'd put the thought in my head, I wondered what I'd find.

Me: *Not worried about that. Dean's dead asleep, draped over my lap.*

Travis: Well, that's unexpected. Something going on there?

If only.

Me: Only that Dean's exhausted and fevered. He was trying to get warm in his sleep. And now that he's sleeping, I don't want to disturb him.

Travis was quiet for a few minutes, though I could see he'd read the text. Eventually, dots appeared.

Travis: You've been there what, two, two and a half hours? Does he feel like he's getting warmer?

Me: No. He's hot, but he feels the same temp he did once he finally settled down.

Travis: Okay. Probably means the fever's peaked. Most fever reducers can be taken every 3-4 hours. If he isn't up in a half hour or so, or if you notice him getting hotter, then wake him up. Otherwise, don't worry too much until you have answers.

Dean stretched, then pulled the rabbit closer to his face. His fingers found the ear and he began to rub the fur between his thumb and index finger.

Me: Or he can wake up now. I'll let you know how he's feeling later.

Travis: Good luck. Tell him we all missed him and hope he feels better soon.

I shut off the screen and carded my hand through his hair, something I'd been absently doing most of the time I'd texted with Travis.

Dean hummed, then his body tensed.

"Hey." I'd tried to whisper the word, but my throat was dry and I'd had to force it out, making it louder than I'd intended.

Dean scrambled off my lap and toward the other side

of the couch. His face was red with embarrassment and pinched in pain, but I didn't know if it was his illness, that his back had seized up while he'd been asleep, or a bit of both. Regardless of the reason, I hated that he was in pain.

It took a few minutes, but he finally looked over at me. "I'm sorry. I don't even remember you sitting down." His eyes widened, showing how bloodshot they were. "Oh no, did I drool on you?"

His concern was cute, but I didn't think he'd want to hear that at the moment. "No, you didn't drool on me." *He'd have been more likely to drool on the rabbit.*

Dean let out a relieved sigh. "That's good." His hand dropped to his lap and landed on the rabbit. The confusion in his eyes and the way his brow turned downward told me he didn't know what he'd landed on.

His eyebrows went from a straight line to two surprised arches on his forehead when he saw the item. "What's this?" His one hand wrapped around its arm, and the fingers of his other began to rub at the ear.

Something kept drawing him to the ear. He'd continually found it since I'd given it to him, even while sleeping.

"Well, if sleepy Dean is to be trusted, his name is Babbit."

"Shit. That wasn't a fever dream?"

I found myself chuckling. "Nope." Sensing his discomfort, I changed the topic. "Travis told me I should have taken your temperature, but I don't know where your thermometer is."

Dean's eyes had gone back to his rabbit, but he

answered me. "It's on the bathroom counter. I took my temp before I took meds last time."

"And when was that?"

Dean blinked, then blinked again. "Uh, before the nap I took before my mom and aunt got here. It had to have been four or five hours ago by now. Hell, I don't even know what time it is."

"It's a little after eight." I stood to go to the bathroom. "Meds in the bathroom too?"

He looked up and nodded. "Yeah. And if it's after eight, it's been closer to six hours. No wonder I feel like shit. Aunt Monica says I should be feeling better soon, though." He yawned and pulled his blanket around his shoulders.

I took that as my cue to get moving. He was also going to need something to eat at some point.

Five minutes later, I'd taken his temperature, given him another dose of fever reducer, and was in the kitchen trying to find something he could eat. He swore he wasn't hungry, but I knew he needed food in his stomach, even if it was just toast.

I heard him yawn three different times while I waited for the toast to finish and the tea to steep. I hadn't stepped into my childhood home in over a decade, but the memory of my mom's toast and tea when I was sick was still vivid. It had always made me feel better, and it was the only thing I could think of to give Dean.

The aroma of the steeping tea reminded me that I needed to call home. I hadn't talked to my parents in nearly a week and Mom would start to worry. For now, I had

Dean to take care of but judging by his frequent yawns, he wasn't going to be awake for long.

Dean was still on the couch when I returned. He'd adjusted to sit cross-legged, his blanket still wrapped around his shoulders and Babbit in his lap. The TV was playing another cartoon, just as confusing as the one he'd been watching earlier. And just like earlier, his eyes were drooping as he watched.

Not wanting to startle him, I nearly whispered as I entered the room. "Hey, Bean."

Dean looked over at me and his nose turned up at the plate in my hand. While I understood not feeling hungry, I also knew it would help him feel better. No matter how adorable his pout was, he wasn't going to get out of eating. I placed the mug on the end table, then sat beside him and handed over the plate. "Eat."

"I'm not hungry."

His pout made him look younger, and the way he blinked up at me with sad, tired eyes wasn't making him look any older. "I know, but you need to eat or you won't start feeling better." When he didn't make a move for the toast, I picked a slice up and held it out to him. "Eat your toast, watch your show, and at the end of the episode, you can go to bed."

He tried to scowl at me, but I was going to count it as a win when he grabbed the slice of toast from my hand and took a bite. I'd put cinnamon and sugar on the toast, a special touch that had always made me smile when my mom made it for me.

I'd forgotten how messy the treat was until a dusting of

cinnamon sugar began falling with every bite. While most of it landed on the small plate, some missed and landed on his rabbit.

The last thing he needed was a sweet, sticky rabbit that would need to be washed before bedtime. I reached over and slid the rabbit from his lap. His eyes flashed with momentary panic that he quickly masked. "Wha…" His question trailed off and his cheeks flushed.

I'd thought of Dean as soon as I saw the rabbit in the store. His immediate attachment to it was just further confirmation of his middle side.

He cleared his throat and nodded toward the rabbit in my hand. "Why'd you get him for me?"

I lifted a shoulder, my thoughts landing on the threadbare stuffed animal that sat on my dresser. I was in my mid-forties and still grabbed it when I was sick. In his current state, accepting that I'd thought he needed something comfortable to snuggle was probably going to be better received than my telling him I'd bought it because all middles needed a stuffy.

"Everyone needs something soft to snuggle when they're not feeling well. You only had Blankie. Now you have Babbit." I pointed to the blanket still wrapped around his shoulders and watched his face heat with embarrassment once again.

The blanket had been all over the house the last few times I'd been there and by the way he'd been reaching for it repeatedly, I knew that it wasn't just a throw blanket.

So much was making sense. What I still couldn't understand was why he said he was a Daddy.

Looking back at his plate, he spoke quietly. "My mom and I call rabbits runny babbits. It's kind of our thing." He finished the first piece of toast and reached for the second. Before putting it in his mouth, he glanced up at me. "Thanks for trying to make me feel better."

His smile was weak and small. The harder he tried to ignore the stuffed animal and focus on the TV, the more I saw his internal struggle, his adult side trying to stay present while his middle side just wanted his stuffed animal.

How would I get him to see that he didn't have to keep pretending to be something he wasn't?

He finished the second piece of toast and put the plate down. With his hands unoccupied, his fingers kept twitching toward where I'd set Babbit, but he'd catch himself before grabbing it. When it became clear he wasn't going to reach for it himself, I decided to take the decision out of his—sugary—hands.

My mom's countless warnings about sticky fingers and comfort items when I was growing up had never left my brain. And just like my mom had done to me, I used the paper towel to wipe his fingers before placing Babbit back in his lap. Dean's face was crimson as I left with his plate and dirty paper towel.

It wasn't until the plate was in the dishwasher that I considered what I'd done. Wiping his hands had been natural at the moment, but had that been the cause of his embarrassment as I left?

I was contemplating how to apologize as I made my way back to the living room, but quickly forgot when I caught a glimpse of him on the couch. I ended up standing just out of his line of sight for nearly five minutes. While I'd been gone, Dean had pulled his blanket and bunny toward his chest and began to sip his tea. The thumb on his free hand continued to rub at the long ear and his eyes never left the cartoon while he drank.

I waited until the show was over to finally step toward the couch. "Okay, Bean. Bedtime. You're falling asleep sitting there. You're going to sleep much better in your bed."

He groaned as he untangled his legs and stood up. "Brush your teeth, change your clothes, and get into bed."

He complained the entire way up the steps but did as I'd instructed. Once the sink turned on upstairs, I took a few minutes to double-check the front door and grab his blanket and Babbit as well as my overnight bag.

Dean was just climbing into bed as I passed the door to his room. I dropped my bag outside his door and walked toward him to give him his items. He gave me a sleepy smile as I placed them next to him. "Thank you."

"Anytime. Need anything else?" He shook his head, his eyes already closed. "Okay, sleep well, Bean."

Halfway to the door, Dean's quiet voice made my feet stop. "Uh, would you mind staying?"

I pointed to the door across the hallway. "I already have an overnight bag with me."

Dean shook his head and patted the bed beside him. "I mean here. Just until I fall asleep? You're right, it's nice to not be alone." He quickly added, "I mean when I'm sick."

My smile couldn't be helped. Wordlessly, I changed

course and headed to the empty side of the bed. Once I'd lain down, he wiggled close enough to me that I could reach out and rub his back.

He hummed and fell asleep quickly, but I continued to rub at his back and watch him sleep. At some point, I fell asleep beside him. Still in my clothes, over the covers, but with Dean's body pressed against mine.

CHAPTER THIRTEEN

DEAN

Hot.

That was all I could think of as my eyes cracked open to a dark room.

Hot and wet. As the sleep cleared from my brain, I knew the wetness was sweat. I was drenched in it, to the point that even my pillowcase was wet. The object my ass was pressed against wasn't helping me cool off.

I reached out, trying to push whatever it was away, only to have it grunt at the contact. Before I could roll over to see what had made the noise, a concerned voice cut the silence of the bedroom. "You okay, Bean?"

Only one person called me Bean, but that didn't explain why Merrick was in my bed. Come to think of it, I barely remembered him coming over.

When I didn't answer, Merrick reached out and ran his hand over my forehead. "Damn, you're soaked."

Tell me something I didn't know.

After a second, he amended the statement. "But cool.

Your fever must finally be breaking. You up for a shower? If you are, I'll strip and change the bed."

His words sent a swirl of contentment through me that I didn't fully understand. Too exhausted to put thought into why and too uncomfortably wet to care, I nodded. A shower would definitely help, and new sheets would be an added bonus. I needed some space from the man who was making me feel things I'd never felt before.

"Yeah, shower sounds good." My clothes stuck to my back as I shuffled across the room to grab new pajamas. Once in the bathroom, I set to work peeling my clothes off, wondering the entire time why I'd gone to bed in layers.

As I rinsed my hair for the second time, Merrick called from the other room. "Hey, where do you keep your sheets?"

"The bottom drawer of the dresser." The downfall of my townhome was lack of closet space. I'd built shelves for my bath towels but had settled on using a dresser drawer for my bedding.

I had stepped out of the spray to grab soap when he called again, this time closer to the bathroom door. "Anything… interesting I should know before I open that drawer?"

What? I blinked a few times as I tried to figure out what he was asking. "What in the h—" Understanding dawned on me and I groaned. "No!"

Not in that drawer anyway.

Merrick didn't respond, so I focused on my shower. The water felt amazing, my body cooling as I stood in the spray. No matter how needed the shower had been or how good it felt, I didn't stay in long. It was still some ungodly hour of the night, and I was exhausted.

After drying off, getting dressed again, and brushing my teeth once more for good measure, I headed back to my room. As promised, my bed was remade with clean bedding. Merrick had changed everything, including the duvet and pillowcases. What I hadn't counted on was him finding, and choosing, the bedding set with game controllers all over it. I also hadn't expected my blanket and the plush rabbit to be prominently displayed on my pillow, or for Merrick to be wearing a pair of pajamas and to be in my bed.

My brain hurt from everything I was seeing. I should have told him that if he wanted to stay, there was a spare room across the hall, but the truth was it had been nice to wake up next to someone... even a friend. I couldn't remember the last time I'd shared a bed with a man, and the firm body I'd woken up against had been comforting. Instead of telling him to leave, I walked over to the bed, climbed in, and tried to hide my embarrassment as I reached for both my blanket and the new stuffed animal.

Merrick had to have figured out that was more than just a throw blanket to me. I only vaguely remembered being given the stuffed animal earlier in the night, but it had felt nice in my arms when I'd woken up.

And there was a memory of quickly giving it a name when Merrick had handed it to me. Once it had a name, it was easy to feel an attachment. Maybe it was the hour, maybe it was the lingering flu, maybe it was something else entirely, but I wasn't ready to put Babbit down.

Without a fever clouding my thoughts, I could admit that it was sweet that Merrick had thought of me. A bit odd that he'd decided I needed a stuffed animal to feel better, but sweet just the same.

And with both items in my hands, I instinctively moved closer to the man who shouldn't have been in my bed and yawned again. "Night, Mer."

"Night, Bean."

My brain was too sluggish to form a comeback to the nickname, and I began drifting off as I attempted to find one. Just before sleep pulled me under, a strong arm wrapped around my stomach and drew me closer. I had to fight a hum of contentment. I'd always been the big spoon, but lying like this, I could understand why being the little spoon was appealing.

The next time my eyes opened, sunlight was fighting the blackout shades in my room and the clock on my dresser read a very blurry 9:49 a.m. The time explained why the spot Merrick had been in however many hours earlier was no longer occupied. He would be long gone, probably elbow deep in renovations at Brodrick's.

I made a mental note to send him a text after I'd had some coffee. It was only right to thank him for giving up his night to hang out with a guy too sick to be decent company. He'd been showing a much gentler side of himself now that he was around more. Even his smiles were coming more freely. Buying a stuffed animal to make someone feel better wasn't something Merrick from a year ago would have done.

Standing in front of the toilet emptying my bladder, I

was able to admit that my aunt was right. I'd been wiped out for nearly two days, but I felt better. Hell, I almost felt back to myself again. That didn't mean I was going to work that day. If I wasn't worried about still being contagious, I would have sent Logan a text to see if he wanted to come over to play video games. The cartoon racing game sounded a lot more fun than the shooting games I typically played. Strategy games were not what my brain needed at the moment.

After flushing the toilet, I washed my hands, splashed some water on my face, and headed out of the bathroom as my stomach rumbled. It was the first time I'd been hungry since Wednesday morning.

Babbit and my blanket were still lying near my pillow as I headed to the door. With nothing more to do than watch TV, I grabbed them and headed down the steps.

As I walked, I wrapped my blanket around my shoulders and tucked Babbit into my arm. By the time I noticed Merrick standing in the kitchen with a cup of coffee on the counter and a plate of scrambled eggs, toast, and sausage beside it, he'd spotted me.

My cheeks were already burning with embarrassment before he raised his coffee cup in my direction. "Morning."

Nothing about the moment made sense. Merrick was standing in my kitchen smiling at me, not bothered by my blanket or Babbit, when he should have been at work.

"Breakfast's ready. I heard you start moving around, so I scrambled some eggs, warmed up the sausage I found in your fridge, and made you some toast."

He pointed toward the seat across the island. "Take a seat."

It took a few seconds to convince my body to move from where my feet had been rooted to the floor. Once seated, he set the plate and mug in front of me, then turned to grab the creamer out of the fridge.

Turning back around, he set the creamer down and moved Babbit from my lap to the seat beside me in one fluid motion.

"Feeling better?"

I focused too intently on pouring the creamer into my mug, giving myself time to take a few deep breaths and gather my thoughts. Once I was sure my voice would come out without cracking, I nodded. "Yeah. Much. Thanks for being here last night. I was feeling pretty awful when you showed up."

His grin spoke volumes, but he waved it off as though he hadn't gone out of his way. "It's no big deal. I'm just glad you're feeling better."

We didn't speak as I ate my breakfast, but when he pulled the empty plate from me, I couldn't help but ask. "Why aren't you at Brodrick's?"

His back was turned toward me as he rinsed the plate, but I saw his shoulders go up in a shrug. "Told Travis that he and Ben were more than capable of handling things for the day. Besides, if they fuck something up, I know where Travis lives and sleeps."

After two days of feeling like death, my laugh was refreshing. "You'd have to get through Caleb first. Do not underestimate the protectiveness of a little."

Merrick threw his head back and laughed. "Believe me, I've spent enough time around Canyon and Larson to not doubt that." His phone rang and he sighed as he fished it out of his pocket. "I need to take this. Go find something to do. You don't need to be sitting here when there's a comfortable couch a few feet away."

As I slid off the stool, I grabbed my blanket and Babbit and heard Merrick's smile as he answered the phone. "Hey, Mom."

The words had my feet slowing, and I turned to watch as he loaded my dishwasher, unaware that I hadn't left. His shoulders had gone a little tense, but his voice sounded warm enough as he greeted her. Merrick didn't talk about his family, so I was surprised to hear him talking to his mom.

He placed a mug in the dishwasher as he spoke. "No, I'm at a friend's house today. He's been sick."

There was a pause in the conversation, and Merrick laughed lightly, though it wasn't as genuine as it had been with me a few seconds earlier. "Yes, tea and toast. Yes, cinnamon sugar too." There was another pause, that time followed by a light chuckle before he spoke. "Well, I brought him one." The smile I could hear in his voice had my nerves calming. "I know. It's still on my dresser."

They talked for a few more minutes, but I was no longer listening. I wanted to know what was on his dresser, but I also wanted to know more about Merrick and his mom. The conversation didn't sound hostile despite the way he'd initially tensed.

So why didn't he talk about them, or growing up?

I was already tiring and accepted I wasn't fully up to par yet, and the couch was calling my name. More caught up in what would be on at ten in the morning rather than expecting something to be on the floor between me and the couch, I kicked a paper bag that I was certain hadn't been there the day before.

Looking down, I noticed it wasn't paper but a blue gift bag. The little tag on the handle caught my attention, and I found myself smiling when I noticed Merrick's chicken scratch scrawled across it. *To: Dean From: Merrick* was barely legible. Then a memory of him pulling Babbit from the bag the night before popped into my head. I remembered the rustling of the bag and then the soft stuffed animal being handed to me.

The heat in my cheeks could only be blamed on slight embarrassment, but at least Merrick was still on the phone. I squeezed Babbit to my chest, a smile forming on my lips and my chest constricting in an odd way as I thought about Merrick buying the stuffed animal.

The plush toy hadn't been something that he'd randomly picked up on a whim. He'd put a lot of thought into it, and that made the gift feel more special than it had a moment before.

The bag was taller than the stuffed animal had warranted, and when I went to push it out of my way, there was a distinct weight that let me know it wasn't empty. I took a seat on the couch and pulled the bag toward me, wondering for a moment if I should wait for Merrick to be off the phone. The thought only lasted a few seconds before curiosity took over and I reached in.

My hand brushed a box and I wrapped my hand around it to pull it out. The LEGO logo caught my eye, but I didn't understand why Merrick had put a Mario LEGO set in the bag.

Staring at the box, I couldn't remember ever having a LEGO set.

I definitely hadn't been the most normal kid. When I was four and the neighbor kid was digging in the sandbox, I'd been taking apart the toaster to figure out how it worked. LEGO sets had never been high on my wish list, not with electronics in the house.

When we moved out of my grandparents' house, I'd taken apart a lot of things. Some weren't able to be put back together, some had been put back together in ways that made them work better, and—as was the case with the blender—others worked a bit too well.

As it turned out, the blender my grandmother got for her wedding didn't do well with a nitrous engine from an RC car. After I put it back together, it only had two speeds: off and pulverize. On the other hand, it made a damn good juice, though no one seemed to appreciate that when they were trying to make a smoothie.

We still didn't talk about the mower I'd dropped a dirt bike engine into. Despite being able to mow my grandparents' yard in less than half the time it used to take, my grandpa didn't appreciate his old riding mower doing fifty on a straightaway. All these years later, I still had to go mow his grass.

He'd once told me I'd be doing it until either he or the mower died. Given that I'd fixed anything that had gone wrong with it since I was fifteen, the odds were the mower would outlast not only him but me too.

There was no reason I needed a LEGO set now. I was well past the age they should have been fun. Yet I was sitting on my couch with a set in my hand and a smile on my face. I flipped the box over again and felt excitement grow when I saw that I could install an app and use this set to play a game on my phone. Oh, this was going to be almost as fun as playing the racing game with Logan.

Did Logan have this set?

"I see you found the rest of your gifts."

My head shot over to where Merrick was leaning against the same wall I'd been leaning on a few minutes earlier. His eyes were sparkling with unmistakable happiness, and the smile on his face was nothing short of breathtaking. Knowing that he'd not only bought these for me but that he'd given them a lot of thought had my gut tightening with pleasure.

Happiness should not make me horny. How long had it been since I'd been with someone if the look Merrick was giving me made arousal stir inside me?

Trying to ignore the stir in my belly, I focused on Merrick. "I don't think that I've ever built a LEGO set."

His eyes showed shock, and he ate up the distance between the wall and couch quickly. "Then I'm glad I picked these up. You and the guys were having a blast playing that racing game. I thought that, since you were sick, you might like something to help pass time." He reached over me and grabbed the bag, overturning it so that the contents spilled out onto my coffee table.

"I might have gone a bit overboard." I was pretty sure he'd said it to himself, but he wasn't wrong. There were numerous sets, and Mario had four different suits to change into. "Which one do you want to start with?"

The question shouldn't have drawn me up short, but I had no idea where to start and ended up staring blankly at the coffee table for a moment.

Merrick's soft chuckle was comforting as he reached for the box containing the classic Mario character. "Well, you need the character to do anything, so we should probably start there."

Twenty minutes later, I'd forgotten all about Merrick as I worked on the box that had big bold letters across the front declaring it the starter set.

CHAPTER FOURTEEN

MERRICK

I knew I was in over my head the moment my lips had made contact with Dean's forehead as I left his house. In that instant, I'd forgotten all about not being his boyfriend or Daddy.

He'd spent most of the day building the LEGO sets or napping, but by dinner, he'd been awake and starving. I'd cooked him dinner, but then had to admit that there wasn't any reason for me to stay. As I grabbed my bag, Dean had met me at the door holding Babbit in his arm.

He'd blushed every time he'd noticed it in his hand, but he hadn't made an effort to take it to his room or leave it on the couch either. He'd played with the LEGO sets for two hours between his last nap and dinner, randomly texting back and forth with Logan the entire time.

Trent had been texting me too, but his had consisted of eye roll emojis and playfully exasperated GIFs. Through it all, Trent had made it clear that he loved the way Logan had been so caught up in what he and Dean were doing. If I was being honest with myself, I'd enjoyed it too.

Then again, I'd spent the entire day watching the man who was normally acutely aware of his every move around anyone, relax and not worry about whether his shirt crept up his back. I'd spent more time examining his scars than I'd spent thinking about the restaurant. And when he'd fallen asleep on the couch after lunch, it had been while I rubbed massage oil into his back.

Leaning forward to give him a gentle kiss on the forehead as we said goodbye hadn't been planned, but it had felt natural. If I hadn't been mistaken, he'd leaned into the touch just slightly, and I knew I'd heard a quiet sigh escape him.

"Don't stay up too late, Bean."

He rolled his eyes. "Don't worry. I'll be in bed early, *Dad*."

It was good to see he was feeling well enough to tease me again, but I'd overstay my welcome if I didn't leave. Theoretically, I should have headed home, but my head wasn't in the right place, and my car automatically headed toward Oak Hill without my planning. I was pulling into Canyon and Larson's driveway before I'd consciously processed where I was going.

I'd barely made it up the driveway, my car not even in Park yet, and Canyon was standing in his doorway, a smirk on his face.

I looked around, trying to see if there was someone else there, but I didn't see anyone as I walked toward his front door. "What the hell? Get super vision or something?"

"Or something. I installed a camera closer to the road. I have no problem telling you all to fuck off because we're having sex, but it's a different story when it's my parents." He laughed at the face I made as he shut the door behind us.

I noticed the lack of Marley's and Lennon's presence immediately, the house eerily quiet. "Where's the brood?"

Canyon let out a belly laugh. "Dexter invited the boys over tonight, and since they have a fenced yard, Larson took the dogs. I suspect they're going to be late. So, what brings you over this way—the complete opposite direction of your home—and unannounced on a Friday evening?" As he spoke, he led us to the kitchen where he was already pulling two glasses from the cabinet as well as a bottle of tequila and a few mixers.

I rubbed at the back of my neck. "Yeah. Sorry about that. I hadn't really thought about where I was going. I was leaving Bean's tonight and kissed him. Next thing I knew, I was pulling into your driveway."

Canyon's hand had paused on the cap of the tequila bottle. Before I'd finished speaking, he'd set the tequila bottle down, put back the margarita glasses, and pulled out a bottle of whiskey and two tumblers. "This definitely isn't a chill-on-the-deck-with-a-margarita chat. This just turned into a whiskey-in-the-study conversation."

He poured a few fingers into each glass before he turned to me. "Or, you know, the living room. The office is now the doghouse… literally." He inclined his head as he picked up the glasses. "Let's go. And grab the whiskey bottle on your way."

I did as instructed and followed him to the living room. The view of Nashville at that time of the evening was stunning and was only going to get better as the sun sank lower. The pinks and purples of the clouds would soon fade to black, and the sky would be illuminated by the breathtaking neon glow of the downtown buildings.

Canyon took a seat beside me, handed over a glass, and propped his ankle over his knee. "Okay. We've got time and we've got drinks. Tell me all about the cutesy nickname and this kissing bombshell?"

I wasn't ready to address the kiss, so I focused on the first point. "What cutesy nickname?"

He shot me an *are you kidding* look that Dean would have been proud of. "You call him Bean all the time."

The only thing shocking in his statement was that no one had pressed me sooner for details. That didn't mean I was going to give them up without a little teasing. "I do not use it all the time!"

Canyon grinned at me. "Doth protest too much."

"You're awful. I showed up to his house one morning and he was wearing a ridiculously oversized T-shirt with a coffee bean on it that said *Cool Bean*. Since I was already bringing him a coffee, it was fitting and it's just sort of stuck. As a bonus, it drives him crazy and gets under his skin."

Canyon bit his cheek in an attempt not to laugh. "Yes. Under his skin. That bashful smile he gives you every time you turn away definitely says you're driving him crazy... crazy with something other than annoyance, maybe."

My blinks of confusion had Canyon laughing so hard he had to set his drink down on the coffee table. When he started pulling himself together, he spoke through his remaining laughter. "You really don't see it, do you? Mer, that's why we were so confused earlier in the week when you told us you needed to find him a boyfriend—or a Daddy. The two of us were convinced you've been gunning for that role." An eyebrow rose in my direction at the last word.

"I'm not equipped to be anyone's anything." After years of telling everyone that I didn't want to date, the change was subtle but there. Canyon might not have known me long, but he already knew me well enough to know something was different.

The humor left his face and he turned himself so he could see me more than the city sprawling out in front of us. "Well, you've told us you're not up for dating, but no one knows why. And despite all the joking around about how you can't get anyone to stay for more than a few days, you and Dean are basically attached at the hip. You dismiss the possibility of a relationship, but you don't get tired of him. From my point of view, it certainly doesn't seem like he's getting tired of you, either."

Did I really want to go there with Canyon? I'd only told Dean about Tom, and at that, I'd been dismissive of the entire thing. If I'd learned anything over the last few years, it was that all of us in the group had hidden huge parts of ourselves since we'd met. Inadvertently, we'd hurt ourselves and our friends along the way. Had it not been for Travis meeting Caleb, there was a chance we all would still be refusing to admit we were anything but gay men happy being single.

With a sigh that felt as though it had come from my toes, I told him about Tom. Not the condensed, flippant, it-is-what-it-is version but the entire thing. From the moment we'd met when he walked into the bar, fresh from a big win in a bartending competition, to his teaching me the trade, all the way to us ending up in bed together for the first time, and finally to my invite to the competition he'd won a few years earlier.

"I was twenty-two." I heard myself say it, but I was so lost in memories, I wasn't paying much attention to the words coming from my mouth. "He was jealous. I knew that I'd been drawing more attention than he was since I had been able to get behind the bar. Two flair bartenders at one gay bar in NYC drew a crowd, but my tips were always higher and my line always longer. What I hadn't realized was how deep his jealousy ran until I got an invite to the competition he'd won, and he didn't. By the time I left on the trip, he'd been obviously faking his support for weeks and flat-out refused to come with me. He said he couldn't leave the bar without two of the best bartenders."

Canyon growled at that but blessedly didn't say anything. If he spoke, I didn't hear it, still lost in memories. "Things weren't the same between us when I returned. The naive boy inside me still wanted to believe that we were forever, though."

The laugh that came next lacked any humor as I remembered the weeks and months of fear and uncertainty that had followed. "You remember the HIV/AIDs epidemic, how scary that shit was. I grew up in Missouri; I'd heard it all. Kids were brutal, their parents worse. That fear didn't get better in New York City as I watched friends die."

I caught Canyon's wince out of the corner of my eye. "Oof, that sucks, Mer. I'm sorry. I remember that fear as I moved to California. It was real."

"Yeah, it really was. It was even worse when I found out that Tom wasn't as committed to *us* as I had been. Hell, he'd never been faithful, and it seemed like I was the only one who hadn't known."

Canyon's grimace spoke volumes.

"Despite having always used condoms, I was scared to death every test I took for over a year. In the back of my mind, there was always a chance. Always a possibility. I still get anxious waiting for results, and I take all the precautions."

Story finally told, I sucked in a breath and looked back over to Canyon. His smile was sad as he shook his head. "That's a hell of a story. Damn, what a wake-up call for a young guy. I can see why that killed your trust."

I collapsed against the back of the couch, feeling drained and ready to sleep, and it was comfortable enough that I could fall asleep right here. I put my whiskey glass to my lips and took a long, slow sip, enjoying the way it burned going down.

"How can I seriously date someone when that fear never goes fully away? That's not fair to either of us. I can't go into a relationship with walls as high as the Batman

Building." I pointed out the window to the iconic focal point of the Nashville skyline.

Canyon's voice sounded far away as he began to speak again. "Unfortunate as it might be, I can see your point. If you're right and he is a middle, he's going to need someone who can go all in. He's going to need a Daddy who's—"

I didn't give him time to finish his thought, cutting him off with the list I already knew by heart. "Understanding. Loyal. Kind. Trustworthy. Dean's hurting, in more ways than one." My lips turned up into a smile. "He needs someone affectionate."

As I spoke, my brain started to kick into overdrive and my stomach muscles unexpectedly tensed.

Dean deserved the man I was describing. He'd always been loyal, almost to a fault. And now that we'd gone down this path, I remembered Travis mentioning that he hadn't liked one of Dean's boyfriends. He swore the man hadn't been good enough for Dean. From what little I remembered, the comment had been made in passing a few times, though there was a memory of the two of them having a disagreement about it. It had been a long time ago, and I clearly remembered that Dean had stayed with his boyfriend until the guy had finally left.

If memory served, that was shortly before his accident.

Realization slammed into me like a brick to the face. Dean was a younger version of myself. Maybe not jaded by a lying, cheating boyfriend, but he'd been devoted and dedicated, and now he didn't trust others. I knew enough to see that I was afraid of being vulnerable to pain like that again. Dean was afraid of the vulnerability he'd feel if someone found out about his scars and the pain he was living with.

We were both messes of different making, careening toward the same end. Dean definitely didn't deserve that ending.

But that left me with another question, uncomfortable to think about and harder to answer. If Dean didn't deserve that ending to his story, why did I?

I drained the whiskey from my glass and held it out to Canyon. "Bartender, pour me another."

Canyon was smirking at me as he poured the next round. "Working something out over there?"

Too lost in my own head, I didn't answer him. I'd punished myself for Tom's shortcomings, but not every man was a cheating asshole. Tom hadn't been my one and only. He'd been my first, but he didn't have to be my last.

There was a chance I'd met my last nearly twenty years earlier and had been too stubborn to see it. Or maybe my last had been too stubborn to see me right there, waiting for him to make me feel again.

Canyon sat beside me as I worked through my feelings, not pushing me to speak. If the smug expression on his face was anything to go by, he knew exactly what I was discovering, something he'd seen well before I'd been ready to accept it myself.

I'd begun to feel again. Those emotions swirling in my stomach when I spent time with Dean were emotions I'd spent two decades running from, each one of them real and poignant. Close enough to the surface to feel and experience but each one fragile enough to turn me to dust if poked too hard.

After years of telling myself I wasn't going to be anyone's anything, it was suddenly clear.

I drained my glass. "I want to be his everything."

Canyon smiled at me. "Glad you finally see that."

Groaning, I held my glass out. "I hope you have a lot more where that came from. I'm going to need it tonight."

"There's more than enough to help you through this breakthrough." He took the glass, then held out his hand. "Hand over the keys and you can have as much as you'd like."

I reached into my pocket for my key fob as Canyon uncapped the bottle. We traded the full glass for the keys and I took another long pull, downing half in one swig. Once these drinks hit, I wasn't going anywhere. Hell, even if I could drive, I didn't trust myself not to knock on Dean's door and tell him that I could be the man he didn't know he needed.

CHAPTER FIFTEEN

DEAN

With a large group of friends, I'd grown accustomed to my phone blowing up with texts. In the last ten days, though, my phone had been blowing up with texts from one person in particular. Merrick was texting me multiple times a day for the most random things.

His new favorite had been making sure I was drinking enough water. Either he had unreasonable expectations or I'd never been truly hydrated before. In the last week, I'd seen as much of the bathroom as I had my desk.

And my phone buzzed religiously at quarter to five and again at five, reminding me to start packing up and then to leave work. The first time, I'd thought it was because he was worried that I was pushing myself too hard after being sick. Nine days later, the texts were still coming. Whatever it was, it wasn't concern about my health. It was something else—I just didn't know what.

However, I was getting used to his frequent texts and

reminders. But as I sat at my desk late Thursday afternoon, I was struggling with something very new to me: a hard-on in my slacks as I reread his last text.

Merrick: *Time to pack it up, Bean.*

At about the same time these persistent texts reminding me to drink water, eat lunch, or not work too long had become a thing, *Bean* had stopped being one of the most annoying names I'd ever gone by. I wasn't going to tell him that I got a smile on my face every time it popped up in text or that my stomach got little butterflies in it each time he said it, but I could admit I liked it.

Me: *Ten minutes, Dad.*

Imagining his grumble made me smile, until I had to reach down and adjust my dick in my fitted pants. Dressing up made me more productive at work, but getting hard in these pants was not something I'd accounted for. Unfortunately, it had been happening more and more frequently in recent days.

Merrick needed something else to focus on. I switched chat screens and tapped a text out.

Me: *Seriously, isn't there something you can be doing to keep Merrick busy?*

Travis: *Hell. No. The fact that he's not all up in my crew's business twenty-four hours a day and we're actually getting this thing done is a miracle in and of itself.*

Me: *Gah! He's driving me nuts!*

And he was. He was making my head confused and my stomach flip-flop on a near hourly basis. I was undeniably attracted to him, but I couldn't figure out why. I knew I wasn't looking for a boy and that I'd be fine in a non-D/s relationship, but if I was going to fall for someone—anyone—I wanted it to be someone who could return my feelings. Merrick had made it clear he couldn't.

Travis: *Few more weeks and we should be to the point that he can start doing his thing in here. He'll be out of your hair by then if Canyon can't help you.*

Why did the thought of Merrick leaving me alone bother me more than his incoming text?

Merrick: *Three minutes. I'll pick you up in thirty, we need to beat the rest of the guys.*

The race to not be the last person at Steve's Tavern each meeting had gotten out of control. To the point that Logan had hung up on me the week before because he needed to leave. I shook my head and tapped out a response.

Me: *Closing my computer now.*

Merrick: *Good job. See you soon.*

My work wasn't done, but I was smiling as I powered down my laptop, slid it into my bag, and turned out the light. Sitting at a stoplight halfway home, I blinked twice. I'd never considered telling Merrick not to come over. I'd never bothered to say he didn't control my work schedule. I'd never thought to not listen to him. I'd just done it.

I'd done it automatically. Without thinking twice. And in the end, that last quick text he'd sent had made me feel good. Pulling into my driveway, reality slammed into me and I hit the brake harder than I'd intended. I'd followed his orders the same way I'd always hoped Evan would follow mine. The years hadn't made me forget all the times Evan had chosen not to do what I'd asked, from the simplest task of getting home before midnight on a work night to eating what I'd made for dinner.

While I'd been with him for a long time—well, longer than I should have been—I'd struggled for most of that time. I'd never felt like I was making him happy and that had bugged me repeatedly. Daddies were supposed to make their boys happy. Then again, it was a two-way street that Evan hadn't followed.

Making Merrick happy was making me happy. Happier than setting any rule or consequence had ever made me.

What did that mean?

I wasn't his Dom, we weren't dating, yet I was finding my mood more and more directly related to Merrick and making him happy.

With the car in Park—my mind had been so scattered I'd checked twice—I finally got out and headed into the house to change. As naturally as I'd tucked my blanket around Babbit as I'd left my room, I reached for one of the oversized T-shirts I'd been wearing for years.

It was halfway over my head when I heard Merrick's voice. Well, not literally, but the words that I'd played on repeat for weeks now. I might as well have had a recording of what he'd said to me after I'd fallen. *"I guess I'm more disappointed that we gave you the impression that we'd treat you differently. A little sad that you've suffered in silence for years. And a lot pissed that you've hidden that body under shirts four sizes too big all this time."*

My movements slowed as I tugged my shirt into place. With it on, I looked over at the mirror.

"Two sizes... right." I rolled my eyes at myself. The

sleeves grazed my elbows and the bottom hem was only an inch or two longer than the shirts that fit well, but it was so wide that Merrick and I could probably share it with room to spare. Hell, this shirt would have been baggy on both Larson and Canyon, and they were the biggest men I knew. And yet I'd still tugged the back of the shirt down so many times that it hung awkwardly low.

Was Merrick right? Had I ever given anyone a chance to treat me differently? I didn't need to ask myself the question. I knew I hadn't. I'd assumed they would and had suffered in silence for years. My desire to not be seen as weak or different had kept them from having a chance to know who I was now. I'd held everyone at arm's length, not just potential hookups, dates, or boyfriends.

Feeling a new type of confidence in myself, I went to change my shirt before my resolve faded. The graphic T-shirt I pulled out hadn't been worn without something else covering it since I'd purchased it.

I wasn't as muscular as Logan or James, but I had a definition that was noticeable through the snug fabric. The foreign feeling of being dressed in a shirt I'd once considered normal spoke to how I'd been hiding, yet paired with the jeans I'd put on, it made me feel more like myself than I had in years.

I turned to my bed. Running a hand over my stomach, I let out a long breath before speaking to the stuffed animal lying there. "Well, what do you think, Babbit?"

A low whistle sounded from my doorway. "That I forgot you had such an amazing body."

My shriek was far from manly, and my heart was

beating nearly out of my chest. I swung around to find Merrick with a pleased smirk on his face. "What the hell? Boundaries!"

His smile was infuriating, but his eyes had focused on my body in a way that made it impossible to ignore the things I'd been trying not to feel around him. "I knocked twice. Then I came in and called your name at least three times. I got worried when you didn't answer. Now I know you were busy having a conversation with Babbit."

"I hate you."

"You love me. And you love Babbit. And if he could talk, he'd tell you the same thing I just did." His smug smile turned fond. "Is it weird that I'm happy you have him to talk things out with?"

"Honestly? Yes. I shouldn't be talking to him at all, much less asking him questions." I was going to pretend that we weren't talking about Babbit with gendered pronouns like an actual person. The conversation was already weird enough without overthinking that part of it.

"Come on, Bean. You look amazing. The guys aren't going to know what to make of you."

I bit my lip, instinctively running a hand along my back. Merrick caught the move and closed the distance between us. "You look great and I'm going to be there the entire time."

His words wrapped around me and made me feel safe and protected. He would be with me. It helped knowing I already had one person on my side. I dipped my head to look down at my outfit again. It was strange to see the outline of my body, even stranger to feel gentle lips pressed against my forehead.

Neither of us moved for longer than we should have, his lips resting on my skin. When he stepped back and we looked at one another, Merrick appeared as surprised as I felt. A faint red had colored his cheeks and he was giving me a small smile that spoke of uncertainty. "You really do look amazing in that."

For the first time since before the car wreck, I felt wanted... all of me. Merrick had seen the scars, he knew my secrets, and he'd never seen me as broken or injured. That feeling that I'd been getting when I talked with Merrick the last week, the one that made my pants tight and my heart tighter, was back in full force. Except this time it wasn't telling me to do anything.

As we looked at each other, his pale eyes turned a misty gray and his pupils dilated. I recognized it immediately as lust and desire, undeniable and palpable. If he was paying half the amount of attention to me as I was to him, he'd see the same reflected in my eyes.

Merrick's hand moved toward my cheek to cup the side of my face, his rough palm rubbing against my well-trimmed beard. "Dammit. Dean, tell me to stop. Tell me to back away. Tell me you don't want this as much as I do."

I didn't say any of those things. Instead, I shook my head. He'd stop this in its tracks—whatever *this* was—if I said anything close to the words he'd told me to.

Taking a leap of faith, I leaned forward, capturing his lips with mine.

It felt like we'd been working toward this moment for

years as we explored each other's lips. Slow, tentative movements, neither of us in control but both needing the connection like we needed oxygen. Then Merrick's hand moved to the back of my neck, his other hand coming up to rest at the top of my ass. His thumb toyed with the top of my jeans but stopped just short of touching my skin.

When my mouth opened, more to gasp in a breath to supply more oxygen to my brain, Merrick took the opportunity to take control of the kiss. His tongue came out, first tracing my lips, then entering my mouth and finding my tongue.

Far from rushed, this was slow and passionate, like we had all the time in the world. We hadn't talked about this; we hadn't discussed anything more than friendship. Hell, we were supposed to be leaving for Steve's. Yet here we were, sharing a kiss that left no doubt where it was headed and taking our time doing so.

Merrick took a step forward, pushing me a step back but never breaking contact. My calves hit the side of my bed and he pressed himself flush against me. In this position, I could feel the bulge in his jeans confirming what I'd already known. He wanted this as much as I did.

The hand that had been wrapped around my neck fell to the front of my pants to grip my erection through my jeans. A keening noise unlike any I'd ever heard escaped my mouth, effectively breaking our kiss and finally allowing me to see more of Merrick's body than his eyes.

A kiss-drunk smile played on his swollen lips as he massaged my erection. "I want this in my mouth."

My knees buckled at his words and we tumbled onto

the bed. The sudden movement could have broken the mood, snapped us back to our senses and made us stop, but the only word I could utter was a frantic plea. "Yes."

Merrick was on his knees in a flash, tugging his shirt over his head and tossing it behind him. I might have heard it hit the closet door, or maybe that was the bathroom door, not that it mattered. All I cared about was freeing my dick from the snug confines of my jeans. Of course, the more of Merrick's body that was exposed, the more the need to see the rest of it was warring for most important.

We popped the button of our jeans at the same time, both of us fighting with the thick material until Merrick finally gave up and stood. In one fluid motion, he had his pants down and underwear off and was reaching for my jeans that were only halfway down my thighs.

I didn't care where my jeans landed once they were off. What mattered was that Merrick was naked and looking at me like he was ready to devour my cock once it was freed from my underwear.

Without pants, underwear, or a dark living room inhibiting the view of his body, I could appreciate the well-groomed thatch of graying hair surrounding his cock. He'd said he wanted to suck me, but I'd happily change places with him at the moment. I didn't want to look away, but I was still in my underwear and there was a noticeable lack of mouths on cocks.

Merrick was staring at me when I looked up. "You good with this?"

I nodded, not trusting my voice to hide just how desperately I *needed* it at the moment.

"Dean." The sharp tone of his voice made me wince internally. He wanted words, and I wanted his mouth wrapped around my dick. I was a pressure cooker, and my release valve was Merrick's mouth.

"Good. So good." *Please don't make me think.* "Your mouth, my cock. Now."

He chuckled as he finally gripped the elastic of my briefs. "Bossy boy."

I wasn't going to take the time to analyze how being called boy made me feel. There had been a flash of indignation at the term. There had also been an equally fleeting, but just as undeniable, feeling of rightness.

This was not the time to think about those things, so I settled on something I hoped would get us back to where we were a few seconds earlier. "If that's what it takes to get my cock in your mouth. Oh, and no pressure or anything, but we should already be at Steve's."

CHAPTER SIXTEEN

MERRICK

I'd never been so willing to be late to Steve's. The bar and our friends had nothing on the man in front of me.

Hooking my fingers in his underwear, I pulled them down his legs, then tossed them over my shoulder. My attention landed on Dean's cock. Just like I remembered, it was perfectly proportioned. For just a moment, I let myself believe that there would be more days like today.

I couldn't allow myself to get too wrapped up in that. Dean was right, we needed to get to Steve's at some point, but I'd promised him an orgasm.

I'd seen his back and heard the stories, but I'd never seen his bare legs before now. I had seen a small glimpse of the scarring, but it was worse than he'd let on. Uneven skin marked the outsides of his legs, and my fingertips were unable to avoid it as I made my way up his thighs.

Dean trembled as I trailed light kisses up his inner thighs, taking more time than needed to reach my target. I wanted him to enjoy every minute of this, see how much I loved his body. He didn't have to tell me that sex with the lights on wasn't something he did. After going through the lengths he had to hide his scars, I knew he was giving me a special gift that I was going to cherish.

My lips found the crease at his thigh, and Dean lifted his legs to allow me better access to his balls, taint, and pucker. Unfortunately, I wasn't going to have enough time to give everything the attention it deserved, but I was going to do my best.

Working my way toward his balls, my chin grazed Dean's smooth skin. The coarse whiskers of my beard drew a long moan from him, and goosebumps rose under my hands. I did it again and was rewarded with the same reaction. "Like that?"

Dean's fingers found my head and he wound them into my hair. "Holy fuck. Yes. Yes, I do."

His words were more intoxicating than the sounds he'd been making. For angling my chin outward, I was rewarded with a constant stream of curses, moans, and gasps as my beard dragged along his balls.

The only thing better than the sounds he made as my beard and lips grazed his skin was the noise he made as I licked from his taint up to his shaft. Dean's cock had enjoyed the feel of my beard as much as he had. The tip of his dick was already coated in salty precum and my tongue started lapping it up.

I rearranged myself to be fully seated between his legs, my knees tucked under me, my arms resting on his thighs. In our new position, I could feel the scarring under his thighs but I resisted the urge to look, not willing to ruin the moment.

Finally, I sucked the tip of his dick into my mouth. A long string of curse words fell from his lips at the contact.

"Mer. Fuck. Merrick. Yes, just like that. Shit. Fucking. Holyfuckinghell, Mer!" I didn't know if I'd cut him off or if he'd been finished, but as I swallowed his length, Dean went silent.

He didn't move, didn't breathe, until my right hand wrapped around my cock and I gave myself a few hard tugs. The movement pulled Dean out of the trance he'd been in and he tugged at my hair. "Oh, hell no. You are not going to waste that load. Flip your ass around. I want to suck you too."

Holy shit, I was going to lose my load right then and there. My balls drew up so fast they ached and I had to squeeze the base of my cock harder than was comfortable to stave the orgasm off. I looked up at Dean, his cock still in my mouth, to find him staring down at me.

"I'm serious. I want to taste you, Merrick." He smirked to himself. "I already know you taste good."

His cock fell from my mouth with a lewd slurp and I gaped up at him. "What?"

"Well, you spilled all over my hand last time." When I continued to stare at him, Dean smiled down at me. "Do you really think I wasn't going to have a taste?"

After tasting him on my tongue, I was kicking myself for not having tasted him then, but before now the thought had never crossed my mind.

Beautiful brown eyes rolled in amusement as Dean stretched to tap my shoulder. "Flip around, Mer."

Sixty-nine was nothing new to me, but there was something about the position with Dean that left me feeling open in a way I couldn't remember. It felt sexy, intimate, and more than a little naughty. Then again, I was having sex with my friend. This was all three of those things.

Dean didn't tease as much as I had. He lapped at my head once before wrapping his lips around my dick and humming. Strong fingers reached up to wrap around my hips and pull me deeper into his mouth. He pulled until my cock hit the back of his throat and he gagged, but he held me in place when I tried to lift my hips.

My mind became more focused on what Dean's mouth was doing to my cock than what my mouth was doing to Dean's cock. Dean had not forgotten the point of the position we were in and rocked his hips upward, fucking my mouth.

On the third upward thrust, a burst of precum hit my tongue, and I remembered what we were supposed to be doing. I redoubled my efforts, taking Dean down to the root once more. I'd been blessed with a lack of a gag reflex, making him easy to swallow. While I was able to get more of him in my mouth than he could take of me, his mouth on my dick was rapidly bringing me close to orgasm.

When my throat constricted around his dick, Dean's resulting hum sent a vibration through my dick and balls and straight up my spine. He pulled my hips into his mouth again, causing him to gag at the same time his dick let out another spurt of precum.

Dammit, I was close. So, so close. Dean's enjoyment only pushed my need to come that much closer. Each time I tried to pull my ass back, he pulled me back in. If I tried to slow down, he bucked harder.

When my need for release had grown unbearable, I brushed a finger across his pucker and felt him go stiff beneath me. For a brief second, I worried I'd gone too far, but then his cock swelled in my mouth and he pulled my hips lower than I'd been yet. My cock slid into his throat as he shot into my mouth.

His cum filled my mouth so completely that I struggled to keep it all in. I had to pull back a bit to accommodate the load, and even then cum dribbled from the sides of my mouth.

With a final pulsation of his cock, Dean collapsed onto the bed. I was on the verge of orgasm, but with Dean sated and relaxed, I hadn't expected him to resume sucking my cock with renewed urgency. His fingers slid from my hips to my crack and he pulled my cheeks apart.

Dean possessed a dexterity most could only dream of, working my cock with his mouth, spreading me open with his hands, and using his fingers to tease my hole at the same time. He continued until the only thing I could think of was coming—my balls drawn tight and my spine tingling with need.

I'd sucked and teased Dean through the most sensitive part of post-orgasm and to the point that his cock was filling again as the first pulse of my cock made me release his on a loud moan. He sputtered beneath me, choking on my cum but refusing to let my cock go until after the final wave of orgasm had passed.

When his mouth on my dick got to be too much for me, I pulled out of his mouth and shivered as I waited for regret to overtake me. Much like that night on his couch, the only thing I felt was sated relief. This time, though, I could detect a sense of belonging through the last of the haze the orgasm had left me with.

Everything felt right until my phone pinged from across the room at the same time as Dean's. I had no idea where I'd left my phone or my pants, and Dean looked just as confused as he glanced around.

My eyes fell on the alarm clock across the room and I groaned in frustration. "It's six twenty. You know that the guys are wondering if we're in a ditch somewhere."

Dean let out a groan that rivaled mine. "We need to tell them we're running late. We know far too many guys in law enforcement. If we don't respond, they are going to have someone knocking on my door for a welfare check."

I rolled onto my back, an arm slung over my eyes. "I hate that you're right." Groping toward where I thought my phone might have been proved fruitless, forcing one of us to have to get up. A glance toward Dean found him with his blanket and Babbit pulled close, his eyes shut and his breathing even, but clearly not sleeping… yet.

Unwilling to disturb his moment of peace, I rolled longways across and ultimately off the bed on a quest to find one of our phones. When I finally found mine, I turned back around to find Dean's eyes tracking my movements, his eyes intently focused below my belly button and a smile on his lips as I moved through the room.

I was about to comment but had only managed to get my mouth open when my phone chimed again. A glance at the screen told me we were running out of time to answer before the cavalry would be arriving. Whether that cavalry would consist of a group of overprotective friends, a chief of police, or a sheriff, I had no idea. Either way, I did not want this moment marred by the arrival of people with far more questions than Dean or I would have answers to.

I tapped my phone to life and speed-read the messages as fast as I could. A long list had come through while we'd been preoccupied, and now they were worried. Judging by Trent's last text, they were also losing patience.

Trent: *Jesus Christ. I'm giving you five minutes. If one of you two doesn't send us a proof of life text, I'm calling Nashville PD.*

Scrubbing my hand down my face, I tried to come up with something to say that would have them standing down while not raising red flags. Another text appeared on my phone, that time not part of the group text.

Canyon: *You know as well as I do that these men gossip like hens and worry like mama bears. You gotta give me something to work with here. Truthfully, I'm a little anxious myself. The last you said, you were going to pick up Dean an hour ago. You better have a good excuse.*

At least Canyon knew a little of what was going on, so I chose to respond to him first.

Me: *It's a damn good excuse. The best, really. But you're just going to have to believe me. Tell them that my car had an unex-*

pected flat. We were going to wait for the tow truck, but it's running late. We'll be there in just a few. Order us dinner.

Canyon: *Fucking hell. You owe me, Mer. You owe me big time.*

And I did. I'd worry about that later. For the time being, I was going to need to work on cleaning up Dean and myself, then rushing to the bar before we were so late that my weak excuse would fall apart completely.

CHAPTER SEVENTEEN

DEAN

We'd been nearly an hour late to Steve's. It was bad enough when one of us was five or ten minutes late, but to have two of us walking in together when everyone already had their plates in front of them had been awkward. We both got weird looks, but when Travis glanced over at Merrick and asked if his car was going to be okay, the tension evaporated. Merrick's chuckle was genuine, even if his voice wasn't as smooth as it normally was.

"Yeah. It's going to be fine. Might be parked in Dean's driveway for the evening, though. Can't believe my spare was flat too! How does that even happen?"

I blinked a few times, trying to figure out what the hell was going on. This was all news to me, but Merrick appeared to have the cover story handled.

Trent's laugh could be heard over the din of the entire bar. "Must have killed you to leave that thing parked anywhere. Even in Dean's neighborhood."

Canyon gave us a look that said he knew more than he was letting on, but I'd happily let Merrick deal with the crazies at the table. He'd obviously come up with something to tell them and was sticking to it. The distraction kept our eagle-eyed friends from mentioning the shirt I was wearing. The shirt that was fitted to my body and not stretched out in awkward ways. I'd take the distraction.

There were only two chairs left, and since Merrick took the spot beside Canyon, that left me to take the seat between him and Logan. Travis was three seats away, far enough that he wouldn't be able to ask me about heading to DASH again or bug me about finding a boy.

Until I let out a sigh of relief at being away from him, I hadn't known how much his questions were weighing on me.

The first time he'd brought it up back at Canyon's house, I'd known I wasn't in the right headspace to be looking for a boyfriend, much less a boy. Over the last few months, the more time I'd spent with Merrick, the more I'd come to think that I'd never be at a point where I wanted a boy again.

My thoughts turned toward earlier in the evening. Merrick on my bed, my begging him to flip around so I could suck him too. *Bossy Boy.* Two words I'd never associated with myself. I wasn't bossy and I wasn't a boy. That didn't change that I'd felt stronger and more in control when I'd heard those words than I ever had before.

It didn't make sense to me.

"Hey, you coming over this weekend?"

Logan's voice drew my attention, but it wasn't until I

noticed he was looking at me that I realized it was me he was speaking to.

"What? Going where? And what's going on?"

Larson's amused chuckle made me look over at him. "Dean's been living on a different planet the last few weeks. You have to send him a private text to have any chance of getting a response from him."

The point wasn't worth arguing. I'd missed a lot in the group text, mostly because it was always insane but also because Merrick usually filled me in on the important things in our private texts. There was no point in sifting through two hundred or more texts a day to pick out things that Merrick had already told me. "What did I miss this time?"

Aiden's head popped around Logan's wide shoulders. "We're having a playdate!"

"Oh. That's cool." Then I thought about it more. "But, uh, why are you inviting me to your playdate? Isn't that something kinda reserved for you all and your Daddies?"

Logan narrowed his eyes at me and I couldn't help the smile that grew on my face as I corrected myself. "Sorry. Isn't that for you, your Daddies, and your handler?"

"One day I'm going to get you all to stop including me with the boys. I'm a pup!"

Aiden snorted. "You're a pup *and* a middle."

I knew what a middle was. But could I see Logan as one? It wasn't like I *couldn't* see him as a middle. I'd just always associated that part of his personality with his pup side.

Logan gave him a dismissive wave of the hand. "You

keep saying that, but I'm a pup. Trent's your Daddy, not mine."

Aiden's eye roll looked like he believed Logan as much as I did at the moment. It wasn't so much what Logan had said as how he'd said it. There was a distinct sadness to his voice when he'd mentioned Trent not being his Daddy. Which left me with even more questions than I'd had when I sat down.

Was Logan a middle? Was he ignoring that side of himself? And if so, why?

Once again, Logan drew me out of my thoughts. "But you're coming, right? I need someone to keep me company. You can hang out with me!"

"I'm not a pup." I avoided the middle topic. Something was swirling inside me, something that I didn't understand myself, and my current company was not the place to analyze those feelings.

Logan bumped my shoulder with his broad one. "Ya don't say? Couldn't have guessed." His grin widened. "Seriously, I had fun hanging out with you last time. You kept them from climbing all over me."

"You also kept him seated. You two got all cozy on the couch and didn't move for hours. I don't remember the last time I saw that man sit still for so long."

Logan stuck a middle finger up at Caleb and in return, Caleb stuck his tongue out at Logan. There was a time that this table had felt more like a group of guys winding down after a long day at work, not like an elementary school playground. At some point, all pretenses of maturity had left the building.

Having always sat between Travis and Trent, this side of the table had felt like an enigma. They got loud, they laughed a lot, and they randomly jumped back into conversations on the other side of the table. Sitting beside them, the entire vibe of dinner was different.

I wasn't discussing work, house issues, or car problems. I was only three seats from where I normally sat but I was talking about a playdate, if I was a human or a pup, and listening to my friends bicker about how relaxed someone was. It was a wonder anyone got anything accomplished.

"Did you not read the text about the playdate?"

I shook my head at Logan's question. "Nope. I must have been at work and it probably got lost in the ridiculous numbers of texts you all send each day." Instead of allowing us to get in a discussion about when or how I missed the text, I turned the focus to the date itself. "When and where is it?"

Logan's body blocked most of Aiden, but I saw his hand poke toward Larson. "Their place. Saturday. Daddy said they're grilling or something."

Larson nodded. "We're going shopping tomorrow. Trav said he'll bring potato salad and cookies. Trent said he's bringing the barbecue chicken—his dad makes the sauce and it's amazing—and chicken nuggets for a certain picky eater." He shot Aiden a pointed stare.

Aiden just nodded his head and grinned. "The sauce really is amazing. But we've had it at least twice a week for three weeks. He made too much and keeps bringing us marinated chicken. Why do you think we're bringing it to your place?"

Logan's mouth hung open. "Wait, you complained and got a different meal? I'm tired of it too! Christ, I need a big juicy burger, some grilled veggies, and maybe some of that potato salad Trav is bringing." He hummed and his stomach let out an audible rumble despite having just polished off a juicy burger, veggies, and the same damn potato salad Travis would be bringing, since I knew it was his mom's recipe and it was served at the bar.

Why had I always spent so much time at the other end of the table? These guys had me forgetting all about our late arrival and what had led to it.

A hand tugged at the hem of my shirt and I looked over to see Merrick pulling it back into place. I'd been so lost in conversation I hadn't noticed my shirt riding up. Merrick gave me a smile and pointed to the burger I hadn't ordered but that had been delivered to the table.

"Eat up. You probably haven't eaten since noon."

He knew exactly when I'd eaten last because he'd messaged to remind me that I needed to take a break to eat.

I turned my attention to my burger, but Dexter's voice from the other side of Caleb had my hands pausing before the food reached my mouth. "Is it just me, or is Merrick putting off some serious *mine* vibes with Dean?"

He'd meant to say the words quietly to Caleb, but Dexter wasn't known for his ability to keep his voice quiet. It didn't seem like his voice had traveled past my spot, but I knew immediately that Logan, Larson, and Aiden had also heard him.

Caleb's lips pressed into a thin line as he shot his best friend a glower. "Seriously?" At least Caleb knew how to keep his voice low. I wouldn't have known what he'd said if I hadn't been reading his lips. "James is so going to have you over his lap if you keep that up."

Larson snorted, clearly close enough to hear Caleb, but Dexter was far from concerned. He shrugged his shoulders and shook his head, though he did manage to keep his voice to an inaudible whisper. However, I was pretty sure that I picked up on something about how James would like the panties he was wearing. I pulled my eyes away from their conversation. Lip reading was both a blessing and a curse at times.

I took an overly large bite of my burger and chewed while I asked myself what was going on between Merrick and me. If Dexter had picked up on the vibe, who else had?

Logan sighed. "Dean and Merrick are good friends, just like we all are. You know that we've all been closer to some people over the years than others. Don't read too much into things." Then he turned in his seat to face me. "But will you come on Saturday?"

The best I could do with my mouth full was a noncommittal shrug. Logan clasped his hands together in front of his face and batted his eyes in my direction.

Why did I bother trying to eat around these guys?

Sputtering and trying not to spit the bite of burger out, I nodded. When I finally had the bite down, I took a sip of my water and glowered at Logan. "I'm pretty sure I've told you before this is *not* the variety of meat I want to die on."

"But you're coming, right? I got those LEGO things you were showing me, but I haven't built it yet. Oh! Can you bring yours? Then we could put our sets together!"

Larson leaned forward in his seat to hear us better. Before I knew it, my dinner was gone, though I think Logan had something to do with the disappearing fries, and we'd gone from talking about LEGO to video games to what movie we were going to watch Saturday evening.

I'd forgotten to pay attention to the other half of the table, too busy laughing and bickering with Logan, Aiden, Larson, and Caleb about movies. Dexter finally crossed his arms in a pout. "Not fair. I want to come."

Caleb leaned into his shoulder with a grin. "But you're going to be with your niece and nephew. You won't be thinking about us at all because those two have you wrapped around their little fingers!"

Dexter beamed as he pushed his chair back. "You know it. And on that note, it's getting late, and James is off tomorrow since those two"—he pointed to Trent and Logan—"are off work Saturday. I want to be able to enjoy every minute of my evening with my man."

Travis was already walking over as Dexter bounced toward James. "And we need to get going too. It's getting late."

How late was it? I picked my phone up from the table to see that it was past nine. I had no idea where the time had gone, but we'd been at the bar longer than normal.

As I slid behind the wheel of my car fifteen minutes later, I glanced over at Merrick. "So much for the days of meeting up at eight or nine before hitting a club, huh?"

With a yawn, he shook his head. "Five months ago this was early for me. Working in the restaurant industry as long as I have, two and three o'clock nights are nothing. That being said, it's shocking how fast things change."

We fell silent as I backed out of the parking space. We made it all the way onto the main road that would lead us back to my house before Merrick spoke again. "Are you going to go to Canyon and Larson's place on Saturday?"

"Maybe? Probably. I mean, it seemed like it was a done deal according to them."

He hummed, but the sun had disappeared and I couldn't see much more than shadows, so I didn't bother looking over. "Logan sounded excited to have you join."

"Yeah. Something about protecting him from the littles." Of course, it was more than that. We'd made plans about what games to play and Larson had been trying to subtly figure out if there were any toys I liked. I'd been honest when I told him I hadn't played much as a kid, which had stumped them all.

Merrick's elbow poked my upper arm. "You and Logan have been closer in the last few weeks than I've ever seen you two. He's good for you, and I think you're good for him. Go and have fun."

That was easier said than done. How weird would it be for me to be the only guy there not attached? What would it be like to knowingly go to one of their playdates and not be hanging out with their Daddies? Correction, Daddies and *handler*.

I liked the idea of going, but I was going to need to think about it. Think about it a lot. The problem was that I wasn't sure what I was thinking and my brain was a bit mixed up. I needed someone to talk with, but I didn't know who.

My life had been a lot easier when the guys just left me alone. And the man sitting beside me, encouraging me to go, was the only reason I'd found myself in this position in the first place.

CHAPTER EIGHTEEN

DEAN

Me: You busy?

I'd been staring at the text for nearly an hour but hadn't hit send. Twelve hours after dinner, I was no closer to having answers than I'd been when Merrick had gotten into the SUV that clearly did not have a flat tire and left my house.

Bits and pieces of the evening before kept replaying in my head with no coherent order. Words and phrases, like *Bossy boy*, *middle*, and *but he's not my Daddy*, popped up over and over again as my brain tried to make sense of the evening. The thoughts and dreams had culminated in my shooting upright at seven that morning, gasping in shock, as the weird dreams all fell into place.

The problem was I still didn't know who to talk to. Logan was the first person my brain went to, but something he'd said the night before at dinner had told me that he wasn't going to be able to help me like I needed. Merrick was the person closest to me at the moment, but talking to him about this would make our already complicated relationship that much more complicated.

The friendly handjob, no emotions attached, wasn't supposed to have gone this far. My emotions were involved now, and I wasn't going to be able to ignore them.

I'd spent my shower trying to figure out who to talk to. Travis was understanding, but I didn't think he'd be the one to help me with this. With Logan and Merrick also out of the question, that left me with one valid option. Except I couldn't seem to bring myself to send the text to Larson.

My battery was below eighty percent and it was just after ten. My laptop was on, I'd pulled up my emails, and I'd opened the file I was supposed to be working on, yet I hadn't touched anything since. How could I focus on work when life as I'd known it was turning on its head?

Three minutes later, my phone getting hot in my hand from the screen being on so long, I sent the text. It was a relief to no longer be worrying about sending it, and I set the phone down on my desk.

Not even a minute later, it chimed.

Larson: *Nope. What's up? Did Mer's car not get fixed yet?*

I nearly asked what the hell he was talking about, then remembered the ridiculous lie Merrick had told. Rolling my eyes at Merrick, at myself, at the entire situation, I tapped out a response.

Me: *Merrick's car is fine. Actually, I need to talk, was hoping you'd be available.*

Larson: *Name the time and place. Canyon took the dogs to run errands today. I'm at the reno I'm working on if you want to come here, or I can meet you somewhere.*

I'd never been so thankful for Larson's easy acceptance of anything thrown his way. I'd never reached out to him before, yet he didn't question me, just offered a solution and an invitation. His current fixer-upper, away from any prying ears, sounded like the perfect place to talk. I was struggling just to figure out how to talk about my thoughts; the fear of someone overhearing would make talking that much harder.

Me: *Mind if I come over now?*

Larson: *I'll leave the front door open. I'm working in the kitchen today.*

He texted the address as I powered down my still-untouched computer. There was no use in pretending I was going to get work done. It didn't matter if I'd just gotten caught up from being sick—I needed to focus on me.

Fifteen minutes later, I found the house in a neighborhood not far from my own townhouse. The homes were bigger than I could justify for myself, but I'd always dreamed of owning one here. The outside of the address Larson gave me was cute but dated, but Logan's truck in the driveway told me I'd found the right house.

Like promised, Larson was in the kitchen in the middle of installing a light fixture. He'd clearly done a lot of work in the house because the inside looked nothing like I'd expected judging by the outside. He never looked over, still focused on what he was doing, but acknowledged me just the same. "Hey. Give me a sec, just finishing this up."

I headed over to the stool along the wall and settled onto it, happy to give him all the time he needed. The hours since I'd woken up hadn't made the thoughts bouncing around in my head any easier to work through, and I didn't think that would change in the next ten seconds or ten minutes. "Take your time."

Larson glanced over, studying my face for a moment before gently letting the fixture go to make sure it would hold. "This can wait. You look like hell."

"Gee, thanks." I knew I hadn't slept well, but I didn't think I looked that bad.

He cocked an eyebrow and gave me a look, daring me to disagree as he washed his hands. When they were dry, he gestured toward a different room. "Come on. Something's got you all out of sorts, and if my suspicions are right, it has something to do with tomorrow."

I huffed. "You don't miss a thing."

He grinned as he pulled open a mini fridge in what I thought was supposed to be an office. The house looked nearly ready to be put on the market.

"Second of nine. In my family, you're primed from a young age to not miss a thing." Not missing a beat, he glanced over his shoulder. "Drink? We've got water, milk, and juice. There's a fridge in the garage that has some soda."

"Water sounds great, thanks."

Larson turned back to the fridge and a few seconds later he was leading me toward the living room, two bottles of water in hand. He gave us just enough time to take a seat on the uncomfortable folding chairs and open our waters before he turned the focus to my presence. "So, what's got you looking like the walking dead and asking to talk at ten in the morning when you should be at work?"

Statistics and data were easy. It all made sense and I could pick it apart piece by piece until I knew exactly how it worked and what was going on. Feelings weren't so easy. And putting those feelings into words was difficult under the best of circumstances. This was far from ideal, so I had no idea how I was going to broach the subject until my mouth opened and words came out. "Won't it be weird for me to show up without a Daddy?"

So that was where we were starting.

Larson rested his elbows on his knees and studied me for a moment. "For us littles? For our Daddies? Or for you?"

My head fell back, the ceiling becoming very interesting all of a sudden. "All of the above?"

"Well, to start with, we invited you, so no, it won't be weird for us. Canyon, Trent, and Travis? Well, I can't speak for them, but I doubt it. You're friends with all of us. And only you can answer the last one."

Tilting my head back toward Larson, I let out a long sigh. "What if…" My voice trailed off. I knew where I wanted the sentence to go, but I didn't know how he was going to react. It took a few seconds to remember that I'd reached out to Larson because he was observant, accepting, and unflappable. Then again, he'd grown up in a family with nine kids and parents who owned a BDSM club. There was probably very little I could say that would surprise him.

I forced myself to take a cleansing breath and put voice

to what I'd only discovered in the last few hours. "I think I'm a middle."

Not even a flicker of surprise crossed his face. If anything, he looked unsurprised. When he didn't say anything, my brain decided to take the silence as an opportunity to spill what had been bouncing around in my brain and keeping me from focusing on anything else.

"Last night at dinner, Aiden called Logan a middle. I know what a middle is. I've been in the community long enough. Hell, even if I hadn't, I've been hanging out with you guys long enough that I would've had to live under a rock not to."

Larson grinned at me. "Very true. We're pretty much a living BDSM manual. But you've always been a Dom, so you're confused."

It wasn't a question, but I found myself nodding. "Truer words have never been spoken. I figured out at a young age that I liked caring for my partners. Maybe being around Trent, Travis, and Merrick so much when I was younger helped me understand that I liked caring for the men I was with, or maybe I would have figured that out on my own. Either way, I knew I liked taking care of people. I liked making them happy. I had a few boys in my twenties. The last one I was with a long time, but we broke up shortly before the wreck. Since then, I haven't been interested in finding a partner."

Larson hummed. It was a low, thoughtful sound that told me he was processing what I'd told him. "Makes sense. Is your lack of interest due to the accident or you?"

I shrugged. I was still trying to figure that out myself.

"Travis has been on me to start dating. Well, on me isn't quite right, but he's brought it up and it's made me feel kind of itchy. Like something doesn't feel right. When I told Merrick about it, he decided that I just needed to find a way to relax. Whether he'll admit it or not, it's because if he's focused on me, no one will bug him about his own love life."

Larson barked out a laugh. "Flawed logic if I've ever heard it, but it sounds about right. Doesn't he realize that if he manages to find you someone, attention is going to turn to him next?"

"I'm pretty sure I told him that same thing, nearly word for word. But in the end, it doesn't matter because I figured out between last night and this morning that I don't want to dominate anyone. I... I like..." Why was this so hard to say?

"You like being taken care of?" Larson's words were gentle, almost coaxing.

"Yes and no. It's all so confusing in my head. When we were supposed to be going to Canyon's mom's for yoga but ended up hanging with you guys, I felt good. It wasn't the relaxing part. Well, not entirely, because that was nice, and I had a lot of fun playing games with you all. But this part of me also got the same happy feeling when I was able to do something for one of you that I used to get when I did something that made one of my boys happy."

Larson's surprise lessened some, his eyes relaxing as he nodded. "Go on."

That wasn't hard to do. Now that I'd started talking, it felt like my thoughts had to come out right away. "Merrick showed up at my office one night to make sure I got out on time. I wasn't quite ready to go, but it didn't matter when I saw the pleased look he got on his face when I packed up my stuff. Then last night, Aiden made that offhand comment. I think that's when it all fell into place."

Larson was grinning now but gestured for me to continue.

"I didn't really play with games or toys as a kid. So hanging out with you all and playing video games was fun. When I was sick, Merrick brought me LEGO sets and I lost hours setting them up and playing with them. It was fun." My sigh was more out of confusion than frustration, though I didn't feel like I was explaining myself well either.

"For a few hours, I didn't feel sick. It was okay to sit in the living room wrapped up in my blanket with Babbit on my lap, toys in front of me, and cartoons in the background. Part of me felt bad that Merrick was cleaning my kitchen and making sure I stayed hydrated and had meds in my system, but part of me felt…"

When I couldn't find the word I was looking for, Larson spoke again. "Cared for?"

"Yeah. Cared for. Safe. I liked it. That's selfish, right? I should be taking care of my partner, not looking to a friend to provide comfort to me when I'm sick." My hair was already a mess, so my hands raking through it again weren't going to make much of a difference. "But I liked it. It felt right. And when Aiden mentioned middles last night, it resonated with me. Of course, I didn't figure that out until this morning."

Larson adjusted in his seat as he thought, then eventually sighed. "Please don't take this the wrong way, because I'm happy you're here and felt comfortable talking to me, but shouldn't you be telling this stuff to Merrick?"

I knew my eyes widened comically, but it was the way my voice cracked when I responded that gave my unease away. "Wha— Why would I do that?"

Now Larson was trying to suppress a grin. "Because, correct me if I'm wrong, Merrick is the one that makes you feel safe. And Merrick is the one that you *like* to please. When you're together, you actively look to him to make choices." He held up a hand before I could dispute it. "I don't think you realize you do it."

I dropped my head into my hands as I groaned. Larson knew the truth, so there was no point in hiding. "Well, I can't talk to Merrick because he doesn't want a boy. Hell, the man doesn't want a relationship! How the fuck could I tell him that I think I'm a middle and the only person I can imagine being my Daddy is him? That's going to go over real well when we had sex last night and never mentioned dating anywhere in there!"

As it turned out, I could shock Larson. His mouth hung open and he blinked at me in confusion. "Holy shit. That's a lot to unpack."

"It's probably better if we didn't right now. I'm struggling enough with understanding that I'm not a Daddy after all these years."

Larson shook his head. If that could make this situation make sense, I'd have figured my shit out hours ago. "Okay, let's focus on that. What did you like about being a Daddy?"

"Easy. I liked caring for my boys and making them happy."

"What else?"

"You mean like punishments? Or routines?"

He nodded a silent encouragement for me to continue.

That was harder to answer. "Routines are nice, but I didn't need them. And I guess for consequences or punishments, I sort of viewed it as my job. It was easier when I knew it was something he really liked and craved."

A long silence stretched between us as Larson gathered his thoughts. He'd obviously thought them over a number of times when his words came out cautiously. "So, in the end, you liked caring for your partners and you liked pleasing them."

I nodded.

"You like pleasing Merrick. You like making us happy too."

I nodded again and Larson smiled. "Why did you choose Daddy Dom and not a stricter form of BDSM? More pain play? Before you say caretaking again, I could give you a list of sites that deal with how beneficial pain play is to those who enjoy it. How they feel cared for, loved, cherished, and how it makes them feel good. So don't tell me it was the caretaking."

That time I had to think harder. I'd been young when I discovered Daddy Doms, but why and how? A light bulb went off in my head a few seconds later. "Travis and Trent! That's how. They'd always hinted at being Doms, maybe not flat-out saying it but alluding to it. And they took care of everything and everyone. They obviously enjoyed it."

A fond memory popped into my head. "Trent was always chasing after Logan, making sure he wasn't going to get himself killed. Travis was always hovering over everyone. It was just natural for them. And then one day, I overheard one of them talking about Daddy Doms and it all made sense. I liked when I made my partners happy and when I could care for them and knew that they liked it."

Larson nodded as though he'd figured something out. "Do you know what I like about being little?"

The abrupt change in topic confused me, so all I could do was shake my head.

He didn't need more encouragement. "Obviously, I like being able to forget the real-world shit. It helps me relax to know that all I need to worry about is the here and now. Those are the givens. Those are what you see on the outside and what people talk about most, but there's something else. I like making Canyon—my Daddy—happy. I like when he smiles at me because I've cleaned up my toys. I like letting him choose my outfits because I know he likes taking care of me. I'm happy when he's happy. I'm happiest when I've done something that I know pleases him."

That time my mouth fell open. Why had I never thought of that before? "I'm not a Dom."

Larson's hands rose in defense. "I never said that!"

"You didn't. I did. And it's the truth. I know I like pleasing my partners. I will do just about anything to make them happy, even things that I don't particularly enjoy." Like punishments and making routines.

No wonder my relationship with Evan had been so rocky. I'd never been a Dom and I didn't like being in charge, but I did it because it made him happy. "I just thought that Doms were the caretakers. They were the ones that made their subs happy. It doesn't make a hell of a lot of sense thinking back on it. Things went so sideways after the accident, finding another relationship or analyzing my feelings never occurred to me."

Things were falling into place so fast, I was struggling to keep my thoughts straight. "Holy shit. I'm not a Dom." I looked up at Larson, whose smile had turned fond at my rambling. "Lars, I'm a sub."

He nodded a few times. "I'm glad you figured that out. I'm sorry that I hid my little side for so long. Maybe you would have figured this out a long time ago."

Despite my shock, I found myself giving him a genuine smile. "Don't be sorry for that. We all have to come out on our own time. You came out when it was right for you. I'm a little behind the curve right now, but I'll figure it out. I want to play video games, or hell, maybe toys could be fun. I want someone else to worry about what time it is and if I should be in bed."

I paused and looked over at Larson, feeling lighter than I had in years. "Thank you."

He blinked. "For what?"

"For taking me seriously. For not brushing me off. For talking to me this morning. I realized when I woke up that I'm a middle, but I was struggling to make it fit with what I thought I knew about myself all these years."

The words had barely left my mouth when I winced. "But that still means I need to find a Daddy that isn't Merrick."

Larson gave me a sad look. "You two can talk later. For now, go home and get some sleep. Come over tomorrow and hang out with us. No pressure at all, from any of us. I'll sit on Trav if he tries to talk to you."

I snorted at the thought. I didn't know if I wanted Travis to say something now or not. However, that was a problem for tomorrow. Larson was right—I was exhausted and bed sounded perfect.

I could deal with everything else later. For now, I needed to sleep.

CHAPTER NINETEEN

MERRICK

I'd been patient. Three hours I'd been patiently waiting for Dean to acknowledge my text. It wasn't like him to go three minutes without reading one of my texts; three hours was nearly unheard of. I'd done everything I could to keep my mind off Dean: focusing on the restaurant, talking with the kitchen manager, and making a plan to get back into the kitchen to start working on menus. I'd fielded some easy questions from the crew and even taken a few calls from a business partner struggling with a restaurant.

Through it all, my mind had only been half on the tasks in front of me. The other half had been stuck on Dean. After nearly dropping a case of glasses, I'd finally admitted to myself that I wasn't going to get anything done until I knew why Dean wasn't responding.

I found Ben—Travis's mini-me—talking to a few crew members out back and made sure to wave to him as I got into my car. His eyes went wide as I put the car in gear. He must have been telepathically linked to Travis because I'd barely made it out of the parking lot when Travis's call rang through.

"H—"

Travis cut me off before I could finish my word. "Where the hell are you off to? I'm supposed to be meeting you there in fifteen minutes! I got stuck at the flooring place."

"Shit. Sorry. I forgot. Rain check."

"What? Merrick, what the hell is going on? Did someone die?"

I sure as hell hoped not. "Gotta go see Dean. He's not answering my texts. He hasn't responded in over three hours."

To my utter amazement, Travis laughed. "That's because he's probably still sleeping."

Unfortunately, the response didn't help my worry any. Dean should have been at work hours ago. "What? How do you know that?" He hadn't told me he wasn't going to work. He hadn't told me he wasn't feeling well.

"Sorry, Mer. Didn't mean to freak you out. I'd called Larson to ask a question about flooring for the restaurant. I wanted his opinion. He'd been telling Dean goodbye when he picked up the phone. He mentioned that he'd had a rough night, had come over to talk about some stuff, and was going home to sleep."

I didn't know if the answer made me feel better or worse.

"Thanks for letting me know. I'm glad to know he's okay, but I'm still taking a rain check. I'll talk with you later."

Travis blew out a frustrated breath. He was annoyed with me and was going to hold it over my head.

Six months earlier, anyone I'd worked with would have had me committed if I'd uttered the next words out of my mouth. Hell, one of my business partners might still if he heard me say it. "You and Ben decide on the flooring. I'm sure whatever you pick out will be great." I hung up the phone before Travis could respond. The only place I wanted to be was Dean's.

The house was dark when I arrived, so I used the garage code in case he was still asleep. He hadn't mentioned not sleeping well the night before, and the fact that he'd been asleep for hours by now made my anxiety higher. The interior of the house was as dark as it had appeared from the outside and despite my announcing myself, it was silent.

In the living room, his blanket was missing from the couch, the TV was off, and the curtains were pulled closed. I called his name again, albeit quietly, as I headed up the steps. His door was open, so I automatically headed that way.

It only took a glance into his bedroom to find him. He was exactly like Travis had told me: sound asleep. I assumed the sports coat, pants, and button-down draped over the foot of the bed were likely what he'd been wearing earlier.

From what I could make out, he was wearing another T-shirt, though it looked to fit better than most of the things he wore. I couldn't see under the bright blue comforter covered in spaceships, or the sheets with vibrant blue stars all over them, but one of his knees was sticking out of the blanket and I could see that his pajama pants were covered in cartoons.

Tucked tightly in his arms, not even draped over his shoulders, was his blanket, with Babbit clutched in the middle.

I found myself leaning against the door frame smiling at his sleeping form yet worried about what had kept him up the night before. I took a glance around his room and spotted the toys I'd bought him when he was sick. They weren't on a shelf as I'd expected but spread out along the floor, one of the Mario characters lying on its side.

My legs moved me into the room on autopilot until I was standing next to his bed. An overwhelming sense of relief washed over me when I placed my hand on his forehead to find no sign of a fever. I still didn't know why he was sleeping when he should have been at work, but at least he didn't appear sick.

It wasn't until he rubbed his forehead against my hand that I noticed I was still touching him and pulled back. If he woke up then, I'd scare the hell out of us both, not having a valid excuse for being in his bedroom without his knowledge.

I'd tried to tell myself that the night before had been casual sex at best. What had he said that first night about friendly handjobs? Friendly blowjobs had to be a thing too. It would be a lot easier to convince myself of that if somewhere along the line, my heart hadn't missed the memo.

I needed to get out of there.

On my way back to the kitchen, I passed the sad room

that was part office, part spare room, and all drab. I'd told him numerous times that he needed to redecorate the space, but he hadn't taken me seriously. A bed with bright sheets, shelves of toys and games, and an area for his video games would be a better use for the space. There were other things to think about than Dean's office area, but thinking of a better use for the space was a lot easier than allowing myself to contemplate why I felt like I'd left my heart upstairs.

Reaching for the door to the garage, I spotted Dean's phone on the counter. That explained why he hadn't responded to my texts.

When my heart tugged again as the garage door closed, I admitted that I needed to talk with someone and, for once, it wasn't a friend I needed.

I pulled my phone out and dialed my mom's number. I couldn't remember the last time I'd called her for advice. I wasn't sure if I'd ever called her for advice, especially not advice on my love life. When I'd come out, she and my dad had been accepting of me, but that was as far as it had gone. They'd never asked me if I was dating, despite lamenting frequently about my younger brother's love life.

Josh was so much younger than me that I had already moved out when he was born. We were both oops babies at opposite ends of life. Now that he was finally out of college, my parents thought he should be settled down, not still jumping from relationship to relationship.

It was my mom's favorite topic lately.

Before coming out, my mom had been my go-to for advice. She always thought things through and if she didn't have a solution readily available, she'd think about it until she did. I couldn't explain why that had changed in high school. While I didn't ask her for advice anymore, when she gave me it unsolicited, it was always solid.

Canyon would politely tell me to put my big boy pants on and tell Dean my feelings, but it wasn't that easy. Travis would hum and listen but would want me to work things out on my own. Trent would probably get interrupted by Aiden, Logan, or work fourteen times before sighing and telling me I was thinking too hard about it. While I could see all their points, it wasn't what I needed at the moment.

As I put my car in reverse, my phone only rang twice before my mom's voice filled my car. "Merrick! What a surprise. Shouldn't you be working?"

I could hear the TV in the background, and if I listened closely, I could almost hear Old Man Jackson's tractor in the field beside the house. I had no idea if he was still alive. He'd been old when I was growing up, but he had always mowed the field religiously on Friday afternoons whether it had needed it or not.

"Took the afternoon off. The guys can handle it."

Mom hummed. She knew I was obsessive about work, after all. It was why I'd missed every holiday, family reunion, or reason to go back in the last decade. "Did you hit your head?"

"No, I got my heart broken."

I pulled into a parking lot and parked toward the back. I couldn't believe I'd said the words to my mom.

"Oh, Mac." The old nickname I'd nearly forgotten about

slipped off her tongue easily as the TV clicked off. "I didn't know you were dating."

A bitter part of my brain had my eyes rolling. *You never asked.* "I'm not. Or wasn't." I scrubbed a hand over my face. Even to myself, I wasn't making sense. I couldn't imagine how she'd feel since I had never told her anything about my dating life. "Sorry. That wasn't what I'd meant to lead with. It must be weighing on my mind more than I realized."

"You don't talk about dating. It's always been a sore subject with you."

"Because I've avoided dating since I was in my early twenties." I wasn't going to go into hookups and casual flings with my mom, but I needed to talk this out. "I fell in love back in New York. He cheated on me, and I've punished every potential relationship for his shortcomings."

We didn't need to be in the same room for me to see her eyebrows fly up her forehead. "That long ago?" She was quiet for a moment, her voice more resolute when she spoke again. "What was so special about that man that made you hold onto him for all this time?"

That was a damn good question.

"I… I don't know. He taught me so much. He introduced me to bartending. He introduced me to the career that shaped my life. We were supposed to be it. Take on the world together."

After a breath, I could admit that it wasn't entirely the truth. "I'd finally found a place that got me, that accepted me. Tom accepted me, the bar accepted me, New York accepted me. They all accepted me as the gay guy who needed people to understand. Sure, I got slurs hurled at me, but there was this group of people that just got it. I'd never had that before. You and dad, you said the right things. You said you loved me and wanted me to be happy. But we all know that you didn't understand. And what could you two have really done if you'd found out about the things said and done to me?"

Mom let out a surprised gasp. "Because you never told us. We found out well after you left."

I swiped at tears that had begun to roll down my cheeks. "You and dad, you live there. That's your home. I knew you two would never leave, and I'd never intended to stay. The last few years of high school had just solidified that. I wasn't going to have you two trying to fight a battle you didn't understand or potentially ruining relationships with people you'd see over and over again."

"Merrick Joseph Carter!" My dad's voice in my ear startled me. I hadn't realized he was anywhere near, much less close enough to hear me. To my surprise, his voice cracked when he spoke again. "First off, if we understood or not, you're our son. We both told you the day you came out to us that nothing had changed. Gay or straight, we were proud of you and loved you. We knew well before you told us, and we'd had plenty of time to digest the information. You, however, came out, then stopped talking about it. The few times we tried, you shut down the conversation so fast, we knew you weren't ready. We didn't push."

I remembered the relief I'd felt telling my parents, and I'd mustered up the courage to tell my best friend. I'd asked him not to tell anyone else. He'd nodded, but in a matter of days the entire town knew. I'd gone from relieved that I had finally told a few people and they had accepted me, to trying to blend into the background of every class or event I went to.

"Second." My dad's voice wavered, the sadness unexpected and painful to hear. "Second, Merrick, I don't care if this place is the only place I've ever lived. I've called these people my family for years. But family—true family—doesn't do that shit. You never gave us a chance to show you that."

Was that true?

"What?"

My mom cleared her throat, then sighed. "Mac, we heard all about the hell you went through. But it was well after you were gone. We heard it from Donnie. He came to talk to us afterward. He said he tried to apologize, but you wouldn't speak to him."

Each time I blinked, new tears fell down my cheeks. If what I was hearing was true, they were right. I'd never given them the chance to support me. I'd never given Donnie a chance to apologize, despite his numerous attempts. Had I lost my best friend due to my own stubbornness? I'd run as soon as the opportunity had presented itself. Just like I'd run from New York after I found out about Tom.

I'd been running ever since. Except that wasn't quite true. I'd been running, but I'd also been coming back. Over and over again, I'd come back to Tennessee. I'd come back to Steve's. I'd come back to Travis, Trent, Larson, and

Dean. The group had grown, but I was still coming back. But I was no longer coming back—I was here. Here to stay. Here to live.

I was also falling. Falling for a man I'd been returning to for nearly twenty years. A man who made my heart swoop in spite of me and my efforts to ignore it. I wasn't just falling, I'd fallen. I'd fallen in love with Dean without trying.

The air from my lungs whooshed out of me like a deflated balloon. "Shit. You're right. I'm sorry. I don't want to keep running from this stuff. I want to give him a chance."

Mom's voice was watery, but I could hear a smile. "Ah, so there is someone. Who is he?"

For the next fifteen minutes, I sat in my car telling my parents about Dean. How we met, how we'd been friends all these years. How the more time I spent with him, the more I fell for him. About how I'd never told him how I felt. More frightening than that, about how I'd all but pushed him away as I continued to tell him that I didn't want more.

When I fell silent, exhausted from the conversation, my brother was the first voice I heard. When he'd gotten there and how much he'd heard, I had no idea, but I needed some of the cocky confidence only a twenty-three-year-old guy could have.

"So you show him, you tell him. Hire a damned skywriter if you have to spell it out. He's single. You're single. You said there's attraction, so go after it. Don't be the bonehead that pushes something good away. For as long as I can remember, it's been Trent, Travis, Larson, and

Dean that you've talked about. Any time you send me a picture, it's of one of them. I've waited for you to get your head out of your ass for years. Ten years ago, I was trying to figure out why you hadn't gotten together with one of them. Then they all started finding boyfriends and you were still stubbornly single."

He huffed in frustration. "If you let some assholes from here or some idiot who never appreciated what he had ruin this for you, *you're* an idiot."

So he'd heard more than I'd realized.

I'd needed to hear those words. I'd needed the bluntness that only a brother could give. My brother was right. I was an idiot if I let this slip away. Well, a bigger idiot than I already was. I hadn't wanted to call one of my friends because I hadn't wanted them to tell me the exact same thing my brother just had. That had to make me an idiot.

"Thanks, Josh. I needed to hear that."

Smugness was clear in his voice. "I'm here for you whenever you need a good dose of reality."

"Hey, guys, thanks. Really. But I need to get going. I just figured out what I need to do."

Josh laughed, Mom gave me a teary goodbye, and Dad reminded me to call more often. There might have been a muttered comment from my mom about stubborn men as the phone clicked off, but my brain was already on another topic altogether.

I needed to let Dean know how I felt.

I'd done such a good job avoiding my feelings that I'd missed when Dean went from my friend, to my best friend, to my boyfriend, to my boy.

That made me his Daddy whether we'd put words to it or not.

It was time I made it clear to him that he was so much more to me than a hookup or a friend. I'd known all along that Dean wanted stability, but I hadn't given him a chance to find that with me.

With the playdate looming the next morning, I needed to let him know that I had his back and that I knew what he needed.

Pointing my car toward the electronics store, I made one more call. "Hey, Logan. What game was it that you and Dean were playing at your place?"

CHAPTER TWENTY

DEAN

I woke up Friday afternoon to a rumbling stomach and a knock on my front door. Not bothering to find my glasses, my phone, or look at the clock, I had no idea what time it was or why Merrick was the one standing on my front porch with a large to-go bag in one hand and a brown paper bag in the other.

After the day I'd had, I hoped the bag contained alcohol.

The afternoon sun was directly behind his head and harsh on my eyes, which had grown accustomed to the dark for the last number of hours. I blinked repeatedly as I tried to bring him into focus. "What are you doing here?"

"Hey, Bean." The smile I could make out on his face was nearly as bright as the sun behind him. The constant stress he held was gone and in its place was a lightness I'd never seen. "Heard you had a rough night and took the day off. Thought you wouldn't want to worry about dinner. Besides, if you're ever going to sleep tonight, you need to get up now."

He stepped inside when I didn't protest his presence. I couldn't help the yawn that escaped as I tried to get my bearings again. "What time is it?" I rubbed my eyes, following Merrick to the kitchen.

"Just before five."

That had me waking up in a hurry. "Five? As in p.m.?" I'd fallen asleep shortly after one. After grabbing lunch at a drive-through on my way home, I had made it as far as the living room before I saw the bookshelf with the building sets that Merrick had brought over.

With my conversation from earlier still fresh in my mind, I couldn't help but wonder how much I would enjoy them when I wasn't sick. The thought wouldn't leave my head, so I had scooped them up and headed upstairs.

As it turned out, when I'd gotten my pajamas on and had my blanket and Babbit, I'd been able to lose myself in play. I'd played for fifteen minutes before I remembered I'd left my phone downstairs, but I hadn't needed the interactive app to enjoy myself. It wasn't until I had begun to drift off that I'd left the toys on the floor and climbed into bed.

At the moment, my stomach was telling me it was nearly dinnertime, but my brain was saying I could have slept a lot longer.

Merrick set the bags on the counter and turned back to me. Given that I'd been following behind him—my nose having decided it was more interested in dinner than my eyes were in sleep—he collided with me. I stumbled slightly and he reached out to steady me. "Whoa, there."

When my feet firmed up again, I expected Merrick to release me, but he pulled me into a hug. My stomach swooped like I was on a rollercoaster at the touch. Then his lips pressed against my forehead, a brief contact that was over too soon, and he stepped back. "What happened, Bean? Why didn't you sleep last night?"

At least the swoopy feeling in my stomach was gone. In its place was a lump of reality I wasn't ready to deal with at the moment. No matter what I said, Merrick would find a way to make it about us, him, or the sex. While it was about all of that, telling him that was only going to fuck up whatever *this* was, and after a night and day of realizations, I wasn't ready for more change.

My smile was forced, but I managed to sound more casual about it than I felt. "Logan's invite to their playdate tomorrow kind of threw me for a loop. I ended up overthinking it."

The eyebrow raised in question told me Merrick didn't fully believe me, but he also didn't press for more. "I told you to go. I hope you're still planning on it."

There was no way to avoid the blush in my cheeks, so I settled on living with it while I nodded slowly. "Yeah. I've just been a little anxious about going alone. It feels weird if they're all in relationships like that and I'm single. Isn't that going to feel strange?"

We were treading into murky territory. I knew it. I wasn't going to ask him if he'd take me, and I definitely wasn't going to admit that I wanted him to. The more he showed up here, the more he showed he cared, the easier it was becoming for me to see him as not only a great boyfriend, but also a Daddy. And that was something I needed to stop wishing for.

Before he could say anything, my stomach rumbled. His brow furrowed and his lips pursed. "Did you have lunch?"

I couldn't help it—I rolled my eyes. "Yes, Dad."

That time, the word didn't elicit the normal reaction from him. Instead of getting annoyed, he relaxed some. "Good. Sit down and I'll get you some dinner." I headed toward the living room where I normally ate, only to be stopped by Merrick clearing his voice behind me. "Counter, Bean. You don't need to watch TV while you eat."

That was what I wanted to do. That was how I ate most meals at home. Sitting in the kitchen with no noise was an awfully lonely way to spend a meal. "I always eat in there."

"Sit your butt in the chair, or you're not getting dinner."

I narrowed my eyes, but when he growled and my dick twitched in my pajama pants, I decided to follow orders before he saw how it was affecting me.

"Thank you." He hummed and gave me a smile before turning back to the bag, and my dick began to swell. I didn't know what was worse at the moment, his seeing my arousal or the fact that his words had caused it.

Complicated, table of one.

In an effort to not reach below the counter and stroke myself to full hardness, I focused on what Merrick was doing. "What did you bring?"

"Tacos."

My stomach rumbled again when the unmistakable smell of seasoned meats and spices hit my nose. "Oh my god. Will you marry me?"

Merrick barked out a laugh, nearly dropping the taco he was plating.

"I see that I must demand a prenup stipulating that dropped tacos are grounds for divorce. Especially from El Pecado. Wait, I'm going to need another clause for nachos!"

Laughing so hard he had to set the plate down, Merrick reached into the bag and pulled out a container of the restaurant's famous nachos. I didn't have to see them to know what they were because they had a special container for them.

"I've died and gone to heaven."

He was still laughing as he slid the box of nachos and a plate of tacos over to me. "How long have I known you? I know your favorites."

That he'd paid enough attention to know my favorites only made my feelings more complicated. I was falling for this man, and I was nothing more than a friend to him. I had to find a way out of this. Maybe it was time for a vacation. An extended stay somewhere far from here. Some space, some time, and maybe once I got home, I'd forget all about these crazy feelings.

"I can go with you tomorrow so you're not alone."

Vacation? What vacation?

Surprise had my mouth answering before thinking it through. "Seriously?"

Merrick shrugged as he pulled a chair around so he could sit across from me. "Why not? You don't want to go alone and I have nothing planned. That takes all the awkwardness away from you not being there with someone." He took a bite of his food before continuing. "If I'm there, you can ask me if you need something, not one of the other guys. I can see why that would be awkward. Besides, I already figured out that you're a lot more like Logan than Trent."

He'd danced around the subject well but had made his point. The surprise must have been clear on my face because Merrick gave me a reassuring smile. "It's okay if you find relaxation, comfort, or pleasure in not being the Dom in a relationship. But if not having a Daddy or a Dom around is going to hold you back from being able to find that place that helps you relax, then I can be there. Not as your Daddy or Dom, but as a friend who understands."

The more Merrick spoke, the more fascinating my nachos became. *Just a friend who understands* summed it up and told me more than anything else that I should be saying no.

Then why was my head nodding in agreement? I didn't want just a friend, but I needed someone there who wasn't going to question why I was hanging out with Logan and the littles instead of with the Doms.

A strong hand gripped my shoulder, pulling my eyes upward to see him now standing beside me, staring at me. "You sure? I don't want to force you to do something you're not ready for. I don't have to go. Hell, you don't have to go if you don't want to."

Caring Merrick was not who I had needed at the moment, because any chance of my saying no, saying that I'd changed my mind and it would be a bad idea, had left with his sincere words. I needed the caring guy as much as

I needed my friend. "No. I really want to go. I think I need it. And I can't imagine asking Canyon, Travis, or Trent for a drink or a snack." My skin nearly crawled at the mere thought of it. "But I want to go. It feels... well, it feels right."

He made a noise of understanding before letting go of my shoulder. "Then I'll go with you."

The excited feeling I was experiencing was how I imagined Logan felt when he got excited. "Yeah." I nodded a few times. "I'd like you to go with me."

"Good." He gave me a playful wink as he sat back down. "Do you want to check out the stuff I bought for you after dinner or at Canyon's tomorrow?"

His bringing me something made me smile. "What'd you bring?"

He pointed to my plate. "If you eat your dinner, you can decide if you want to see it tonight or wait."

Did he have any idea how that sounded? Teasingly calling him Dad had become second nature, but now that he knew I would rather have a Daddy than be one, it made each of his actions more confusing.

Twenty minutes later, I'd done the dishes while Merrick put the leftovers away, and when the kitchen was cleaned up, he grabbed the bag and led me to the living room. "Do you want to see what I brought? Or do you want to wait until tomorrow?"

It hadn't been a very fair question for him to ask me. "Um, now?"

"Don't sound so sure of yourself."

Inclining my head, I shot him a glare. "Well, I'm excited,

but I don't know what it is, which makes me a little nervous."

Merrick held the bag out for me. "Here. I think you and Logan will probably have fun with this tomorrow."

Whatever was in the bag was dense. It wasn't huge, but it weighed more than I'd expected it to. I placed the bag on my lap and reached in to pull the box out. It took more than a few seconds to believe what I was seeing. When I finally convinced myself I was holding what I was, I turned to Merrick with wide eyes. "You bought me a Switch?"

He nodded. "Yeah, Logan told me you didn't have one yet. But that's what you guys were playing that night on the couch, right?"

My head was going up and down, but no words would come from my mouth.

"I called him today to get an idea of something you could play tomorrow. I ended up getting a long explanation of why you had to have this thing in order to play the game with him. You know, it was a lot easier when things just had two controllers and no internet connection."

"Hate to break it to you, *Pops*, but those days are long behind us. I mean, you can still play some of those games without having two systems, but a lot of them are single-player games that you can connect to a server to play."

"And you've already lost me." He reached into the bag and removed something I'd missed.

"And the game?" I might have squealed in excitement. "Thank you! Actually, I'm kind of surprised you were able to find the game. It's really popular."

"Ha! Let me tell you, Logan has some mad skills when it

comes to finding in-stock game things. Apparently, there are some stores that are less popular than others, so they often have more stock than the other stores or something. He went into the reasoning, but I was more focused on figuring out what he was telling me to buy than why he was telling me to go to Ashwood to buy it."

My head shot up from the box I was staring at. "Ashwood?" Ashwood was over half an hour from here and he would've passed numerous other stores along the way.

A blush spread across Merrick's cheeks, making his eyes appear silver. "Logan said that was where they would have it, and they did." He pointed to the game in my hand. "Do you need to set it up or something before tomorrow?"

"I probably should. But I left my glasses upstairs."

Merrick stood. "I'll grab them. You work on the packaging. If it's anything like the last two I unpackaged for my friend's kid, it will take you the next hour to get open." He was up the steps before I could think to stop him, returning a few minutes later with Babbit, my blanket, and my glasses. "You left these up there too. Thought you might want them."

His confidence had returned while my cheeks flamed with embarrassment, yet I still reached for all three. Unboxing the game hadn't been that difficult, but setting it up proved to be an exercise in patience that required passwords, my phone, a connection to Wi-Fi, and a credit card. By the time I got it set up and created a profile for the game, it was nearly eight and Merrick had made himself comfortable on the couch beside me, watching a movie that I was pretty sure my mom had dragged me to see when I was too young to stay home alone.

It took another hour to get the game to a place where I felt like I had a good enough grasp on it that I could join Logan the next day. The entire time, Merrick had rubbed my back or shoulders, sending confusing feelings and emotions through me. Even when my T-shirt had ridden up and his hands had made contact with my skin, I didn't recoil like I always had.

There was something about his touch that didn't hurt me the way I always used to hurt when someone touched me. If anything, it felt good enough that I leaned a little closer, trying to soak up the affection he was showing. If I could only have this level of comfort with someone for a little bit, I wasn't going to squander it.

We sat in comfortable silence until Merrick's movie ended. I hadn't paid attention to it, more interested in the game than the action on the screen. I actually hadn't noticed the movie was over until the living room went dark. By then, I felt like I had a good start to my world and was looking forward to playing the game with someone else the next day.

"Have fun?" His voice was warm, but I could hear tiredness in it.

"Yeah. You sound exhausted, though. Might be *your* bedtime." I'd nearly added *Dad* but knew I couldn't keep joking like that with him. It was getting too real, too easy to imagine. And sitting as we were, it would be way too easy to let my heart get even further ahead of my brain.

The hand that had been rubbing my lower back snaked

around and squeezed my side playfully, causing me to twist and yelp. His chuckle was genuine and his voice was warm as he spoke. "Late enough that I know you need to go to bed. Big day tomorrow. You're going to want your rest."

I'd already begun to exit the game and glanced at the time at the top of the screen. "It's not even eleven. And it's a Friday. I don't have to be at Canyon's until nearly lunchtime tomorrow."

With my eyes finally adjusting to the dark, I could see just enough of Merrick's features to make out the stubborn set of his jaw and eyes. "Bedtime." His finger came up and booped me gently on the nose.

To my surprise, a giggle escaped me. I couldn't remember the last time I'd giggled like that, but it felt right in the situation. "Only old people go to bed this early on a Friday night!"

"Old people and boys who have busy days ahead. Go get ready for bed."

I wanted to protest, but my need to see him smile was deeper than my desire to argue, and I found myself standing up to put the game in its dock. "Ugh, only because I can see how much you need sleep." As I made my way up the steps, I tried to hide my yawn, but from the sound of Merrick's snicker, I had to assume he'd heard.

If I hurried, there was a chance we could have a repeat of the night before. The thought had me moving through my bedtime routine a bit faster than normal. Merrick was in my room with my blanket and Babbit when I stepped out of the bathroom, but he was fully dressed and determination was set in his eyes. "Bedtime, Bean."

My eyes didn't even attempt to roll. It was hard to argue for sex when the man in front of me was standing next to the toys I'd been playing with earlier and holding a blanket and stuffed animal I slept with. I reached for the items in his hand as I passed, but he gave a little shake of his head and pointed toward the bed.

"In."

Awkward.

He had to use his foot to push a few of the toys out of the way as he made his way to my side of the bed to hand me my things. Of course, he didn't just hand me the items and leave. No, he handed me Babbit, then draped my blanket over my shoulders the same way I did when I slept alone, then pulled my blankets up around me.

I hadn't thought anything of putting the vibrant sheets on my bed when I'd changed the bedding earlier in the week, but with Merrick effectively tucking me in, I was feeling younger than my years. And as he pulled the blanket with rockets and spaceships up, a strange vulnerability came over me like Merrick was seeing my soul, not just my bed.

When I was settled, Merrick brushed his hand across my forehead and allowed his thumb to rub gently over my skin for a few extra seconds. "Sleep well, Bean."

"Stay?" The word surprised me, but I meant it. I wasn't looking for sex of any sort—that plan had left as he'd tucked me in—I just didn't want to be alone that night. My room, my house, the world in general felt too big.

I didn't know when I'd gotten so tired, but my eyes felt

heavy as he whispered an agreement. "Just let me run to the bathroom and get out of my jeans."

If my plea for him to stay hadn't been enough, I followed the statement up with something I'd never thought of saying to a man before. "There are pajamas in the second drawer. They should fit you fine." My eyes closed again, sleep tugging at me. "And they don't all have cartoons on them."

Merrick's laugh followed him to my bathroom. "Your pajamas are perfect."

Even though I never felt him climb into bed, I fell asleep hearing him move around my bathroom and for a moment, my world felt right.

CHAPTER TWENTY-ONE

❦

MERRICK

My eyes cracked open just after seven. For a moment, I panicked when it felt like a boulder was on my chest, making my breathing difficult. Then the velvety soft fur of Babbit brushed my cheek as Dean worked it between his fingers in his sleep.

No longer panicked, I took in my surroundings.

I'd gone to sleep on the far side of the bed, trying to give Dean as much space as possible. While I hadn't moved much, he had rolled all the way across the bed and was now sound asleep on top of me. Most of his upper body rested on my chest while the hand clutching his rabbit had been flung over his head.

He'd been so earnest as I'd tucked him in, there was no way I'd have been able to turn down his request to stay. The shift had been subtle but there nonetheless, happening as I pulled the blankets around him. He'd looked small in the bed, and his big brown eyes had held uncertainty. I knew before he'd asked that he wouldn't want to be left alone.

So I agreed. In the light of day, as I lay there rubbing his back, I couldn't imagine being anywhere else. Even my apartment didn't rank on the list. I'd had the forethought to stop between the store and Dean's, so Mooch was fine. We would need to stop at my place on our way to Canyon's and, at some point, discuss where sleepovers would be happening in the future.

Of course, that rested on us actually talking about the future. Dean was just discovering his submissive side and I was barely scratching the surface of understanding what it meant to be a Daddy. I knew I was his Daddy—formal title or not—and I needed to take control and talk about where we saw our relationship going, but it was going to wait until later.

Dean needed to be able to relax for the day, not worry about titles or our relationship status. I wanted him to have fun with Logan, Aiden, Caleb, and Larson. I wasn't going to complicate things before leaving the house.

He needed today to finally learn who he was when he wasn't being Dean, Daddy, or any of the various hats he hid himself under. He deserved the chance to explore and get to know himself as a middle. And I needed to be ready to make decisions and take control from the start. That meant getting up and making my boy breakfast.

Getting out of bed proved more difficult than it should have been when Dean wouldn't roll over. His sleepy refusal and persistent need to be attached to me had me smiling, despite my bladder's protest at his weight that was now resting on it. "Just roll over a bit."

Babbit got pulled closer to his face, but he burrowed deeper into my chest and gave a muffled protest before finally rolling over and off of me.

Muffled as it was, the words were still easy enough to make out. "Umph. Daddy, stay."

His breathing evened out immediately, and for a moment I couldn't move. I replayed the words in my head as a peacefulness settled inside me. I'd accomplished a lot in my life between leaving home and becoming the owner of Brodrick's. I'd been an award-winning competitive bartender, a college graduate, and a successful entrepreneur. Not one of those moments had brought me the contented happiness and purpose that one word had.

With Dean finally sleeping at my side instead of on top of me, I was able to roll over and replace my body with the pillow I'd been sleeping on. He didn't move as I left the room wearing the only pair of flannel pajama pants I'd found in his drawer. His choice in T-shirts and loungewear made a lot more sense now. Had I not figured it out before digging through his pajama drawer, I would have definitely suspected something was up afterward. The haphazardly filled drawer was a stark contrast to the pristine organization of the closet his work clothes hung in.

I'd gone pee and made it halfway to the kitchen when I snorted a laugh. His pajama drawer looked identical to the one I'd had as a teenager. Back then, the disorganization and wrinkles hadn't bothered me. I'd grown increasingly aware of the state of my clothing and had eventually decided that the extra few minutes it took to hang or properly fold my clothes was a worthwhile trade-off. Dean's work clothes and T-shirts had obviously been deemed worth the effort to hang, but the clothes that he liked to relax in weren't as important.

To a degree, it made sense. It wasn't how I worked, but I could understand it. When he relaxed, he didn't have to be on, and his pajama drawer reflected that.

As I began rummaging through the kitchen for breakfast foods, my mind was trying to come up with ways to entice Dean to keep his dresser more organized. After five minutes of searching, I hadn't come up with an idea for either. All I knew for certain was that Dean needed to go to the grocery store.

It took a phone call to my mom for her French toast recipe, but it was all I could think of when he only had a few eggs, a half-empty half gallon of milk, and a loaf of bread in the house.

The first batch had just come off the griddle when Dean, all sleep rumpled and confused, stumbled into the kitchen with his blanket wrapped around his shoulders and Babbit in his arms.

I'd had a suspicion that he'd like the rabbit's soft fur when I picked it up the first time. When he'd gotten sick, part of me hoped it would bring him comfort while he wasn't feeling well, just like my old battered stuffed animals had given me countless times over my life. What I hadn't expected was that he'd become attached to it.

"Smells good." He used the hand holding his rabbit to rub at his eyes.

I wasn't going to call attention to how cute he looked at the moment; however, I was happy to let my heart beat a bit faster and a smile play on my lips.

Without another word, he headed to the coffee pot, then stared at it in confusion for a solid ten seconds as I tended to the breakfast still on the stove.

"I know it wasn't just bready goodness that woke me up. I smelled coffee, but there's none in the pot. Where'd you put it?"

A quick glance toward the sink was all he needed to see my freshly emptied mug. His brown eyes widened and he crossed his arms, yet he failed to look menacing while clutching a fluffy rabbit. "You drank the coffee and didn't make more!"

I couldn't decide if it had been a question or a statement, but I nodded regardless. "You don't need coffee today, Bean."

His mouth fell open to protest, but I didn't give him a chance to get started. "Today, the goal is to help you figure out your middle side. I'm here to be the one who helps you make decisions. My first decision is that you don't need coffee until you've had a chance to learn more about yourself. I've spent enough time around Canyon, Travis, and Trent to know that their boys don't get coffee when they're having little days."

His eyes narrowed in annoyance. "I'm not a little."

"Neither is Logan, but I know Trent watches how much coffee he has, especially if they're going to a playdate or the club."

As I turned back to the griddle, I heard him pull out one

of the chairs from under the counter. Despite being pleased that he'd taken a seat in the kitchen instead of heading to the living room, I tried to keep my smirk hidden from the annoyed man across the room. He sounded truly dejected as he grumbled. "Teenagers can have coffee."

Forcing a straight face wasn't easy at the moment. "But how old are you when you aren't Dean the accountant?"

Watching him closely, he didn't appear to have an answer to my question.

"Enjoying video games isn't enough to call yourself a middle or give yourself an age. It's something you like, but it's not just middles that like video games. I'm not telling you that you're not going to find your happy place as a pain-in-the-ass teenager, but I'm also not putting all my money on that."

There had been too many things that I'd seen recently that pointed to him identifying more as an older child or tween. "Let's get through today. If you can honestly tell me that you felt like a stubborn, moody, petulant teenager all day, then next time you can have coffee."

He grumbled something that could have meant anything. I chose to take it as hesitant acceptance and slid a plate and silverware toward him.

Canyon would have cut Larson's breakfast into pieces, but I suspected that Dean would get annoyed with me if I did that. Instead of offering, I grabbed my own plate and cut my serving before pouring syrup on it. I kept an eye on Dean while I did so, watching as he carefully set his blanket and rabbit on the chair beside him.

The glass of milk I slid across the counter before beginning to eat my breakfast thawed a bit of his mood. I was learning that Dean was more of a prickly cactus than cuddle bug when he woke up. I would need to remember that in the future.

He reached for the glass, then paused and glanced up at me, mischief sparkling in his eyes and a smirk on his face. "Since you're putting your foot down on the coffee thing, can't this at least be chocolate milk?"

Had there been food in my mouth, I would have choked. "You're taking this a little far, don't you think?"

Without his plastic-framed glasses, his exaggerated eyebrow waggle was even more amusing, and I had to fight not to laugh. "Am I? You're the one who just told me that I needed to figure out what my submissive side needs. Aiden, Caleb, and Larson all get chocolate milk."

Before I could argue that, he amended the statement quickly. "And so do Logan and Dexter." He finished by sticking his tongue out at me and I lost my ability to hold in my laughter.

"You're going to be a handful." I wanted to tell him that chocolate milk with French toast would be too much sugar, yet I was already reaching for the glass. "Do you have chocolate syrup?"

The light blush that spread across Dean's cheeks as he pointed to the fridge had me smiling again. The only thing that surprised me at this point was that he was just figuring out that he was a middle. I found the syrup tucked in beside the ketchup and mustard. A healthy squeeze of chocolate syrup and a few seconds of stirring later, and I was pushing the glass back toward him. "Finish your breakfast. We need to stop off at my place and check on Mooch before we leave."

Dean's eyes widened at my statement. "You should have gone home last night! Will he be okay? Is it okay to leave him that long?" He scratched his head. "I don't know anything about caring for pets. I know their anatomy, and the different classifications, and life expectancy of different breeds, as well as the problems they face in the wild versus being indoors. But I've never had a cat or dog. Cats are more self-sufficient, though. So he'd probably be fine overnight, at least as long as he had food and water." His head shot up. "Did he have enough food and water to get him through the night? Does he need any medications?"

Christ, the genius couldn't stop his brain. How the hell Jenny had been able to raise a kid like him was a mystery to me. I finally had to interrupt him. "Bean, hold up. You're getting ahead of yourself." When he finally shut his mouth, I continued. "Mooch is fine. I swung by the apartment last night before coming over here to give him food and water and even scooped the litter box. He doesn't need any meds, and he likes his space."

Besides, I wasn't sure if he'd fully forgiven me for starting work at the restaurant and being gone hours at a time. He'd gotten used to me being home a lot when I'd first taken him in. Now he gave me the cold shoulder a lot. As long as he had food, water, and clean litter, he was fine.

By the way Dean began eating faster, I didn't know if I should have told him about Mooch. It was a moot point now. He finished his breakfast quickly and dumped his plate and cup in the sink. "Let me go grab a quick shower."

He'd already turned to head out of the kitchen before I'd been able to swallow the bite of food in my mouth. "Whoa there! Plate and cup in the dishwasher, please."

I watched as his shoulders drooped some before he turned and headed back to the sink to rinse his dishes and put them in the dishwasher. With that done, he was back out of the room in seconds, his blankie and Babbit in his hands.

I'd just finished putting my own dishes into the dishwasher and washing the griddle off when the shower turned off. That was my cue to get moving. I needed to get my clothes on from the day before and make sure Dean had a bag packed for the playdate.

The bathroom door was cracked when I entered his room to find my clothes. I left him alone as I dressed and looked around for a bag to pack his things in. Finding nothing, I called into the bathroom. "Hey, what do you want to use to take your toys in today?"

His head popped into the room, his brow turned downward. "What toys?"

I pointed at the toys scattered on the floor by the bed. "I know Logan is excited to play with those, and your video game needs to come too." *And his blanket and rabbit,* though I thought he might not want to admit that he'd want them with him, so I wasn't going to include those in the spoken list.

"Oh. Uh." His face twitched as he thought, then his eyes

popped open and he stepped out of the bathroom. "I've got a bag in my closet."

He was already in a pair of joggers but hadn't put a shirt on, and he didn't seem to notice that he was walking around the room with his entire torso on display. A faded scar I figured was from the accident started between his hip bone and belly button and disappeared into the waistband of his pants. The scarring on his back wasn't as bad as he seemed to think it was. Yes, it was noticeable and some parts were raised and more discolored than others, but they didn't stand out either.

Larson's story about the accident came back to me, and my heart hurt for Dean all over again. I wanted to wrap him up in my arms and tell him he never had to be ashamed of his body again, but I also wanted to plant a huge kiss on him and tell him how proud I was that he hadn't thought twice about stepping out of the bathroom without a shirt on.

He disappeared into the closet and reappeared a few seconds later, a shirt on and a backpack in his hands. He'd chosen a graphic tee with a game controller on the front. The shirt fit him well, showing off the definition he'd hidden for years.

Paired with the joggers, he looked ready to relax for the day. If it weren't for the stubble on his face and tattoos covering his arm, he'd look just like a kid getting ready to go to a friend's house to play.

My eyes must have lingered on his tattoos too long because he ran his right hand over them. "They cover the scars."

I blinked in surprise at the admission. "I've always wanted to do something about the scars on my back, ass, and thighs, but they usually hurt to touch. I don't want to think about what a tattoo gun would feel like."

The truth was painful to hear. The fact that a man as gorgeous as Dean could be ashamed of any part of his body was a difficult pill to swallow. He barely had the words out and I had him wrapped in my arms as though the embrace could take his insecurities away.

His chuckle made me pull back. "What's that for?"

"I'm honestly not sure. I don't know if I needed the hug or I thought you did, but I hate that you think your scars are so defining."

Dean leaned forward, appearing to go in for a kiss, but changed his mind at the last second and went for a hug. "Thank you." After a moment longer, he stepped back. "I need to finish getting ready if we're going to go check on Mooch."

He disappeared into the bathroom again, leaving me to pack his bag for him. On a whim, I added pajamas and a change of clothes, not sure where the day might lead us.

CHAPTER TWENTY-TWO

DEAN

If I hadn't known that Merrick had rented his place for as long as he had, I'd never have believed it. The white walls were mostly bare and the living areas lacked any personality. The man got on me for the state of my office slash guest room being depressing, but this place was like a hospital room.

The only things that made it look like anyone lived here were the cat toys spread across the floor, the two bowls that contained Mooch's food and water, and the cat condo with a large gray-and-white cat splayed across the top. Mooch's head lifted as the door shut behind us.

Merrick greeted the cat with a light head scratch. "Hey, Mooch. Did you enjoy the place to yourself last night?"

The cat gave a mew and began to stretch out to an impressive size.

Merrick let the cat do his thing, then turned to me. "There's a cup in his food bag. Would you give him a full scoop and refill his water while I shower?"

"Yeah, not a problem."

The smile I received for my agreement would have made me do anything for him. I knew it was a dangerous thought because Merrick couldn't be mine. He didn't want to be anyone's, but that didn't change my brain's inconvenient decision that he was my Daddy. His words as he headed down the hallway didn't help me erase the thoughts. "Thank you, Bean. I'll be quick. Make yourself at home."

It took a minute to find Mooch's food sealed in a clear plastic container in the pantry and another minute to get him fed and replace his water. Then I had nothing else to do, so I pulled out my phone and sank down onto his couch.

Mooch had jumped from the tower and went to his bowl. From what I knew about cats, they usually liked to be left alone, so I turned my attention to my phone and the texts that Larson, Logan, Aiden, and Caleb were already exchanging. At some point, they'd added me to a separate group chat that only included them and Dexter, though Dexter had been quiet that day.

I hadn't yet managed to get caught up on the conversation from that morning when Mooch jumped onto the couch and walked onto my lap without hesitation. Surprised, I watched him for a few minutes before I finally placed my hand on his back for a pet.

Two strokes down his back, and Mooch had begun to purr. A few strokes more and he lay down, claiming my lap as his bed. Thankfully, I was able to use the swipe text feature to text one-handed because every time I took my hand off his back, Mooch reached up and batted at me, demanding more attention.

Logan*: Trent bought me some of those LEGO sets like you have. Are you bringing yours? I thought we could connect them and make a huge course.*

Me*: Uh, I think Merrick put them in my bag.*

Logan*: Sweet! Trent told me he'd pack mine.*

Larson*: Wait, Merrick and Trent packed your bags?*

Aiden*: But Logan swears Trent isn't his Daddy too.*

Logan*: He's not my Daddy, he's your Daddy.*

Caleb*: I can see Aiden's eyes rolling from here.*

I chuckled at them. I saw Aiden's point, though. Trent did do a lot for Logan, even if neither man realized it. And better yet, Logan was more interesting than Merrick and me, so they didn't press for more.

Larson*: What time are you all getting here again? I'm waiting for Daddy to finish getting ready. We need to go to the rehab house this morning. He forgot his favorite water bottle there yesterday... I might have distracted him a bit.*

Logan*: Ohhh, Lars, I didn't know you had it in you!*

Aiden*: Tell us more.*

Caleb*: Doubt he minded that distraction.*

I was laughing out loud as I swiped a response.

Me*: We're at Merrick's right now. We have to drive by that house on the way to your place. Is there any way we can pick the water bottle up?*

Larson*: I could give you the garage code. But are you sure you want to do that? We can go, it's just going to take us a few extra minutes.*

I looked down at the cat on my lap.

Me: As long as Mooch lets me up when Merrick's ready to go. It's still early, so the stop will keep us from being way too early to your place. Especially if Canyon isn't ready.

A text from Larson popped up outside of our group text while I was still swiping the next text out. A quick glance at the preview showed the garage code, followed by a bunch of emojis that I was going to take to mean thanks. I finished my text to the other guys and tapped send.

Me: He was making breakfast before eight this morning. I woke up when I smelled coffee, but the jerk wouldn't let me have any. At least I got chocolate milk.

Merrick's bedroom door opened as my phone blew up with texts. I glanced down and cursed myself. Logan was no longer more interesting than me.

Logan: Whoa, sleepover?

Aiden: I repeat, tell us more!

Caleb: Yeah, I concur. More details are required! He was setting boundaries with you?? This is newsworthy!

Larson: For once, I agree with all of them. Sleepover with Mer? You guys are getting cozy.

"Ready to go?"

Mooch looked over at Merrick, and I turned away from the phone to find him standing by the couch. A pair of jeans that were distressed in all the right places was hugging his legs, and he was wearing a light gray fitted T-shirt with the sleeves rolled up.

On anyone else, the look would have been ridiculous, but on Merrick it was hot. A tattoo visible where his shirts normally covered, hair artfully mussed, beard freshly trimmed—he looked like he was heading to a photo shoot, not a day playing pretend Daddy to a guy who needed encouragement to figure himself out.

My mouth hung open as my entire vocabulary escaped me. All I could manage was a nod of agreement while I swallowed thickly. Finally, my brain started to work and I remembered how to speak. "Yeah. Ready when you are. As long as your cat lets me get up. And we need to stop at Larson's rehab place to get Canyon's water bottle that he left there yesterday when they got *distracted*." I overemphasized the last word with air quotes around it.

The movement disturbed Mooch, who mewled loudly in protest before jumping off my lap and climbing onto his cat condo again.

Merrick nodded as he headed to the kitchen. I watched as he double-checked the bowls and nodded to himself again. "Thank you for filling his food and water. That was a big help."

It hadn't been that big of a deal, but by the way he thanked me, it sounded like I'd gone above and beyond for him. It was also too easy for me to imagine him thanking me for helping Daddy out. I had to choose my words carefully when I responded. Randomly saying, "You're welcome, Daddy," would likely ruin the day and make things awkward between us. I ended up saying the words three times in my head before I finally opened my mouth. "You're welcome. It wasn't a big deal."

The faint smile on his face as I spoke made me wonder if he knew how hard it was for me to censor my words. But I was more focused on the pride I'd felt not blurting out *Daddy* to give much more thought to his smile.

"Well, I appreciate it nonetheless. And since Mooch is set for the day, I think it's time to get out of here."

I managed a faint nod, gave Mooch one last pet as I passed, and followed Merrick out the door. I had to give him directions to the house Larson was working on. He'd made a lot of progress after I'd left the day before and the sparkling kitchen that greeted us pulled a hum out of me.

"You've been wide-eyed since I pulled onto this street."

The duck of my head and the shy blush that followed had him tilting his head in my direction. When he didn't speak but also didn't look away, I knew I had to say something. "Yeah. I've always loved this neighborhood. Gramma and Pap live a few blocks away. When I was little, we used to walk here. A lot of Gramma's and Mom's friends lived over here. When I got older, Mom used to say she would love to move here one day. She busted her ass to raise me, and when she could finally afford to move out, this neighborhood wasn't in the cards. Now that she has the money, she likes her little house and says these homes would be too big for one person. I agree with her on the size thing, which is why I've never moved here despite having the money and loving the neighborhood."

Merrick was listening to me, but he was also looking around the house. "It's a cute place. And you're right; the neighborhood is beautiful."

Without thinking, I grabbed his hand and led him through the house to where Larson had said the water bottle would be. I wasn't going to think about what they'd managed to get up to in the master bedroom, but I was going to allow myself a moment to imagine my bed in the space overlooking the little creek that ran through the backyard.

After locating the water bottle, the two of us spent time looking at the rest of the house. In each room, we talked about how we'd use it or how we'd decorate it. Merrick had laughed heartily when he'd seen the room Larson had gotten our water bottles from. "This is a proper office."

Crossing my arms, I looked around the space. It was big and airy and I liked the light blue walls and soft carpet that had been installed, but I wasn't going to tell him that. "My office is fine!"

"Your office is boring. I still maintain you don't *need* an office anyway. You do your work at the co-op space. And it should be staying there. That space could be utilized so much better. You could make it an escape for yourself."

His words trailed off, and I was left to look at a man lost in thought, wondering where he was going with that and what exactly he meant by escape. Before I could ask, he shook his head. "This house really is beautiful."

My agreement was automatic. "I'd live here in a heartbeat if I didn't feel like it would be too lonely."

Merrick squeezed my hand in his, pulling my attention down to where they were linked at our sides. I barely remembered grabbing his hand minutes earlier. The gesture had been natural and had felt right at the time. Even now that my attention had been drawn to it, it didn't feel wrong.

"Come on, Bean, let's get going. Canyon wants his water bottle and you have a playdate to get to."

He didn't drop my hand as we left the house, not even

as I paused to shut the garage or as we approached the car. He held onto my hand until we reached the passenger's side of the car and he opened the door for me. I almost asked if I was big enough to sit in the front, but the question got stuck in my throat as I looked up and saw him smiling at me. "Buckle up."

Merrick waited until I'd clicked the buckle into place before nodding his head and shutting the door. I chastised my imagination when I swore I'd heard him say, "Good boy," as the door shut. My crush was getting out of control.

He was in the car before I could shake the feeling. Instead of talking about the house, Merrick turned the conversation toward the day ahead, asking questions about what was planned, what I was looking forward to, and if I knew of anything I'd need from him that day.

The longer we talked, the more the conversation gradually eased into things I was excited about. When we pulled into the driveway, I was no longer worried about what Canyon, Travis, or Trent would think and more excited to share the games I'd brought with Logan and the others if they were up to it.

Merrick's voice had held a smile for most of the drive. It wasn't until we'd parked at the top of the hill the house sat on that I stopped talking long enough to realize I'd dominated the conversation for most of the second half of the trip. Yet Merrick was still smiling each time he managed to get a word or two in. My mouth clamping shut had his smile growing.

"Larson's excited too." He used his head to motion to the front door where Larson was standing. Marley and

Lennon were sitting to either side of him like giant statues. Lennon would stay at Larson's side, but Marley was a mixed bag. He'd taken a liking to me from early on, but Merrick still swore the dog was plotting ways to make him into a snack.

Whenever I'd seen Larson playing in the past, he'd worn cotton shorts and childish T-shirts. Today he was dressed in a pair of cargo shorts and a green T-shirt with the words In My Defense I Was Left Unsupervised printed across the front. It was even funnier given that he was standing in the doorway with a half-eaten donut in one hand, a smear of filling on his chin, and was apparently oblivious to Marley eating the bagel in his other hand.

Confirming my suspicion, Larson's eyes widened when Marley pulled the last bite of bagel from his hand just as we got out of the car. From the driveway, I could hear Larson call into the house. "Daddy! Merrick and Dean are here." He conveniently left out that Marley had eaten his bagel, but I wasn't going to be the one to tell Canyon that.

Canyon appeared in the doorway, took one look at Larson, shook his head, and disappeared just as quickly. Merrick joined me on the walkway to the front door with the bag he'd packed for the day slung over his shoulder. "Phone, Bean." He held out his hand as I stared at him. He raised an eyebrow and stared back. "You are not going to spend all day checking emails or texts. Besides, almost everyone is here anyway."

"But the LEGO game is on my phone." A weak excuse at best, and I was already reaching into my pocket for it.

Merrick didn't take his eyes off me. "If you want to play that game, you can come get your phone."

Handing it over felt good. Not only did it make him smile at me, it was freeing. There was no way I could get sucked into work or the adult world if texts, calls, or emails came in.

"Hey!" Larson was nearly vibrating even as Canyon returned with a washcloth to wipe his face. He wiggled and moved his face from side to side in an attempt to see around the washcloth but Canyon wasn't deterred.

"Calm down, little bit. Your face is a mess. I swear, I just ran to the bathroom. How did you get jelly all over your face?"

Larson's shoulders drooped in resignation. "It wasn't *all* over! You're just being extra thorough."

Canyon rolled his eyes playfully at Larson's protest. When he finally decided that Larson was cleaned up, he turned to us. "Hey, guys. Come on in. Larson's been anxious for someone to show up. Even a hike this morning didn't get his mind off of it." He turned back to Larson. "Why don't you take Dean inside. We'll hang out here and wait for the other guys to arrive."

That was all the encouragement Larson needed and he reached out for my hand. I took it with only a quick glance back to find Merrick grinning at me. He gave a nearly imperceptible nod, and I was following Larson through the house.

We were in Larson's play area before I figured out that Merrick and Canyon had likely planned our early arrival to give me a chance to relax. With the two of them elsewhere and only Larson, who already knew my secret, in front of me, it was easier to sit down on the floor beside him.

He pulled a box of cars and racetrack pieces from a shelf. "Are these good? We can also play video games, but I thought you might want to save that for when Logan gets here. He's going to be excited to have someone to play with who gets him a bit more."

I reached for a few of the cars. There was a bright blue convertible and a green muscle car that caught my eye. "These are cool. I never had many toys growing up. I mean, I did, but I didn't play with them. There were always more interesting things to do."

Larson beamed as he scrambled to his feet faster than I thought a man his size should be able to. He disappeared around a corner. I heard a door open then close, and a few seconds later he returned with a rolled mat. "I have this too! I like to be able to build the town on the rug but thought you might like the tracks because they make the cars go faster. But if you haven't had a chance to play with this stuff, this might be fun too."

His acceptance of whatever I was in the mood for made it easier to find that place I'd been at in the car, when all I wanted to do was get here and have fun with my friends. Not the fun where I talked with the guys and discussed work and life, but the fun where I got to play with the littles and not worry about those things for a while.

It only took a few minutes to figure out what Larson meant by the rug making the cars slower, but after a second of contemplation, I decided to set up a track just to the side of the rug. Much like the houses and buildings that Larson was adding, I was adding a racetrack where the cars could go faster.

At some point, I'd curled my legs under me and was sitting on my knees as I built the track. Larson had finished the town and joined me, offering pieces and suggestions as we went. I was having fun and didn't notice that my back had stiffened up from the position until I turned to grab a piece and winced reflexively as tight muscles strained.

"Shoot. Are you okay?" Larson's voice was filled with worry, the same as his eyes. "Should we be doing this at the table?"

"I'm fine." The words came out harsher than they should have, but Larson didn't recoil. Instead, he closed his eyes and sighed.

When his words came again, they weren't delivered in the same tone he'd been using since we'd arrived. They were crisp, matter-of-fact, and all adult. "Listen, I'm not going to ruin the day, but I know you hurt. This isn't the right time, and I know this is supposed to be a stress-free day, but I was there that night."

My mouth hung open in shock.

Larson just nodded as he continued. "I know now that I should have said something a long time ago, but I knew you didn't want to talk about it. Our crew got called to the scene. When I recognized your license plate—" He trailed off for a second, as though he couldn't find the right words. "I'm not going there today. I rode with you to the hospital. I know the extent of your injuries. It's okay if sitting on the floor is too much. You don't have to play the tough guy all the time."

He gave me a slightly watery smile. "That's what's great about age play. You don't have to be the adult the world around us expects. It's okay to get upset, to be scared, to show pain, or need a little more attention. It's okay to let your guard down." He bit his lip for a second before he finished quietly. "None of us are going to think differently of you." A faint blush spread across his cheeks. "I'm sorry I didn't say that a lot sooner."

I was rendered speechless. Not just at the admission, but at the acceptance Larson was showing me. His admission felt a lot less impactful than his promise that it was okay to admit that I hurt sometimes. Ignoring anything that might pull us further from a few minutes earlier than we already were, I settled on a nod of my head and a quiet admission of my own. "Thank you. I hurt sometimes. Okay, I hurt a lot of the time. But it isn't so bad that we need to go to the kitchen. I just need to remember to move a little more."

With a blush that matched his, I gave him a genuine smile. "Thank you, really. For thinking about me and caring. And honestly, thank you for telling me. I don't think I would have been ready to hear that before now, but it means a lot."

Larson shuffled forward and gave me a giant hug. His huge arms made me feel tiny in comparison, but I found myself returning the hug with a smile on my face. We didn't separate until Logan's cheerful voice filled the room. "Group hug!" Before we could pull apart, Logan had thrown his arms around us, and two additional sets of arms joined. At some point, we fell into a heap laughing. The serious mood that had hung between Larson and me a moment before had been broken, and I found myself relaxing around my friends for the first time in years.

CHAPTER TWENTY-THREE

MERRICK

Aiden, Trent, and Logan pulled in just behind Travis and Caleb. Logan was hurrying up the walk with a giant gift bag and a grin on his face that told me he was up to something. I shot Trent a questioning look, but he only shrugged. "He won't tell anyone." He was weighed down by two bags and what appeared to be a heavy blanket.

He made to step inside, but Canyon patted the bench beside him. "Take a load off. Literally. We're giving them some time to settle down in there."

Trent placed the blanket and bags down on the bench, then took a seat himself. "How do parents do this? My sister and her husband lug all this shit into my parents' house when they bring the kids to spend the night. Hell, Mom already has half of it, but does that matter? Nooooo. This one likes *this* and that one likes *that*." He rolled his eyes dramatically. "Two bags and Logan's weighted blanket are enough for me!"

Travis put his bag down and took a seat next to Trent,

clapping him on the back. "I think it might be something to do with Logan and Aiden's stuff being a bit bigger and weighing more than kids' stuff." He pointed at the blanket. "And what made you bring that, anyway? He never takes that out of the house."

A fond look crossed Trent's face. "Logan's been acting weird lately. Is clingy the right word? I don't know how to describe it, but he's been going between normal Curious slash hyper Logan and kind of quieter and more reserved. He will swear up and down that he's not attached to this thing, but then he drags it all over the house and can't sleep without it."

Trent gave a casual shrug. "If, by some miracle, he tires himself out, I wanted to make sure he had his blanket. No matter how much he rolled his eyes at me when I brought it to the truck."

Trent's words hit close to home. I knew he was talking about Logan, but he could well have been talking about Dean. I'd packed his blanket and rabbit because I knew he'd want them if he got tired, whether he'd tell anyone or not.

Since we'd been spending more time together, he'd gone from the normal guy I'd known for all these years to a snarky, sarcastic guy who rolled his eyes and huffed more than he used words to communicate, to a guy happy to lose himself in cartoons, toys, and snuggles on the couch with his blanket and Babbit.

Aiden's teasing words at dinner about Logan being a middle came back to me. He'd spoken quietly enough that I knew he hadn't intended for anyone at the other end of the table to hear them. Given that there had been a convenient lull in our conversation, I'd heard but only barely made his words out. At the time, I'd heard middle and had thought more about Dean than Logan. Then we'd started talking again and I'd forgotten all about what Aiden had said. Now the snippet of conversation had come back to me, and I was replaying it with my focus on Logan instead of Dean. I could see Aiden's point and I could clearly remember the hint of resignation in Logan's voice when he'd told Aiden that Trent wasn't his Daddy. Were they as clueless as Dean and I had been?

It was hard to imagine those two not realizing something that important, but what did I know? Dean was just discovering his middle side while I was only just beginning to discover I was a Daddy. Or maybe just *Dean's* Daddy.

"Earth to Merrick."

I blinked back to the conversation to see Canyon waving his hand in front of my face. "Whoa. Sorry, got lost in thought."

Canyon chuckled. "I'd say so. We were getting ready to head inside before the boys eat all the donuts in there. Larson doesn't need another donut today."

Trent groaned, the bags and Logan's blanket already in his arms. "And Logan *definitely* doesn't need that much sugar. He'll be bouncing off the walls."

We walked into the house to a cacophony of sound from near the kitchen. I worried that they had gotten into the donuts and would be on sugar highs the rest of the day. When we followed the sound, all five of them were gathered on the floor next to the fireplace. A rug that had streets filled with cars and tiny felted mushroom homes was surrounded by Aiden, Larson, and Dean, each of them moving a different car around the roads. From where I stood, it looked like they were heading to the same spot, a giant car track set up next to the rug.

A few feet away, Caleb and Logan had dumped out a bucket of LEGO bricks and were building little cars as fast as they could find wheels.

I'd been around their playdates before, and they had never been this loud. Larson, Aiden, and Caleb didn't seem to be as little as they normally were when they got together. The quiet conversations and giggles I'd come to expect from afternoon playdates had been replaced with talking about favorite games, what they were building, where they were going, and the occasional outburst about a car beating them to a store or a house. The noise only got louder as all five made it over to the racetrack.

From what I'd gathered of their conversation, this was supposed to be a drag race for the cars.

Dean's palm made contact with his forehead. "Shoot! I don't have my phone. I don't have a timer!"

Logan groaned as well. "*Daddy* made us give him ours too."

Aiden rolled his eyes at Logan, but Larson was scrambling to his feet. "I have a stopwatch in the garage. I use it when I'm lifting." He got to his feet, not paying attention to anything but getting to the stopwatch, and didn't stop until he saw us standing there. "Oh! Hi. I need to get my stopwatch. We're having a race."

He made it almost to the door before Logan's words

stopped him. "Oh! You're finally inside. Now I can give Larson his present!"

Larson stopped in his tracks and turned around. "Stopwatch?"

Logan looked at the bag. "But I got you a present! It's been killing me not to give it to you before they got their asses in here."

Aiden bumped his shoulder into Logan's. "You said a bad word."

I had to put my hand to my mouth to not laugh. A quick glance around showed that I was not the only one struggling to keep from laughing at the interaction.

Logan stuck his tongue out at his boyfriend. "I get to say bad words."

Trent finally spoke up, ending the conversation quickly. "*Pup.*" His low, warning tone had Logan turning toward him. "You need to watch your language around the boys."

Logan glowered at Trent. While he didn't argue with him, he did cross his arms and pout. "Fine. But I still want to give him his gift!"

Larson could have already gotten the stopwatch and been back in the time they'd been bickering. Canyon finally stopped the argument by holding up a stopwatch he pulled from a drawer. "Here, we've got an extra. Problem solved. And Larson can come back and get his gift… whatever that might be."

Logan bounced on his knees before springing up and nearly sprinting toward the hallway. He was back before Larson had made it back to the rug. "Open. Open!"

Caleb scooted away from the rug, getting more

comfortable on the floor beside Dean, and shook his head. "He's worse than Dexter's niece and nephew."

It was then that I realized Dean's lower back was exposed and I warred with myself as to whether I should tug it down or leave it alone. Canyon's hand landed on my shoulder. "Don't do it. Just let him be in the moment."

I thought about his words as Larson reached into the gift bag that Logan had thrust into his hands. Canyon might not have been the only one who had noticed, but Travis's furrowed brow as he looked Dean's way could have been something to do with Caleb, or completely unrelated to anything going on at the moment.

Larson finally pulled an item out of the bag, and it expanded to be a black shirt with his woodshop's information on the back in bold tan writing. None of us could figure out why he was laughing as hard as he was until he turned it around. The design on the front was the same color, but above the saw blade that had the logo of his shop on it were the words "Like my wood? Come see it at…"

I'd had no idea eyes could get as wide as Trent's did at that moment.

By the way Logan was wiggling and bouncing his legs, I had a feeling that the surprises weren't over yet. Not leaving us in suspense long, Larson pulled numerous shirts out of the bag, all with the same design.

"There's actually a shirt for all of us. I just didn't know how to give them to everyone. I hope you like it." Logan glanced behind him, an uncharacteristic vulnerability in his smile as his eyes found Trent.

Trent gave Logan a smile and a nod, and the worry in

Logan's face disappeared, leaving only a bright smile in its place. At least until it was replaced with surprise as Larson nearly tackle hugged him to the floor, repeatedly thanking him for the shirt.

It didn't matter how ridiculous they were; I knew every one of us would wear them.

After a few minutes, a number of hugs, and even more giggles from the boys, they settled down to get back to their game. Canyon cleared his throat. "Let's get lunch ready. They're going to be complaining that they're hungry before long."

The next ninety minutes were spent making lunch in the outdoor kitchen so we didn't bother the men playing. Once it was done, we began filling their plates. I knew Dean well enough to know to pass over the tricolored pasta salad but add the pasta salad made with macaroni noodles.

Nothing about doing that was awkward and none of the other guys thought twice about my plating Dean's lunch. When I was done, his food was all placed carefully. Things got close and touched in places, but they weren't as haphazardly piled as my own plate would be. Looking around, I realized Dean's plate wasn't close to as cleanly plated as the ones Trent was carrying. He'd filled them both carefully, though one was definitely piled higher than the other and obviously Logan's.

He glanced back and gave me an exaggerated sigh. "Ah, you've got it easy. Logan hates food touching. He always has. It just took me until Aiden came along for me to figure that out. There are more divided plates in our house now than most parents of toddlers have. Of course, Logan's are all solid colored instead of bright patterns like Aiden's."

His smile was fond as he turned to go into the house. I couldn't help my eye roll at them. They really were *that* clueless.

Canyon's deep voice easily carried over the laughter of the boys gathered around the racetrack. "Lunchtime! Come on over to the table."

Logan's head popped up first, his blue eyes barely visible over the counter. "Can we eat over here?"

Trent actually snorted at the request. "Not a chance, pup. There will be no greasy fingerprints all over Larson's toys. You seem to forget that I live with you two. Our boy has a gift of wearing as much food as he gets in his mouth."

Dean's head appeared beside Logan's. The first thing I noticed was how bright his eyes were. He was happier and more relaxed than I'd ever seen him, his smile only growing wider when he spotted the plate in my hand. His glance flickered to the toys for a second, then he looked back and spoke directly to me. "Do we need to clean up before lunch?"

As he asked the question, I understood why he'd been nervous to come alone. The innocence of the question, the uncertainty in his voice, and his inability to figure out the right thing to do were clear. And the fact that he'd looked directly at me for those answers showed how much he trusted me. He might not have called me Daddy, but he was asking his Daddy for guidance.

"You'll need to clean up before we leave, but for now eat before things get cold."

The uncertainty in his eyes cleared as I spoke, leaving me feeling pride in not only him, but in myself too.

A moment later, the five were rushing to the table to eat. As a whole, the group still wasn't as little as they normally were. I'd seen a few rush off to the bathroom a few times, and Travis had reminded Caleb to go at least once since we'd arrived. Despite none of them being overly little, Trent still secured a bib around Aiden's neck.

Before leaving, Trent bent over and kissed the top of Aiden's head, then Logan's, and warned them to behave. I found myself longing to be able to bend over and kiss the top of Dean's head and watch him grin like his friends had.

At least I got to see a bright smile when I handed him the plastic tumbler with apple juice in it. I'd seen apple juice at his house enough to know that he liked it. When Canyon had asked what to get Dean for a drink, I'd passed the insight on without a second thought. I definitely thought about it when I saw his face light up when he noticed what was in the cup.

He didn't speak, but his smile spoke volumes. With each glance from Dean, I felt a restless part of my soul settle. The first chance we had, we were going to have a serious talk, though it could wait a little longer. For the rest of the day, my only plan was to enjoy where we were.

CHAPTER TWENTY-FOUR

DEAN

My knees ached from sitting on them while we played on the rug but, for the first time in longer than I could remember, my back didn't hurt. Merrick had taken to rubbing my back any time I was around him. His fingers were always gentle and I rarely found myself uncomfortable. The more he'd done it, the better my back had felt, and the easier it loosened up when it did get tight for some reason.

If I let myself think about it much longer, I was going to start paying more attention to the way Merrick kept giving me encouraging smiles and was always nearby if I needed something. Those moments made my stomach flutter each time.

Aiden, Larson, and Caleb had moved from the cars to playing with dinosaurs and army men. Those hadn't held my interest much, so I'd been slowly putting away the cars and tracks, trying to figure out what to do next. Logan must have been on the same page because he'd disappeared to the back porch a few minutes earlier and I hadn't seen him since.

Still feeling uneasy about talking with Canyon, Travis, and Trent, I hadn't wanted to follow. Once he'd been gone a handful of minutes, I decided Logan wasn't coming back and began scanning the room for something that would hold my attention. A stack of coloring books and crayons looked like a nice distraction, and I could sit at the table or on the love seat beside the rug to save my knees and back.

Focused on finding a coloring book I liked, I hadn't noticed Logan coming back inside. When he tapped my shoulder, I nearly jumped out of my skin. "Sorry. I went out to ask if we could play video games. Trent and your… uh, Merrick said we could! Canyon said we can go to the living room and play." He glanced toward the other three. "They'll get all distracted by the video games and bug us. It happens every time I start playing a game."

If it wasn't bad enough that I'd nearly called Merrick Daddy a number of times already, Logan had almost slipped up as well. We weren't doing a very good job of being just friends if Logan had picked up on my feelings.

Before I could agree to the plan, the back door opened and Trent and Merrick walked in. They gave us smiles as they headed through the house, and Logan gripped my elbow. "Quick, before they notice." He motioned with his chin toward the other three while leading me through the kitchen and toward the living room.

The living room had an amazing view of the entire property as well as Nashville. We settled onto the large couch, the view of downtown Nashville sprawled in front of us with our backs facing the patio the others were sitting on.

We were debating if we'd be here long enough to see Nashville light up like a giant Christmas tree after sunset when Trent and Merrick walked in. In one arm, Trent had the giant blanket that we'd covered up with at their place and in his other arm was a backpack. Merrick had only brought the backpack, but I couldn't help thinking it appeared fuller than it should have from the toys and my Switch.

Logan scooted closer to me and motioned for Trent to drape the heavy blanket over both of us. "There, now maybe you'll actually stay seated for ten minutes. Every time I've looked in here for the last hour, you've been somewhere else or bouncing in place." He leaned down and kissed Logan's forehead. "I was starting to wonder if you needed your hood and knee pads for a bit."

I didn't hear the rest of the conversation because Merrick set the bag he was carrying on the couch beside me. "Having fun, Bean?"

"Yeah. Thanks for coming with me."

Merrick nodded, masking an emotion I couldn't quite read, but I did catch that he rubbed idly at his chest for a moment before turning his attention back to the bag. I almost missed the quiet words he spoke more to the bag than me. "Anytime."

Hope sparked inside me. Maybe I wasn't making the connection up or falling for someone I couldn't have. Maybe Merrick felt the same things for me. Maybe we could find a way—

My thoughts were cut off when he produced my blanket and Babbit and placed them on my lap. "What? Why?"

The corner of his lip turned upward. "I kind of figured the two of you needed some quiet time, and I know how much these mean to you. I can't remember the last time I saw you relaxing without them."

I fought to keep my embarrassment in check, but the heat in my cheeks let me know I wasn't doing a very good job. Then Merrick reached out and smoothed my hair back. "Relax, Bean. Figure out what you like. You were having a lot of fun playing with the other guys, but now you and Logan can have some quiet time too." He leaned in closer and nearly whispered to me. "And Logan is sharing his blankie with you."

My eyes widened as I looked at the blanket covering my lap. It was so heavy. How could this be his blanket?

Merrick chuckled. "Yeah. Trent says Logan doesn't sleep without it."

At least my embarrassment faded as I processed the words. So many questions for Logan. Then the bright red game controller was placed in my hands. "Do you need anything else?"

"My phone?"

Laughter filled the room, but I couldn't figure out what was so funny about the statement. Finally, Merrick pulled himself together and shook his head. "If you want to play the Mario game, let me know. You guys can go to the kitchen and you can have your phones in there. Until then, no phones."

Narrowing my eyes, I made to protest, but Logan's singsong voice cut the words off before they had a chance to make it out of my mouth. "Thank you, *Daddy*!"

Trent huffed. "Pup." The word had been delivered as a warning, but Logan only smiled brighter. After a few seconds, Trent ruffled his hair. "Be a good pup with Dean."

Logan's blond hair had grown out and it flopped as he nodded eagerly. The two left the room and Logan sobered as he turned his game on. "Join?"

I pressed the power button on my own game. Logan didn't stay quiet long, turning toward me before either of our games had finished loading. "Your bunny is cute. I have a prairie dog at home."

"Thanks." Logan was smiling again, and there was no evidence of judgment in his tone. "His name is Babbit." I had no idea what possessed me to admit that, but it was out there and I wanted to crawl into a hole.

Logan wiggled a bit and pointed to my screen, reminding me to play the game that had finally loaded. "Pierre's in a drawer in my old room."

Something about being alone with Logan made my filter nonexistent, causing me to say the first thing that popped into my head. "Why?"

A friend request popped up on the screen from Logan and I'd accepted it before he spoke again. "Trent got it for me a few years ago. It was right after I'd discovered my pup side. He said it was cute, like me."

I heard the fondness in Logan's voice as I chased his character through the village. Bumping my shoulder into his, I teased a bit. "That's because you *are* cute. Especially when you're not bouncing all over the place and yelling."

He let out a hearty laugh. "I've heard that a few times. My blanket helps, though. And at night I have Aiden and Trent. Sometimes, I forget where I am or to censor my reactions when I get excited."

"But you have Trent for that too."

Logan's puppy, wearing a pair of overalls in the same color aqua as Logan's puppy hood, stopped and grabbed apples from a tree. The little dog handed one to my duck. "Gives us energy."

We got lost in our game for a few minutes before Logan spoke quietly. "I do. But he's got Aiden to look after too, so I try not to make more work for him. I'm enough work just as I am."

It took a few minutes for me to figure out what he was alluding to but eventually I landed on what I thought he was getting at. "Is that why you've never told him you want him to be your Daddy? Because you don't want to add more to his plate?"

Logan's character walked straight into the side of a house. He didn't bother correcting his path as he set the game on his lap. The movement made me look up from my screen to find him staring at me. "What are you talking about?"

I didn't bother trying to backtrack because I needed to know. I was discovering this whole new side of myself and needed someone who understood. Awkward as it was, I pushed ahead. "Well, Aiden said you're a middle at dinner. It makes sense. You don't have a problem playing with them"—I motioned into the other room where I could still hear the three playing with their dinosaur toys—"but you also like to play video games. And I see how you look to Trent for answers sometimes. And you listen to him. A lot like..." My voice trailed off before I could say *like me*.

As it turned out, I didn't need to. Logan finished the sentence for me. "A lot like you do with Merrick?"

My voice refused to work, so I settled on a nod instead.

Logan let go of the game completely, then leaned back against the couch. "We're a mess."

"Merrick swears he doesn't want a boyfriend." Well, at least my voice was back.

He snorted at my answer. "Has he told himself that? I hadn't figured it out until you two were so late to dinner, but it's obvious that he's into you. The way he looks at you now is way more than even a simple *damn, he's hot*. If you haven't noticed that he looks at you like you hung the fucking moon and stars, you're blind."

"I kind of thought I was making it up."

Logan rolled his eyes at me. "Nope."

"But you're already with Trent and Aiden. It's got to be less complicated for you. You three are relationship goals. Aiden knows you're a middle. It sounds like you do too." Patting the blanket covering us, I continued. "I have a feeling Trent knows too."

His hand waved about, nearly making contact with my face before I caught it and pushed it down between us. "Holding my hand down does not help me think."

I hadn't expected the giggle that came from me as I held

firmly to his hand. "Well, if you break my glasses, I'm not going to be able to see."

"Then your not-Daddy would probably get frustrated with me."

"And your not-Daddy would be frustrated too."

Logan slumped against my shoulder. "I don't want to rock the boat. I never thought I'd get Trent in the first place. Somehow, I ended up with Trent *and* Aiden. I've got two amazing boyfriends and I'm happier than I've ever been. I don't need more to be happy. What we have is enough."

From my position, it sounded like Logan was trying to convince himself of that more than me.

"Besides, Trent's the sheriff, he's Aiden's Daddy, he's my handler when I'm a pup. He's also my sounding board for any problem, and constantly watching out for me at work, at home, and at the club. He already worries that I'm going to rush into something dangerous and get myself killed. I don't want to make things awkward. I don't want things to change exactly. It's so confusing in my head."

His right hand flew up and knocked a pillow off the couch. He hadn't been kidding about being unable to think without moving his hands. At least I wasn't going to end up with a black eye or bloody nose if I held his left hand down while he gathered his thoughts.

Sighing, I couldn't help but agree with Logan about part of it. "I get confusing."

"I don't need him to take care of me. I really can function on my own. There are just some times that I get distracted or it feels like a lot. That's why I like Curious. He doesn't have to think. But there's also part of me that kind of needs that release without being a pup. That makes no sense, does it?"

"More than you think, honestly." And it did. It made a lot of sense to me. Having to totally switch mindsets to relax would be stressful for me. I was already figuring out that not having to make every decision was freeing. I didn't have to be a different person—or persona—or in a special outfit for Merrick to step in and tell me to eat, go home, or head to bed. As weird as it still was to me, I liked those times.

Logan's sigh sounded like he'd been holding it in for a long time. "Sometimes, I kind of need Trent to help me make decisions or tell me when to stop. And I do like when he puts his foot down and tucks me in some nights. Without that, I'd just keep going without noticing I was exhausted. And I love when he pulls me toward him for a hug or a cuddle. It helps my brain stop racing. Part of me wants to tell him that, but a bigger part of me is afraid it's going to be the thing that pushes him away."

I let out a sigh that matched Logan's. "I get that too. I know I need to talk to Merrick, but I'm afraid things will change."

Logan hummed. "Yup." Then he leaned a little closer, as though what he was going to say was a secret, but he still spoke louder than necessary. "To make matters worse, I still don't feel submissive. But he naturally takes control and it feels… right I guess. Things quiet in my brain and I don't feel so jumpy. If I get all sarcastic and call him Daddy sometimes, it keeps me from saying it sincerely. And he only gets playfully frustrated."

My heart hurt for Logan, and I found myself leaning into him. "I get that. I stopped teasingly calling Mer Dad when I realized what I really wanted to call him was Daddy."

We sat in silence for a moment before I gathered my thoughts. "Do you think Trent would really get mad if you called him Daddy and weren't being sarcastic?"

"Honestly? I don't know. Maybe? Probably not. I think I'm building it up in my head."

"You sound like me."

He turned toward me, the muscles beneath my hand going slack. "I put the dog in my drawer when we moved into Trent's room. We already took over his bed with my blanket and Aiden's stuff. I tried not to bring my blanket —it's so big and heavy—but Trent kept bringing it over. I'm kind of surprised he never saw the dog. Guess I hid that well." The look on Logan's face rivaled any sad puppy face I'd ever seen. "He'd basically given us his entire bed, what would he have thought if he'd seen *that* too?"

"That the custom bed I've been eyeing up since Aiden first spent the night with us was a higher priority."

Trent's voice made us both jump in surprise. He looked as sad as Logan, and I wanted to find a way to comfort them both. "Pup, why didn't you tell me all this?"

Logan's mouth opened and shut a few times as Trent made his way over to us.

To my surprise, Merrick was standing to the other side

of Trent. Trent's body had blocked my view of him until he had started walking toward Logan.

Merrick looked disappointed as he made his way to me. We might as well have been completely alone in the house for all I noticed Logan and Trent talking beside us.

"I'm sorry." He wrapped an arm around me, pulling me close to his body. "I should have talked to you earlier, when I figured things out for myself."

My fingers worked at the soft fur on Babbit's ear. I didn't know where this was going or how much he'd heard. Hell, I didn't know what he'd figured out. It had taken me thirty-five years to understand that I needed to be able to escape my head by handing control to someone else. He was ten years older, with more experience. As long as I'd known him, he'd steadfastly insisted that he didn't want a boyfriend.

I should have protected my heart better when I'd first realized I felt more than friendship toward him. I should have stopped things before they ever got to the point that I couldn't see myself with another Daddy. He never should have gotten close enough to know that my blanket wasn't just a random couch throw or to figure out that I'd not only needed this day but that I'd needed someone—needed him—with me. My heart had gotten involved and I'd allowed myself to ignore the inevitable heartbreak.

It looked as though I wouldn't be able to ignore it any longer. Reality had caught up with me and I couldn't see a way out of this that didn't end in a broken heart and a lost friendship.

Fuck, we'd been stupid.

A finger ran down my cheek, then warm lips made contact with my forehead. "You deserve so much more than what I've given you so far. I hope I'll get the chance to make that up to you. I want to be around as more than a friend with benefits or just someone you trust. It took me a little while to figure that out."

"Wait." Had I heard him right? Thirty seconds earlier, I'd been bracing myself for the moment he told me he was sorry he'd led me on. What he was saying didn't sound like a goodbye. Far from it. "What about single and happy?"

He ran a hand through his silver hair but refused to let go of me. "I was wrong. It wasn't a Tom thing, or a Dean thing, or a life thing. It was all a Merrick thing. The only thing that I can blame you for is making me feel things I hadn't felt in years. And maybe giving me the push to figure out that it was all me holding myself back."

CHAPTER TWENTY-FIVE

MERRICK

Trent and Logan had moved to another room to talk, probably with Aiden if I had to take a guess. At the moment, I didn't care if they were sitting next to us or not. Dean was my only priority. He had been for longer than I'd allowed myself to admit. From the little bit of the conversation I'd overheard, it was clear I'd fucked up.

My plan to talk with him at some point this weekend when he'd had plenty of time to digest the day had been thrown to hell. The talk was happening now, ready or not.

Dean bit his bottom lip as he stared at me for longer than was comfortable. The flesh was red and swollen when he released it only to utter one word. "What?"

I pressed my lips to his forehead, inhaling the scent that was pure Dean. I could tell he'd sweat earlier, but the saltiness on my lips wasn't unwelcome. "I have this habit of holding things in and running when life gets tough. I ran from home. I ran from New York. I ran from my family and other relationships. I never gave anyone a chance to fight for me."

My chuckle came out closer to a scoff. "Not that I'd have wanted Tom to fight for me. That was over. But I never gave my parents a chance to have my back. I didn't tell them how awful it was when the school discovered I was gay. I didn't give my best friend a chance to apologize or explain. I didn't give my friends at the bar a chance to ask me to stay. The going got tough, and I got going."

Dean gripped my hand, his slender fingers appearing small against mine. He didn't say anything, but I took the fact that he was still sitting next to me as a good sign. It took me a moment to gather my thoughts, knowing that I needed to get this right. "Then I found this group of guys in Tennessee." I looked directly into his eyes, watching his pupils dilate and contract as he stared back at me. "Goofy, loud, funny, fierce. Shit, they hooked me. Through thick and thin. I ran, they called. I left, they beckoned. For years, I kept coming back. Over and over, through ups and downs, relationships and breakups. Emergency room visits and surgeries. I kept finding myself back here until one day I didn't want to leave again. I'd found the place that I knew accepted me, no matter what."

He squeezed my hand gently, and his words were almost whispered. "You're stuck with us."

I felt my head nod in agreement. "I am. And there's one particular guy here who's kinda gotten under my skin."

Color filled Dean's cheeks at the comment, and it was too hard to resist rubbing my thumb over one. "But old habits die hard and I sort of forgot to tell him as much."

"Really?" The question sounded more like a plea.

"Yeah. Really. All of it. I've spent the entire day deciding when and how to talk with you. I figured out weeks ago that you were meant for me, but I kept making excuses as to why it wouldn't work. I hope I didn't wait too long?"

Dean's pursed lips made me worry. He hadn't said he was mine, but he hadn't said I was too late either. He licked his lips and looked at his lap. After a few slow breaths, Dean looked into my eyes. "I guess that all depends."

My heart beat harder than I thought possible, definitely harder than was safe for a man my age. "On what?"

His eyes cleared, his back straightened, and he spoke clearly, though I could hear the worry in his voice. "On you."

"Me?" I didn't know if it was humanly possible for my eyes to get wider. I'd just told him I'd been wrong and that I wanted him.

"Yeah. Can you handle being Merrick my boyfriend *and* Daddy? I wasn't just saying that I wanted you to come today because I know you aren't going to judge me. I wanted you to be here today because I can't see anyone else being in your place right now. But I'm not just looking for a boyfriend, Merrick. It's taken me all this time to figure out that I'm happiest when someone else takes control. It's not something I can ignore now that I've figured it out."

I fought to contain the relief threatening to escape as a laugh. "If anything, I could see myself being bossier than I've been. I'm all in, Bean. You've been my boy since the moment I heard about that Tony superhero guy."

Dean blinked at me. "Tony? Are you talking about Tony Stark?"

"Yes! That guy. Thank fuck you know who he is."

Dean's chuckle didn't hide his confusion, but at least he was smiling. "I don't know what Tony Stark or Iron Man has to do with me, but I guess I'll take it?"

I waved my hand in front of my face. "It's a long story. You should probably ask Larson if you actually want to understand any of it. But while he was talking about the secretary being his Mommy or something like that, he mentioned middles, and it all fell into place."

"I don't know if I'm going to ask Larson or not at this point."

Shrugging, I could only smile at the entire thing. "It really doesn't matter. In the end, that was what helped me figure it out. That and a long conversation with Canyon and my family. Each person I spoke to had a different piece of the puzzle falling into place. By the time I tucked you in last night, I already saw myself as your Daddy. If there'd been any lingering doubt, it would have been erased when you called me Daddy this morning."

The grin that had been growing on Dean's face as I spoke vanished. "Wait. I did what?"

Pulling him to my side so that I could wrap my arm around him, I kissed his temple, then his jaw, and finally his swollen lip. It took all my willpower to not turn the kiss into more than just a meeting of lips. "As I tried to get out of bed this morning, you called me Daddy. Believe me, if I wasn't committed to us, I'd have been out the door before you were fully awake."

Looking around the house, I could see Larson and Caleb sitting on the patio with their Daddies. Caleb's eyes were drooping shut as Canyon read the two a book. Trent, Aiden, and Logan hadn't reappeared yet, but I knew they were somewhere having their own important discussion. "As part of this group, I've known for years that *Daddy* is a special title. What I hadn't understood was just how special it was when someone you truly care about says it. After I heard it from your lips, I knew I was all in."

I lightly pressed my finger to his nose. "I plan on being your Daddy for as long as you'll be my Bean."

He somehow managed to smile despite having cheeks so red they looked like they'd catch fire at any second. Then his head began to bob rapidly. Tears welled in his eyes, but he wrapped his arms around my body and buried his face in my neck before I could ask why. The only thing I could do was hug him tight as he pulled himself together.

We were finally reminded that we weren't alone when a door shut and feet shuffled toward the kitchen. A moment later, Larson appeared. I watched as he went to the fridge to grab something, then turned and briefly glanced into the living room. Then he did a comical double take at seeing our embrace.

"Did you two finally figure it out?"

Dean lifted his head from my shoulder, but there were no words from him, so I answered for us. "It seems that way."

"Finally!" He turned on his heel and hurried toward the patio calling for Canyon. "Daddy, guess what!"

I wiped my thumb over Dean's cheeks. "Fifteen seconds and the entire house is going to know."

He barked out a laugh. "You wish. Eight, max."

"Are you okay with that? We can leave now if you want."

Canyon's voice carried in from the patio. "It's about damn time. I thought we were going to have to lock them in a room and refuse them food and water before they finally admitted their feelings."

Dean dropped his head, but his shoulders were shaking with laughter, not tears. "No reason to leave. They all know now. Besides, I think Larson mentioned cupcakes later."

"To be fair, I think they all knew before today." I gave his shoulders a final squeeze as I stood up. "I'd been coming in to give you water. Do you need anything else?"

"Uh, it would help if my game partner was here. Other than that, I can't think of anything I need."

There was uncertainty in his eyes again. We'd been through a lot in the last half hour, so it wasn't surprising that he was feeling a little out of sorts. "How about I grab you a snack to get you through until dinner? I'm pretty sure there's plenty of leftovers in the kitchen."

"Did you hear my stomach?" Dean looked down and rubbed his flat belly.

I couldn't deny that I was relieved to be laughing at the moment. When I'd first sat down on the couch, the fear that I'd lost my chance had been real. "Just a bit. I swear I fed you lunch a few hours ago, and it wasn't small."

Dean's grin lit the room more than the picture windows ever could. "I'm a growing boy."

I was still grinning as I made my way to the kitchen to find him something to eat. It looked as though he wasn't the only one hungry since Travis was at the counter putting peanut butter on graham crackers. "I take it things went well?"

He handed a plate and clean knife over to me. "Yeah. I think we figured it out."

Travis smiled, though it looked sad. "I'm glad. I can see you two are happy together. I feel awful that I've been pushing him to find a boy. I'm thankful you saw what we missed and followed your gut."

"If it helps, I think Dean missed it too." It was easier to focus on spreading the peanut butter than looking at Travis, so that was where my eyes stayed. "I think that, if it wasn't for you finding Caleb, none of us would have figured ourselves out. We all lived the stereotypical, oblivious male lives until Caleb shook the group up. He saw things in a different way than we had, and in a lot of ways, he's helped us all understand ourselves better."

I could have waxed poetic about how important all of the guys were to me and how they'd given me the freedom and security I'd needed all these years. Part of me wanted to announce to the entire room that they were my family and I loved them all.

Travis hummed as he made little sandwiches out of the crackers, then broke them into rectangular pieces before arranging them carefully on a plate. "I know I lucked out with him, but looking around the house, I think we all got pretty lucky."

There wasn't much I could say to that, so I hummed an agreement as I finished Dean's snack. "I'm going to take this back to the other room. I think he needs some space for a bit."

"Understandable. I'm going to go give these to Larson and Cal before they revolt. Cal was almost asleep after the story Canyon read, but Larson's yell woke him up. Now he's hungry. I'll take care of my boy; you go take care of yours."

My grin was so wide my face hurt. "I plan to." It took me a few minutes to clean up, then I returned to the living room to find Dean where I'd left him. His blanket and rabbit were in his lap as he focused on the game in his hands.

He looked up as my shadow moved across the screen. His eyes went wide with happiness when he saw the plate. "My grandma makes those for me. They're my favorite." The snack was enough for him to put the game in his lap in exchange for the plate. "Thank you."

He reached for one of the rectangles and just before popping it into his mouth, he forced out, "Daddy." His cheeks flooded with red. It hadn't been easy for him to say, yet he'd managed.

Pride and happiness swelled inside me. "You're very welcome, Bean. Do you want me to hang out in here with you?"

The blush faded as Dean looked around the room. "You're welcome to. But I don't need you to. Besides, I'm sure the other guys are bursting with questions." He wrinkled his nose at the thought. "I'll be honest. I'm not ready to talk to them about it. I kind of want to stay here and lose myself in my game again and forget about all of that. Is it bad that I feel like I need some alone time?"

The pride I felt just kept growing. "As long as you're not trying to push me away, I can understand the need for space."

Dean looked over, another tiny sandwich halfway to his mouth, and shook his head. His posture wasn't as stiff, his eyes weren't as serious, and his smile wasn't as tentative.

"Promise. I just want to play my game."

"Alright. I'll be on the patio if you need me."

His eye roll told me he thought I was being ridiculous, but when he spoke, I could hear the sincerity in his voice. "Thank you."

Our conversation had pulled him back to reality before he'd been ready. I didn't need anyone to tell me that Dean needed time to process everything we'd discussed, and he was going to work through it best by giving his adult brain a rest.

There weren't as many questions as I'd expected when I returned to my seat on the patio. Canyon gave me a wink and Travis nodded his head in my direction.

The two were a lot more interested in what was taking Logan, Aiden, and Trent so long and where they'd gone off to. I couldn't help wondering how Trent was going to handle two boys. I'd always thought the three were chaotic as they were. I was still contemplating the chaos of their home when Trent sank into the seat beside me.

"When will that man figure out that he's not a bother? Fucking hell, I feel like an asshole. All this time telling him to stop calling me Daddy when what he needed was me to be his Daddy." He scrubbed his hands over his face and groaned.

Travis didn't immediately answer, instead looking around like he was expecting someone to pop out of nowhere. "Where're your boys?"

Trent threw his thumb over his shoulder. "Aiden fell asleep, and Logan went to find Dean. They were starting their game again when I left the room."

With Trent's words, Travis noticeably relaxed and began to speak. "You're going to have to show him he's not too much. How many times has that man been told he's too hyper, too crazy, too loud, too... much?"

"All the time. Christ, even I tell him to tone it down."

Travis chuckled. "But you're his Trent. You've been the most important person in his life since high school. We all know that Logan's always been worried about not being what you need. You guys have this natural balance that I'm not sure any of us could manage, yet you do it effortlessly. Maybe it's always been there, maybe he's just discovering it, but Logan needs more than he has in the past. I can understand why he's worried."

Frustration radiated off Trent, but I got the feeling it wasn't directed at the change in their dynamics, just at not being able to fix everything immediately. It was a feeling I understood well. He threw his hands in the air, though he kept his voice low. "It's not that I'm worried about him being too much; it's that I don't know what he needs. He's never been submissive. He doesn't like pain play. It's not like he's looking for a Dom in the traditional sense, and he's not looking for someone to spank his ass or put him in time-out. I can't figure out how to give him what he needs without smothering him, yet he wants me to make choices and take control. I have to make things better and I don't know how."

Logically, I knew Trent was speaking about himself and Logan, but I could easily see that being Dean and me. Pain play of any sort was off the table. We didn't need to discuss that. At times, he still struggled with my hands rubbing his back, though I'd noticed he didn't wince nearly as often now as he used to. So how did I set boundaries and show him I cared?

My mind was racing to recall every article I'd read on age play, especially where middles were involved. "Consistency!" The word was out before the thought had fully formed, and I became the focus of the men around the patio.

Three heads turned my way, and Trent's eyebrow rose in question. "What about it?"

Now that my brain had latched onto the thought, it was clear in my head. "When my brother was a teenager, he used to bitch all the time that my mom made him go to bed at midnight on school nights. One phone call, when my mom admitted she was tired of the fight, I asked why she fought it. She told me it was because she was giving him constant reminders that she cared. My brother might not have known it, but the consistency of the argument was my mom continuing to show him love."

My friends were listening intently, but I could tell they hadn't figured out how my thoughts related to anything. They'd get there, but they needed to see the entire picture. "When I was growing up, it was a rule that I did the dishes after dinner. I hated it for the longest time. Then in high school, I started to appreciate it. Not necessarily doing the dishes but the predictability of it. It never changed. I knew what was expected of me, and I did it. The few times I wasn't able to, I felt all out of sorts."

Canyon nodded thoughtfully, and his voice came out softer than normal. "I think I see where you're getting at."

"When I left home, the thing I missed most was doing the dishes with my mom in the kitchen. There were no more hugs, no more nightly chats, no more laughs. Even though I didn't tell my parents how bad shit was outside of the house, in the house I was always loved and accepted. It didn't matter if I yelled and lashed out because I was angry at something, I still had to do the dishes. It didn't matter if I fucked up and got my ass sent to my room or grounded. Mom would still knock on my door, give me a hug, and tell me she loved me... even if I didn't love myself at the time. Then she'd tell me to get my ass downstairs to wash the dishes.

"Middles need structure and routines. They still need to know that there is someone there when they need it, and they need that space to be protected and cared for when the world gets too much."

Trent slapped his thigh, the sound echoing through the trees. "Oh, that makes sense! It doesn't have to be a control or domination thing. Logan might just need the predictability, schedules, and routines. Damn, you're brilliant! Expectations and consequences. That was one of my mom's favorite things to remind us of as kids. I think my brother spent more time being grounded from the TV than watching it."

Travis snorted. "I'm sure you were so much better."

As they bickered, I was already planning how to implement my own set of rules, expectations, and consequences with Dean.

Hours later, when Canyon handed out the promised cupcakes—decorated to look like mushrooms—all the boys were tired. Logan and Dean came out from the living room where they'd stayed huddled on the couch, but even they yawned the entire way through dessert.

Wiping a smear of frosting from Dean's nose, I took the opportunity to give him a quick kiss. "Come on, Bean. Let's get you home."

He nodded and slid out of the chair. A few minutes later, we were leaving the house, Dean walking beside me with Blankie and Babbit in his arms and his backpack slung over my shoulder.

I'd thought he'd fallen asleep almost immediately, but before we made it to the highway, he spoke through a stifled yawn. "Can we stay at your place?"

"You sure?"

"Uh huh. Mooch shouldn't have to spend two nights alone." The statement was followed by a soft snore. Following his request, I directed us toward my apartment where Dean headed directly to my bed, pausing only long enough to say good night to Mooch.

CHAPTER TWENTY-SIX

DEAN

A tickle under my nose roused me from sleep. At first, I twitched my nose, trying to make the feeling go away. When that didn't work, I moved my face, only to have my eyelids tickled. Finally moving my hand, I made to brush whatever was on my face away and found a fine layer of hair.

Then the body attached to the hair vibrated as a laugh reverberated in my ear. My eyes shot open, my heart rate climbing at the unexpected person in my bed. The fear eased quickly when a strong arm wrapped around me and silver hair came into focus. I'd already figured out who I was using as a pillow before Merrick spoke. "You are a very tactile sleeper."

I adjusted so I could see his face, though Merrick's arm held me close. "Actually, I'm not usually. I've never liked people touching me while I sleep."

My head bounced a few times as he playfully flexed the bicep I was now resting on. "Maybe you don't like people touching *you*, but you certainly like using *me* as a pillow. I barely made it into bed and you were getting comfortable on me."

Not only had I slept the entire night, but I had no memory of getting into bed. I had my blanket and Babbit in my hands, but I could feel sheets instead of pajama pants against my legs. Looking down, I recognized the shirt I'd been wearing the day before, and when I lifted up the unfamiliar sheets, I was only wearing a pair of briefs.

As though he could read my mind, Merrick squeezed me in a reassuring embrace. "You were out of it last night. The day hit you hard. I tried to get you to change into your pajamas, but the best I could manage was convincing you to take your pants off after you insisted on telling Mooch good night."

That explained why the bed was all wrong. Pieces of the previous evening were coming back. There was a hazy memory of being worried about Mooch and instructing Merrick to go to his house, but nothing after that. Hell, I hardly remembered climbing into his car when we left Canyon's.

"Let's go to the kitchen so I can make us some breakfast."

This was beginning to feel a lot like the morning before. "Can I have coffee this time?"

I hadn't realized that Mooch was on the bed with us until Merrick's laughter startled him from sleep, causing him to growl and jump down. "I think coffee's fine. We have a lot to talk about anyway. I don't want to risk you falling asleep on me."

If he heard my grumbles, he did a good job ignoring them. I understood that we needed to talk, but it wasn't like I was looking forward to it. I'd heard about the awkward conversations the other guys had had as they worked out the details of their relationships. Wasn't it enough that I'd told Merrick I wanted him to be my Daddy?

Maybe the fact that we hadn't rolled out of bed yet and I was already pouting over the need to have it was exactly why we needed the conversation. "At least I get coffee."

He finally let me go and got up. "If you're lucky, you'll get Mooch cuddles too."

"Mooch!" The idea of hanging out with the cat was the motivation I'd needed. I made it as far as throwing back the covers when I remembered that I was only wearing a T-shirt and a pair of briefs. Merrick had seen me undressed before, but first thing in the morning, without sleep, lust, or post-orgasm bliss distracting me, I felt more vulnerable and exposed than when I'd been naked in front of him on Thursday night.

"Damn, that is one sexy ass."

I reflexively moved my hands over my backside, trying to cover as many of the scars as I could. He was by my side before I could find my bag. Still only wearing a pair of cotton shorts, he wrapped me in his arms.

Unable to meet his eyes, I focused on the tattoos covering his bicep—a tree with flowers on it, and above it the phrase "Hope will never be silent" was written in Latin. I'd never noticed the phrase before but could tell it was older, and it piqued my curiosity.

I almost laughed when the absurdity of the moment hit me. I was translating a tattoo from Latin to English while also being embarrassed by my exposed body.

"Dean, listen to me." His voice was steady and firm, drawing my attention from his tattoos to his voice. Thankfully, he didn't tell me to look at him because I wasn't ready for that. "*You* are what I find irresistible. Your personality, your smiles, your honesty; it's all pulled me in. Your scars are part of you. They are as much a part of you as your nose or your eyes. You can't change those things, and you can't change the scars."

I couldn't bring myself to look in his eyes, though I appreciated his words and could admit I'd needed to hear them.

He pulled back, his hands resting on my upper arms. "When you see me without a shirt on, do you only see the big-ass scar running up the back of my left bicep?"

I forgot all about being uncomfortable, my head shooting upward to look at him. "Wait, what scar?"

Merrick turned to give me a full view of a gnarly scar that ran from his elbow to his shoulder. "A constant reminder to stay out of trees."

When he turned back around, he was serious again. "Sure, your scars are more visible, but I really don't think they're as bad as you've made them out to be. They were a surprise at first, but I've seen them all. And when I look at you, I don't see them. I see muscular thighs, a gorgeous ass, firm abs that I'd have killed for at twenty-five. I won't even bring up thirty-five… or especially forty-five."

He patted his stomach. It was perfect in my eyes. A little

softer than mine, no defined abdominal lines, with graying hair, but no less perfect.

My eyes got bigger as the meaning sunk in. "Oh."

Merrick chuckled. "For being such a genius, you can be a little slow sometimes."

I pushed at his shoulder. "Shut up. I haven't had my coffee yet." Then I leaned forward and kissed him, allowing it to linger long enough that my cock was beginning to fill when he pulled back.

"While I like where this is going, it's not going to get us any closer to talking. I'm pretty sure Canyon will chew me out if we don't have a talk before moving things to the bed."

"The talk can wait thirty minutes."

Merrick's expression hardened and with it, my dick went from half-hard to fully hard. "Kitchen. I'm going to get us food and coffee, then we're going to go talk. Afterward, we can see what you're in the mood for."

I palmed my dick through my briefs. "That's nowhere near as fun as my idea."

Clearing his throat, he waited until I looked at him to speak. "Hands off your dick."

My cock twitched at the instruction, but my hand fell to my side just the same.

"Good boy. No touching that dick without permission."

What would happen if I came in my underwear without touching myself?

Merrick choked on air. "And this is why we need to talk." He raised an eyebrow in my direction, then pointed to the bag I'd been looking for a few minutes earlier. "Pants on, then to the kitchen. Now."

As I turned toward my bag, I caught a glimpse of the impressive bulge in Merrick's pants. At least I wasn't the only one who found this hot. Unfortunately, his matching arousal didn't change his resolve to have a conversation first. "Go."

Merrick headed to the bathroom as I pulled on a pair of sweats that had been packed in my bag. He'd thought of everything the day before, right down to a change of clothes.

A few minutes later, he appeared in the kitchen looking way too good for having only just woken up. With a kiss to my forehead, he placed my blanket and rabbit on my lap, then headed for the coffee maker. "Glad you decided to get to the kitchen like I told you, but you forgot these."

Fingering Babbit's ear, I tilted my head to study Merrick... my Daddy. "You don't mind?"

He turned around, a bag of coffee beans still in his hand. "I got you Babbit. I'm the one that keeps handing both of them to you and packed them in your bag. If I had a problem with either, I wouldn't be doing those things. You aren't as clever as you think you are, Bean. Blankie is way too loved to be some random throw blanket."

My cheeks flushed. "I never gave it a name."

Merrick shrugged as he turned back around. "Well, I did. Because he should have a name." The grinder started before I could respond and by the time it stopped, Merrick was ready to change the subject. "But there's more to being your Daddy than chasing you around with Blankie and Babbit."

While I wanted to say that was enough, because I liked that he always had them nearby and wasn't particularly looking forward to the conversation, I knew it wouldn't be enough for either of us.

"Okay. I'll buy that. But what are you thinking? You already remind me to eat lunch and leave work. And then you bug the hell out of me until I go to bed at night." I finished the sentence with a wink and grin to let him know that I didn't mind the poking and prodding.

He'd naturally started bugging me about my schedule and despite not saying as much, I appreciated it. There had been something reassuring about the predictable texts. They weren't like the ones my mom used to send when I'd first moved out, worrying that I'd get so caught up in studies that I'd forget to go to classes or eat.

I'd hated those reminders because they made me feel incompetent. Merrick's had never made me feel that way, only cared for.

He spent a few seconds rummaging in a cabinet before answering. When he turned around, he was holding a box of pancake mix. "Well, I guess that kind of depends on what you need from me as well. Your input is going to help me decide. What I can tell you is that I think a schedule and expectations will be good for you."

My brow furrowed. "Why?"

"Well, for starters, I've done a lot of reading recently." He set the box on the counter, then ducked down to look in a cabinet. He hadn't come back up and his voice sounded funny as he spoke more to the cabinet than me. "Ah-ha!" He reappeared with a griddle in one hand and a mixing bowl in the other. "I knew I had these."

It became clear that doing something else while he talked was making this conversation easier for him. I could understand it, but it was still strange looking at the door of a refrigerator instead of a face. "Anyway, my understanding is that middles and littles both still need routines, predictability, and stability. Where a little needs Daddy to be more involved in roleplay, middles need to know Daddy is there for them and still holding them accountable with expectations and consequences."

My nose turned up just as he shut the door. "Don't like that idea?"

I was going to reserve judgment until I had answers, but I hadn't been able to hide my initial reaction. "What type of consequences and expectations?"

He busied himself at the counter, facing me but looking into the bowl as he added ingredients. "I was thinking a lot about bedtimes."

"Ugh." *Cue teenage annoyance.* At least I could handle that part well.

Merrick finally looked up at me. "Really? Right now, you're supposed to be the grown-up Dean."

The coffee maker hissed as the last drops finally made their way into the carafe. "Coffee!"

"Deeean." The warning in Merrick's voice made him sound more like Trent telling his pup to behave than Merrick frustrated with his boyfriend. I was pretty sure I'd just discovered Merrick's Daddy voice.

And it was hot.

That didn't mean I should push my luck, though. Especially not before we'd finished this conversation. My goal was still to get back into bed.

"Sorry, sorry. I really don't mean to huff and roll my eyes. It's just natural around you."

He shook his head. "You're going to push buttons."

"I'm listening. Promise. Grown-up discussion. Expectations, accountability." I intentionally left out consequences, but I should have known my Daddy wasn't going to forget that one.

"And consequences." He gave me another stern look before returning to the pancake batter.

"Yes, consequences." I didn't like the idea of consequences much. They always sounded painful. Caleb, Aiden, and Dexter were not very good at keeping their mouths shut about how much they liked the spankings they got. I wiggled in my seat at the thought of him striking my ass. My skin ached thinking about it.

I must have gotten lost in my thoughts because Merrick cleared his throat and I glanced up to find him looking directly at me, his lips pressed together with worry. When he knew he had my attention, he took a breath. "This isn't going to work if you get lost in your head and don't talk to me."

Communication was something I didn't have a great track record with. Evan and I had never had a conversation like this. Maybe if we had, we'd have figured out we weren't right for one another before things went downhill.

Sighing heavily, I dropped my eyes slightly. It wasn't the

move of a petulant teen but of a grown man who fully understood that his boyfriend was right. No sooner did I open my mouth than words started flowing quickly. "You're right. I'm sorry. I'm not all that great at talking about my feelings. The truth is I got caught up on consequences. I know that some of the guys love them, but the thought of them makes me uncomfortable. And I don't like pain."

He'd already reached across the counter and grabbed my hand before I'd finished speaking. "The thought of a spanking never crossed my mind. I knew you wouldn't find pleasure in them. They would be more of a punishment—a cruel one at that. I'd thought more along the lines of going to bed early, no dessert, losing game time."

I honestly didn't know if the early bedtime or loss of gaming was better or worse than a spanking. "Straight to the heart. At least a spanking is over quickly."

My words had Merrick laughing as he turned to tend to the griddle. I didn't know when the pancakes had been put on it, but they were ready to flip. "It should scare you into behaving yourself and going to bed on time."

"Alright, you've got my attention. What are the expectations?"

CHAPTER TWENTY-SEVEN

MERRICK

Dean hadn't loved some of my ideas. He'd been most hesitant on weeknight bedtimes. What he hadn't thought about was that I'd basically had him going to bed before eleven almost every weeknight already. For the last two weeks, I'd texted around ten thirty to tell him it was getting late. Like clockwork, he'd complain for two texts and by the third, he'd be agreeing to turn his game off after that round. A few nights I'd nearly forgotten to check in, only to have him shoot me a text to tell me he was tired and heading to bed.

"Eleven? I didn't have to go to bed at eleven when I was fifteen!"

"That's because you'd graduated high school by then. It's kind of hard to tell a guy going to college that he needs to go to sleep at eleven. Correct me if I'm wrong, but when you're my submissive, you don't want to be the guy in college or responsible for his own career. When I tell you to do something and you do it, it makes you feel good."

I topped off our coffee mugs and slid the last pancake onto Dean's plate. He'd eaten the first three like he hadn't eaten in days. "I guess so, yeah. It feels like you're thinking about me, and I like that. Part of me likes that you don't give up, even when I'm being dismissive or stubborn."

I'd figured that out already, but I was impressed that he had picked up on it himself. Since I'd heard Larson talking about middles, everything I'd read and learned had fit Dean perfectly. That he liked when I took control didn't surprise me. It surprised me even less that he was sometimes obstinate about it.

Wanting Dean to know how happy I was with his admission, I allowed pride to show on my face and in my words. "I'm glad you see that. I've seen it too. And I'm confident that it's going to feel a lot better now that we have defined rules. It's one thing for your annoyingly bossy friend to tell you to go to bed. It's another to have Daddy tell you it's bedtime."

A light flush spread across his face, but his smile told me he agreed. "Okay, I can agree with that one. Wait, what about the weekends? Do I still have to go to bed at eleven?"

His worry about weekend bedtimes was unexpectedly sweet. He needed the expectations I'd been planning more than he knew. "I think weekends can be your time. But if I think you're not taking care of yourself, or if there are plans on Saturday or Sunday morning, you are going to have to go to bed earlier."

He sipped at his coffee as he thought over what I'd said. I could see he wanted to disagree, but when he didn't come up with an argument he was willing to voice, he set the mug down and nodded. "That's reasonable."

"I'm glad you think so. You're also in charge of cleaning up the kitchen after meals when we're together. If we're eating here or at your house, you need to clean up."

This time, he wasn't going to agree as easily. "What? I do that anyway. Well, at home at least. But expected? What if we get interrupted? Or *something* comes up suddenly?" I struggled to contain my laughter when he glanced pointedly to his lap. Though I found myself sobering quickly when his eyes shot up to mine, true worry in his expression. "What if people are over?"

Answers to the first few questions weren't as important as addressing his current fear. "You put the dishes in the dishwasher? We clean up the kitchen after a meal. That's just how it works."

"But what if they don't *know*?"

He was pleading with me to understand, but for a few seconds, all I could think was why they wouldn't know that dishes got put into the dishwasher. I'd nearly asked the dumbest question ever when I figured out what he meant. I resisted the urge to comfort him, knowing that at the moment what he needed was someone to reassure him. "Bean, when you go to a friend's house for dinner, do they put the dishes in the dishwasher?"

Dean nodded slowly.

"And does that mean that their Mommy or Daddy gave them that rule?"

His eyes widened and he shook his head. "No. That's just something you do." Before I could respond, Dean's hand hit his forehead. "I just had one of those slow moments, huh?"

That time I did laugh, but not until he'd already begun to laugh at himself.

"Sorry, I got caught up in my head. This is all new and sometimes it feels a little scary. Logically, I know I put the dishes in the dishwasher after every meal. But when you told me I *had* to, it felt a lot more like a kid having rules than an adult having responsibilities." He shook his head at himself. "And that's the point, isn't it? I have a rule and there's an expectation that I follow it. If I do, I make Daddy happy. If I don't, I get a consequence."

"Bingo. This isn't to stress you out. I am pretty sure that I could have naturally implemented everything without having this conversation and you wouldn't have batted an eye. But for me, I like knowing that we've agreed on them and you're choosing to follow them." Then I winked. "Or not. Hell, maybe you'll find you like going to bed early or washing my car."

Dean's mouth fell open. "Washing your car? What about mine?"

He was so easy to tease, though I did like the idea of making him wash the cars as a consequence, at least when the weather was nice. "Calm down. We'll discuss that one later. I pulled it from thin air, but I think it could be a good one."

Dean crossed his arms, but with Blankie and Babbit trapped between them and his chest, he didn't manage to look very cross. "Fine. What else?"

"Communication."

There went the eye roll again, but he followed it up with words that were more sincere, even if they were a little confused. "We're doing that now. We already said we need to talk to make sure we're on the same page. I'm pretty sure that's how this conversation started."

Dean wasn't the only one who could roll his eyes and I found myself doing the same to him. "I mean that I want you to check in with me. I'm not trying to take over your life, but when you go somewhere, I want you to send me a text before you leave and I expect a text when you arrive. I'm trying not to micromanage, but I know I'll worry regardless."

To my surprise, Dean smiled, big and genuine. "I can do that. I actually kind of like that. It can get lonely living alone. My mom loves me, I love her, but she's definitely not texting me to check that I made it home."

"I like it too. And we can always add and change things as necessary."

Dean scratched his head and looked a little bashful for a few seconds before meeting my eyes again. "Yeah. That works for me. Um, is it weird that all this talk about rules and expectations made me horny?"

I slid his empty plate away from him. "And you can't touch that without permission."

Dean's eyes widened. "Whaaa?"

"Did we not talk about that one?" The corner of my mouth turned up in a smirk.

He shook his head. "Hell no, we didn't! I am rather fond of my dick, and touching it. We have a very satisfying relationship."

"You can still have that relationship... as long as you ask permission first."

For a few seconds, I was pretty sure that I'd overstepped. Dean didn't say anything as he glanced between me and his lap. I was about to tell him we could talk about it if he wanted when he sighed. "My logical brain is screaming at me to say no, but if I take a minute to think about it, there's something really hot about it."

He glanced back to his lap, his frown turning into a mischievous grin that lacked the hesitancy of a few minutes earlier and the innocence of the day before. The man across from me was definitely my horny boyfriend, and his words only highlighted that. "How about we go to bed and I can see just how much my dick likes the idea, Daddy?"

Schooling my reactions—both in my face and in my pants—was nearly impossible. I wanted to drop everything and drag him to my bedroom, but that defeated the purpose of everything we'd talked about that morning. There was a bowl, a few measuring cups, a measuring spoon, and our dishes and silverware in the sink, and I'd just told him it was his job to take care of them.

Being a Daddy was going to be hard work. "How about you show me after the dishwasher is loaded."

Dean's mouth fell open. "Bwah?"

"We just talked about expectations. Besides, I need to put the butter and syrup away and wipe up the counter where we ate."

His mouth shut and he looked at me as he worked

something out in his head. "You're going to help clean the kitchen?"

"Dishes aren't the only thing that need to be cleaned up after a meal. Besides, if we work together, it gets done faster, and we have a chance to talk about whatever we want." Post-meal cleanup with someone never failed to put me in a good mood. We hadn't talked about forever, but the fact that we were sharing this at all said that I was already thinking long term. This was something I didn't share with people.

He stood up from the chair, set his items on the seat, and made his way to the sink. "Like how much sex we're going to have when we're done?"

The syrup bottle almost slipped from my hand. I recovered quickly and placed it in the fridge. "Bean." At the sink, Dean was batting his eyes and smiling at me like he couldn't figure out why I'd nearly dropped the bottle.

It was a good thing there were only a few dishes to do. I didn't know how long either of us was going to be able to follow the rules we'd just agreed on. His mind hadn't given up on sexy things happening and thanks to his comments, mine had joined his back in bed.

"See, sex is safer. If you had broken that bottle of syrup, I would've been done with the dishes before you had your part of the kitchen cleaned."

With so few things in the sink, he'd have the dishwasher done before me regardless. "If you're not careful, you're going to be cleaning the kitchen by yourself."

Dean sobered. "This rules thing kind of sucks."

It wasn't hard to spot the erection impatiently pressing

against his underwear and sweats. "Have you told that to your cock?"

A wet hand waved through the air, then toward his crotch. "He has a mind of his own. His opinions don't always match reality." Dean grabbed the next plate from the sink, and as he was turning to put it in the dishwasher, he spoke just loudly enough that I could hear. "They just might at this particular moment, though."

My assertion was holding true: he was a handful, in more than one way.

Dean did his job well, though I might have rushed my tasks a bit. As soon as he shut the dishwasher, I tossed the rag I'd been using to hastily wipe the counter into the sink. The kitchen was done enough for me. "Come on. I think someone's earned a reward."

"Thank fuck."

"Language." Dean's groan was far more aroused than annoyed, and my cock twitched. I liked the effect my control was having on him.

Halfway to the bedroom, I stumbled. Thankfully, Dean was ahead of me and didn't see my less than graceful steps. We'd never talked about position preference. I liked to bottom from time to time, but I liked to top more. The extra few seconds it took me to get to my doorway had given Dean enough time inside to already be searching the top of my nightstand.

"What the f—udge?" His back was toward me, so I knew he hadn't seen me walk in, yet he was still trying to watch his language. We were both more natural in our roles than either of us had originally expected we'd be. He blew out a breath, his lips making a raspberry sound as he did so. "What single man doesn't keep lube on the nightstand?"

"The one whose foreskin is intact. I don't need it for a handjob. I keep the lube with my toys. I'm guessing, as a previously single man yourself, you wouldn't keep your toys on top of your nightstand."

His eyes sparkled with delight. "Well, it depends on the toy. My dildo, probably not. The vibrating cock ring, well, that's small enough that even you haven't noticed it."

"I see I'm going to need to be nosier when I'm at your place."

"Next time. Right now, where are your toys?"

"Drawer. Right in front of you."

He raised his eyebrows, silently asking if he could open it. At my nod, he pulled the drawer open and looked inside. I only had to wonder for a moment what he thought about the contents. Most items wouldn't be surprising—a few dildos, a prostate massager, a few different-sized plugs— but I hadn't met a guy yet who had expected to see the vibrant blue-and-white tentacle dildo.

A few seconds after opening the drawer, Dean turned around with the lube and the tentacle in his hands. "I have always wanted to try one of these. Now I don't know if I should use my fingers or this"—he wiggled the dildo—"to stretch myself."

My brain shorted out for a few seconds. Dean wasn't balking at the find, more excited to try it himself. He'd answered the question about if he bottomed, but he'd been so certain he was going to stretch himself, I couldn't ignore the statement.

"Who said anything about you stretching yourself?"

He blinked at me a few times. "Well, I want your cock in me. In order for that to happen, I need to be stretched. It's been so long since I've had anyone inside me, there's no way I'm going to be able to take you without prep."

I closed the distance between us and gently removed the items from his hands. "Is there a reason you're going to prep yourself? If you're not comfortable with me inside you, you are welcome to my ass. I'm vers. I might have a slight preference to top but at the moment, as long as we come, I don't particularly care how we reach that point. Hell, I'm good with just doing more of what we've already done."

His mouth opened and shut a few times, then he shook his head as though he was clearing cobwebs from it. "Um, I've always stretched myself."

I set the items on the bed, sat down beside them, and pulled Dean so that he was straddling my lap. "Have your partners always prepped themselves?"

The look of confusion on his face would have been funny at any other point. It was rare to stump Dean like that, but in this case it was more depressing than amusing. He wiggled slightly on my lap. His cock hadn't gone soft, though mine wasn't as excited as it had been in the kitchen. "No. I mean, there have been a few guys who were already prepped ahead of time, but if we're not in a hurry, I've always enjoyed it."

Ignoring the sour thought of Dean having meaningless, rushed hookups, I focused on the here and now. "Are you opposed to being stretched by someone else?"

"No. Nothing against it. I've just never had anyone offer before."

I swore I wasn't going to growl. No matter how much I wanted to. I wanted to see his ass stretch slowly as I worked the tentacle in and out of his body. The fantasy was bringing my dick back to life. But the first time someone stretched him, showed him the love and care that he'd always deserved, it shouldn't be with a toy.

Mind made up, I reached for the dildo beside us. "It's a very fun toy and the little suction cups drive me insane." I traced a finger along the bulbous cups. "And I can't wait to show you how mind-blowing it is."

His cock pressed against my stomach, pulsating at the mere thought. "But today, if you want me inside you, I'm going to show you what it feels like to be cared for by your boyfriend."

"My Daddy." His voice had come out as nothing more than a whisper, and he buried his face in my shoulder.

Pride surged through me and with it, love. That time, I didn't hide from the flutter in my chest or the way my skin felt too small. I allowed myself to embrace the feeling as I moved to nip at his neck. Dean squirmed and laughed when I found a particularly ticklish spot.

Patting his thigh gently, I encouraged him off my lap. "You're right. But Daddy can't get you stretched if you're sitting on my lap." I planned to show him just what selfish assholes his past lovers had been and just how good I could make this for him.

Dean wiggled off me but paused with his lips and brow scrunched in question. "Where do you want me?"

"Right there is perfect." He was sitting on the bed beside me, his legs dangling over the edge. From that position, I could move his legs however I needed to get him in the best position and allow me the best angle into his body. It was time for Dean to know what it was like to be cared for.

I didn't say it, but I knew I wasn't thinking just in terms of sex. Dean had wormed his way into my heart, one snuggle, laugh, and admission at a time. I was going to spend the rest of my life caring for the man in front of me, and I was going to be happy doing it.

CHAPTER TWENTY-EIGHT

DEAN

Oh, holy hell. That first breach of Merrick's finger felt like he'd just strummed every nerve in my body like a guitar. I swore I vibrated. I spent about an eighth of a second trying to convince myself it was due to the release of tension that had built as we talked about expectations and sex but quickly decided it had nothing to do with the conversation and everything to do with Merrick.

Embarrassment had initially swept through me as I thought about how ridiculous I must have sounded when I told him I'd never had someone else's fingers inside me. His concern about my limits and resolve to rectify the situation quickly had been a sweet gesture that helped ease my discomfort.

He hadn't come out and said it but he'd been worried about my own body image issues. They were going to linger for a long time, but with Merrick, they no longer felt like they defined me.

He'd already proven numerous times before that he'd stop or change things up if I gave the slightest indication that something hurt. That knowledge was how I knew that what I was feeling as he began to stretch me was not tension. This entire body thrum of anticipation, excitement, and pleasure was all because of who I was with and how damn right my world felt.

I wasn't going to allow myself to get caught up in emotions or declarations of love, so I let the next best things spill from my mouth.

"Jesus. Fucking. Oh, shit. Fuck. Th-Mer-holyfuckingshit." As I babbled, he twisted the digits inside me and I hollered. "That's-that's, ungh!"

Thankfully, the words that accompanied his wicked grin weren't about my questionable use of language. "That's barely two fingers. I haven't even gotten the second all the way in."

Yes, it had been longer than I cared to admit since I'd allowed a man anywhere near my ass, but that didn't mean *I* hadn't played with myself. His tentacle dildo was hot, but I had a few toys at home that rivaled its length and width, just notably lacking the suction cups and shape.

With my feet resting against the mattress, I had enough leverage to rock my hips downward onto Merrick's fingers. The slight burn wasn't uncomfortable, the pleasure from being full overriding everything else. "Now you have."

Merrick couldn't decide if he wanted to argue with me or laugh. As long as it got his dick into my ass, I wouldn't be bothered by either. My hips chased his fingers until he laughed. "You're not very patient."

"You're taking forever!"

He shook his head, spreading the fingers in my ass slightly and sending my head backward on the bed. "I'm taking care of you. I'm showing you just how amazing this is when someone else does it for you."

My head popped off the bed to focus on him. "So I get to do this to you next?"

Gray eyes narrowed at me. "At some point. Probably not this morning, though."

I grumbled but understood his point. At thirty-five, my recovery time wasn't what it had been a few short years earlier. "Someday, I'm going to drive you insane. But right now, I need you in me." I'd never been so close to coming untouched and with nothing more than a few fingers in my ass.

Merrick spread his fingers again, the burn of the stretch lost to the sensation of cool lube sliding down my taint. I'd expected to feel it run all the way down my crease, but it stopped at my entrance and I felt additional fullness as his third finger slid inside me. There was no mistaking the moan that escaped me as anything but pleasured.

His fingers were bringing me pleasure I'd never known, but they weren't enough. I needed more, and not just of his touch or his dick inside me. I needed the closeness with Merrick like I'd never needed closeness with anyone before.

I knew I shouldn't have been thinking about past relationships, but uninvited memories of sex with Evan came to mind. Yet I couldn't come up with a single memory of feeling the need I was experiencing now. The simple answer was that it hadn't ever been there. Sex had felt good, it was nice, but it had never been an axis-shifting moment. We'd whispered the right things to one another, but the passion and desire had never felt like this.

I needed Merrick and I needed to give him all of me. No more holding back. As long as I'd known him, he had been anti-dating. He wasn't only showing me trust that I wouldn't hurt him, he'd opened his eyes to a world he hadn't understood. He'd seen what I hadn't and had given me the push I'd needed while patiently waiting for me to figure it out. He was already there when I realized what I'd needed was *him*. He was the missing link, the person that made all the parts of me that never fit into a nice little box finally fit.

I needed him more than ever. "Fingers out. I'm stretched." I propped myself up on my elbows enough that I could see the surprise in his eyes. "You've done your job. I need to feel *you* inside me, not your fingers."

"I've barely started!"

I shook my head. "No, you've finished. Fingers out, dick in."

The sheer emptiness when he removed his fingers left me unable to catch my breath for a few seconds. My muscles protested, pulsating rapidly in search of the friction and fullness they wanted. But the reprieve gave me a chance to adjust my position.

I'd spent seven years hiding my body from everyone—myself included—and that was going to end now. This wasn't where I'd expected I'd find my self-confidence, but when Merrick turned toward his nightstand for a condom, I flipped onto my hands and knees. Everything I'd hidden for years was exposed to him, with the lights on and sun shining through the window.

Unable to bring myself to look over my shoulder, I focused on the tuft of cat fur on the bedding beneath me. Merrick's sudden inhale told me he'd turned back around. "Oh." The single-syllable whisper held reverence and understanding, and despite clearing his throat a few times, his voice was still choked when he spoke again. "Thank you."

It wasn't a long acknowledgement of how hard this moment was for me, but his sincerity was better than any rehearsed speech he could have given. His touch was barely more than a graze as he ran a hand over the scars on my upper thigh and butt. "Tell me if it hurts."

I nodded. "Promise." Merrick had never given me reason to think he'd ever do anything to hurt me. It had taken time, but I knew now that the pain I'd been feeling all these years wasn't as much physical as psychological.

In the beginning, it had been so painful it was nauseating at times. But over time, that pain had faded but left me *expecting* it. It wasn't until Merrick started giving me massages that I had been able to tell the difference in the sensations.

What I felt now was years of neglected muscles and scar

tissue and a lingering feeling of being an idiot for not listening to everyone about taking care of myself better.

His hand glided effortlessly from my ass to my hip, leaving a damp trail in its wake. He'd put lube on his hands to help ease friction on my back, just like he'd done to the condom covering his dick.

It took a few seconds for my brain to convince my muscles to relax, but with a gentle push, Merrick began to slide into me.

From the sound of his groan, it had to have felt as good to him as it did to me. My breath came in ragged pants as my body adjusted. My earlier need to be filled with more than fingers wasn't enough to ease the additional stretch. Once he'd breached my rim, Merrick moved slowly, easing his way inside as he allowed my body time to adjust. When his balls touched mine, I was well past the pain and into pleasure.

"You feel so good." He slipped the hand that had been massaging the top of my hole to my hip. "Ready to move?"

With my head still bent downward, I watched as the bead of precum on my tip became a string connecting me to the bed. "Oh my god, please. Please move." I didn't doubt that I was yet to know the pleasure he'd bring me, but as he pulled back, stars danced in front of my eyes.

And then he was inside me again. His balls slapped against my taint, and I keened. Pleasure, stretch, emotion—it all crashed into me with each thrust until I was finally unable to resist the urge to push back into him.

A fine sheen of sweat coated my chest and back as we worked as a team. Our staccato breathing was only occasionally broken by a word or two in order to beg for more or harder. When I couldn't resist the need to touch myself any longer, I reached a hand under me, only to have it batted away.

Merrick spoke between thrusts, each word forced and broken. "Want. To. Come?"

Looking over my shoulder, I caught sight of Merrick—my Daddy—his forehead damp with sweat, cheeks flushed with a combination of exertion and arousal, his eyes only half-open as he moved in and out. Words became more difficult to find, but I managed to get my thought out. "So much. Yes. Need to come."

Merrick let go of my hip, leaning over my back to grip my cock in his hand, but I had a better idea. With a grunt and a few careful movements, I managed to get myself up on my knees, my back pressed against Merrick's front. We both gasped as the angle of his thrusts changed. He hit deeper inside me, the head of his dick rubbing against the front of my channel and nailing my prostate with each thrust.

I reached behind me. One hand found the back of his neck to pull our heads closer, the other gripped his hip, desperate to keep him inside me and moving as we were. Merrick's arms reached around me, effectively locking us together, the position reminiscent of an embrace. One hand confidently wrapped around my cock as the other moved to my chest, his thumb and forefinger working my nipple to an erect peak.

A few strokes later, we began to lose our rhythm, both of us frantic to come but stubborn enough to not want to spill first. I lost the battle to hold off when Merrick's beard grazed the side of my neck, his breath ghosting over the shell of my ear. "Come for me, Dean. Let me know if you like this." Then his teeth made contact with the side of my neck, biting hard enough that I knew there would be a mark later while also sending shockwaves of pleasure through my body.

My orgasm was inevitable as my dick filled beyond my ability to control it, and the first spurt of cum shot from me. Merrick moved his mouth to capture my screams, but I was too far lost in the moment to kiss him back. I rode my orgasm out, screaming and moaning into his mouth before finally sagging against him. With his hand still wrapped around my cock, a combination of lube and cum allowing it to continue to slide easily along my softening dick, his hips began to buck frantically.

He broke our kiss with a grunt as he slammed into me again. His cock swelled inside me, causing my dick to try desperately to fill again.

"Fuuuuuck." Merrick's strained voice cracked as he released into the condom. He pushed hard against my backside, frantically stroking my now-sensitive cock through his own release. By the time he finished, I was twitching and squirming in his arms, unsure if I liked the overstimulation or hated it.

"Oops, sorry. Got a little carried away there."

"Don't be sorry for that. It was hot, just intense. I think I need a shower and a nap now."

"Both can be arranged. You able to move yet? I need to take care of this condom, then we can get in the shower."

* * *

I awoke sometime later when Merrick answered his phone. It took me a few seconds to pick up on the conversation, but my interest was quickly piqued just by hearing Merrick's side.

"No, he's not going to *cut me a deal*. I'll pay list price."

There was a pause, then Merrick huffed. "Fine, what he was *going* to list it for."

I could hear someone speaking on the other end but not well enough to make out who it was or what they were saying. Finally, Merrick spoke again. "Fine. That works." The pause was shorter and Merrick nodded his head as he listened. "Have him call me when he has some time to chat. I appreciate it. Thanks."

He hung up the phone and rolled over to spoon me. This position was beginning to feel natural. I couldn't deny how safe it made me feel and now that we were openly dating, I could also admit that it was welcomed.

Fighting off a yawn and the lingering fog from our nap, I let my curiosity take over. "Who was it?"

My body got pulled flush against his and he hummed. "More sleep."

"You can't leave me hanging like that! I'll never rest."

For a few seconds, I thought he'd already drifted off, but eventually he put me out of my misery. "It was Canyon. I've been thinking a lot about that house Larson is working on. I talked with him about it yesterday afternoon and he talked to Larson about it today. All this talk about commitment and not running made me realize that it was time to set real roots here. I've lived in apartments and hotels my entire adult life. I have things keeping me here." He squeezed me tighter. "I have someone."

My heart did that weird flutter thing again and I rolled onto my side to face him. "Yeah? You're going to stay for me?"

His grin didn't hide the uncertainty in his eyes or the worry in his voice. "If you'll have me."

"Of course I'll have you. You're my Daddy, after all." I pressed my lips to his and enjoyed the firmness of his as he kissed me in return.

His lips turned up in a smile, breaking our kiss. "Damn right I am. Which makes you my Bean." He pecked my lips, pulling back quickly. "I thought you could help me decorate it. If you're going to keep me, I figure you should have a say in what it looks like... but only if you don't try to decorate it like your office."

In our position, it was difficult to wrap myself around him in the way I wanted. Eventually, I pushed him onto his back and climbed on top of him. Straddling him with my hands on his chest, I looked into his eyes and smiled so hard my cheeks hurt. "I like that plan. And I think you were the one that told me my work had to stay at work."

He placed his hands on my hips, his features relaxing as I spoke. "Your Daddy is a very wise man."

A giggle bubbled from me as I leaned down to kiss him. Our connection lingered for a while, though never turning into anything more desperate. Pulling back, I heard myself whisper, "I love you."

So much for no crazy declarations. When his eyes

widened, I tried to backpedal. "I know it's too soon. Shit, we barely started dating a day ago. I don't even think it's been a day. It's okay if you don't feel the same." Groaning, I fell to the side and pulled my blanket over my head.

A few seconds later, the blanket moved and Merrick's face appeared in front of mine. He was grinning, chuckling actually, as he looked into my eyes. "We aren't two twenty-year-old kids still green to the world. We're two men who have lived entire lives. It's okay to know what you want. It's okay to feel what you feel. What makes it even better is when the feelings are returned."

I blinked a few times. The comment earlier about being smart but slow was haunting me again. I knew I was missing something and my brain was just beginning to work it out when Merrick took pity on me. "Dean, I love you too."

"You do?" I threw my hand over my mouth as soon as the words were out, wishing like hell I could take the statement back.

Merrick didn't seem to think my reaction had been ridiculous. "I do. I can't get enough of you. You brighten up my life and make me want to stay. You're so much more than my friend. You're my boyfriend, my Bean, my dildo-tree-painting boy—"

I held up my hand. "It was a dickiduous forest!"

He laughed. "I'm sorry, please forgive me. What I'm trying to say is, too soon or not, I love you."

His words filled me with joy. Orgasm earlier or not, my cock was beginning to fill. I had a boyfriend, a Daddy, a man in my life that loved me. And I loved him. After a kiss that left us both breathless, I rocked my hips into his. "I think it's my turn to make you feel good." I slid between his legs, swiping the lube from the nightstand on my way down, thankful we hadn't gotten dressed again after our shower. "I want you to feel how much I love you."

CHAPTER TWENTY-NINE

MERRICK

Halfway through my forties, I had yet to reach the point where I was too mature to whine to my best friend. "This sucks!"

Canyon's booming voice reverberated through the phone. "You were the one who decided to buy Brodrick's."

I was standing in the stockroom taking a breather before I said something to the bar staff that I'd regret. Over the last three weeks, Brodrick's had been transformed by Travis's crew, and I'd brought the staff back for training. With opening day in just over a week, it was important to get things right.

"I don't regret buying Brodrick's, but I've hardly seen Dean all week."

"Ah. I see. Missing your boy. Well, I can assure you that he left work when you told him to. He ate dinner here at the house with us and is now with Larson and Marley at your new place. They're picking out siding colors and discussing landscaping. Larson wanted to show him some wall colors while he's there, then he was planning on heading back to his place to play a video game with Logan."

I couldn't help but smile. Dean had become a social butterfly. He'd always been willing to join us but hadn't spent a lot of time alone with any of us. Lately, he'd been more active in not only the group chats but hanging out with the guys as well.

At first, I'd worried that he'd be uncomfortable around Travis, Trent, James, and Canyon, but that worry had turned out to be unfounded.

The previous week Dean had met Travis for dinner, and he'd gone to Trent's on Saturday to do his bookkeeping. I'd been shocked to hear that both Aiden and Logan had been out on a date together at the time, especially since it had taken Dean three hours to get back to his place. When he'd finally texted me that he was home, he'd told me that he and Trent had started to chat and lost track of time.

"I just want to get this place in order. If we break one more bottle tonight, I'm going to lose my mind." Thankfully, none of them had been expensive bottles, but every broken bottle was one more that I had to replace and five minutes longer I was going to be there while we cleaned up the broken glass.

"Patience, young Padawan."

I rolled my eyes at my friend. He and Larson could have entire conversations in movie quotes. I was lucky if I had ever heard the quote, much less quote a movie myself. "I'm running out of it." There was a drink shaker on the shelf beside me and I grabbed it and began spinning it in my hand.

While I'd shifted focus to something more sustainable as a career, bartending had remained a passion of mine. After breaking up with Tom, competitions had ceased to be enjoyable. However, I still liked to mix drinks. I wasn't as fast as I was when I was in my twenties, and a little rusty on some of the more complicated moves, but I was still good at it. It was always a fun party trick to perform for friends. With only a single tin shaker and one available hand, my moves were limited, but I could do a palm spin in my sleep, and tossing and catching an empty tin was second nature.

"Get back out there, get your shit done, and get home to your boy. Dean knows you're busy, and he knows that this isn't going to last forever, but your Bean still needs you."

I groaned, flipping the cup over my hand and allowing it to roll over my thumb a few times. "I know, I know. I swear, I'm just tired and grumpy."

"Give your boy a call, get your work done, and get back to him."

Finally feeling more centered, I allowed myself one more sigh. "Okay. Thanks for talking me off the edge."

"Anytime. Now, go whip them into shape." Canyon disconnected the call while laughing at me, not that I could blame him.

I rolled the tin up my forearm, let it slide back down into my palm, then flicked it upward, over my shoulder, and caught it with my free hand. When I spun around, my newest bartender was standing in the doorway, slack-jawed.

Anxiety roiled in my gut. How much had she heard? Before I could ask, Zoey pointed at my hand and spoke excitedly. "Holy crap. How'd you do that? Can you do more? That's so cool!"

I blinked a few times. Her green eyes were wide and excited, clearly eager for an answer. When my answer didn't come quickly, she ran a hand through her purple hair. "Sorry, didn't mean to scare you. I'd been coming back to tell you that we got the glass cleaned up and the ice well changed out. Then I saw you flick the shaker up and around. It's really cool. Do you know more tricks like that?"

"Yeah. I've got a few." My smirk gave me away, and it only served to make Zoey more excited.

"Will you show us? My guilty pleasure is watching those flair bartending competitions on YouTube. They're amazing. I've always wanted to learn!"

Her excitement brought back memories of my fascination with Tom when he showed up at the bar, his flashy moves mesmerizing me, his edgy style addictive. I'd come to expect anger or resentment when I thought of him, but that time there was only a fondness for the path that his presence in my life had led me to.

Tennessee, friends, a home, a bar, a boyfriend. The memory of kissing Dean goodbye that morning filled my thoughts. He'd still been sleepy as I'd handed him the travel mug of coffee. "A bean for Bean."

No more eye rolls accompanied the name. He smiled

and kissed me gently. "Have a good day, Daddy." As he turned to head out the door, he was hugging his coffee like he'd been hugging Babbit when he woke up.

"Let's go. I think I might be able to teach you something."

Zoey's squeal of delight was nearly enough to make my ears ring. "Yeeeessssssssssss!" She turned on her heels and hurried down the hall yelling to the rest of the bartenders there. "Merrick's going to show us tricks!"

My attention was drawn to the storeroom, and I looked to see what we had on hand that I could use. Some of the tricks were easy enough that I was pretty sure even Wyatt, the server-turned-bartender-turned-butterfingers, could master. At least tins only bounced and at worst dented.

I'd start slow.

By the time I brought a crate of supplies to the bar, the entire staff had lined up, eagerly awaiting my demonstration. My eyebrows rose, looking to Zoey for answers. "What the hell? Did you tell them I was giving away free booze?"

She giggled. "Nope. I told them you had tricks. Turns out, you've been holding out on us, Mr. Carter! *And* Dane is a damn good secret keeper. At least until he let it slip that you probably know more than a trick or two. Seriously?"

I set the crate down and held up my hand to stop her. The more she chattered, the more excited everyone else became. "First and foremost, that was a different lifetime ago, so don't be expecting me to be able to pull off half the tricks these guys competing today can. Second, it's a hobby now, but once upon a time, I was fairly well known."

"Bullshit."

The voice pulled my attention away from my staff, and I looked up to see Dean and Larson standing in the doorway. "Bean!" There was no hiding my happiness at seeing my boy standing in my restaurant.

Dean and Larson came over to the bar, Dean beaming as I leaned over the wood surface to give him a kiss. "What are you two doing here?"

He was still grinning as he reached for a seat. "Came to say hi before heading home. Now it appears I'm staying for a show." Looking at my staff, he winked playfully. "Don't believe him. He's just being modest."

Larson's eager nods were not helping the excitement in the room.

"Fine. Let it be known that these two are way overstating my skills."

Dean and Larson stuck their tongues out at me.

Zoey rolled her hand, signaling for me to stop stalling. "Let us be the judges of that, boss man."

"Yeah, Mer. Don't keep the people waiting!"

Removing the items I'd brought with me, I glanced over at Larson. "You know, you used to be quiet."

Dean let out a giggle that sounded far too innocent for my boy. "I like this Larson better." He patted Larson's bicep, then bumped a shoulder into him as Larson's cheeks turned red.

I needed to get this moving if we were ever going to get out of here. Having Dean on the stool across the counter made me that much more determined to wrap up at a reasonable hour.

"Alright. Fine. Let's see what I remember." Dean, Larson, and I all knew I was playing up my rusty skills. There was no way I was up to competition level, but I wasn't bad. I'd just kept practicing, mainly with friends.

With every item I pulled from the crate, a memory came back to me. The first time I saw Tom showing off. Our first kiss after I'd mastered my first tin flip. The elation of the invite to my first competition. The melancholy of the last. As I pulled bottles of liquor from the shelves and began to do a survey of the work surface, the memories shifted to meeting Dean in college. When he came out to us. Late night study sessions. The awe I'd always felt at his intelligence and the way his mind worked. The jokes, the smiles, the first time I heard him call me Daddy.

Showing up to his house last week to find Mooch, his tower, his food bowls, and litter box all there and Dean snuggling my cat on his couch with a guilty grin on his face.

My eyes found my boy across the bar. He was wearing a pair of jeans and a T-shirt that fit him, his legs bouncing with energy as he spoke with Larson.

Absently, I flipped a tin upward, catching it easily and grinning. I'd come to accept that my past had happened for a reason, and I was here because of it. This was the last step in making it full circle—behind a bar, an audience composed of more than just my closest friends on the other side, and a smile on my face.

I was feeling at home as I picked up a second tin and spun it on my palm. I was home, the pieces of my life all put back together, thanks in large part to the man across the room from me.

"Come on, Mer. Don't keep them waiting. Show them what you got!" Dean's call had everyone laughing, but it reminded me that I had a job to do.

"Alright, alright." Intentionally flicking the tin harder than I should have, I watched it fall and feigned surprise.

Larson's voice was unmistakable as I focused on the fallen cup. "Har, har, har." I glanced up in time to see him look over at Dean. "Your man thinks he's funny. Maybe we should call the circus and tell them we found one of their clowns."

Dean pursed his lips. "I think I'll keep the clown. I kind of like him here. In my bed. I miss him enough when he's late getting back."

That time, dropping the jigger hadn't been planned. I hadn't hidden our relationship from my employees, so his appearance wasn't a surprise to them, nor was our kiss. His open admission of where he liked me and how he didn't like the late nights had been a surprise, but only to me.

He wasn't the only one.

The head cook groaned. "I'm starting to wonder what kind of show we're going to be getting."

After throwing a piece of ice in his direction, I held up my hands. "Alright, alright."

With a last glance over my surface, I cracked my neck, and started to move. I wasn't going to be juggling bottles or dancing around on stage. But I could give them a show with things they could all easily do behind the bar with a little practice. Years of repetition allowed me to flick a hurricane glass off the bar with my left hand, bounce the base off my left elbow, and catch it—right side up—with my left. It was on a napkin and I was halfway through tin prep before my employees had a chance to do anything more than drop their jaws.

The easiest moves I'd mastered were still the ones that impressed the most. The crisp, clean flicks and flips of the tins that resulted in an ice-filled shaker were what finally made the oohs and aahs start. I'd done these moves so many times that they were as natural as lifting a fork to my mouth. Turning my hand slightly, I lifted the bottle of dark rum from the well in front of me, rotated it around, and strategically flashed the label of the bottle before rotating it back to pour into the small tin.

Each move elicited another reaction from my audience, right down to the way I flipped the empty tin around my forearm a few times after pouring the contents into the glass. A round of applause and cheers came as I garnished the drink and slid it across to Zoey.

She gave it a tentative sip before humming an approval. When Wyatt reached for the glass to try it, she batted his hand away playfully. "You saw how he made it. Do it yourself!"

We laughed, but Wyatt went pale. "I'll never be able to do that without tricks. I'm going to be lucky to pour a virgin screwdriver at this point."

I watched as Dean's eyes went wide at the statement, despite everyone else laughing. After a quick wipe down of the bar surface, I shot a wink at Wyatt. "We'll get you there." Hopefully, I sounded more confident than I felt. I wasn't sure if he was cut out to be a bartender. It was perplexing since everyone had told me he'd always done well behind the bar when they were in a pinch, despite having always been a server before I took over.

I took the momentary distraction to make my way over to Dean. "What's up? You look like you swallowed a fly."

He shook his head. "Stepped in a pile of shit might be more likely."

"Language, Bean."

Blinking through a light blush, Dean nearly whispered his response. "Sorry, Daddy." His next words lacked the same cute blush but were delivered just as quietly. "So, uh, the nervous guy?"

I glanced over my shoulder where Wyatt was sitting, still trying to bribe Zoey out of her drink. "Wyatt?"

Dean lifted a shoulder. "Not sure of his name. Uh, he's been a server here a long time."

"Yeah. He's a good guy. Everyone loves him. Though he's got butterfingers behind the bar."

The way Dean bit his lip nervously, I knew he was about to drop a bombshell on me. I just didn't know what it was going to be. Even after he spoke, I wasn't sure I believed him. "Uh, he's overheard some very interesting conversations over the years."

Any server who had been around for more than a few weeks had heard some interesting conversations. My eyebrow lifted. "And?"

Larson snort-laughed as Dean finally sighed and spelled it out in very clear terms. "He heard Travis and me talking one time about being Daddies. He's been weird around us since. And I know he's overheard other private conversations between different guys over the years. He always gets super awkward, turns neon red, and runs the other way when we come around."

That last part sounded a lot like the Wyatt I'd come to know. It also explained a lot. Which meant I had to decide if I approached him or let him approach me. I wasn't about to lose a guy everyone loved because he was nervous around the guys.

He was a good worker, trying to make ends meet while raising his brother and sister. He needed this job and Brodrick's needed him.

I leaned over and gave Dean a kiss on the forehead. "Thank you for telling me that, Bean. I think I'm going to need to talk with him before things get more awkward."

He nodded. "Good plan." He shook his head and let out a huff. "The guy has confused sub written all over him, or at least he has in the past. If it's going to help, you can talk to him about us."

"Thank you, but I'll try not to go into details unless I have to. There are some boundaries employers don't need to cross. However, I hear you and Logan have a date with a video game. You should probably get out of here so you aren't late."

Dean grinned. "We do! Aiden's at a shoot and Trent's working."

And my boy was ready to be done adulting for the day. "Okay. Head home. Remember bedtime at ten thirty."

He huffed and groaned but reluctantly nodded. "Yes, Daddy."

"Good boy." I leaned forward and gave him a kiss. "Love you."

His smile brightened. "Love you too."

A few seconds later, Dean and Larson were out the door and I was left to focus on my staff, Wyatt included. What was I going to do with the new information?

CHAPTER THIRTY

DEAN

"What were you and Larson up to tonight?"

"Do we seriously have no secrets?" I punched a button, my duck collecting another apple.

Logan was nearby, harvesting his own crops while we chatted. "Have we ever?"

"Probably more than we should've."

Logan laughed. "Okay, you have a point."

I grinned as I thought of the evening. "We were at the house. He asked me to pick out colors for the siding. It's the next thing to be changed. Oh, and picking out wall colors. Then we went to Brodrick's for a few minutes. Now I'm here."

I directed my character toward the marketplace. We'd been playing for over an hour, and aside from a few texts letting me know that Daddy was still at work, it had been a pretty quiet evening. The only other voice I'd heard all night had been Trent's reminding Logan that he was expected to be in bed by eleven.

Logan had huffed and grumbled but ultimately sighed and told Trent he'd go to bed. It was still a little strange to hear Logan call Trent Daddy without overt sarcasm.

Of course, when Trent was telling him to follow rules, Logan always sounded exasperated. Then the "Love you, Daddy" as Trent left the house was genuine. Just as genuine was his groan of embarrassment when Trent reminded him that his stuffy, Pierre, didn't belong on the bench in the hallway. Trent was grumbling that he didn't want a call that evening complaining that he couldn't find his dog.

Not like I was going to say anything. I was sitting in the living room, Mooch on my lap, my blanket around my shoulders, and Babbit tucked into my elbow.

I was happy that they had started working their own stuff out. Logan had definitely seemed less bouncy the last few weeks, to the point that he'd sat through the entire dinner last week without bouncing around. Everyone had noticed the change. Aiden had beamed with undeniable pride when Logan let Trent make decisions for him or let him step in to remind him to keep his voice down.

My phone pinged and I looked down.

Daddy: *Bedtime is coming up. If you're still playing your game, you need to wrap up and tell Logan good night. He has to go to sleep too.*

I sighed loudly enough that it caught Logan's attention over the noise of our game. "What's up?"

"Bedtime's coming up. Just got a text. But he's not going to be home."

Logan hummed. "Going to sleep alone isn't fun."

"Your bedtime's soon too, though."

Logan blew a raspberry. "Trent isn't going to care. I get the psychology behind it, and it feels good when he's home and puts his foot down sometimes. But it's not like he's going to care what time I go to bed when he's not here."

"If I don't go to bed on time, I have to go to bed early on the weekend." I wrinkled my nose at the thought. It hadn't been bad going to bed at a decent hour when Merrick was home, but with work picking up, going to bed alone wasn't fun.

I had spent the last two nights telling myself that he had a job that would keep him away from home at weird hours sometimes. At least he wasn't traveling like he used to, but I'd grown accustomed to Merrick's presence in my bed. Truthfully, I'd grown accustomed to my Daddy being home in the evenings.

"Yuck. Trent threatened that. But what he doesn't know won't hurt him. Tell me more about the house? Are you moving in with Mer when it's ready?"

I forgot all about Daddy's warning to go to bed early as I told Logan all about the house and our plans. Now that he'd put my bucket of toys in my office instead of the bedroom, I was starting to see his point about my office being drab. Then again, I didn't like playing in my office anyway. It reminded me of being an adult and kept pulling me away from my play.

Time slipped by as we talked about the house and our plans. Logan had just asked when we were going to move in when a throat cleared in the doorway. I forgot all about the question as I looked over to see a very frustrated Daddy staring at me. "Bean."

I winced. From the tone of his voice, I'd missed bedtime. "Hi, Daddy?"

He gave a resigned sigh as he shook his head at me. "TV off. Tell Logan good night."

"Yes, Daddy." I didn't want to disappoint him any more than I already had. Until now, I'd been good about following rules. Tonight I'd been lonely and Logan had been a good distraction. The distraction didn't make up for the look on Daddy's face at the moment. "I gotta go."

"I heard. Later."

The room fell into silence as I exited the game and turned the TV off. My phone was sitting beside me, the screen blinking that I had eight missed messages. The anxious feeling in my stomach was unlike anything I'd ever experienced as a kid.

My mom and I'd had disagreements, and I'd been grounded a few times. Gramma and Pap had also gotten frustrated with me, leaving me to spend plenty of time weeding the garden, doing extra chores, or in my room. None of those felt as grave as disappointing my Daddy.

It took effort to look over at him. He was still in the doorway, his arms crossed over his chest, staring at me. His eyes had circles under them, and his hair was a mess. He stifled a yawn as he stood there watching me.

Seeing how tired he was only made things worse. He was exhausted and wanted to go to bed, and now he had to be Daddy and deal with me. I gripped Babbit's ear, trying to find a way to make it better. All I could come up with was an apology. "Sorry, Daddy. I lost track of time. We were talking and playing. I saw the text reminding me to wrap up, but then we started talking about something else."

His face never changed as he listened to me. "I noticed. That doesn't mean that it excuses your behavior."

My head hung low and tears pricked behind my eyelids. "I know. I'm sorry."

"Come on. It's time to get ready for bed."

I didn't want to make him have to tell me again, so I moved Mooch and gathered my things quickly before climbing the steps. He was just inside my doorway, pointing me toward the bathroom. "Go brush your teeth. I'll get your pajamas."

My bedtime routine felt more like a death sentence. I was aware of every movement and step, paying more attention to doing them right than fast. He'd had such a long day and I'd made it worse instead of better. As I stepped out of the bathroom, the uneasy feeling in my stomach finally made sense. I was scared and anxious and just as disappointed in myself as he was.

I knew I would have to go to bed early the next night, but what if it was too much for him? What if having to follow through on consequences when he had so many other things on his plate was just too much? Would he still want a boy who didn't listen?

I'd worked myself up to the point where I was nearly in tears when I stepped out of the bathroom.

The first thing I saw was Daddy sitting on the bed holding my pajama shirt. If it was too much, he wouldn't be there. I held onto that thought as tightly as I was gripping Babbit as I slowly made my way over to him. To my surprise, he reached for my T-shirt and I let him tug it over my head. When the baggy T-shirt was off, he placed a kiss on my forehead. "Pajama pants, underwear, or nothing?"

Swallowing a few times before I trusted my voice not to break, I still ended up whispering my response. "Pants."

He nodded and reached behind him for my pajama pants, a pair covered in superheroes that matched the T-shirt he'd pulled over my head. Despite my nerves, I found myself smiling at the gesture.

"You going to get your pants off, or should I do it for you?" He didn't sound mad, but he wasn't teasing like he normally did either.

My only response was a shake of my head as I reached for the button of my jeans. My fingers shook slightly as I rushed to work the button and zipper open quickly, then pulled my pants and underwear down in one motion. I was left standing in my bedroom in just a baggy T-shirt that covered my very uninterested dick.

Daddy held my pants out in a way that gave me the option of taking them from him or stepping into them as he held them. Needing the connection and closeness, I stepped into them and let him work them up my legs. Once they were on, Daddy handed over my blanket and Babbit and turned toward the bed to pull the covers on my side back.

Climbing in, I decided that if I hadn't blown it already, I would do everything I could not to mess up in the future.

My head hit the pillow and the blankets were already being pulled up. "Good night, Bean. I love you."

Tears pricked at my eyes. *It couldn't be that bad if he said he loved me.*

"I'll be to bed in a few minutes. I need to get myself ready."

Words tumbled out of my mouth. "Wait, you're staying?"

His brows pulled downward so far they nearly met in the center of his forehead. "I'd planned on it, at least if you still want me to."

"But you're upset with me."

The bed dipped and I opened my eyes to see Daddy sitting beside me. "Bean, I need you to listen carefully."

He waited until I looked up at him. Without my glasses on, he was always blurry, but with the tears in my eyes, it was hard to see him at all. I was able to make out his hand reaching toward me, and I couldn't deny it felt nice when he placed it on my head and rubbed gently. "No one is perfect. I will never expect perfection, either as Daddy or as Merrick. We talked about rules and consequences, and you agreed."

My chin was trembling before I opened my mouth. "I-I-I…" I forced myself to take a deep breath. Pulling both Babbit and my blanket tightly to my chest, their familiar feel in my hands finally provided enough comfort that I could speak again. "I like the rules. They're nice. But I didn't know I'd feel so bad for not following them." Having spoken the words, the weight that had been sitting on my chest since I heard Daddy clear his throat in the living room finally began to ease.

Strong hands massaged my scalp. "We're both still

finding our footing here. Maybe you didn't mean to ignore my texts. Maybe you were pushing the limits a little. Maybe you were trying to figure out how this is going to work in the long run. Maybe it was a little of all of those things. Let's take our personal rules out of the equation for a minute. If I wasn't Daddy and you weren't my boy—we were just Merrick and Dean, two boyfriends with totally vanilla lives—do you think that we'd never disappoint the other person?"

The answer was so obvious, I found myself shaking my head quickly. "That's ridiculous. Of course we would."

Daddy hummed. "Exactly. At some point, I'd disappoint you. You'd disappoint me. Maybe we'd have a fight. Maybe we wouldn't speak to each other for a few hours."

I gave a weak nod and sniffled.

He used a thumb to wipe away a tear that had managed to pool at the corner of my eye. "This isn't any different. What is different is that we already talked about how we're going to handle these bumps. If it's too much, you need to tell me. If it's easier, we can have safewords for the future. Right now, the consequence for not listening is no video games tomorrow and early bedtime. That's it. If we need to talk more before or after, we will. But once you wake up on Saturday, it's all over. Until then, and even afterward, I'm still Daddy, I'm still Merrick, and nothing is going to change for us."

I gave a weak nod, too tired and emotional for anything else.

He rubbed at my scalp a few more minutes and eventually gave a reassuring smile. "I'll be back in just a few minutes. Promise. Try to get some sleep. It's late."

His words had been clear, but my brain was struggling to believe that. I'd messed up. Was going to bed early the next night really going to fix it? Exhaustion was louder than my worries and began to cloud my thoughts.

My brain was hatching a plan as Daddy came to bed and I began to drift off. The last thing I remembered was mumbling a quiet "Night, Daddy. Love you."

He might have responded, but if he did, I was already asleep.

Sleep wasn't long-lived. Not even six hours later, I was wide awake. I'd woken up plastered to Daddy. His arm had been wrapped around me and I was warm and comfortable, just like every other morning. Except this morning, I couldn't stay in bed. The thoughts I'd had as I drifted off to sleep were still fresh in my mind and refused to allow me to rest longer.

He had a better hold on me than was reasonable for a man who was asleep, but I eventually managed to slip from his grip and replace my body with Babbit. Once out of bed, I tiptoed out the door, skipping my bathroom for my morning pee and heading down the steps to the hall bath.

A few minutes later, I was in the kitchen. Daddy made me pancakes or waffles on the weekend. It was fun to wake up smelling the sweet batter and sausage or bacon cooking.

Daddy usually stuck with scrambled eggs and sausage, telling me that he didn't like pancakes or waffles as much as I did, but he was happy to make them for me. The only time he would eat just as much of his breakfast as I did was when he made French toast.

He'd made it for me the weekend before and put strawberries on top. We didn't have any strawberries left because I'd eaten them all during the week. We did have blueberries, though.

Opening the cupboard, I remembered he'd used a special bread that we didn't have any more of. We did have a loaf of my favorite soft wheat bread from the bakery that I was positive would work.

My biggest stumbling block was that I wasn't normally a breakfast maker and had never made French toast before. The previous weekend, I'd sat at the counter playing a video game and talking to Daddy and had hardly paid attention to what he'd been doing.

I was pretty sure there had been eggs and milk, and he had to have put something else in there because it had smelled sweet and there had been a spiced taste to it. When the fridge dinged at me, warning me that it had been open too long, I shut the door and admitted I needed to look up the recipe. Except I'd left my phone upstairs, so my tablet would have to do.

Five minutes later, I'd found countless recipes, all of them with very strong opinions on which ingredients were best. This was nowhere near as easy as my Daddy made it look. I was already frustrated and hadn't put anything in the bowl yet. The fourth recipe I found wasn't as opinionated and particular about the type of eggs, milk, or bread used. It basically amounted to a few basic spices whisked with milk and eggs. Once that was ready, all I would have to do would be dip the bread into the mixture and cook it on a hot pan.

Ten minutes later, I learned that it wasn't as easy as the recipe made it look. The batter was wet and the bread fell apart when I tried to pick it up. When I finally got the first two pieces—that by then had turned into six—onto the pan, the griddle was too hot and the batter smoked and burned quickly.

Determined to save breakfast, I turned the burner down and dipped another piece of bread into the batter, careful to not let it soak as long that time. The smoke detector took that moment to warn me that the hallway was filling with smoke.

"I know, I know! Give me a minute and I'll open a window. I need to get this on the pan!"

In the middle of my tirade at the smoke detector, a sleepy, rumbly voice came into the kitchen. "Do I even want to know what's going on here?"

I jumped and gasped, dropping the egg-soaked piece of bread on the floor. My elbow hit the bowl I'd been dipping the bread into, and I watched helplessly as it soaked my pajamas before clattering to the floor.

It ended faster than it had begun. Breakfast was already ruined and now the smoke detector was going off, Daddy went from sleepy to startled, and the full-blown cry I had managed to avoid the night before could no longer be stopped.

My first sniffle had barely escaped when arms wrapped around me and pulled me close, gooey wet pajamas and all. "Bean. What's going on? You're never up this early. You don't like to make breakfast, the kitchen is filled with smoke, and I think those charred squares on that plate were supposed to be edible."

"I was making you breakfast!" If I'd whined more than spoken, Daddy didn't call me out on it. The truth was, at the moment, I just needed someone to make it better.

"It's not even six thirty. Why are you trying to make breakfast? Especially without any coffee."

I smacked my forehead with an open palm. "I forgot the coffee!"

Daddy's chuckle was warm, even with the disaster all around us. "I think you left half your brain in bed."

"Breakfast."

"Might need to be cereal."

Tears came again as the frustration of the previous night was released. When my sobbing slowed, we were rocking back and forth and Daddy was whispering soothing words in my ear. I picked up that he loved me and he would listen when I was ready to talk. There were some curses he'd directed at himself between reassuring me that everything was fine.

The tears stopped and I wrapped my arms around his back. "I messed up."

CHAPTER THIRTY-ONE

MERRICK

Dean had been fitful all night, tossing, turning, and occasionally whimpering. He'd been upset when he fell asleep and I'd planned to talk to him more that morning. Then I woke up to find a stuffed animal in my arms, a cold bed, the smell of smoke, and clanking coming from the kitchen.

Plans changed.

Aside from burning bread on the stove and Dean muttering about this not looking complicated when I had made it, the kitchen had still been relatively clean. Or it had been clean until I'd scared him, now there was egg batter on the floor.

Then again, aside from the one night Dean had been feeling particularly young and had dragged the few buckets of toys from his office to spill them across the living room floor, he was always tidy. It wasn't surprising he was equally neat while cooking.

It also wasn't surprising he'd been having a hard time

with the bread. Whatever he'd been dipping it into looked suspiciously thin, and the bread he had been using was so soft that it barely held up to jelly being spread on it. Though that still didn't explain what had led to the charcoal briquettes that might once have been pieces of bread.

Ten minutes later, still soaked in spiced egg milk, Dean finally cried himself out. I wanted to tell him that it wasn't worth crying over spilled milk, but I knew that whatever had him this upset wasn't burned bread or spiced pajamas.

As we swayed back and forth, I thought back to when I was about sixteen and struggling with my sexuality. An ignorant comment from the health teacher about homosexuality being a choice had sent me over the edge and into a very uncharacteristic tirade, ranting about how he was wrong, no one would *choose* to be gay, and that just because we lived in conservative mid-America didn't mean we had to be ignorant. Before I'd clamped my mouth shut, I'd known I'd overstepped, so getting sent to the principal's office hadn't been a surprise.

The dread had only grown more as the principal called home and my dad was the one who answered. With my mom out shopping, he was left to come to the school to pick me up for the rest of the day. My world was crashing down around me. My dad was obviously worried about me since I'd never been in trouble at school, and to make matters worse, the call had come in while my dad had been fixing a metal link to the sign that hung at the entrance to the farm.

His rare few hours of downtime had been interrupted by my outburst and the welding project had been cut short.

When we got home, he was needed back in the field and had to leave the project for another day.

Despite being interrupted, he'd tried to get me to open up the entire way home, first with small talk about the welding project, then prying a little more about the events of the day. Not ready to talk, I'd stayed silent. In my silence, the guilt had continued to grow throughout the evening and into the night.

Looking back on the situation, I could have fixed everything by talking with my parents, but instead, I'd thought I could show him I was sorry while not discussing anything and fix the sign myself.

I'd watched or helped him countless times over my life. In my mind, finishing the weld and hanging the sign would be easy work. And it was. At least until I got the sign hung and pulled the truck away to admire my work.

The beautiful metal sign hung for all of ten seconds before the link snapped. I'd watched in horror as it fell to the ground, hit the unforgiving dirt-and-gravel driveway, and the corner bent awkwardly. Of course, my dad had taken that moment to come see why the truck was at the bottom of the driveway.

Just like the man in my arms was crying over a ruined breakfast, I'd found myself wrapped in my dad's strong arms as I cried over the damaged sign. And just like I hadn't really been crying over the sign, I knew my boy wasn't crying over a ruined breakfast.

That night, as it'd felt like the world was crashing down around me, I'd come out to my dad's shoulder, sniffling and snuffling as I finally told him everything that I'd been holding inside and why I'd tried to fix the sign.

With the memory fresh, I didn't think twice when Dean did the same thing I had. "I didn't listen. I didn't go to bed when I should have. I didn't text you back last night."

His words were muffled by my shoulder, but the house was as quiet as it had been that night on the farm. I pulled him closer, just as my dad had me, trying to provide comfort and reassurance as he worked through his feelings.

"And-and-and I was lonely and mi-missed you. Maybe it wasn't all a mistake. B-but I disappointed you and felt bad and I don't want to be too much trouble." His shoulders heaved again, and I dug my fingertips into tense shoulder muscles. "You like French toast, so I thought that if I made you breakfast, you'd be happy with me again."

As my adult boyfriend, Dean was fully capable of talking his thoughts and fears out. We'd had discussions in the past, from previous boyfriends to the accident. But the night before, he hadn't been my boyfriend—he'd been my boy. He'd been lonely and, if I had to guess, didn't want to make me feel guilty for working so much but didn't know how to put all those thoughts into words. He'd put them into actions instead and hadn't followed the rules.

He'd gotten my attention, but it didn't seem like he'd been ready for the natural consequences.

With the admission out, he sagged against me. Standing by the bed of the truck, my dad had told me he wasn't a mind reader. Nearly thirty years later, I fully understood the guilt he'd expressed for not realizing I was struggling sooner.

Kissing the side of Dean's head, I chose my words carefully. "When you feel out of sorts, you need to talk to me. I can't promise you that I could have gotten home earlier yesterday, but I could have talked with you about it and we could have made a plan together."

Dean sighed and pushed back to look at me. His eyes were bloodshot and puffy and his glasses had spots of tears on them, but his cheeks were finally dry. "It was fun talking to Logan last night, though."

I snorted a laugh. I couldn't help it. I'd woken up to my phone vibrating with a text from Trent. He'd been bitching that Aiden had come home to find Logan awake at nearly one in the morning. "Well, you two can both have fun going to bed early tonight."

My boy's nose wrinkled. "I really have to go to bed early tonight?"

"Yes. You still have to go to bed early tonight. But we can try to salvage breakfast. I'll even make sure to get home early tonight so we can spend time together before bedtime."

Dean's smile was enough to make me move heaven and earth to make sure I was home by five.

With my help, we were able to leave the house with bellies full of—edible—French toast that went a long way to improving both our moods. Dean was all smiles as he got into his car, freshly showered and wearing a pair of light gray dress pants that left absolutely nothing to the imagination. Given the temperature that morning, he'd opted against the sports coat, and his purple dress shirt was just as fitted as his pants. It wasn't fair that his ass looked so damn good and I could do nothing but wait until later on to touch him again.

With Dean out of the house and me anxious to get back home for the night, I found myself at Brodrick's before nine. It was too early to be mixing strong drinks, but I was enjoying the quiet time as I played with a mimosa recipe.

As I worked, I got lost in thought about the staff the night before. They'd all had fun practicing the tricks I'd shown them. Even Wyatt had found a rhythm toward the end of the night. Between his growing confidence and the rubberized practice bottles I'd dug out from the storage room that morning, I was hopeful that cleaning broken glass from the counters, floor, and ice well was a thing of the past.

My focus was on the strawberry mimosa I was creating, so I missed the person sliding onto the stool across from me. I finished the drink off with a fresh strawberry garnish, spun the straw around my finger a few times, and popped it in. Sometimes less was more, and in this case, it was exactly what the vibrant pink drink in front of me needed.

"Holy crap, that looks too good to drink!"

I jumped in surprise and looked up to see a startled Wyatt sitting at the bar. My ass hit the back counter and my hand covered my heart to make sure I could still feel it beating. When I fully processed who was sitting there, I took a deep breath. "Wyatt?"

He flushed. "Guilty as charged."

"It's"—I looked at my watch—"nine ten. What are you doing here?"

The tomato red his cheeks turned put any blush I'd ever seen on Dean, Caleb, or Larson to shame. His hands became fascinating and he picked at the skin around his thumbnail. "Um, I just dropped the kids off at school and saw your car here?"

Wyatt would make a killing behind the bar if he could gain confidence. His curly strawberry blond hair made him look younger than his twenty-three years. It was sometimes hard to remember that he was responsible for two teenagers.

Dean could be a handful on his own, and we were both adults. Holding him as he fell apart in the kitchen that morning had rattled me, and I knew I wouldn't have been able to handle it at Wyatt's age, especially with *real* teenagers. Siblings or not, he had his hands full.

"I need to get home early tonight. It's been a rough week for both of us. Thought I'd get a little work done early today, then I got sidetracked when this recipe popped into my head."

Wyatt nodded, though his eyes weren't focused. I knew he was trying to figure out how to say something, so I thought I'd rip the bandage off. "Dean told me last night that he remembers you from past visits."

His flapping mouth, stuttered words, and the way even his ears blushed told me I'd hit the nail on the head. "He-I-well..." His head dropped to the wood counter and for a moment, I worried he'd pass out. I'd just reached out to touch his shoulder when his head shot up and he spit words out so fast they were barely coherent. "He was talking to his friend and said he's a Daddy. But if that's the case, then that makes you his boy and I can't see you as a boy. And the way he looks at you doesn't make me think he's your Daddy and—" He cut himself off with a gasp and his hands flew to his mouth.

Instinctively, I looked behind me to see if someone had come in to elicit such a startled response from him. When I saw no one, I turned back around and focused on the man on the other side of the counter. "Wyatt, are you okay?"

He covered his eyes and moaned. "Oh my god. I shouldn't have said anything! What if he hadn't told you? What if you had no idea? Holy shit, did I just ruin your relationship?"

The poor guy had worked himself into a frenzy and if I didn't step in and calm him down, I didn't doubt he'd be out the door in a heartbeat. He'd already begun pushing back from the counter, shaking his head while apologizing.

"Wyatt. Wyatt!" I had to raise my voice to get him to stop talking and look at me. "You're fine. You haven't told me anything I didn't already know."

He stopped, his mouth clamping shut with an audible clack of teeth. His wide eyes begged for more answers, but he was pursing his lips so tightly they'd turned white.

Taking a deep breath, I tried to answer in the vaguest terms I could. This wasn't my strong suit. I was still learning the ropes of Daddy/boy and D/s relationships myself. This would have been a place where Canyon or Travis would have been much better suited, but they weren't here.

"You're right. I'm not Dean's boy and he isn't my Daddy." The light chuckle that escaped my mouth was mostly due to the discomfort of the situation.

"I guess you can say that we all learn things about ourselves as we move through life. What's right in your twenties might not be right in your thirties. What you think you know about yourself the first forty-five years of life might not be as accurate as you once thought."

Wyatt studied me closely, as though he didn't quite believe what I was saying. "Wait, he's not your Daddy… you're… *his?*" On the last word, his voice rose as high as his eyebrows.

To my surprise, he deflated like a balloon being popped with a pin. "Fuck. I probably just crossed way too many lines, didn't I?"

The conversation had reached awkward, and being behind the bar, I felt more like a judge than a boss or even a friend. I knew it wasn't good practice to make friends with employees, but Wyatt needed a friend more than a boss

Taking the seat beside him, I swung around so my back was against the edge of the bar and I was facing him. "First off, your job is safe. I don't know you well, but I know everyone loves you."

"Seriously?"

"Seriously. And second, I'm an open ear if you need to chat." Thinking better of the statement, I amended it quickly. "And I bet Dean would be happy to talk with you if you'd be more comfortable."

Not that his blush had ever completely faded, but his cheeks reddened again. At least that time they didn't look like a cartoon right before exploding. He slowly blinked as he took in my words, then kept his eyes closed in thought. They were still shut when he spoke quietly. "Thanks. I'll, uh, think about it. I'm not sure I know what to even talk about."

Opening his eyes, he forced a smile. "I'll leave you be. You've got stuff to do if you want to get out of here this evening."

He'd already made it halfway to the front door when I called out to him. If I let Wyatt leave, I'd kick myself in the ass the rest of the day. "Want some practice behind the bar?"

Terror flashed in his eyes, already shaking his head before I could finish the question.

"You sure? I pulled these out earlier. I thought they might help." I tossed one of the unbreakable bottles his way. It was heavy like a liquor bottle would be, and I could fill it with water to simulate what it would feel like full.

Wyatt yelped and jumped away from the bottle until it bounced on the floor a few times. "Wait... what?"

Seeing his smile as he figured out what was at his feet gave me the same feeling of warmth as when I put a smile on Dean's face, though it didn't result in an inconvenient erection in my jeans. I knew I'd done the right thing and would be able to take one worry off Wyatt's plate.

Canyon had once said that being a Daddy wasn't just a title or a role; it was a state of being. For the first time, I understood exactly what he meant. My need to care for people wasn't directed only at Dean. Yes, I wanted to take care of my boy in a very different way than I wanted to take care of Wyatt, but being able to give him a little confidence was as satisfying as when Dean let me step in to help him.

I was more productive the entire day, and Wyatt managed to get over his awkwardness. The rest of the staff fed on that energy, and soon I was heading home to spend a bit of time with Dean.

CHAPTER THIRTY-TWO

DEAN

My productivity ground to a halt that afternoon despite my best efforts. Logan had been texting me since three, complaining that Trent was trying to tell him he was going to bed early.

I'd been stuck between teasing him and trying to get work done. But the more Logan complained about his *Daddy* being mean, the more distracted my thoughts had become.

A stressful night, a very early and long morning, and it being Friday on top of that had my brain fighting to stay on the tasks in front of me. Every time Logan sent another pouty text about how mean Trent was, a bit of guilt coiled inside me. At four I decided it was a lost cause and closed down all my tabs and programs.

Logan: *If Daddy is going to make all these rules and be serious about it, do you think I can get more LEGO?*

Me: *I don't think that's how that works.*

Logan: *But I have to go to bed early! And he's hovering today!*

My laughter was getting harder to contain as he continued to complain.

Me: *He always hovers. Didn't you agree to the rules?*

His response took a few minutes longer than I'd expected, and when it finally came in, I could nearly hear his sigh.

Logan: *... Yes...*

Me: *Are you second guessing?*

I needed to ask the question, but even as I did, it seemed highly unlikely to be the case.

Logan: *No. Not really. Is it weird that I kind of like it? I could never give him as much control as Aiden. I'm totally not going to stop foreplay to text him and ask if I can orgasm. It works for them, and I still get to come whenever I want when Trent isn't home.*

Me: *Whoa there. I know we share a lot, but I don't need to know about this much.*

Logan: *Whoops, sorry, got carried away. I think, before last night, I kind of thought that he was just humoring me. Part of me really didn't think he'd care. What's the difference between eleven and twelve fifty anyway?*

Getting to stay up late on a Friday? I managed to not type my thoughts.

Logan: *What about you?*

Me: *I have to go to bed early.*

Me: *I knew he'd be serious about it. He's sent me a text every single night to get into bed on time. It wasn't hard when no one was distracting me. And I guess I was a little lonely last night.*

My phone rang and I jumped slightly before seeing Logan's name on the caller ID. "Hello?"

"Did you tell him that before? Aiden gets himself in trouble for that stuff all the time. He doesn't tell Trent or me that he's struggling, and when he starts acting out, he gets a punishment and it all comes out. Then Trent feels guilty, and I feel bad."

I spun myself in my chair as I thought about what Logan said. "Not so much. But I'm a reasonable adult. I know that sometimes work commitments are unavoidable. And he's opening his own restaurant! Of course he needs time to get it all in order."

The raspberry Logan blew in my ear made me wince. "But you're also a middle and his submissive. Sometimes, it doesn't matter what your adult brain says—that other part of your brain needs more reassurance. That's okay."

A smile played on my lips. "Talking from experience?"

"Maybe a bit. Trent might have picked up a shift last night, and there's a chance I didn't tell him I'd been looking forward to spending time with him. He'd gone out with Aiden the last two nights I worked, but I haven't had much time with just Trent lately. I was frustrated and avoided talking about it."

"Ohhh." I got that. It made a lot of sense. Though I felt bad that Logan hadn't been able to tell Trent what was going on in his head. A lot like I hadn't been able to tell Merrick.

Our conversation got interrupted by Trent. His voice wasn't far from the phone and I could hear his disappointment in it when he spoke. "Pup, why didn't you say something?"

Logan squeaked in surprise then cursed when something crashed behind him. "Da-Trent!"

"I'm going to let you go." I didn't wait for an answer and hung up the phone, glad I didn't have to be in the room to hear that conversation.

There were technically thirty minutes left in my day. There was a chance I could get something done without Logan bugging me every five minutes, but I wasn't feeling it. I spun my chair back to face my computer and found Merrick in the doorway, leaning against the frame with a smile on his face.

"Daddy!" I couldn't get out of my chair fast enough and nearly flung my arms around him.

He wrapped his arms around me, never missing a beat. "Hey there, Bean. Not that I mind such an excited greeting, but to what do I owe it to?"

Remembering how sad Logan had sounded a minute earlier, I pushed my head into his neck and breathed in deeply. "I've just missed you."

He gave me a squeeze. "You know you can always text or call."

My cheeks noticeably heated. "I didn't want to bother you."

His answering hum told me that a discussion was coming, but for the time being, he tabled it in exchange for an easier topic. "Well, I guess you're in luck because today was productive and I don't feel bad cutting out early. Thought we could go get pizza before heading home."

For the first time since he walked in the door, I realized I was in my office. I tried to look past Merrick to see who was still here, but he just shook his head. "Laptop, Bean. No one's here. I can't believe you're still here, honestly. The place was dark when I got here."

Extricating myself from his grip, I headed over to the desk to shut my laptop down and grab my bag. "Logan's been distracting."

"Is that who you were on the phone with?"

"Yeah. He's pouting that he has to go to bed early tonight. But he did help me see that I don't always handle situations like I should."

Daddy hummed in agreement. "Like ignoring texts?"

I slung my bag over my shoulder and went to grab his hand. "Or not talking when something's bothering me. Adult thoughts and middle thoughts get a little mixed up sometimes."

"I could see how that would happen. We can talk about it over pizza."

"Ham and pineapple. No pepperoni or sausage."

He held the door for me, then waited patiently as I locked the building up. "Since when don't you like sausage and pepperoni?"

"I like it sometimes. But sometimes it's spicy." My middle was particular, and after the last twenty-four hours, very close to the surface. "But ham and pineapple is never spicy."

* * *

With a belly full of good pizza and a can of soda, I was content enough to not pout that Merrick had a beer with dinner. And once he'd grabbed my blanket, Babbit, and a bucket of LEGOs, I couldn't convince myself that alcohol sounded appealing.

He hadn't pulled the Mario sets out but the bucket of bricks that had been growing consistently over the last few weeks. It was still a challenge to shut my brain off, and I always wanted to make something more fantastic than the last creation.

When my eyes fell on little windowpanes, I knew what I was going to make. Halfway to the garage, Daddy's voice caught my attention. "Bean, your toys are here. Where are you going?"

Calling over my shoulder, I continued toward the door. "The garage!"

"Why?" Humor filled his voice and without turning to look at him, I knew he was smiling at me.

A glance backward confirmed the smile. "For my electronics kits." *Duh.*

He stood up from the couch, laughter dancing in his eyes. "I have a feeling I'm going to regret asking this… but why do you need your electronics kits right now?"

"To give the house lights and make the garage door go up and down."

By the way he blinked at me, I wondered if my words hadn't been as clear as my thoughts. Daddy moved my hand from the door, shaking his head in amusement. "Bean, you're not going to have time to wire an entire house tonight."

That's what he thought. But he was already directing me back to the living room. "Sit down here. If you get bored, we can talk about plans for our real new house."

My attention moved from the electronics, to my toys, to our house so fast my head spun for a second. "What about the house?" I was once again sitting on the floor in front of my toy bucket but looking at Daddy.

"Well, we need to come up with a theme for your room."

My nose turned up. "But I like sleeping with you!" A quick glance toward Babbit and Blankie had me adding to that. "So do they." Suddenly bashful, I ducked my head.

Daddy slid onto the floor beside me, handing me a base plate. "Not the room for you to sleep in. I happen to like having you next to me every night. I meant the room for your toys and games."

"Oh." That made more sense. I reached into the bin and pulled out a few long bricks. "Space." It wasn't like me to have a lot of opinions about decor—as was witnessed by my office—but I'd done a lot of thinking about the office area in the new house.

Since figuring out I was a middle, I'd discovered I had a wide range of headspaces. Earlier in the day, texting with Logan, I'd definitely felt more like a teenager avoiding doing my homework than a business owner. As the evening had gone by, I'd felt younger. It didn't feel awkward to be sitting on the floor with a bucket of LEGO bricks beside me as I dug through them and talked with Daddy about my new room.

"Tell me about what you see."

With that little bit of encouragement, all the ideas that I'd kept in my head about how much fun a space-themed bedroom would be came tumbling out as I built a more basic house than the one I'd originally planned. It had a door, a few windows, and a flat roof. I finally gave up digging for the wheels and dumped the bucket out beside me.

"I always thought it would be cool to have a whole bookshelf with space books." I grabbed two sets of wheels from the pile. "And I saw this really cool beanbag a few years ago that looked like the moon. I almost bought it. Oh, and there's this whole thing that matches my comforter and sheets. There's throw pillows and a throw blanket and these stuffed planets."

I grabbed a windshield from the pile. "I almost painted my room dark blue. I always wanted a space room when I was a kid, but we lived in my grandparents' house for a long time. By the time we had a place we could decorate and paint, I was too old for space stuff."

A yawn escaped as I placed a person in the front seat of the car I'd built. Daddy hadn't said anything more than asking for clarification on ideas as I worked, but he was still sitting next to me.

After sorting through the bricks for a few seconds, I finally huffed. "Do you see a tree?"

He didn't answer as he looked but finally plucked one from the edge of the pile. "Like this?"

"Exactly!" I placed a kiss on his cheek as I took it from his hand. "Thank you, Daddy."

He rubbed my hair. "You're welcome. Few more

minutes to play, then you need to get cleaned up. Bedtime is rapidly approaching."

Hopefully, my sigh hid my stifled yawn as I turned back to my toys. "Okay."

I could have pushed myself to stay up longer, but after staying up late the night before, not sleeping well, waking up early, and then the weird emotional roller coaster I'd been on that day, I was tired when Daddy told me to clean my toys up. There was even a chance I sighed as he pulled the blankets around me and kissed me good night. "See you in the morning, Bean."

Another yawn escaped as I tried to tell him good night. When it finally passed, I cracked my eyes open. "Night, Daddy. Love you."

"Love you too." He placed Babbit in my arms and draped Blankie over my shoulders. On his way out of the room, he flicked the light off but left the door open.

Before he could get far, I needed to make sure of one thing. "Daddy? When I get up in the morning, I won't be in trouble anymore?"

He appeared in the doorway, the hallway light casting a soft glow behind him as he studied me for a few seconds. "You aren't in trouble now. This is just a consequence for not following the rules. So you know that Daddy cares enough to follow through and hold you accountable for your actions."

My head struggled to nod, so I used words. "Oh. Okay. Good. I like that you care." My eyes were too heavy to stay open, so I let them drift closed and sleep overtook me.

CHAPTER THIRTY-THREE

MERRICK

For the first thirty minutes Dean was asleep, I enjoyed watching TV that wasn't a video game or a cartoon. Then I began wondering if I'd missed the next episode of the cartoon Dean liked. After listening to the show so frequently, I'd somehow gotten accustomed to it and now followed the plot.

When I got up to pee, I ended up upstairs checking on Dean. He was sleeping soundly, so I couldn't even talk with him. It was time to admit I was bored.

Settling back onto the couch, stubbornly refusing to get ready for bed, I pulled out my phone.

Me: I've been single most of my life. Why is it that I've forgotten what to do with myself when Dean is in bed and I'm awake?

The response came back almost immediately, telling me that Trent was likely in the same situation.

Trent: *It's been so long since I've had a night off and neither* *one of the guys awake with me. I'm losing my mind. I almost let Logan stay up.*

Me: *Dean was falling asleep before I tucked him in. I don't think it would have mattered.*

Trent: *Logan was pushing his luck all night. I overheard him talking with Dean this afternoon, he was upset I took a shift last night. He also didn't think I'd make him go to bed early tonight. I'm telling you, this middle stuff is a lot harder than caring for a little. When Aiden gets moody, a stern look or a timeout is all it takes for him to be singing like a bird. I practically have to read Logan's mind. It's everything he says and doesn't say.*

I found myself grinning. It was a good way to describe Dean as well. Though I was happy Dean wasn't as rambunctious or mischievous as Logan. It was hard enough to keep track of Logan the adult. From what I'd seen of Curious the pup, he was a handful, but at least he didn't talk. Logan the middle was likely to be nearly as hyper as Curious but with a large vocabulary and opinions to match.

Trent sent another text and I had to scroll up to make sure I hadn't actually typed my thoughts.

Trent: *Curious is so much easier to deal with than a slightly non-traditional middle. He still doesn't like being considered submissive, but he needs routines and structure and reassurance. I've always known he's a little insecure about his personality—worried that he's going to be too much for people—but I never truly understood just how much he needs to be told he's not. It's like he's internalized every single time someone told him to chill out or calm down. He needs a constant reminder that he's not* *going to be too much, but he's not going to come out and say he needs that either.*

Me: *You just have to show him. I know, I know, easier said than done. I wasn't expecting Dean to never fully turn off his middle side. There's a lot of looking to me for things, and sometimes I forget that it's not just adult Dean that I'm dealing with.*

Trent: *Ah, I know that feeling. Especially with Aiden. You'll get there. You both will. Logan's just stubborn. Though, I kinda miss the stubborn ass right now. It's too quiet in the house.*

Me: *That's why I texted you.*

I laughed at the two of us. We were quite a pair, both bored to death while our boys slept. It was funny until I stood to get a beer from the fridge and stepped on a LEGO that had been left on the floor.

Cursing the little nubbin that could double as a medieval torture device, I gave up on the beer and sat down on the couch with a sketch pad and pencil, designing the room Dean had described earlier in the night. With a futon for gaming or napping, some well-placed storage, a table to put his toys on, and a nice TV for gaming or watching cartoons, Dean would be set, and my feet would be safe again.

I'd forgotten all about texting with Trent as I worked. When I finally yawned and looked at the time, it was nearing one in the morning. Dean had gone to bed three hours earlier. It would be unreasonable to expect him to sleep in the next morning.

My suspicion as I got ready for bed turned out to be correct. After nine hours of sleep, he was awake. Parts of him more than others.

I woke up with a moan and a rocking motion against my ass. Without Dean on top of me, I'd actually been able to roll to my left side for the first time in weeks. Since I'd stripped naked before bed, too tired to fight with pajamas, the position had given him full access to my ass, with my cock hard and leaking between my stomach and the bed. For a brief moment, I'd thought it was a dream, but when I felt hips rock into me again, I knew it was Dean.

Reaching behind me, I gripped his ass through the pajama pants he'd fallen asleep in as he rocked again. His cock had pocked through the fly giving our skin full contact, and I heard a gasp as warm breath ghosted over the back of my neck.

"I could get used to wake-ups like this one."

Dean's sleepy laugh told me he wasn't quite as awake as his dick was. After another squeeze to his ass, a gasp turned into a moan followed by a sharp thrust forward. The head of his cock grazed over my hole, raising goosebumps that ran from my shoulders to my knees.

My hips pushed back, my ass seeking more friction regardless of the lack of prep or how much I wanted more sleep.

He kneaded my ass cheek, his thumb dipping into my crease. "I want in this ass." Dean's sleepy voice was filled with possession that made my heart speed up.

Between the rutting, kneading, and his sexy growl, I found myself alternating between rutting against the pillow in front of me and pushing back into his thrusts. "Hell yes. Yours for the taking." He rutted against me a few more times before rolling us as a unit.

Resting on my ass, his thighs to either side of my body, I felt him move to rummage through the drawer in his nightstand. The entire time he searched, he rocked against me.

His body lifted from mine for a moment, then I caught sight of his underwear fling across the room before he straddled me again. When I finally heard the unmistakable sound of lube being poured into Dean's hand and felt it trickle onto my ass, I wasn't sure how long I'd be able to hold off. He slid two fingers inside me, stretching and rotating as he explored the tightness of my hole.

I was so ready to be filled, the last thing in my head was the thought of tensing. Just the opposite happened as I began to push onto his fingers, desperate for any contact with my dick or prostate.

"Damn, you're loose. One more finger, then you can have this." He slapped his sheathed cock against my ass cheek as he slid a third finger into me. The sound of his cock against my skin, the stretch of his fingers, the familiar —yet shockingly out of place—feel of the latex against my skin, all worked together to push an entirely unique fantasy into my brain and out of my mouth.

"Shit. Dean. So good, baby. So, so good. Want to feel you in me. All of you. Can't wait to do this without a barrier between us."

Sudden stillness in my ass followed the statement and he had a hitch in his voice when he spoke. "What?"

Without stimulation, my brain caught up to my mouth. My first instinct was to deny it, tell him that I'd been caught up in the moment, but that would have been a lie. It wasn't easy, but I forced myself upward without pushing Dean's fingers from my ass, twisting just enough to look into my boy's eyes. "Yeah, Dean. I want that. Not today, but I want that with you. My ass belongs to you and only you."

Dean put a hand over his heart. While his words were sarcastic, I could see emotion shimmering in his eyes. "Well, if that isn't the sweetest thing anyone has ever said to me." Then he crooked his fingers just so and nailed my prostate. Around my moan, I heard him speak. "As soon as we're cleaned up, we're finding a clinic."

I would have laughed, but he removed his fingers and the sudden loss pulled an entirely different moan from my body. The head of Dean's cock was lined up with my hole as he whispered above me. "I can't wait anymore. I need in you so we can take a nap, then make some calls. Maybe a shower somewhere in there."

He pushed in, applying enough pressure that his head breached my entrance, then slowed as he drove in steadily until his balls rested against my ass. His gentle movements gave me plenty of time to think about what it would be like without something between us.

The fear that had always accompanied the thought was nowhere to be found. Each push forward brought the image more alive until I was pushing back to meet him thrust for thrust, begging to be filled as Dean's pace picked up until he was pounding into me. Beneath me, the pillow was wet with precum, the slickness allowing me to hump it as frantically as Dean was doing to my ass.

"Come for me, Mer." The words were barely audible as he frantically thrust. "I'm so close. I need to feel you come.

Please, Daddy, come first, pull me over." I didn't know if he'd meant to utter the last sentence aloud, but the words were out.

The last of my control shattered and my body convulsed as I shot into the pillow. Dean's yell drowned out my throaty roar as my ass contracted tightly around his dick. "Fucking. Yes. Your ass is so tight."

He bucked into me with frantic, shallow thrusts until he stilled above me. Even as I shot another volley of cum into the pillow, I could feel the condom fill inside me as he released.

Dean collapsed on my back, his dick sliding out of me with the movement. Our bodies stuck together with sweat, and he muttered and cursed as he fought with removing the condom. The giant sigh he gave as he finally rested fully against my back let me know he'd managed to take care of it.

There was still a lot of cleanup—of me, the bed, and him—that would need to happen sooner rather than later, but for now we were clean enough.

As our breathing slowed, Dean rolled off my back. Feeling his eyes on me, I turned my head to find him studying me closely. I began to ask what he was thinking, but the words didn't have a chance to form before he spoke, his voice barely more than a whisper. "It's okay if that's not what you want."

I blinked. "Don't want what?"

His fingers twitched a few times before he placed them on my arm. His eyes closed as he gathered his words. "If you don't want to stop using condoms. I completely understand if you don't. I know it's a thing that bothers you, so it's okay if those were just words spoken in the moment." He opened his eyes again, allowing me to see the sincerity in them.

I adjusted so that I could look at him better, making sure I had his full attention and had gathered my thoughts before I opened my mouth. "I meant it in the moment, and I mean it now. I want to share that with you. You're the first person I've ever wanted to remove the barriers for. And I don't mean just leaving condoms behind. I don't want to protect myself from you. With you, there's no need. I trust you."

Tears welled in his eyes as he listened to me with a gentle smile on his lips.

It wasn't often that I was this forthcoming, and if I didn't get it all out now, it would be hard to say it later. "I've trusted you since I met you. I trust you today. I'll trust you in fifty years. You're so much more to me than my boyfriend and my boy. You're my world. You're the man who deserves all of me, and I plan on giving you that. Today, tomorrow, forever. I love you, and I always will."

Dean swiped at the tears that were now running freely down his face. A dry chuckle escaped as he began to speak. "I had this big speech prepared in my head about how I understood your reservations and respected them. Now I don't know what to say to that."

He pressed his lips against mine, gently and without pressure for anything deeper. When we separated, he was smiling again, though it was watery and his voice cracked a few times as he spoke. "You'll always have my world and my heart. I fell in love with you as a friend almost as soon as I met you, and that love has only grown. Until recently, I didn't know it was possible to love someone as much as I love you. Like you said, you're more than my boyfriend and more than my Daddy. You're my best friend, my lover, the person that knows me better than I know myself. I'll always protect your world, just like I know you'll protect mine. Today, tomorrow, always."

There were no more words to be said as we curled into each other's embrace. It had taken us time to find ourselves. With a little trust and a lot of help from our friends, we'd found not only ourselves but each other as well. I'd lived long enough to know when something was right, and the two of us just were.

I must have drifted off at some point because I woke to Dean giggling quietly in my arms. Cracking my eyes open, I saw him tapping at his phone screen. "What's so funny?"

He rolled over, Babbit and Blankie clutched to his chest, and grinned at me. "Mom's going to be here in two hours. She wants to take us out to celebrate figuring our 'shit out.' Oh, and she also says that if we'd listened to her years ago, we could have saved a lot of time."

It was my turn to laugh. "Jenny's not going to let that one go, is she?"

Dean shook his head. "And Aunt Monica's going to be worse."

Knowing he was right but having nothing to counter the statement with, I reached out and squeezed his side. "Come on, Bean. Let's get cleaned up. If we stay like this much longer, we're never going to get the smell of sex off us."

"Ugh, fine. But only because I have to pee." He wriggled to the side of the bed and looked back at me before getting up. "You know, I might need Daddy's help getting cleaned up."

His playful wink had me moving to get up despite my body's screams for more sleep. We were going to be lucky to have the bedding changed before Jenny arrived, but I couldn't find it in me to care. I had my boy waiting on me, and the rest of the world could wait on us.

~*~

Coming January, 2022: *Seth* (https://readerlinks.com/l/2095111), book 3 in the Johnson Family Rules series. If you haven't had had a chance to meet Zander and Nathan, make sure to begin reading the series here (http://readerlinks.com/l/2085979). This huge, blended, and eccentric family has a surprise at every corner and love to share. Dive in today!

If this is your first visit to the middle of Tennessee with me, then welcome. Here's a list of books in which the side characters from this book appear.

Want to learn more about how Caleb and Travis got together? Pick up *Desires* (http://readerlinks.com/l/

2079528) today and discover the moment Caleb, a sweet, shy, and skittish little, found his happily ever after with a workaholic construction worker, Travis.

CURIOUS ABOUT HOW two best friends who couldn't find a way to make a relationship work finally found love with a third? Read all about Trent, Logan, and Aiden in *Curiosity* (http://readerlinks.com/l/2079527). A serious Dom, a bouncy pup, and a sweet little find out that together they are stronger than apart.

DEXTER'S A HANDFUL and James is a closed-off grouch. But when they live next to each other, it's impossible to avoid one another, especially when they share so many of the same friends. Find out how a little satin, a lot of sass, and a sprinkling of grouchy bear turns into a romance too sweet to pass up. Start reading *Attraction* (http://readerlinks.com/l/2079526) today.

LARSON AND CANYON played a huge part in *Secrets* (http://readerlinks.com/l/2079525), if you haven't read their story yet, make sure to pick up *Secrets* today. You won't want to miss how this giant little and his super sweet Daddy discovered happiness in the most unexpected way.

A Note from Carly

Dear Reader,

First, thanks for picking up *Submission*. Second, an apology in advance, because this is going to be a long note!

This series has spanned years, and I've experienced so much growth as an author throughout writing these books. Looking back on the last two and a half years, I can't begin to tell you how much Caleb and Travis changed my life. Cliché, right? But it's the truth. I am not the same person I was at the beginning of this series.

These guys, all of them, have grown and changed throughout the books and years. None of them are with who I expected them to end up with when I started writing these books. Logan and Trent weren't supposed to have Aiden. Dexter was never supposed to get a book, I had NO idea who Larson would end up with. Merrick was supposed to end up with Wyatt, and Dean with Ben and Asher (… oh and did you know that Ben and Asher are brothers?)

As I finish *Undisclosed* and reflect on where these guys came from and where they ended up, Dean and Merrick's pairing was the perfect end to this series. Two broken men finding happiness together, discovering that things change, and much like a fine wine, they get better with age.

And just like the guys, my life has changed since I wrote *Desires*. I've grown and changed as both a writer and person. I've learned who I am as a writer, and what works for me. I've learned to follow my gut, not worry about the word count, and somewhere along the way, I learned a little about comma usage. (Not much, but some!)

This series would never have been possible without my editors—Susie and Jennifer (yes, two of them over the course of this series), numerous friends who cheered me on—Taylor, Charlie, Annabeth, Kat, and others. My PA-turned-close-friend, Charity, has kept me sane and on task, and has been an amazing alpha reader and shoulder to cry on when things are going insane.

Thank you to each and every one of you for giving Middle Tennessee and the *Undisclosed* men a try. While it's goodbye for now, it's not goodbye forever. The guys will be back.

Please consider leaving a review (readerlinks.com/l/1891032) of *Submission*. As an independent author, reviews are invaluable and help other readers find my books.

Make sure to flip to the next page and follow me on social media, my newsletter, or both so you don't miss a release. In the coming months, I'm planning to revisit some old favorites and introduce a new series!

With Love,

Carly

ABOUT THE AUTHOR

Carly Marie has had stories, characters, and plots bouncing around in her head for as long as she can remember. She began writing in high school and found it so cathartic that she's made time for it ever since. With the discovery of M/M romance, Carly knew she'd found her home. She was surprised to learn not everyone has sexy characters in their heads, begging for their stories to be written. With that knowledge, a little push from her husband, and a lot of encouragement from newfound friends, she jumped into the world of publishing.

Carly lives in Ohio with her husband, four girls, two cats, and more chickens than she can count. The numerous plot bunnies that run through her head on a daily basis ensure that she will continue to write and share her stories for years to come.

Keep up to date on all the latest by following me at:
Mailing List: Carly's Connection
Website: www.authorcarlymarie.com

Printed in Great Britain
by Amazon